Suffragist
Hellraiser

Suffragist Hellraiser

SHARON MARGOLIS

authorHOUSE®

AuthorHouse™
1663 Liberty Drive
Bloomington, IN 47403
www.authorhouse.com
Phone: 1-800-839-8640

Published by AuthorHouse   04/27/2015

ISBN: 978-1-4772-2789-3 (sc)
ISBN: 978-1-4772-4447-0 (e)

Print information available on the last page.

CHAPTER I

The undulating Montezuma Hills appeared black against the night sky. Wispy, high clouds veiled the face of the half-moon, filtering its silver-white light and a warm breeze whispered of spring turning to summer. The bright beam of the single headlight from the 1902 Pierce Arrow Motorette was all that allowed Kate Moore to see the deeply rutted dirt road. As she headed home toward the town of River Run, she could not hear her own carefree humming above the clatter of the motorcar.

Kate stomped the gas pedal to the floor, pushing the Motorette to its top speed. She guessed it rattled down the road at twelve miles per hour, a respectable rate for the eight-year-old machine, but not nearly as exciting as whizzing along at twice this speed in her mother's new automobile in New York. A twinge of regret for her hasty departure from that city pricked her heart. Ruthlessly, she obliterated the emotion by concentrating on navigating the dark road.

A sudden, hard bump propelled her toward the roof of the car. She felt the thwack on the top of her head as her huge-brimmed, flower-bedecked hat hit the leather awning.

Kate heard the explosive bang from behind her reverberate off the hills in a chain of echoes. As the auto tilted toward the left rear wheel, she groaned with vexation and stopped the engine. The motorcar ceased its rattling. Night sounds surrounded her; crickets, a hooting owl, the breeze rustling through a nearby tree.

Ordinarily, she would not be frightened by a quiet night, but alone and far from town her imagination conjured up flesh eating beasts and renegade men eager to pounce on a lone woman. Sliding her hand under the seat, she was reassured by the smooth feel of a metal gun barrel. The pistol was small, but she could protect herself if the need arose.

Kate knew what the problem was before she got out of the car to inspect it. She was an old hand at patching blown out rubber tires. With determination, she marched to the rear of the auto and kicked the sagging tire. Her colorful language damning rutted rural roads rebounded off the hills.

Standing with her gloved hands on her hips, she glanced back down the road. She recalled that Abigail Penny and Eulalia Ericson had left the women's suffrage meeting after her, but they would not be coming along in the slow moving buggy for quite a while.

Resignedly, Kate untied her unwieldy, beribboned hat and tossed it across the car seat. Her leather driving gloves quickly followed. She wished to do away with the pinching whalebone corset as well. It would be much easier for her to work without all the feminine trappings of fashion.

After opening the toolbox on the rear of the Motorette, she removed the jack. To her satisfaction, work went quickly.

She was so engrossed in applying the patch to the tube that the rhythm of a horse's hooves did not register until the animal and its rider were nearly upon her. In a hurry, she moved toward the front of the auto where she could easily reach under the car seat. The horse stopped a few feet from her, but in the dark, she could see no more than a shadow of the rider.

"What have we here? Are you lost, little girl?" A man's deep voice came at her with a teasing lilt.

Kate bristled, "little girl" indeed.

"It's none of your concern what's going on here. Just move along," she managed in a calm tone.

"Are you nervous? You should feel real nervous out here in the dark . . . alone." Kate caught her breath in apprehension as the man dismounted and stepped slowly toward her. "No telling who might be just waiting for a sweet little thing like you to come along."

Kate was more than nervous. She could hear her heart thudding in her chest and her hands were slick with sweat. As his slow, purposeful stride brought the stranger closer she grasped the gun and brought it down to hide behind her skirt. He was so near she could make out his six foot, broad-shouldered, intimidating size. Still, he kept coming. Her arm shook as she lifted the gun out in front of her. The barrel end was only a yard from his shirt buttons.

"No further," Kate ordered as she cocked the pistol. "I know how to use this."

Abruptly, the man stopped. "Easy, now. I was just trying to make a point, not molest you." She noticed that caution and respect replaced the bravado in his voice. "Point that gun away from me and let's talk."

"Let's not talk. Just climb back on your horse and get out of here." Finding no reason to trust him, she still leveled the pistol at his heart. Adrenalin raced through her, stiffening her trigger finger with tension.

"I won't hurt you. I'm the Chief of Police from River Run. Now put the gun away." There was a hard edge to the command. He clearly expected to be obeyed.

"Prove it." Her voice was crisp, belying the anxious quaking deep in her belly.

She watched as slowly he reached his hand up to his shirt pocket and removed something from inside it. Metal caught the moonlight. Kate stepped closer and saw it was a badge.

Obviously, River Run's town council had selected a new Chief of Police during her absence. Last week she had returned to California after living in New York for six years. When she had left, she remembered Zack Peach holding the office and this man was definitely not Zack.

Looking up at the shadowed face hovering above her, she distinguished the startling light eyes and brown hair that was too long, a wild lock tumbling across his forehead. A lightning bolt of recognition jolted through her. John Gallagher. Except for the few hardened angles of his face that aged his boyish handsomeness, he looked much the same as he had six years ago. He had been a new police officer then, recruited from his father's farm somewhere up the Sacramento River.

Disconcertingly, she had the same physical reaction to him now as she had when she was fifteen. Only this time there was no confusion. She understood the heat that spread from the core of her womanhood, making her want to touch him. It had been many months since a man had made her feel this way, not since Trevor Freebush. That despicable fortune hunter and all men were her enemies.

The lawman's commanding voice, low and tense, interrupted her train of thought. "Take that gun away from my chest. Then hand it to me . . . butt first."

Kate realized that the pistol was still poised to kill him. She lowered the barrel to aim at a more intimate part of his anatomy.

"Are you nervous?" The corner of her mouth tugged up in a mischievous half-smile. "You should feel real nervous, trying to frighten a harmless woman. There's no telling what she might do in self-defense."

Gallagher's teeth ground together. He was losing patience with the cheeky brat. With her tiny stature, machine oil smudged across her delicate features and wheat-blond hair swept up and pinned down into a ladylike do, the woman looked about as dangerous as a three-week-old kitten. He reckoned she was just having fun at his expense, but she was playing a dangerous game. He had no intentions of losing his manhood because some female twit caused an accident.

Stretching his arm out toward her, Gallagher turned his hand palm up. His deadly cold eyes nailed her.

"Give it over. Now."

He stared her down, controlled violence causing his biceps to spasm. From her expression of amusement, he knew she enjoyed watching him squirm. Gallagher was close to the breaking point.

Silent curses echoed in his head as she ignored his waiting hand, uncocked the weapon and slowly reached behind her to place it on the car seat. Her eyes steadily held his. She had obeyed, but not entirely.

Gallagher's eyes narrowed and he silently vowed to squash her. The small act of defiance showed more pluck than he thought was acceptable in a lady . . . and she most definitely was a lady.

His glance took in the petite figure in the grimy dustcoat. The top of her proudly held head did not reach his shoulder, yet she seemed to look down at him. Moonlight accentuated the pampered fair complexion and fine bone structure of her face. Even though he was annoyed, he had to admit she was appealing.

Behind the show of bravado, he suspected a scared little girl. There had been a flicker of deep pain in her eyes before she had put down the gun. She was no shallow innocent. A seed of recognition intruded on his thoughts. He had seen that hurt look somewhere before.

"Who are you? And what are you doing out here alone?" His voice was gruff. He doubted she would answer if he didn't sound in command.

"I'm Katherine Moore and I was on my way home to River Run. As you can see, my car has a flat tire. Now that your questions are answered, you can leave and I can get back to work."

He watched her turn from him and head for the rear of the auto. Moore from River Run. He remembered now. Nathan Moore, from The Hill, had been killed in an accident. There had been a scandal and his socialite widow had left for New York with her daughter. He wondered how much this gutsy lady knew about her father's private life. His gaze searched out the young woman who was wrestling with the rubber tube.

"Could you use some help with that?" he offered.

"I can do this myself."

"Suit yourself." Gallagher leaned comfortably against the side of the Pierce-Arrow. "I'll just stand here, then, and frighten away the bogeyman."

"The only bogeyman around here is you and it would suit me fine to see your back as you ride away," she spat at him.

He unsettled her with his presence. His masculinity reached out to batter her defenses and she could not allow that. The longer he remained with her the more of a danger he became.

"You remind me of a cat I had once." His voice was deep and mellow, floating to her on the evening breeze. "She was a tiny, little thing, the runt of the litter. I was partial to her, always did like calicoes. We called her Spunky. Even as a kitten she was real feisty, hissing and clawing at everything and everybody. I remember she used to go after the dogs."

"Mr. Gallagher." Kate stopped her work to look at him as he lounged against the auto. "If this story has a point, please get to it."

"Yes, ma'am." He smiled, his teeth flashing white in the moonlight, and then continued to speak in his slow, easy way. "The dogs wouldn't hurt her, maybe bark and snap at her some. That's about all. Now, Spunky knew she was safe picking on the dogs. One night, she went after a strange dog in our field. It was a coyote, but she couldn't tell the difference."

There was a long silence as Kate waited for the story to go on. She looked up to meet his eyes. The end of the tale was evident to her before he told it.

"All we found the next day were a few tufts of calico fur and coyote tracks."

"Are you a coyote, by any chance?" Her mouth had a sour twist.

"I might be, if I'm pushed too far."

She studied him for a long while, taking his measure. His lips slightly curved up as though something amused him, but the eyes were calculating and stern. A premonition warned her that Gallagher had no patience for nonsense. This homespun lawman, in spite of his homey farm stories and easy smile, could be a dangerous adversary in more than one way. His unyielding temperament was evident in his steady gaze. A worse problem was her powerful physical reaction to his blatant maleness. Kate would be fighting him and herself at the same time.

She forced her attention back to the patched tire. It was ready to be put back on the rim and pumped up. She worked quickly and efficiently. On occasion, her gaze flickered toward the man who stood nearby. He had lit a cheroot and was relaxing while he smoked. His eyes never left her. The aroma of burning tobacco drifted past her nostrils as warm, comforting emotions floated up to surprise her.

Papa used to smoke that brand, she thought with a bittersweet pang of nostalgia. But he was gone now and she still missed him sorely. Firmly, Kate pushed the memory from her mind. It was perilous to allow sentimentality to distract her when she needed a clear head.

Kate heard the horse drawn buggy coming long before she could see it. She sighed with relief. Now that Abigail and Eulalia were arriving, she could rid herself of that pesky Mr. Gallagher. She would convince the two schoolteachers that it was not proper for her to be alone out here with a man.

The buggy had hardly stopped when the driver, a drab, brown sparrow of a woman, spoke. "Are you all right, Katherine?"

"It's only a flat tire, Abigail. I'm almost done fixing it."

Before Kate could say more, footsteps came up from behind her and a baritone voice sounded from above.

"Good evening, ladies. It seems to be a busy night for roaming around in the dark."

"Good evening, Mr. Gallagher." Abigail sent him a friendly nod. "There was a suffrage club meeting tonight. Quite a few of us from town attended. How lucky for Katherine that you happened along."

Kate grimaced. Lucky was not the word she would have chosen.

"I was riding back from a visit with my folks when I came upon Miss Moore. She's been interesting company. It's getting late and I'm sure you ladies want to get home. I'll make sure Miss Moore gets back to town safely," he assured them.

"Could you please stay for a little while longer?" Kate addressed the women, but glanced in Gallagher's direction. "For propriety's sake."

"It seems Miss Moore has her doubts about my intentions. Please reassure her that she's safe with the Chief of Police." His voice held an offended tone. She was certain a chaperon was the last thing he wanted.

Eulalia, the sweet-faced young blonde lady sitting beside Abigail, spoke for the first time.

"I am certain Katherine trusts you as we all do and is only concerned with her reputation."

"In that case, I know her friends wouldn't hurt her reputation by gossiping about us." Kate watched the women stiffen at his words. "Of course if Miss Moore is afraid to be alone with me, then maybe one of you should stay."

Kate was incredulous. That slippery-tongued snake had backed her into a corner. She could not accept aid from the women without hinting that she feared their gossip. It would also be an admission that he scared her and neither could be further from the truth. She had never cared what society thought of her and no man would make her cower.

"That won't be necessary. I've changed my mind." Kate's chin thrust out.

Gallagher stifled a grin, but victory glittered in his eyes. The little stinker was no match for him. He had to concede, though, that she kept the game interesting.

"I am sure you will be safe with Mr. Gallagher, Katherine. We will see you next week at the meeting." Gallagher watched with satisfaction as Abigail lifted the reins and started the horses toward town, a chorus of "Good evenings" floating on the night air.

He was alone again with that aggravating female.

As soon as the ladies were gone, she returned to work on the tire, which irritated him no end. Being ignored was more of an insult than if she had slapped him.

"That was a tricky move, trying to get one of the ladies to stay here." While she wrestled with the tire, he stood close beside her, determined to gain her attention. "I think you'll appreciate no one else being around when I scold you."

"Scold me? Whatever for? You're the one who's behaving like a horse's behind." As she spoke her work continued, her tone careless as though his rising temper were no concern of hers.

Gallagher was tired, the hour was late, and his patience was at low ebb. It was time to take charge and put this brat in her place.

Kate was startled when his powerful hand clamped onto her arm and swung her around to face him. Her chin was firmly held in his other hand and tilted up so she was forced to look into his glinting eyes. There was no mistaking his foul mood, but she did not feel threatened. Her thoughts were consumed by the heat emanating from his flesh on her arm and face. His hold was forceful yet not painful and she had to concentrate to understand what he was saying.

"I will talk and you will not say one word." His voice was controlled, each word spit out in a puff of breath that tickled her face. "The game is over and I win. When I'm through bawling you out, you'll get into your car and I'll finish fixing your tire. You'll say 'thank you' and drive home where you belong."

Gallagher paused for a moment, his grasp on her chin turning gentle, one finger sliding over the soft underside toward her throat. She swallowed convulsively at the electric force of his touch on her tender skin. "A young girl like you shouldn't be out here alone at night. Any drifter could come along and you could be robbed, beaten, murdered, raped, or all of those things. We could've been out here tomorrow morning searching for your body. I don't know what your mama was thinking to let you out alone. She should know better. In fact, I've got a mind to see her tomorrow and tell her so."

His hand left her face, but she could not determine whether she felt relief or disappointment. When Kate could concentrate on something other than his touch, she was appalled at his vivid description of what might happen to an unprotected woman out at night. No gentleman would be so explicit. And how dare he touch her without permission? Besides, she was not a child to be scolded and, now that his distracting hand was removed from her jaw, she intended to tell him so.

"For your information, Mr. Gallagher, I am twenty-one years old and able to take care of myself. My mama, as you call her, is in New York and likely to stay there. You are an arrogant, overbearing bully who ..."

Kate never completed her sentence. His hand clamped over her mouth, warm fingers against her lips in a near caress. He seemed to lean over her, the magnetic draw of his expanded pupils pulling her closer to him. Her heart pounded in her ears, sounding a warning bell. This man was dangerous! There was no controlling her body or thoughts when he was so near.

She was surprised and confused with conflicting emotions when he caught her behind the knees and lifted her off the ground. A few long strides brought them to the front of the auto and, as he deposited her inside, her bottom hit the driver's seat with a thump. When Kate turned to berate him, he was headed toward the nearly repaired rear tire.

On second thought, she reasoned, maybe continuing her contact with him, even on a verbal basis, was not a good idea. She needed time alone to counteract his powerful physical affect on her.

Without conscious thought Kate reached into her reticule and stroked the string of yellow, glass beads hidden there. Her father had given them to her when she was a child so she would have something to do with her hands when she needed to sit still. They had become a source of comfort when she felt agitated and she kept them with her constantly. She needed the soothing presence of those beads now.

That beast of a policeman had the manners of a rampaging gorilla, yet he appealed to her on a basic level that defied explanation. There was more to the attraction than his good looks. Common sense told her to steer clear of him in the future, but her plans for the suffrage cause would render that impossible. She hoped when they clashed again, he would not use her physical pull toward him as a weapon.

Gallagher soon reappeared beside her. In an effort to avoid feeling the effects of his masculine aura Kate turned her gaze away from him.

"The tire is back on. You can go home whenever you're ready. If you run into any more trouble, I won't be far behind you." His manner was easy with no trace of his earlier annoyance.

"Thank you, Mr. Gallagher, for your concern." Her voice sounded strained to her own ears. She wondered how she sounded to him.

When Kate started to get out of the auto to crank up the engine, he motioned to her to stay put and he went to do it for her. Shortly, the Pierce-Arrow was clank-banging down the dirt road toward River Run. A sigh of short-lived relief escaped her as she drove away from the unsettling encounter.

As chairwoman of the suffrage association's newly formed Action Committee, Kate's rabble-rousing plans would eventually bring her into conflict with the local law enforcement. Judging by tonight's experience, locking horns with Police Chief John Gallagher could prove to be a nerve-knotting contest of wills. Remembering the titillating sensation of his hand on her face and that he had not hurt her no matter how angry he became, she looked forward to the daring challenge.

CHAPTER II

The house was a huge Victorian confection with turrets, gables, and gingerbread trim tossed together at random, porches and balconies starting and stopping without symmetrical plan. Wild tangles of weeds and overgrown honeysuckle bushes crowded the front porch and walls, lending the mansion a derelict air.

A blistering noonday sun beat down on Kate's head as she cut back the bushes that crept over the banister and spilled onto the front porch. Her wide-brimmed straw hat shaded her face but did not keep the heat from penetrating through the crown. She ignored the discomfort, welcoming the physical exertion. Unfortunately, the exhausting work did not hold back her troubled thoughts.

Clipping viciously at the trailing honeysuckle, she recalled her meeting earlier in the week with Jeffrey Carlisle. She equated her visit with her father's lawyer to being dunked into a freezing lake. He had explained her precarious financial situation in discouraging detail. Kate still found it difficult to believe the inheritance from her father was hardly enough to keep her going for a year. And that didn't include the niceties she was used to, such as a maid, a telephone, and gasoline for her motorcar.

Crushing a handful of blossoms in her fist, she again heard the lawyer's laughter when she had mentioned running a boarding house for a genteel clientele. He had suggested she sell the house and return to New York. Kate wanted to loosen his perfect teeth with her fist and rip off his carefully tended mustache. The condescending ass!

She jutted her chin out in a defiant gesture. Against Carlisle's advice, she had started preparations for the boarding house. As soon as the house was put to rights, she would place an advertisement for renters in the *River Run Gazette*.

A rivulet of perspiration trickled down her nose and she swiped at it with her forearm. The weather was unusually hot for the end of June, prompting memories of the way she used to sneak out of the house to play down by the cool river with the children of the Southside shanties. Her father had not minded those escapades, but her ever-proper mother had been livid. After all, what would the neighbors say about such goings on?

At the thought of her snooty neighbors, Kate clipped at the overgrown bushes with a vengeance. Since her return, she had been unaccountably snubbed by people who had been friends of her parents. Twice she had caught Beatrice Slater, who lived directly across the street, peeking at her through the window, only to pull away and shut the drapes when Kate waved to her. With determination, she forced all troublesome thoughts of her neighbors from her mind and applied herself to trimming the shrubbery.

Kate heard the front gate swing open and click shut. Heavy footsteps rhythmically tapped on the stone path behind her and she turned to identify her visitor. Captain Tom! Kate dropped the shrub clippers and ran to greet the old man. She hugged him and felt his bear-like arms around her shoulders, returning the pressure. Pleasure was evident in his gleaming blue eyes as she stepped back to look at him.

"I'm happy you came today," Kate said. "Come inside and have something cool to drink. Blanca made some lemonade."

"That sounds real good. These old legs ain't used to climbin' hills no more."

"Don't tell me you walked all the way from the docks." She looped her arm around his elbow and led him toward the porch.

"No. Hitched a ride into town on one of them new fangled motor trucks. Dangdest ride I ever had. We musta been goin' twenty-five miles an hour. Don't know what this world is comin' to."

Kate was overjoyed to see Captain Macaphee. He had worked for her father's freighting company as a riverboat captain for more than a generation and Kate considered him like a grandfather. She remembered last week, on the day of her arrival, her bicycle ride down to the river and the rickety old houseboat where he lived. Her homecoming would not have been complete without his welcome.

Today, she could not help noticing that his full gray beard was neatly trimmed and his casual clothing was spotless and pressed. The cracked leather shoes were spit shined. He obviously had taken extra care with his grooming for this visit.

As they reached the house, Kate removed her straw hat, releasing the tawny curls that were carelessly pinned on top of her head. She hung the hat on the wooden rack just inside the doorway to the hall. Tom handed her his captain's cap, baring his pink scalp with the few wispy hairs sprouting on the top and the longish, gray fringe around the back and sides.

She noted his discomfort as he looked around the hallway. Although he had been a close friend of her father, Kate recalled he had rarely visited this house on The Hill, and then only on business. Her mother had treated him as an underling, never offering him refreshment or a seat in her parlor.

"Come into the back sitting-room while I get the lemonade." Kate said, while leading Tom down the hallway.

Kate understood the tear in the corner of his eye and the slightly upturned lips. She remembered the bittersweet memories invading her when she had returned to the house after so many years; not knowing whether to laugh or cry and doing a little of both. Before they entered the formal parlor, she patted his weathered and gnarled fingers.

Tom seemed to hang back from the elegance of the room with its rose-colored silk sofas and tapestry-cushioned, straight-backed chairs. She settled him comfortably in a wingchair before leaving the room to get the drinks.

Sunlight streamed through the open kitchen windows when Kate entered. She smiled at the woman who stood at the table slicing leftover roast beef for their lunch. The return of her mother's housekeeper was a stroke of marvelous luck. Throughout Kate's childhood, the motherly servant had been a haven of warmth in the otherwise coldly correct household.

Blanca Mendez looked up from her work for an instant. Lively, deep brown eyes glanced in Kate's direction, then she returned to her task. Gray streaks accented the black hair that was pulled back into a loose bun. Her short figure was softly rounded with cuddly padding.

"Your cooking is getting better. This roast you made last night is muy bueno." There was a lilting, Spanish rhythm to Blanca's speech.

"You're a good teacher. I couldn't cook at all when I got here. By the way, we have company for lunch. Captain Macaphee just arrived."

Kate walked to the wooden icebox, took out the jar of lemonade, and set it on the table. She took two glasses from the cupboard and filled them with the sweet-tart liquid. In her mother's home, serving the guests would have been a maid's task, but Kate was learning to serve herself and do housework as well. There was too much work for Blanca to do everything. She dipped her hand into the can of crackers and laid a few on a plate.

Without warning, a brown streak whizzed out of the cupboard, ran across her hand and disappeared under the iron stove. Kate shrieked and threw her hands up to cover her face. Sight of the mouse opened a trap door to let loose a monstrous specter.

Behind closed eyes, she saw herself lying on a narrow cot, alone in a filthy room. Pain in her lower body was unbearable, the sensation deadening effects of ether wearing off. The dead fetus that Trevor had planted in her womb lay on the floor, wrapped in bloody newspaper. In the far corner of the room, a huge rat sat on its hind legs, its nose twitching as it caught the scent of her blood.

Tears collected in the corners of her eyes as Kate forced herself free of the memory. She could not allow the pain of her stepfather, Ralph Keeler's, betrayal to take hold of her, or the inner strength she had painstakingly built might crumble.

As though from a distance, she heard Blanca's concerned voice calling to her.

"Are you all right, Chica?"

Kate slammed shut the door on the hurtful memory and responded. "Yes. It was only another mouse. Those traps I set don't seem to be working."

"Tomorrow, I will bring you a cat. Ours had kittens a few months ago and little Flora is a good mouser," Blanca offered, continuing to slice the meat.

Kate thanked her and composed herself enough to place the lemonade and crackers on a tray and carry it to the parlor. The terrible images were gone, but her hands still trembled when she rejoined her guest.

Captain Tom was standing at the window looking into the garden. His back was to the room, as though it was not worthy of his attention while glorious nature put on a better show outside.

"We can go into the garden after lunch," Kate suggested. "I haven't gotten to trimming it yet, but it will still be pleasant out there."

She lay the tray on a small table and handed a frosty glass to the captain.

"There's somethin' beautiful about nature growin' wild that dies when you try to tame it. Sort of like a bird singin' in a cage. I'd rather hear it crowin' sittin' in a tree," Tom's voice was gruff.

"I know what you mean. Living in New York City is as far from nature as you can get. To me, it was like living in a stone tomb. Some people love big city life, but I felt smothered. Seeing the Sacramento River again was like being reborn."

"You take after your daddy. He loved the river, too."

"Yes. He loved the river, but it took his life."

"Sometimes I wonder about that." The captain paused and looked away, but not before Kate noticed the haunted glaze over his eyes. "I don't know if I should tell you what happened that night. Your mother forbid me to talk to you alone after the funeral."

During the years since her father's death, she had clung desperately to her father's memory. It had helped her to cope with life. She relied upon his ethereal presence now nearly as much as when he was alive. His death never seemed real to her.

"I want to hear what happened. She shut me away from people until we left for New York and refused to talk about the night he died. Please, tell me about it."

He nodded and took her tiny hands in his huge, rough ones. Kate sat beside him on the nearest sofa, taking strength from his fingers still linked with hers.

"I found Nate in the shallows near his overturned rowboat. Looked like the boat hit him a good one on the head when it turned over. Knocked him out cold and he went in headfirst. Drowned. At least, that's the way Chief Zack Peach saw it."

Kate conjured up the sight of her father's lifeless body floating in the Sacramento River with the back of his skull bashed in. Her throat worked in huge gulping swallows. Her mouth trembled with her struggle to hold back the threatening tears. She turned her face away from her old friend so he would not see her distress.

"It was a calm night," he continued. "Your daddy knew boats and the river. Chances of an accident like that happenin' to him that night are near zero. Besides, that light boat couldn't have hit him with enough force to do that much damage."

"What do you think happened?" Kate pressed when Tom paused.

"I think someone killed him and dumped him in the river to make it look like an accident."

The shock of such a revelation clubbed her already faltering composure and she covered her mouth with her hands to stifle the sobs that wrenched from her throat. She felt the captain's arm circle her shoulders in an attempt to comfort her.

"I'm sorry, Kitten. I shouldn't be tellin' you such things."

When she stopped reeling from the emotional storm, her curiosity came forward.

"Who would want to kill him?"

"I don't know, but I think Peach was too quick to shove the file in the back of his drawer and forget it. He liked things quiet, especially when it got near to his retirement."

She felt that her father's memory was slighted by the unwillingness of the police to run a proper inquiry. The least she should do for him was clear up any shadowy speculation about his death.

"Do you think we could start an investigation? It's been six years since it happened. Information would probably be difficult to come by, but I could try."

Kate watched conflicting emotions cross Tom's face, none of which she could read. When he finally spoke, his manner was gentle with a combination of sadness and regret.

"Only thing you would find is trouble. The law forgot about it years ago. If there was a killer and he's still around here, you might make him nervous enough to come after you."

Like a bulldog with a bone, she would not let go.

"You mentioned a file. Was there really a police report?"

"I expect so. Peach was pretty efficient about such things, but I don't know if Gallagher would still have it."

Kate felt the heat rush to her face at the mention of the young lawman's name. She turned away from the captain so he would not see her flush. It had not occurred to her until now that if she wanted to see a police report, she would have to ask a favor of that irritating beast. The thought rankled.

Captain Tom's forehead wrinkled in puzzlement.

"Why're you blushin' like that? Did I say somethin' wrong?" he asked.

"No. It's not you. I met Mr. Gallagher a couple of nights ago and we're not exactly on friendly terms." She heard her own disgust in the tightness of her voice.

"Exactly what terms are you on?"

"He's the most annoying jackass I've ever met. The thought of seeing him again makes me want to smash something." The captain's secretive smile chafed her. She would die of mortification if he guessed how devastatingly attractive she found the lawman.

"What did he do? Or shouldn't I ask?" Kate tried to ignore the captain's blue eyes, which were alight with humor.

She felt the heat in her cheeks and knew they were scarlet. Knowing she would embarrass herself further by relating the incident, she opted to change the subject.

"That uncivilized lout is not worth discussing." She stood and said, "Come into the dining room and I'll check on lunch."

"Will you be askin' to see Peach's report on the accident?"

Tom followed Kate from the parlor.

"Yes. I'm too curious to be put off by a few minutes of unpleasantness."

Tom's face wrinkled with laugh lines, leaving Kate with the impression that he thought she wanted to see Gallagher again as much as she wanted to read that report. But, of course, he was wrong, she denied to herself.

When they entered the dining room, Kate recognized the discomfort on the captain's face. He stopped just inside the door and silently surveyed the long, mahogany table covered with the rich, lace cloth. Two elegant, silver candlesticks graced its center. She suspected that he would be happier if they ate in the kitchen, but how could she suggest it without insulting her old friend?

Tom's next words settled the problem.

"This is a mighty big table for the two of us and a long way to carry everythin'. I'd be happy to eat in the kitchen. That is, if Blanca don't mind us joinin' her."

"That's a wonderful idea. Actually, I've been eating in the kitchen since I got back." Kate linked her arm with his and guided him to the doorway at the opposite end of the room. "Mother would have a fainting spell if she knew. She used to scold me for filching cookies in the kitchen and speaking to the servants."

Kate watched Blanca's eyes round in surprise as she entered the room with her guest.

"Captain Macaphee prefers to eat in the kitchen," she explained.

"This way I get to eat with two beautiful ladies." He winked at Blanca and flashed her a smile.

Kate remembered that on the rare occasions the captain had come to the house to see her father, he had taken every opportunity to tease the housekeeper and make her blush.

"Some things never change. You are still chasing skirts." The housekeeper waved her hand as if she did not believe his compliment, but her eyes lowered coyly. "Sit down and I will set the table."

"Set it for three," he said.

Blanca smiled and nodded.

Comfortable warmth flowered inside of Kate as she watched these two people. They were the closest to family she had in River Run. Her own mother did not give her the same feelings of security and belonging that she felt right now. If not for the newly posed mystery about her father's supposed drowning, she would feel content in the loving atmosphere.

The next morning, Kate pedaled her bicycle down Superior Avenue, the main street in River Run. She had passed the elegant part of the downtown area containing City Hall, the new Nickelodeon Theater for motion pictures, and Willis Park Square. As she got closer to the river, the buildings became shabbier. She stopped the bicycle and propped it against the wooden building.

Through the grimy window, she saw the Chief of Police reading, his booted feet resting on his desk. With a few brisk hand movements Kate straightened her long, black skirt and flowered hat. She squared her shoulders and lifted her chin before opening the door and entering the jailhouse office.

John Gallagher heard the door squeak and looked up from reading a report from the Town Council. He was surprised to see the little sharp-tongued imp from the other night march boldly into the room. Her appearance this morning contrasted sharply to her dishevelment as she had wrestled with the automobile tire the last time he had seen her. Now, golden highlights gleamed from her high, neatly tucked-in hairdo and her pearl-like complexion was not marred with streaks of black grease.

Remembering his manners, he slowly swung his boots off the desk and stood. His face lit up with an easy smile. He would enjoy a good sparring session.

"Good morning, Miss Moore. What can I do for you? I hope you didn't blow out another tire."

"Good morning, Mr. Gallagher. My tires are fine, thank you. I am here on business." Her announcement projected a cool formality, holding him at a distance.

"Have a seat." He motioned toward a chair opposite his desk.

She sat, but did not look relaxed. He came around to the front of his desk to casually perch on its corner.

"My mother refused to discuss my father's accident with me. I understand there was a report written on it by Chief Peach. I was hoping it might answer some of my questions. May I see it, please?" Kate's voice trembled with emotion.

"Sure, you can see it." Gallagher rose from the desk. "Chasing it down may take a while so just sit tight."

Poor little thing, he thought as he walked to the wooden file cabinets in back of the room. She's bound to find out about her father's affair sometime. I just hope it isn't now. Weepy females make me nervous.

As Kate waited, she surveyed the sparsely furnished office. There were two large desks, a few chairs, and file cabinets. A rifle rack on the wall held three rifles. Wanted posters were displayed on a bulletin board and a potbellied stove with a coffee pot on it stood in a corner. The room appeared dingy from the thick layer of dust that coated everything. Her glance settled on the back of the police chief as he riffled through files in the bottom drawer. He was hunkered down and her attention caught on his dark pants pulled tight around his firm buttocks. He stood up, breaking her concentration.

She heard scratching at the back door which Gallagher opened, and let in a large, yellow-beige dog. The mongrel's tail wagged in greeting.

"How you doing, Rufus, old boy?" Gallagher ruffled the fur around the animal's neck.

Kate saw the dog's nose twitch as the dog caught the scent of a stranger in the room. When he loped cautiously toward her to investigate, she put her hand out and he sniffed her fingers. He nuzzled her other hand that held the yellow glass beads in her lap and she removed her white gloves to stroke the short hairs on the top of his head. Rufus was huge but not threatening.

"If Rufus bothers you, let me know. I'll put him in the other room," Gallagher offered.

"He's fine where he is," Kate assured him.

He nodded and returned to his search for the report. She waited only a few more minutes before he stood with the sought papers in his hand.

"You'll have to read this here. We don't allow reports to be taken from the office or we'd be missing half our files," he explained as she accepted the report from him.

"I understand." She nodded.

At first she had trouble deciphering the handwritten pages, but the reading grew easier as she became used to Zach Peach's rambling scrawl. Her hand compulsively traced the smooth surface of the beads in her lap as she read the facts surrounding her father's death. As the report became graphic, her sight swam in unshed tears and the written words blurred. Occasionally, she had to blink her eyes before continuing.

Most of the information she already knew. The few fresh details she did pick up posed more questions than they answered. For one thing, Henry Slater, who was her neighbor from across the street and owner of the Montezuma Cannery, was questioned as to his whereabouts at the time of the accident. It was proven that he was in his office at the cannery at that hour. She wondered why he was questioned. Also, no mention was made of where her father could have been going or from where he had been returning when he died.

Gallagher peeked out from behind the papers he had picked up to hold in front of his face as though he were reading. It was difficult for him to believe this self-composed gentlewoman, who sat demurely in front of him with the dog resting on her feet, was the same fire breathing dragon lady who had scorched him a few evenings before. The other night she had been unpredictable and exciting. Today, she was sweet, vulnerable, and way out of his class. He was drawn to both sides of her personality.

"Mr. Gallagher." Kate called for his attention. "It says here that Henry Slater was asked where he was on the night of my father's death. Why was he questioned?"

He stalled for time by slowly putting down the papers in his hand and sitting up straight to look at her. There was no way to answer honestly without hurting her. A half-truth would just make her more curious.

"I wouldn't know," he lied. "Zack was in charge of the investigation."

"Do you know where I can reach him? This is important to me."

His protective instincts surged forward. She looked so fragile, her luminous eyes near to tears and delicate fingers nervously toying with the yellow beads. He detested lying to her, but would hate himself more if he hurt her with the truth about her father.

"He moved up north somewhere, but I don't know where exactly. I don't know who else might be able to help you."

Disappointment reflected in her downcast eyes. There was something suspicious about the missing information in the report, and the tension she sensed in the man sitting across from her. Kate was certain he was not being truthful. Her intuition supported Captain Tom's belief that her father's death was not an accident.

Perhaps Blanca could answer her questions about Mr. Slater. Her daughter, Dorothea, worked for him at the cannery. Kate was more determined than ever to find out what happened to her father that night.

Gallagher caught the flicker of distrust in her expression before it was replaced with stubbornness. Now he recognized the spirited combatant from the dark country road. It was evident to him that she was on to his deceit.

"I will find out what I want to know without your help," she informed him. "Tenacity is one of my strong points."

He watched her tug the gloves onto her tiny hands and drop the beads into her reticule. The young lady moved with purpose. There was no doubt in his mind she would do whatever she set her mind to. He admired her spunk and wished he could spare her the heartache she would eventually uncover.

When Kate stood, Rufus lifted himself off her feet and she patted him on the neck in farewell. As Gallagher took the report she held out to him, she noticed how the veins stood out on his strong, tanned hand. Fleetingly, she recalled the feel of it on her face and back. Heat rose to her neck and retreat seemed like a wise plan.

"I'm sorry I couldn't do more for you, Miss Moore," Gallagher said as he followed her to the front door.

"I have discovered quite a bit," she said. Now, I am sure there is something being hidden, Kate added in her thoughts.

He held the door open for her as she passed through. His eyebrow quirked up in surprise as his dainty visitor walked to her bicycle, stood it up straight, and straddled the seat. She owned an auto, yet she chose to ride an old bicycle. Her choice of transportation pleased him.

The road was rough and the wheels bumped in a mad rhythm as she pedaled. His attention focused on her sweetly rounded rump as it bounced up and down on the leather cushion. He watched until she was out of sight.

The exercise helped to relieve Kate's tension as she cycled through the town headed for home. Questions tumbled through her mind. Why was her father out on the river at that time of night? Where was he going? What did Henry Slater have to do with it? Was her father's death really an accident? If it was murder, who would want to kill him? Finally, what information was John Gallagher holding back from her? The more questions she asked, the more confused her thinking became. She shut her eyes for a moment to clear away the cobwebs and an image of the young lawman appeared. Instantly, her eyes flicked open. That disturbing man invaded her thoughts without warning. With great effort, she banished him from her mind, only to have his image pop up again unexpectedly and with unsettling frequency.

CHAPTER III

As usual on a summer evening, after dinner strollers congregated in downtown River Run at Willis Park. The modest oasis consisted of a lawn, a few scattered live oak trees, a dozen wooden benches, and flowerbeds installed and tended by the Ladies' Aid Society. At seven o'clock, the sun was well into its descent, allowing a cool breeze to refresh the promenaders.

Kate marched purposefully through the park with a sturdy wooden soapbox tucked under her arm. With a feeling of tempered triumph she recalled the suffrage meeting last Thursday evening. Her proposal to lecture in the park and later invade the male sanctum of a Town Council meeting had faced a mixed reception. A vote had approved her plan by the narrowest of margins.

Now, ready to put her plan in motion, she glanced at her two stalwart helpers. Abigail Penny, the tiny, energetic school teacher, and Caroline Parkhurst, a nineteen year-old socialite from The Hill, strode beside her like soldiers facing battle. The ladies' apparent determination caused a swell of pride in Kate's throat until she remembered that no one would accompany her to brave the Town Council meeting, later in the evening. She would have to face the bull corral of City Hall alone.

Flanked by her two eager helpers, Kate took one complete turn around the park, noting likely locations for her impromptu stage, and evaluating the competition. She stopped for a few moments to listen to Wilhelmina Christian, the mayor's snobbish wife, holding forth on the evils of hard liquor. The town's first lady was in her usual tightly corseted glory, with a gargantuan, artificial garden of flowers and birds balanced atop her head. Kate found the buxom temperance activist's delivery to be moving and impressive. She grudgingly acknowledged the powerful voice and intelligent reasoning. Wicked Willy was a force to be reckoned with.

Choosing a busy byway near the park entrance for her lecture, Kate set down her soapbox. She eyed her two helpers as they clutched their fliers and pasted on strained smiles. Abigail, the spinster schoolteacher, was more colorless than usual with her nervous pallor accentuated by the dull brown of her high-necked dress. The tiny woman looked ready to faint from tension. Caroline, on the other hand, looked aglow with nervous excitement. Tall, with reed slim grace, the sweet-faced young lady's huge blue eyes darted in every direction. Even her mahogany hair, done up in a lofty pompadour, exuded pent-up energy. Kate thought they looked more nervous than she herself felt.

"Don't worry. This is a quiet town. Besides, any remarks will be aimed at me. You will both be safe," she assured them.

Slipping her hand into her reticule, she rubbed the yellow beads for good luck before briskly stepping onto the soapbox. She introduced herself, projecting the full timber of her voice over her potential audience.

As she spoke, Kate watched Caroline and Abigail hand out fliers, which announced the need for women to vote. She knew it was the first time in this town since 1896, that a women was speaking publicly on this issue and resistance would be high. It did not surprise her when ladies, accompanied by their husbands or beaus, tried to slow down and listen, but were firmly moved along. She felt gratified when a few small groups of women stopped to pay polite attention. Not so encouraging was the handful of men dressed in rough work clothes who stood on the side with mischievous grins and amused sparkles in their eyes. Kate recognized in them the traits of troublemakers. She silently willed them to leave, but they did not oblige her.

Passion gave force to her words as she related the plight of unmarried women, especially widows with children. "Denied the protection of a man, their only options are to work for pitiful wages in deplorable conditions or to enter a profession that a lady does not mention in public."

As Kate expected, feminine eyebrows rose at the allusion to prostitution.

"Bein' a whore can't be that bad," one of the rough men called out. "All you got to do is lay on your back." There was raucous laughter from his companions.

"Their children die of starvation and lack of medical attention." Kate continued as though the rowdy men did not exist.

She hoped they would not chase away her audience with their vulgarity. "There is no law to protect such women and children because men do not think it is important enough. Women should be given the right to help make laws that protect us."

One of the unkempt men loudly commented, "What you need is a husband and a coupla kids to keep you at home and shut you up. A woman got no business tellin' a man how to run things."

Kate realized that disregarding the hecklers would not discourage them. They apparently enjoyed the attention they attracted from the audience. She decided on a more direct approach.

"If these crude, unwashed clowns are examples of the power that runs our town and nation, then we are in more trouble than I thought." She smiled at the listeners as though she just good-naturedly poked fun at the men.

There was a smattering of laughter and a few handclaps. Someone hooted in appreciation.

"She got you that time." Kate was pleased that the comment came from a well-dressed man.

The face of the man who had received the verbal slap turned dark with rage. "Somebody ought to put that bitch in her place," he said, taking a threatening step forward.

At first, Kate was unaware of physical danger. No man in his right mind would hit a woman in front of a crowd. Then she saw his unsteady stance and spidery red veins in his eyes. He had been drinking. Panic squeezed at her stomach, but she stood firm.

"I do not mind defending my beliefs, but I refuse to debate with a bottle of alcohol. Perhaps you could convince your friends to have their fun in a more appropriate place." She appealed to the third man who stood with the ruffians. He did not seem as intoxicated as his two companions who were razzing her.

There were a few jeers aimed toward the unruly men from the watchers. A sizable group formed to see what the commotion was about and the man whom Kate addressed looked uneasily at the unfriendly townsfolk. Firmly, he latched onto his friends' arms and propelled them toward the park exit.

Kate looked at Abigail and Caroline. Their faces were deathly pale. They looked shaken and she smiled at them in reassurance. Her own confidence was in sad condition, but she still had a job to do. Valiantly, she picked up the thread of her lecture and continued.

Most of the people who had joined to watch the ruckus left when the speech was resumed and many of those who stayed were not sympathetic to her cause. She could read their apathy or disapproval in their unsmiling features, but they were listening and that was encouragement. As her gaze flitted from face to face, frequently stopping to make eye contact, she came across a condescending glare that pierced to her core. Taking into focus the humorless face that surrounded those eyes, she recognized Wilhelmina Christian. The huge woman's mouth was pursed as that of a fish and her nose wrinkled, as though she smelled something offensive. The sour expression of the temperance leader showed her displeasure with the views she was now hearing. Wicked Willy was not known for being close-mouthed and Kate fervently hoped she would not become a target for the woman's sharp tongue. In the next instant her hope was squashed.

"God does not want women to vote."

The words shot out, commanding everyone's attention. Kate stared at Mrs. Christian. Battle lines were drawn and no quarter would be given.

"He may not want you to vote, but He hasn't said a word to me about it." Her lips curved in a smile as though her opponent's comment was amusing.

Snickers erupted in the audience. Wilhelmina glared at Kate, who felt the malice stabbing at her from her adversary's slit eyes.

"You want to vote like a man. Are you willing to go out to work like a man and tell all women to do the same? If you want to have the same rights as a man, you should have the same responsibilities," the provoking matron declared. "I, for one, enjoy my favored status in society that allows me to be a lady."

Kate sensed the interest for this line of attack from the female listeners and the approval from the few men in the audience.

"For many women, working like a man would be a relief. How many men would be willing to stay home and do laundry, wash floors, clean toilets and talk to children all day? Not to mention, changing diapers and catering to a husband like a servant. Who says a woman doesn't work hard?"

The tirade was interrupted by sparse applause. Kate noticed one woman abruptly stop clapping when her husband's elbow jabbed her ribs.

"As for being a lady, that is determined by how a woman behaves, not how she is treated." Kate's eyes drilled into Wilhemina's flushed face. "Your 'favored status' comes from your husband's money. Most women aren't so fortunate. Some have no man to provide for them and are forced to earn their own way. There are few respectable jobs open to them. In their case, there is no 'favored status'."

Kate watched as Wilhelmina elbowed a path through the assemblage until the huge woman stopped only a few inches in front of her. Even though she stood on a box, Kate was still shorter than the imposing figure hiding her from view of the spectators. She rose on tiptoe and thrust her chin out to make up for the deficit in her height.

"Are you saying people treat me like a lady only because my husband has money?" the older woman stormed. Birds and butterflies on her flamboyant hat danced with every indignant toss of her head. "How dare you talk to me that way? I'll have you know, my husband is the mayor of this town!"

"I'm happy to know that the mayor is a man of patience and fortitude. He would need a wagonload of both to put up with you," Kate flung back.

The sound of hooting laughter signaled to Kate the gathering of a delighted crowd.

"No man would put up with you at all, Miss Katherine Moore. It's no wonder you're still not married. You'd best change your ways, young lady, or you'll spend your life alone."

"I would rather live alone and accomplish something with my life, than marry and boast of my husband's achievements as though they were my own. Tell me, what do you do besides tell people not to drink liquor? I hear the Mayor likes a nip now and then."

Laughter crescendoed then receded like a wave. The aviary sitting on Wilhelmina's head did a wild jig as she shook with fury. Her nostrils flared. Kate wondered if Wicked Willy would clout her. It was clear to her the enraged woman dearly wanted to.

A high, firm voice behind Mrs. Christian caught Kate's attention. "Ladies! Ladies! You must stop fighting this instant. You are disgracing yourselves. This will not serve either of your causes," she recognized Abigail's scolding as though she were speaking to her third grade class.

"Stay out of this, Miss Penny," the mayor's wife snapped. "I will not be interfered with."

"Certainly, you are too dignified to let yourself be drawn into this spectacle, Mrs. Christian." The schoolteacher persisted.

Kate almost felt sorry for the teacher as the Mayor's wife focused the full force of her devastating glare on the intruder. "Abigail Penny, if you do not stop badgering me, your job in this town will be history."

Uncertainty registered on the suffragist's pale features and she took a few steps back. Her lips turned white and were clenched shut.

Kate's temper flared higher as she saw the haughty smirk that adorned Wicked Willy's over-wide mouth. A strong urge to avenge her colleague's embarrassment overrode any thought of caution.

"It seems you are wrong, Miss Penny." Kate fought to keep her voice light. "Everyone can see Mrs. Christian enjoys making a spectacle of herself. She does it so well."

Loud muttering from the rear of the crowd intruded on Kate's thoughts, but she could not see over or around Wilhelmina to discover the cause of the disturbance.

"We'll see who is making a spectacle. I'll have you arrested." The mayor's wife licked her lips, seemingly in anticipation of the delicious thought.

When the large woman stepped aside, Kate saw a young man quickly working his way through the crowd. Caroline Parkhurst followed closely behind him, speaking as they walked. She wondered who he was until he stood before her and the sinking sun reflected off the metal badge pinned to his shirt. He was the law.

A quick appraisal of his imposing build reminded her of a bulldog, with his massive shoulders and chest set upon narrow hips. Dark, unruly hair showed from under a broad brimmed hat. Judging from his youthful features she guessed his age to be a year or two older than herself.

"Officer Taylor, arrest this hussy. She insulted me," demanded Mrs. Christian.

"Hold on a minute, ma'am, and we'll get this all straightened out." Jason Taylor's voice was reassuring but stern. He turned to the onlookers. "Everyone go on about your business. The show is over."

While the curious people slowly dispersed, the policeman waited patiently. Soon only Kate, her two friends, and Wilhelmina remained. Kate opened her mouth to speak until Taylor held his hands up, palms out to ward off explanations.

"I don't care who started this or what you called each other. You should both be ashamed of yourselves, carrying on in public. This is a quiet town and it's my job to keep it that way. Now, you both go on home and cool off."

"How dare you speak to me in that tone of voice, young man. Do you know who I am? I'll have your job for this," Wilhelmina huffed.

"I know who you are, Mrs. Christian. You're welcome to speak to Chief Gallagher at any time. His office is just down the street." Jason spoke politely, his voice devoid of emotion.

The matron's face was nearly purple with pent-up venom and vexation, to Kate's immense satisfaction.

"You'll hear from your superior. Don't think you won't," she declared. Abruptly, she turned her back to the officer and strutted from the park as fast as her hobble skirt allowed her.

Kate watched the angry retreat with concealed amusement. The sight of her opponent's frustration was delightful and this confrontation with a policeman did not upset her in the least. She had hardly listened to his light scolding. It was fun compared to the verbal and physical manhandling she had endured from the officers in New York. Actually, she felt grateful to have the squabble with Wicked Willy cut short. The Town Council meeting she planned to attend was due to start in a few minutes and she had to hurry.

"Thank you for the advice, sir." She smiled sweetly at the young man. "I shall go home and think about my actions. I can't imagine what got into me."

Kate almost retched at her own falseness, but Officer Taylor did not seem to notice. His mouth remained in a firm line but his gray eyes sparkled in appreciation. He is a handsome man in a rustic sort of way, she thought. The tingle of romantic interest was absent and she dismissed the fleeting notion.

Jason cleared his throat and tipped his hat. His gaze took in the three suffragists. "Good evening, ladies." He spoke with courtesy before walking out of the park.

Abigail and Caroline flanked Kate, both talking at once.

"What a disaster!" the teacher exclaimed and threw up her hands.

"It was so exciting!" Caroline grabbed her heroine's arm with enthusiasm.

Kate registered the conflicting views of the incident. This was their first experience with such matters and they had nothing to measure it against. She needed to put the events into perspective for them.

"What happened here was very ordinary compared with other situations I've been in. We got our message across. The debate with Mrs. Christian went quite well, I thought, until it degenerated into a shouting match, and you both handled the event with common sense. I am well satisfied."

The two helpers stared at Kate dumbfounded as she picked up the soapbox and tucked it under her arm. Obviously, they did not consider the event ordinary.

Abigail cleared her throat before she spoke. "I had no idea that a simple lecture would cause such an uproar. My participation will have to be re-evaluated."

"Does that mean you might not be willing to stand with me?" Kate felt her body sag with disappointment. She had come to think of the sensible schoolteacher as her lieutenant.

"Not at all," Miss Penny hastened to reassure her. "I meant that I might have to take more risks than I had originally intended. My self-respect does not permit me to stay silent while others carry the flag."

Kate breathed deeply with relief, then turned to Caroline. The young woman was still aglow with elation.

"If this is just a hint of the excitement that's possible, then I can hardly wait for our next lecture."

The veteran campaigner viewed her aides' determination and eagerness with a healthy dose of skepticism. She wondered if these untried troops would face heavy fire without flinching. In the thick of battle she needed soldiers she could depend upon. Only time would tell.

A quick glance at her lapel watch told her she had to hurry.

"I must get to City Hall for the council meeting. Will either of you join me?" Kate did not expect assent.

Her two companions mumbled excuses and regret as they retreated toward the park exit. Their actions were no more than she had anticipated. In spite of their show of bravado and enthusiasm, they were not willing to charge with her into the lion's den.

Masculine voices in loud argument drifted out of the open door to the meeting room of City Hall. River Run was not yet a city, but its seat of government had been named with a healthy dose of optimism. The pungent aroma of cigar smoke attacked Kate's nostrils as she crossed the entrance hall headed for the noisy council chamber. Without pausing at the doorway, she marched into the crowded room with a determined strut, passed the back rows of seats where it would be easy to hide, and settled in the front in full view of everyone.

Proceedings had already begun. This fact worked in her favor since it would cause a major disruption to eject her. She would not go quietly.

Her keen eyes scanned the smoke-dimmed room to take in relevant details. Directly in front of her four men sat on a low platform behind a table. They were the members of the Town Council. She recognized the huge bulk of Mayor Arnold Christian, who also ran the local bank. His thinning hair was neatly parted in the middle and brushed back from his florid face. He exuded sincere friendliness and self-confidence and the citizenry expressed their fondness for him by keeping him in the mayor's office for the last fifteen years. Beside the mayor sat Hank Slater, owner of the cannery and Kate's neighbor from across the street. His face showed large, coarse features topped with shaggy, brown hair. A loose jacket hung from his massive shoulders. He reminded her of a trained bear; possessed of immense latent power, but not threatening. The appearance of his name in the report of her father's death prompted her to wonder if he might be a threat after all. Her gaze shifted to

Jeffrey Carlisle who sat in the next chair. This impeccably dressed middle-aged dandy had been the Moore family's lawyer and still handled her affairs. His hair was slicked down and glowed with oil. The handlebar mustache was rigid with wax. She looked at him and had a sudden desire to wash her hands. Matthew Winkleman occupied the last seat. White blonde hair and a pale complexion gave the merchant the bland appearance of a worm.

The deep timbred ruckus in the room rapidly diminished. Then it was quiet. Kate could hear her own breath. She looked around the man-packed room for the cause of the miraculous phenomenon. All eyes were focused on her. A few of the looks were hostile, but most were just curious.

"Good evening, gentlemen. Don't mind me. I just want to see government in action." She leveled a blinding smile at the mayor, then turned coyly away. Although her nerves jangled at the idea of men looking down upon all things female, she felt no remorse at using her own femininity to her advantage. She was simply fighting by their rules.

Mayor Christian, always the diplomat, spoke evenly. "I don't see the harm in letting the lady stay, so long as she keeps in her place."

There was a low murmur of cautious assent. Kate bristled at the thought of "keeping in her place". She was certain her idea of a woman's place was galaxies away from the mayor's concept.

"Let's get back to the subject." Arnold Christian deftly directed the discussion back to placement of street lamps at the south end of town.

Kate was content to let the attention slip away from her for the moment, for she needed the time to finish assessing her surroundings and plan her next move.

At close inspection, she saw that most of the men in the room were either roughly dressed shopkeepers from the less privileged south side of town, or Portuguese shepherds from the Montezuma Hills. Vague memory of an article in the "River Run Gazette" flitted through her awareness. It had dealt with the shepherds' children attending the River Run schools. That would explain the hill men's presence.

As her scrutiny passed around the room, an unkempt man sitting in a corner caught her eye. A glowing cigar butt protruded from his whiskered face. Through the heavy tobacco smoke, she recognized Sam Wakely, owner of the town's only newspaper. Kate considered this an opportunity to get free publicity for women's suffrage. Her appearance at the meeting alone was cause for comment in the publication. The commotion she intended to provoke would be exciting news for this dull little town. An exhilarating tingle spread through her as she prepared her strategy.

She allowed the matter of street lights for the south of town to be settled without her comment. It would not serve her purpose to be ejected before she could put forth her views on the education issue. Finally, the mayor approached the subject of the schools.

"River Run has been accepting children from the Montezuma Hills into its schools. There were only a few of those children until Sacramento passed the mandatory education law. Now, our schools are being crowded with more children from our own south district as well as from the hills. We can't afford to build another school. Matthew Winkleman has looked into the situation and he has a few things to say about it."

The mayor sat down and the slight-framed merchant stood. His thin voice did not carry well and the background whispering was shushed so everyone could hear him.

Winkleman gave the facts and figures. It was expensive for the town schools to teach the extra children.

Kate concentrated on the comments and opinions voiced by the men. The town people were in favor of ejecting the shepherds' children from the schools. Their parents would have to hire a teacher for a one room school. A suggestion was made for the shepherds to pay toward the education in town, but the price was prohibitive. Angry heat rose to flush her face. They were reducing the quality of children's futures to dollars and cents. It was hard reality, but she did not have to like it. She pulled her soapbox out from under her seat. During a lull in the discussion, she stepped up onto her impromptu platform so she could be seen above the men. Her full voice projected through the chamber.

"I recognize your concern for the cost of education, but we are dealing with children's futures here. A one room school could not possibly have the advantages of our town's schools. Surely, there must be a way to finance the extra students."

"Money ain't easy to come by, but I guess you wouldn't know that," a roughly dressed man from the south district called out. He pointedly eyed her expensive suit and tastefully decorated hat. There was a mumbled undercurrent of agreement.

"But what about the welfare of the children? They deserve more than one meeting for this decision. Someone must look into ways to raise the money," she demanded.

"You got no right to come in here and tell us what to do. This is what too much education does to women. Makes 'em forget where they belong," a man from the back of the room flung at her.

The mayor called for attention. "Miss Moore, if you want to remain here, you must be quiet. You were not invited to speak. Please, sit down."

"Mr. Mayor, good sense is worthy of consideration whether it is offered by a man or a woman," she persisted.

"I never heard good sense from a woman yet," a deep voice rang out. To her chagrin, general laughter followed.

"I will not warn you again." Mr. Christian's hard gaze spiked Kate.

She decided a temporary retreat was favorable to expulsion. Her chin thrust out as she rigidly descended from the box and seated herself. The meeting continued with the mayor's announcement that the council would take all information into consideration when it made the decision on the school issue.

He brought up the next topic for discussion. Should a newly married woman teacher be allowed to continue in her job? The case under discussion was Eulalia Ericson who was soon to be wed.

Kate recalled the pretty blond teacher who had arrived at the suffrage meeting with Abigail. She was concerned about losing her job. This would be an excellent opportunity to support the rights of women.

Jeffrey Carlisle, the lawyer, explained the situation to the listeners. The reason for not employing a married female teacher was that her family's needs would take precedence over her work. Normally, the teacher would be asked to leave without a thought to the matter. Unfortunately, the supply of quality teachers willing to work in such a small town as River Run was sadly limited at this time. Should they bend the rules and keep Miss Ericson on?

Several remarks were made about setting a bad precedent. Kate burned. In her view, the entire discussion was idiotic. She stomped onto her soapbox again, her nerves crackling with indignation.

"Gentlemen, I can't believe what I am hearing. Where is your logic?" Passion emphasized her speech.

Men demanded that she sit down. Boos and catcalls nearly drowned out her words. She refused to let the rude reception dent her determination and continued the harangue without slowing.

Arnold Christian rose to his feet. "Miss Moore, you have abused your welcome. Now you must leave."

Kate ignored the mayor. She would leave when the choice was hers, not before. Less than a minute later, Jeffrey Carlisle purposefully came around from behind the table to stand before her. A dark cloud seemed to pass across the dandified lawyer's face as he reached for her arm. She automatically recoiled from his grasping, pale fingers. Her reaction was due more to revulsion at the thought of his touch than fear of being ejected from the meeting. The unexpected feeling surprised her. She had no aversion to most people's touch. Her stomach roiled in distaste when his long fingers clamped onto her arm. Quelling her inflamed nerve endings, she hastily picked up the box before he maneuvered her through the room.

"You would do well to stay clear of men's business." He firmly propelled her toward the door at the back of the room. Kate restrained herself from biting his hand.

"This meeting is everyone's business," she rejoined.

Once in the quiet hallway, Kate tried to pull from Carlisle's grasp. The pressure on her arm tightened as his fingers dug into her flesh. He bustled her quickly outside onto the City Hall steps.

"Don't come back," he threw at her as he turned to re-enter the building.

Kate heard the door click closed behind her. Fresh, sweet air filled her smoke-clogged nostrils. A soft, cool night breeze refreshed her overtaxed senses. The sound of deep voices wafted through an open window from the side yard which reminded her that this evening's job was not finished.

"I won't let them beat me," she told herself.

Determination stiffened her back as she strode briskly up the steps and grabbed the doorknob. It would not turn. Carlisle had locked the bolt. Her eyes glittered with deviltry as she remembered the open window.

With gleeful anticipation, Kate prowled around to the side of the building until she stood directly beneath the window. Tobacco smoke billowed out to blend into the darkness. The ledge was too high for her to reach. She stood her soapbox on the ground with its long side up and tested its sturdiness by leaning on it. Yes, it would hold her weight. Her palms braced against the building for support as she climbed onto the box. Smooth wood greeted her fingers when she grabbed for the window ledge, but the shift of her body unbalanced the box, toppling it with a clatter. Kate dangled from the window and her legs tangled in her petticoat. Using every bit of her strength, she heaved her wiry body through the open window to rest across the sill.

Noise, smoke and light bombarded her senses. A face prickly with whiskers came into focus beside her. Sam Wakely, the newspaper owner, watched as she struggled. Surprise and amusement registered in his dark brown eyes. His meaty hand reached out to offer her aid.

"No one could accuse you of being a quitter, Katydid."

Kate flinched at the use of his childhood nickname for her. Sam had been her father's friend and she had an abiding affection for the unpretentious rascal. His witness to her awkward position was not an embarrassment. He had never judged her. She grasped his proffered hand, letting him help her into the room.

"Thanks, Sam. I had myself in a tight spot for a minute."

"You haven't changed a bit. Still getting into mischief. How long do you think it will be before they kick you out again?"

"I hope to get a few licks in before they do."

"Then you'd best go to it, girl. The mayor just spotted you and he doesn't look happy."

Her glimpse toward the council table proved him right. Arnold Christian spoke to Winkleman, the merchant, but his gaze bored through Kate. They held eye contact, exchanging a fierce, silent challenge. She stretched taller with courage and moved toward her former seat at the front of the room. Winkleman hurried from the chamber, tossing the persistent female a condescending glare on his way out. A plot against her had been hatched. Curiosity itched at her, but she had no time to dwell on it.

Kate resumed her previous seat as though it belonged to her. Insistent grumbling rippled around her as if she were a pebble plopped into a pond. A satisfied smile stretched her wide mouth. Without saying a word, she had caused a disturbance that threatened to disrupt the proceedings.

From the corner of her eye she saw council member Winkleman re-enter the room and nod assurance to the mayor. The colorless worm's eyes glittered maliciously as they found Kate and bored into her. She shivered with foreboding. That unpleasant little man did not have her happiness in mind.

"Gentlemen," Mayor Christian announced. "It seems our unwelcome visitor has returned. I promise you, the situation will soon be remedied. Until it is, let us proceed with business."

Suddenly, it struck Kate what was happening. The police had been called to remove her. She looked at Sam Wakely sitting near the window, contemplating her with considerable amusement. He was certain to print a story about her disturbing the council meeting. This foray into the men's world would accomplish much. Her attention reverted back to the speaker at the front table. When the mayor affirmed the decision to allow Eulalia Ericson to continue teaching after her wedding, Kate enthusiastically applauded. The sharp clamor of her rapidly beating hands resounded through the room. She felt the men's disapproval swirling around her like a poison cloud and reveled in it. Time was short and any agitation she could promote might well be her last.

An abrupt shift in the mood of the men brought her to swift attention. They were shouting encouragement and whooping with gleeful eagerness. Kate could not see the cause for their celebration, but it did not bode well for her. The mayor called out to someone in the back of the room who had just arrived. It was impossible for her to hear the conversation above the expectant babble of voices. Men stood, blocking her view. one by one, they stepped aside and she looked up into the steady blue gaze of John Gallagher.

CHAPTER IV

An unladylike oath threatened to escape from Kate's lips. She would much have preferred to deal with young Officer Taylor on whom her feminine trickery would not be wasted. This cold-eyed ogre was too perceptive and unpredictable to be manipulated.

"Miss Moore, it's time for you to leave. You can make it easy on both of us by coming along with me quietly." Gallagher's voice was low and easy, but she sensed the steel behind it.

"This is a public meeting, Mr. Gallagher. I'm not breaking any laws by being here. There is no reason to arrest me." Kate's tone dripped with honey. Hoping to lead him into a game of wits, she labored to suppress a naughty smirk.

"I'm not arresting you, just removing a public nuisance. You can walk out or be carried. Which will it be?" His uncompromising attitude had her at a loss for words. This was no idle threat.

Before Kate could answer him, his hand closed around her arm in an unyielding grip and she felt herself being hauled from the seat. She struggled against his hold until the no-nonsense glint in his narrowed eyes convinced her the attempt was useless. Perhaps she could salvage this quickly degenerating episode with a show of dignity.

"Your manhandling is quite unnecessary, Mr. Gallagher. I can reach the door under my own power."

When he did not loosen his grasp, she glanced meaningfully at his offending hand. After a moment's hesitation he freed her arm and stepped aside to let her pass. Straightening herself to regal bearing, Kate marched through the room. Nearing the council table, she nailed each member in turn with a sharply honed gaze.

"Good evening, gentlemen. Thank you for your hospitality." Icicles clung to her words.

Gallagher admired the lady's courage and pride as, with cool dignity, she ignored men's jeering comments bombarding her from all directions. Her facial expression was shuttered and he could only guess at her angry, rebellious thoughts. He had seen her temper up close and imagined she was now a boiling cauldron of hidden emotions that would soon come spilling out onto him.

In the empty hall outside the meeting chamber, she stopped short and turned toward him.

"You said you aren't arresting me. Does that mean I am free to go now?" Her voice sounded strong with purpose.

"No. You'll sit in my office until the meeting is over. The council doesn't want you back in that room tonight."

"If I'm not under arrest, you have no right to force me and I won't go. Taking me at gunpoint won't work. I know you wouldn't shoot a defenseless woman."

He recognized the obstinate set of her chin and knew reasoning would be a wasted effort. He reached into his back pocket for the handcuffs.

"There are many things I would call you, lady, but defenseless isn't one of them."

Shock scrambled Kate's composure when she saw his hand come forward with the cuffs dangling from his fingers.

"Surely, you wouldn't use those on me." The telltale tremble in her voice annoyed her.

"I'll do whatever I have to. It's your choice."

Sensing his determination, she backed away from him, hiding her hands behind her skirt. Vile epithets flooded her mind, but she stifled them, waiting for her self control to return before making her next move.

"If you come near me with those shackles, I'll scream bloody murder and half the men in the next room will come to my defense."

"They'd come out here to cheer me on."

Suddenly, he reached behind her and grabbed her hand. His warm palm on the knuckles of her fist sent an electric tremor through her arm. Ignoring her body's heated reaction to his touch, Kate tried to pull her hand from his grasp without success. Frustration beating her senses to a froth, she kicked him on the shin,

Gallagher let out a surprised gasp as the pain coursed through his leg. Reflexes tightened his grip on her convulsively. As the hurt receded, he held back the impulse to retaliate with violence. If his attacker had been a man, his fist would be connecting with a jaw right now. But he had never hit a woman and had no intention of starting with this one, no matter the provocation. It struck him that this wild-eyed female was a monumental hypocrite. She demanded the respect given to men, but relied on a man's respect for the frailty of women in order to avoid physical punishment. To his way of thinking, she needed a lesson in fair play.

Surprised at her gall, he saw her foot snake out at him again. No way would he stand still for more of her punishment. While she was balanced on one leg, he grabbed her ankle in mid air. Her bottom hit the tiled floor with a resounding thud, her legs sprawled out in front of her like a rag doll. The black stockinged limbs were visible up to the knees. Her prim hat sat askew atop a myriad of escaped honey colored ringlets. Astonishment and indignation showed in her wide open eyes and crimson cheeks.

In spite of his trying to control himself, rumbling, raucous laughter spilled from him like water in a brook. Still chuckling, he extended his hand to help her up, but she batted it away. He watched with amusement as she wrestled with her petticoats while trying to stand up.

Gallagher marveled at her rapid change of roles. One moment she was a kicking, spitting hellion and the next she resembled a sulking ragamuffin. She was more entertaining than a circus.

"You are no gentleman," Kate announced after righting herself.

"I'm a gentleman when there's a lady present." He took firm possession of her upper arm and steered her across the hall toward the front door. "No more games. My patience is running thin."

Kate opened her mouth to protest his roughness when she noticed the handcuffs still clutched in his hand. She had to weigh the situation. No doubt this barbarian would use the restraints on her if she attacked him again or tried to get away. Would he tolerate verbal abuse if she cooperated by promising to walk with him to the jail? The metal bracelets would not lock her lips, in any case.

"You don't have to drag me. I won't cause any more trouble."

His eyebrow raised in doubt, but his hand dropped from her shoulder. She breathed easier when he retired the handcuffs to a back pocket.

They descended the steps of City Hall in silence. A sweet night breeze cleansed the cigar smoke from her lungs, replacing it with the scent of grass and pungent jasmine. Kate inhaled deeply in an attempt to capture a piece of the evening's tranquillity. Her bout with the Town Council was finished for now, but the day's conflict was not yet over.

From the corner of her eye, she glimpsed the shadowed profile of the man who walked beside her. A street light accented the rugged angles and lines of the police chief's features. Her blood stirred and she hastily looked away. He posed more of a challenge for her than any council meeting could. She would be fighting against him and her traitorous body's responses.

The silence between them hung heavily, his temporary victory chafing her pride. Well, she would not allow him to wallow in his smugness for long.

"There's no law against women speaking at town meetings. The men who wanted me gone created the problem, yet I was the one removed. You obeyed the council without hearing my side." She kept her tone deceptively relaxed. "Is it comfortable being tucked away in the council's pocket?"

His footsteps halted and she turned to see the expression on his face. Blue ice sparked from his eyes and his jaw muscles flexed in a wild rhythm.

"You'd best watch your mouth." Gallegher's words were measured. An undercurrent of violence flavored his voice, causing her to shiver with apprehension. "I would truly enjoy teaching you some manners."

Kate recoiled as his warm hand captured her neck in a firm grip. Her heartbeat accelerated to a gallop with fear and reaction to his melting touch. She instinctively knew he would not physically hurt her, but the threat of his thumb trailing fire as it wandered across her throat gave testimony to the seriousness of his intent. His gaze burned into her, demanding obedience.

"Do you understand?" Gallagher sensed her retreat.

He watched her head nod slightly in answer. For the moment, she was subdued, but experience had taught him not to trust this devious female. He knew she would be ripping her claws into him again before the night was over. Now, he must concentrate on getting her to his office without wringing her neck.

Reluctantly, he released his fingers from the softness of her throat, downy errant curls brushing against the back of his hand. A disconcerting truth struck him. Even during her most annoying behavior, she had the capacity to arouse his male need. Inwardly railing at his weakness, he took firm hold of his prisoner's narrow arm and hustled her to a rapid pace.

While his long stride comfortably settled into the gait, Kate was forced to hustle to keep from being dragged, the high heels on her shoes throwing her off balance. When she stumbled, only the support of his hand kept her from falling. His step slowed a bit, but not to her satisfaction. Her lips parted to complain about the harsh treatment until she read the no-nonsense set to his chin. Grim stoicism settled over her as she silently struggled to match his speed.

As they entered the jailhouse office, Kate squinted at the glare from the bare electric bulb dangling from the ceiling. Her eyes were still accustomed to the night.

"Sit." Gallagher pointed to the wooden chair facing his desk.

The sharp tone of his voice offended her, but the seat was too inviting to refuse. Their grueling pace on the way from City Hall left her in urgent need of a rest. Considering his strong reaction to her barb, she had half expected to be sitting in a barred cell. Her legs tingled with relief as she lowered herself onto the chair.

He stood in front of the desk, leaning back against it, arms folded across his chest. His scrutiny scorched through her like a forest fire, torching everything in its path.

"You've really got nerve, lady, disrupting a government meeting, striking a police officer, and brawling in public with the mayor's wife. I can't understand how such a small girl could get into so much trouble in so little time."

An angry red light flashed before her eyes.

"I am not a little girl to be scolded for misbehaving. I was exercising my constitutional right to free speech. As for kicking that brute of an officer, he deserved it." In spite of her growing wariness of the police chief, caution was not her strong suit. She suspected she would regret verbally wrangling with him, but her tongue seemed to have a life of its own, speaking her mind with no thought to consequences.

"You have no respect for the law."

"You're wrong. I have great respect for the law. It's men I have no respect for," she shot back. "They use the law against those weaker than themselves. Men use women however they please without concern for our welfare."

Gallagher noticed a dark shadow pass over her animated features. The light, sparkling eyes turned to deep pools of pain. Angry determination marked the tilt of her chin and straight line of her generous mouth.

Vengeance can give a person devastating force. Too bad people use their power to destroy instead of build, he thought.

"Fighting with men will do you as much good as a dog howling at the moon. You'd do well to learn your place."

"I know my place and it's not under some man's foot." Her words were flung out, heavy with defiance. "I will not be brow beaten."

The unlikely idea of this sharp-tongued witch being brow beaten aroused Gallagher's sense of humor. Hearty laughter shook from deep within him.

"Any man brave enough to marry you should be given a medal."

Considering the sparks flying from her eyes, he expected her to blow up like a volcano.

"When and whom I marry is no concern of yours. I would prefer the privacy of a cell to your boorish conversation."

"Sorry. There's a drunk sleeping it off in the back room. It's no place for a lady. You'll have to suffer with my boorish company." His smile was insincere. Her discomfort amused him. His shots were hitting their mark and he relished watching her squirm.

"And you will have to suffer with my curiosity." Her candy sweet voice warned him that her claws were bared. "You never did tell me how it feels to be owned by the Town Council. It must be lucrative, covering over their dirty work."

Kate watched the policeman push away from the desk and slowly advance on her. A fist of anxiety ground into her stomach as a thunder cloud seemed to gather over his head. His hands gripped the armrests of her chair, imprisoning her in the seat, his imposing frame towering over her, his masculine presence overpowering. Her vision was filled with the wide expanse of his shirt and stubble covered jaw. A musky scent uniquely his triggered her body's heated female response. The sleeve of his cotton shirt nearly touched her face, and she almost leaned over to feel it against her cheek. When his deep voice rumbled from above her, she had difficulty concentrating on the words.

"For two years I fought with every man on that council, almost losing my job because of it. I refused to take bribes or do unethical favors for them. Maybe that was how this town was run before, but not now." He took a deep controlling breath. "You just earned yourself a shadow. Step out of line and I'll cart you off to jail. I won't have my honor insulted. Nobody owns me. Not the council. Not anyone."

His fingers felt warm against her chin as he tilted her face up so she must look into his stabbing gaze. Kate's lids closed to shut out the visual attack as anger, fear and sensual hunger played havoc with her control. She fought valiantly to regain her equilibrium.

"Now you'll sit here and behave yourself until it's time to leave," he commanded.

He stepped back from her, turning toward his desk, but the unsettling influence of his physical nearness remained. Struggling against the power he had over her senses, she stood and flung stinging words at his retreating back, trying to deny her confusion.

"Does it make you feel manly, intimidating me with your body? You're twice my size, but that doesn't make you my master. Only a coward would resort to such methods."

He turned to stare at her, his lips compressed, jaw muscles working. His menacing expression hit her with stunning impact and she backed away from him. With an unexpected leap he was beside her, his iron grip trapping her wrist, the chair she had been sitting in easily lifted in his other hand. She could discern no hint of his intentions as he stomped across the room dragging her behind him. Her heart drummed with fear.

When Gallagher plunked the chair down facing the corner of two walls, Kate felt the heat of embarrassment flood her face. She had been three years old the last time her mother had made her sit in a corner. The thought of such demeaning treatment was intolerable to her. She strained against the persistent force his hands exerted on her shoulders as he pushed her down onto the chair.

"Sit here and don't dare move," he warned.

Kate's outrage overflowed. When he turned and started toward his desk, she stood up to hurl her anger at him.

"You can't do this to me. I'm not a child. How dare you treat me like this!"

As she started to walk away from the corner, he pushed her back onto the seat. Bolting up again, she nearly upended the wooden chair and herself. Investigating an ominous weight on her wrist, she discovered handcuffs linked her securely to the piece of furniture. It was a moment before the full impact settled in. Then molten fury burst from her like an erupting volcano.

Gallagher stood at a safe distance enjoying the performance. Now that he had won the duel, he could afford to admire her magnificent spirit. Her tiny feet pummeled the wall in front of her as her free hand pounded the chair arm. Inventive insults spewed from between her gritted teeth. Never before had he seen a grown woman throw such a glorious fit of temper. He was amazed that one small female could create such a clamor. And that colorful language. Where had a lady from The Hill picked up such vulgarity?

The uproar ceased as suddenly as it had begun and Kate's narrow shoulders slumped forward, her head bent in dejection. Her fragile neck, dotted with wispy curls, aroused his protective instincts, and he longed to lay a comforting hand on the silky flesh.

Gallagher, you're a fool, he told himself, turning away from the enticing woman-child. If he softened now, she would be at his throat again in an instant. An idea pushed his lips into a half smile. Opening the back door, he whistled and Rufus loped into the room and greeted Gallegher with a flapping tail and wet hand licks. Without a word, he led the overgrown yellow dog to the sulking woman in the corner.

Kate was so engrossed in her gloom that the first she knew of her visitor was the warm, drenching tongue on her face. Fetid dog breath attacked her nostrils. With her free arm, she pushed his head down onto her lap and buried her face in the soothing fur of his ruff. Rufus whimpered in sympathy. She clung to him like a friend, soaking in his animal warmth. It had been many years since she had last indulged in the release of a full blown tantrum. Then, she had known the relief of tears in the devastating aftermath. She could not allow herself that luxury in the presence of the detestable offal who had cuffed her to the chair.

She dug her hand into her reticule in search of the familiar comfort of the strand of yellow beads. The smooth, glass pellets felt cool against her fingertips as she lifted them out of the cloth bag. Memories of her father's supporting strength accompanied her emotional attachment to the simple necklace. "Make your anger work for you," he had told her. "Use it to make yourself strong against your enemies."

With renewed vitality Kate sat up straight and pushed Rufus off her skirt. His furry body settled across her feet in a gesture of protection and affection. She ventured a peek at the dog's mean-spirited master.

He sat behind his desk observing the gentle interplay of the young woman and the huge mongrel. A prick of jealousy stabbed at him as her delicate face nuzzled the fur at Rufus' neck. When the dog left her lap, he noticed the mustard colored beads in her hand. Recognition was instantaneous. She had toyed with that same necklace the last time she was in his office. A movement of her head brought his attention to her face. Gallagher was amused to see anger glitter in her eyes as though she had not crumbled into a sagging heap a few moments before. Their gazes met in a measuring inspection. He refused to give her the satisfaction of breaking eye contact first, and openly grinned when she sniffed in distaste and turned away. At least she's quiet, he thought, wondering how long the silence would last. His nerve endings tingled with the anticipation of their next clash.

Kate stared at the dingy wall and clenched her fists with determination. This rout had to be turned into a victory. Her experiences with the suffragists in New York had taught her to use dignity and pride when dealing with difficult situations. At this point, convincing him that she had any dignity whatever would be a monumental feat. Her pride, on the other hand, was in unlimited supply. She conjured up delicious plans for revenge but none of them would stand a chance against her opponent's physical strength and legal power.

When she heard the front door open and heavy footsteps thump into the room, Kate remained facing the wall. She was in no mood to greet anyone while in her present state of disgrace. She stifled a groan when the new arrival brought attention to her.

"That's one mean looking desperado you got there, John." Officer Taylor's chuckle grated on her ears. "What did she do, rob the bank?"

"She took on the Town Council and half the saloon owners from the Southside. You don't want to tangle with her, Jase," the police chief advised.

"Maybe I would," Jason commented. "I like my women with a dash of pepper."

Turning her head slightly, Kate watched the burly, young officer approach her. She remembered their earlier encounter in the park, his firm but polite handling of the confrontation. This gentle teasing was a side of his personality she had not seen before.

"Your preferences in women are of no concern to me, Mr. Taylor," she informed him, hoping the bite in her tone would dampen his playful mood.

The amused expression on his face turned suddenly dark.

"What's going on here, John? Why is she handcuffed to the chair?" His voice was tight with annoyance.

"I had to quiet her down. It isn't hurting her. Forget it."

The unfounded anger that Gallagher felt when Jason looked at the Moore woman with that special fire in his eyes, was a new experience. He wanted to get rid of the intruder, throw him out the door, punch his face, strangle him with his bare hands.

"This is no way to treat a lady, boss. She's so tiny there's no way she could hurt you. Look at her and tell me you can't handle her without cuffs."

Gallagher glanced at her and admitted to himself that she appeared as innocent and gentle as a newborn lamb, but his original opinion of her was borne out when she snarled at the deputy and took a verbal chunk out of his hide.

"He can't handle me with them, without them he is helpless. As for you, Mr. Taylor, your lecherous glances and condescending manner are an insult to womanhood. I don't need you to fight my battles."

Gallagher watched with satisfaction as his prisoner vented her spleen on her unsuspecting champion. The incredulous expression on Taylor's face tickled him. Hearty laughter rolled from him, filling the room.

Kate stared at him blankly until she realized that he was laughing at her.

"Shut up, you braying jackass," she shot at him.

The laughter continued louder. Rage bolted through her slight body. If she had not been cuffed to the chair, the Chief of Police would have felt her palm smashing against his cheek.

She was vaguely aware of the telephone bell jangling on the wall and Jason walking across the room to answer it.

"John, it's the mayor. He says the meeting is over and you can let Miss Moore go home now."

"Tell him thanks."

Kate watched as Gallagher stood up and walked toward her. His hand touched hers when he removed the metal cuff, sending an electric charge up her arm. Irritation at her body's startled reaction to his touch churned in her belly. She abruptly stood and pushed the chair back from the corner. The sooner she could leave his disturbing presence, the happier she would be. Rufus hauled himself off her feet and scampered out of her way.

"I can walk her home," Jason offered. His eagerness annoyed her.

"She's my responsibility. I'll make sure she gets home safely."

"That will not be necessary. My automobile is waiting for me near Willis Park. I will be quite safe without you."

Kate was eager to leave the two lawmen behind so she could relax and sort out her thoughts. The last thing she wanted was an escort to prolong the harrowing ordeal.

"Then I'll walk with you to your auto."

When she opened her mouth to protest, Gallagher's forefinger pressed against her lips before the words were out. Only the scintillating sensation of his flesh touching the sensitive area curbed her mad desire to bite the silencing digit.

"No arguments. I'm going with you."

Kate recognized the stubborn set of his jaw and knew she would be forced to tolerate his presence a while longer. Astonishingly, a part of her was pleased. Annoyed with herself for the traitorous warm feelings sneaking under her guard, she pulled away from him and headed for the door. He would certainly follow, but she would not give him the gratification of her consent.

Superior Avenue was nearly deserted after dark. Men's laughter and boisterous voices spilled from the pool hall across the street. Gallagher's long stride easily kept up with the tiny woman's hurried pace. He studied her finely etched profile, iridescent in the silver moonlight, shadows emphasizing the smooth plains of her delicate cheek and full curve of her lips. God, she was beautiful!

Her face turned toward him and he met her saucy glare straight on. For an instant, the cold light in her eyes melted and poured a golden stream of tenderness over him. The illusion appeared and evaporated with such haste that he almost disbelieved he had seen it. A vivid memory of that night on the road and the passion he sensed lay smoldering inside her dismissed the last of his doubts. Under that thorny battle armor was a sweet, loving treasure. He wondered if he could find a way to win her without getting too bloodied. The challenge was intriguing.

Kate faced away from him to block out the exasperating man's image. Why did he have to look so enticingly masculine in the subtle moonlight? How could she rail at him when her blood was racing in anticipation of a kiss that must not happen? Her confused emotions were a hopeless tangle.

"How could your mother allow you to live here alone?" Gallagher asked. "or did you run away from home?"

"I didn't have to run away. My stepfather insisted that I leave. My suffragist activities embarrassed him." Kate's words were brisk to keep the pain from her voice. Her mother's part in banishing her still hurt too much to admit to anyone.

Fleetingly, she wondered why she felt the urge to discuss her personal life with this man whom she had done little but fight with since their first meeting. Confiding in him seemed so comfortable that she could not help but indulge the impulse.

"It seems you aren't the only one who doesn't appreciate my adventuresome ways," she continued. "Actually, I'm enjoying my freedom. There's no one at home waiting to scold me tonight or try to stop me the next time I decide to ruffle a few feathers."

Gallagher ignored the remark about future ruffled feathers. He was intent on recalling his own departure from his parents' home.

"That first taste of freedom can be mighty sweet," he agreed. "My father kicked me out when I was sixteen. I traveled a little, drank a lot, worked when I wanted. The only bad time was Christmas away from home, remembering my mother's mince pie and the little kids stringing popcorn for the tree."

He grew silent, wrapped in his memories.

Kate was startled by his gentle expression as he thought of his family. She remembered that he had been returning from a visit with them the night she had met him on the road.

"You went back to them. Why?"

"I never went back there to live. Farming wasn't for me, but I love them and they love me, even if we don't think alike."

The last phrase rolled around in her head. Was that true? Could people love each other through the hurt? She doubted her mother would ever love her unless she behaved like a lady, and the possibility of that happening was near zero. Her father had taught her to respect and enjoy down-to-earth people, their work and pastimes. Social status meant nothing to her and everything to her mother. In spite of their differences, Kate still held frantically to the hope that her mother would someday love her.

"Maybe we've done too much to each other to ever forgive." Her words were barely audible, as though she might not want anyone to hear them.

"I don't believe that. The love between parents and children is hard to kill."

Kate wanted to accept that comforting idea. She would have to think about it when she was alone. Now, she had to deal with emotions of a different sort. In the last few minutes, her pique at the man walking beside her had dissolved, along with the defense it afforded against his physical appeal. He exuded strength and she basked in it like a cat in the springtime sun.

Kate stopped beside the Pierce Arrow waiting for her under a street lamp. Her glance in Gallagher's direction found him openly staring at her. His expression was intent as his eyes lingeringly drank in her lips, nose, eyes. Expecting a kiss, she backed away in panic as he took a step toward her, but he moved too fast for her to escape.

She felt herself pulled forward and lifted off the ground by his well muscled arm around her waist. Warm, soft lips captured her mouth. As she squirmed to break his hold, her breasts rubbed against his chest, her apprehension overshadowed by the exciting heat radiating through her from those twin peaks.

A moan escaped from her throat as fire ignited low in her belly. His mouth pushed urgently against her lips and she parted them, her mind ceasing to think coherently as she surrendered to sensation. He tasted pleasantly of aromatic pipe tobacco and she wanted to devour him. Her fingers found the soft hair at the back of his neck and burrowed into it. His tongue tentatively entered her mouth and explored, raising her desire to a fevered pitch. The bulge of his hard manhood straining against his pants brushed her leg and she knew he was also affected by the electric storm they generated.

Abruptly, Kate stood on her own feet again, held away from his warmth at arm's distance. Her first reaction was a sense of loss. Then she remembered where she was and with whom she was. Her thoughts were tangled and she was too shaken to straighten them out. This spellbinding male animal could stealthily creep under her barricade and hurt her like that weasel Trevor had. She must never again allow a man to get close enough to hurt her.

The need to run from his magnetism and her own wayward feelings prompted her to leave without another word, but she would not have him think she was a coward. She would offer one more jibe before departing.

"I'm leaving. You'll have to find some other woman to brutalize."

Gallagher's eyes were closed as he struggled for control of his body. At her taunt, he opened them to look at her. He was pleased that her witch's mask was back in place. Her surprisingly passionate response to his kiss had spurred him to take it to a depth he had not intended. The hurt young woman under that prickly facade made him uneasy with a confusion of unfamiliar feelings. He was more comfortable with her temperamental side.

An instant before she had drawn back from him, he had recognized the fear in her rounded eyes. Why was she afraid of him? Earlier, when he had threatened and raged, she had defied him at every opportunity. Could she fear his gentleness?

"I think I'll let the other women off easy and save all of my cussedness for you. Stay out of mischief or you'll find out what I do to naughty little girls." Gallagher fought against his inclination to grin. He knew she loathed being referred to as a child.

"Your threats don't scare me, Mr. Gallegher. I do what I must, regardless of the consequences. If you get in my way, you'll find me an untiring adversary."

"Is this a challenge, Miss Moore?" After all she had suffered this evening, he had difficulty believing she had so much brass left.

"Take it as you like. I will win the vote no matter your efforts to thwart me. You are merely an obstacle to be walked around or climbed over, like a tree or a rock. Nothing more."

Her taunt stirred his male instinct to dominate her until it breathed like a living creature. He rejected going another round with her in the middle of Superior Avenue in full view of anyone who cared to watch. When they fought to the finish, it would be a bare knuckle free for all and he wanted no interference.

"I take it as a declaration of war and you'd best get your tail home before I catch it in the wringer. Get in the auto. I'll crank her up."

Kate considered refusing his offer, but decided that accepting his dismissal was preferable to spending more time in his presence. She was still trembling inside from their kiss. Yet the temptation to sling a parting shot was too strong to deny.

"For your sake, I hope you don't plan on a war of wits. You don't have much of an arsenal."

"Don't claim victory too soon, lady. I won't fight by your rules."

When he reached up to gently smooth her cheek with his finger, danger alarms clanged in her brain. Kate needed to get some distance between them . . . fast. Her back resembling a ramrod, she marched to the driver's side of the auto and climbed in. She waited silently while he rotated the crank.

As the motorcar started, Kate had an insane impulse to run the machine over him, but common sense ruled. He stepped lithely to the sidewalk and his smug expression as he stood watching her ride away, chewed at her pride. She vowed not to let him win the war.

CHAPTER V

Numbers danced on the sheet of paper, evading Kate's every attempt to focus. In surrender, she dropped her pen on the desk and leaned back in the leather chair, feeling dwarfed in the man-sized furniture. Her father's presence wrapped around her in a comforting hug. She sniffed at the supple leather for a whiff of his scent, but inhaled instead the heady aroma of roses wafting to her from a vase on the desk.

Kate considered the delicate blushing pink flowers and how well they blended in with the light, feminine touch she had used to transform her father's masculine study. A framed seascape replaced the buck's head hunting trophy, lacy sheers hung in place of heavy, burgundy drapes, and plants brightened the bookcase.

Bringing herself back to the business at hand, Kate glanced at the figures on the paper in front of her. She wondered with a sense of desperation how house repairs and running expenses could add up to such an appalling sum. At this rate Papa's legacy would be gone before the year was out. Her only choice was to take in boarders as soon as possible. Perhaps Abigail Penny would be interested in becoming her first tenant. Kate brightened at the prospect.

Her glance caught the envelope she had thrown down on a far corner of the desk. The address was written in her mother's ornate hand. Much to Kate's relief, telephone lines from California went only as far as Chicago, keeping her mother in New York from reaching her by phone. Written words were easier to ignore than her mother's demanding voice. Or were they?

She had read the letter upon receiving it yesterday and had been trying to forget it ever since. Burning it had crossed her mind, but the guilt pangs she would suffer would not be worth the satisfaction of watching the flames.

Why does she insist on rubbing my nose in the dirt? Kate asked herself, remembering the letter's reference to her unfortunate romance with Trevor Freebush. Does she get pleasure from hurting me? That possibility was too painful for her to contemplate and she pushed the notion aside.

Kate considered her written reply to her mother's letter, imagining the disapproving frown on her mother's face as she read that rowdy suffrage activities had landed her daughter in the custody of the police chief. She laughed at how the plans to run a boardinghouse would shock her mother to the core of her snobbish heart. More pressing business requiring her attention, Kate set a reply to the letter aside for the present.

She wrote a column of figures estimating the cost of a trip to San Francisco to attend the 1910 California Women's Suffrage Convention being held the following month. The sum at the bottom of the long list of numbers was depressing.

Perhaps she could visit with the Endicotts for a few days instead of staying at a hotel. A warm glow welled up inside of her at the thought of seeing Priscilla Endicott, her closest friend at Durham's Ladies' Academy in San Francisco. She also looked forward to visiting with the elder Endicotts who had rescued Kate from the comfortless dormitory by inviting her to spend weekends with them. Now Prissy was married and she and her husband lived with her in-laws in their mansion.

Not wanting to impose on people she had never met, Kate decided to stay with Priscilla's parents. This evening she would telephone the Endicotts and make arrangements.

Her decision made, she leaned back into the over-sized chair, again allowing her thoughts to drift toward her father. Two weeks had passed since she had seen the police report on his death. During that time, she had spoken to Dorothea Mendez, Blanca's daughter, about Henry Slater. The factory worker knew little about her employer's private life, but had briefed her on the deplorable working conditions at the cannery. Kate was appalled at what she heard. Now she had two reasons to speak to the man.

This being Sunday, she thought Henry Slater might be at home. Aware that approaching him on the delicate subjects of her father's death and working conditions at his factory would be far beyond the bounds of proper conduct, but to her way of thinking, the niceties of polite society did not apply when important issues were at stake.

With enthusiasm, she marched to the entry hall and picked up the wide-brimmed hat that matched the ecru linen dress she wore. Kate secured the hat to her hair with a pearl-tipped hatpin and slipped lace gloves over her hands. A quick glance in the wall mirror reflected her elegant charm. She would appear the perfect lady to gain entrance into the Slaters' home.

Like a soldier, Kate threw back her shoulders, bracing herself for battle, and opened the door.

The Slaters' front parlor was arranged with large, comfortable furniture, devoid of the fringes, knick-knacks and gilt common in so many fashionable Edwardian homes. From her vantage point as she sat in a straight-backed chair, Kate admired the room for its uncluttered honesty. The housekeeper had shown her here to wait, then gone to announce the guest to her employer.

Kate watched Henry Slater enter the room and stand before her. His tall, barrel-chested physique was imposing. He had not bothered to put on his suit jacket and his shirt sleeves were rolled up, baring well-furred forearms. His informal appearance and impatient scowl impressed upon Kate his lack of respect for her, but she was not deterred.

"Good afternoon, Mr. Slater. I hoped to speak with you for a few minutes." She forced politeness into her tone.

"Is this a social call or do you have a purpose in being here?" His deep, rumbling voice sounded abrupt to her.

"I'm here to discuss the employees at the cannery. It has come to my attention that many of the women are not pleased with the conditions they are forced to work under."

"No one is forcing anyone to work at the cannery. My girls are free to leave any time they want. There'd be three people waiting in the hiring line for every job they'd leave. You don't understand anything about business or working. I suggest you mind your own affairs, young lady." She detected no anger in the reply, only head-patting condescension.

"You can't hold people down forever. I wouldn't be surprised if your workers unionized. All they need is strong leadership from someone who isn't afraid of you." Kate caught a flicker of alarm on his face before annoyance appeared in the glint of his steel gray eyes.

"I hope for your sake, that wasn't a threat. Organizing a union can be dangerous. It's no job for a lady."

"I am not in the business of union agitation, Mr. Slater. My intention was to avoid such unpleasantness with a discussion of possible changes in working conditions."

A quick succession of emotions sped across his coarse features, beginning with silent shock and ending with restrained rage. Before he could answer, muffled footsteps sounded on the carpet and Beatrice Slater entered the room.

"Who has come to visit, Hank?" she asked, stepping to her husband's side.

After six years, seeing the Slaters standing side by side, Kate was struck anew by the incongruous match of the woman's cultured grace with her mate's burly crudity. With a creamy complexion accented against her dark hair, Bea was impressively attractive, even though the bloom of youth had faded.

Kate's curiosity piqued as her neighbor's luminous brown eyes flew wide in panic and she turned to flee, but Henry's hold on his wife's arm prevented her escape. Mrs. Slater's bodice rose as she sucked in a long, steadying breath and shut her eyes.

Wondering at the woman's distraction at seeing her, Kate was reminded of Beatrice watching her through the bedroom window, then closing the drapes. What could be disturbing her?

"Good afternoon, Mrs. Slater."

"Good afternoon," Bea choked out.

"The young lady was just leaving," Slater announced.

Determined not to leave before her mission was accomplished, Kate stood her ground. "There is just one thing I would like to ask you before I go. I read the police report about my father's death. Why were you questioned?" Kate expected to get the answer from the expression on his face, not from his words.

Beatrice covered her trembling lips with her fingers, jerked free of her husband's grasp and fled from the room.

"I have no idea why Chief Peach questioned me. I was at the cannery all that evening." His voice shook with barely contained emotion. "Your business here is through and you will leave now. In the future, you will stay away from me and my wife."

Kate watched him stomp from the parlor. She read rage, pain and frustration flitting across his face through the holes in his control. The rage and frustration she could understand, but the pain was a mystery. Mrs. Slater's high strung reaction was another puzzle. Others knew something she did not and she was determined to keep asking until she discovered what it was.

As she stood and started from the room, a maid appeared to show her to the door. Once outside, she allowed a deep breath of relief to escape between her teeth. The confrontation was more harrowing than she had expected. Since she had gone on the attack without preamble, she had expected Henry Slater's belligerence, but Beatrice's near pass with convulsions at the sight of her had been a surprise. She wondered what could have caused the irrational response.

Sunlight struck her as she left the shelter of the porch and strode along the path crossing the lawn.

Kate struggled with her depressing thoughts. Life was not as simple as she had thought when she was a child. The man she previously considered as "friendly Mr. Slater" actually ran a sweat shop, her father was in financial trouble at the time of his death, Police Chief Peach took bribes from members of the Town Council, and her father's death might not have been an accident. She hoped that future revelations about the town's people, and her parents in particular, would not be as disappointing as she believed they might be.

The kernel of a deliciously outlandish idea took root in the fertility of Kate's mind. Happily, she rubbed her hands together in anticipation of accomplishing many goals with one daring act. She would further the cause of women's suffrage, bring the plight of the cannery workers to public scrutiny and further irritate Henry Slater, whom she suspected of having something unsavory to do with the death of her father.

CHAPTER VI

At twenty minutes to seven in the morning, the sun was already dispelling the mist over the river. A bleak, two story brick building jutted out from the lower warehouses surrounding it. Workers trickled through the outside wooden gate, but were reluctant to enter the building. There was still plenty of time to get to their work stations before the seven of clock starting bell.

An automobile stopped outside the fence and the three lady passengers removed their dustcoats. The fine quality of their fashions contrasted sharply with the coarse, durable clothing of the cannery employees. Curious stares followed the movements of the women climbing down from the Pierce-Arrow.

Kate nearly gagged at the pungent smell of cooked and rotting tomatoes. The air reeked of the stench. She had no doubt of what the cannery was producing.

In an attempt not to appear over-dressed to the cannery workers, she chose to wear a white blouse with only one row of lace and a plain dark blue skirt, but the delicate fabric and excellent fit betrayed her costume's expense. After a cursory inspection of the fence, Kate addressed her companions, Caroline Parkhurst and Rebecca Willis, also a resident of The Hill.

"Come, ladies. Our duty awaits."

When she started to march through the gate, Miss Willis grabbed her arm. Kate turned to Rebecca, struggling to suppress her annoyance. She had her doubts whether the twenty-eight-year old spinster had the gumption to follow through with today's plan. Rebecca was reported to be of a dull, bookish nature. Her unadorned gray dress, pale eyes peering from behind spectacles, and brown hair severely pulled back into a bun reinforced Kate's doubts.

"If we enter that yard, we could be arrested for trespassing."

"Yes, that is a possibility, but the women are congregating there. We have an audience waiting for us. Besides, Mr. Slater knows us personally and he wouldn't have us arrested." Kate's last remark was a falsehood designed to subdue Rebecca's apprehensions. One of her objectives this morning was to create a disturbance worthy of police involvement and a column in the *Gazette*. She fumed, remembering that Sam Wakely had ignored her appearance at the Town Council meeting. The newspaper publisher had refused to give the suffrage cause free publicity unless an issue he deemed more important was also involved.

"Come now, Becca. Where is your sense of adventure?" Caroline prodded. "Women will never get the vote if we do not put ourselves forward." Kate stepped back from the gated entrance as Caroline passed through.

She noticed Miss Willis' eyes register distress behind her wire-rimmed spectacles. "Have courage, Becca," Kate heard her whisper to herself as she tentatively crossed the gateway.

Kate set down her peach crate platform to the side of the building's entrance where a crowd of listeners would bar the doorway and create a nuisance. Such a location would also be impossible for the workers to ignore. She hopped up onto the wooden box and, projecting her voice to the far reaches of the yard, introduced herself and her assistants.

At first, Kate was aware of the hostility in the workers' comments. She suspected they did not appreciate intruders into their territory, especially women who had never dirtied their hands with manual labor and wore hats that cost more than they earned in a month.

"Are all of your managers men? Do any of you hard working women have any chance of becoming a manager? How much is a man paid for shifting crates of fruit around? I bet it's more than any woman earns for doing a job just as difficult."

Kate's words seemed ignored by the women she addressed until a burly man stepped in front of her. His beard-stubbled chin nearly touched her face. She was almost brought to her knees with a whiff of his unwashed body and dragon breath.

"There ain't no woman here can lift a crate like a man. We're better'n them so's we get paid more an' we're smarter'n them so's we get to be boss. Now quit your caterwaulin' and git outta here!"

A rush of satisfaction warmed Kate's heart as a loud protest, mostly in Portuguese, erupted from behind him and pebbles pelted his back. The man retaliated with a barrage of foul language while he retreated into the building. Kate could not suppress a smile. Her assailant had done her a favor. The women considered her an outsider until all womanhood was attacked. Now she was one of them.

"That pea-brained grizzly bear can vote to make your laws, but you are not given that privilege. Is he smarter than you are? I doubt it. So long as women are unable to vote, we will be paid less than men, denied managerial jobs, and forced to work under insufferable conditions." Kate continued.

A glance toward her helpers reinforced her confidence. Female employees accepted the printed fliers.

"You women who stay home have life easy," a man called out from the increasing crowd. "How can you stand here telling these working girls what to do, when you haven't worked a day in your life? If these girls complain, they could lose their jobs. What do you big-mouthed trouble makers lose?"

"When women are able to vote, we will change conditions by passing laws. No one would lose a job because of it. Tell me, sir, are you married?" She addressed her detractor.

"Yes, and I support my family. My wife doesn't have to work," he answered with pride.

"How nice for her. All she has to do is wash and iron the clothes, do the shopping, cook, clean the dishes, scrub the floors, mend the clothes, clean the house, take care of the children and obey your orders." Her eyes gleamed like a cat that had feathers hanging from its mouth. "I wonder what she does with all her spare time."

Applause and laughter filled the yard. Briefly she looked at her lapel watch. In three minutes the factory starting whistle would sound and most of the female workers were still in the yard. Kate hoped to keep them from their jobs long enough to draw attention from the management. Without the cooperation of the female employees her plan would fail.

"Ladies, this is an opportunity to display your pride and let Mr. Slater know you have a strong voice. Stand with me," she implored.

A few women entered the building. Kate knew it was late and most of those who were not swayed by her speech were already at their work stations. The majority of the cannery employees still stood in the yard. Two women guarded the door, discouraging last minute defectors from leaving the ranks. Kate recognized Dorothea Mendez as one of the enforcers. She was not familiar with the other woman.

Her already taut nerves were stretched further by the whistle to start work. As if on cue, a thin young man sporting a magnificent handlebar mustache and pomaded hair parted down the middle appeared at the door to the building. She did not recognize him, but judging from the uncertainty obvious on Dorothea's face, he was an important man here.

"Everyone to your place at once. We will not put up with such behavior. For every minute you're out here, we'll dock your pay," the man announced.

"That is a ridiculous threat. They will just work later at the end of the day because you don't want your tomatoes to rot. I've heard how you lock the doors so they can't leave in the evening," Kate said with a pugnacious thrust of her chin.

She was not disturbed by the disdainful glower the young man turned in her direction.

"So it's Miss Moore who's responsible for this unruliness. I might have guessed it was you after witnessing your disgraceful performance at the town meeting."

"Please introduce yourself, sir. I would like to know who I'll have the pleasure of insulting."

"My name is Matthew Liszt and I'm a manager here. You're trespassing on company property. If you don't remove yourself, I'll personally escort you out by force."

His menacing words and stance were promising signs to Kate. Her intention to evoke violence here was near fulfillment. She was still uncertain of the support of the women in the crowd, but she would test that without delay.

"Spoken like a true man of courage. Truthfully, you look too dandified to muss your hair dealing with the likes of me."

Kate was pleased with the reaction. A few titters from the employees brought red heat to the manager's face. He started forward, a rigid set to his stride, but was soon stopped by a barricade of sturdy women's backs. They would not let him through to reach her. With an amazed expression, he looked around at the more than one hundred women standing in the yard.

Triumph illuminated Kate's soul. Urgently, she searched the edge of the gathering for Caroline. Once she sighted her helper, she waved her arm. Cary nodded her head in acknowledgment of the prearranged signal and left the premises.

Now that her friend had gone to make the phone call to inform Sam Wakely of a disturbance at the Montezuma Cannery, her task was to keep the situation lively until he arrived. Before returning her attention to the beleaguered Mr. Liszt, she sought a glimpse of Rebecca, hoping not to find her in a panic. She was jolted at the sight of the usually colorless, self-effacing lady pushing herself among the crowd to hand out fliers and voice her enthusiasm for the suffrage cause. With her face flushed from excitement, Rebecca appeared almost pretty to Kate.

"Miss Moore, if you don't leave immediately, I shall call the police to deal with you," the manager warned from the safety of the doorway.

"So you would call in a replacement to do your dirty work. Do you think a badge would make any difference? You can't stop what's happening here. If Mr. Slater doesn't improve conditions now, he'll be forced to do it when women get the vote and help make the laws," she answered.

"You've made your point and I can't see the benefit to you or anyone else of prolonging this unfortunate incident. In a few moments Mr. Slater will take charge here and, I assure you, he won't treat you with the same patience I have shown. Please be reasonable."

She almost laughed at his desperate plea. Doubtlessly, Slater would appear to take charge for his unsuccessful underling who could not handle a mere female uprising. The young man had more cause for distress at his boss' appearance than she did.

"I would welcome the opportunity to debate with Mr. Slater. As for your patience, I haven't seen much evidence of it. All you've done is issue threats. Arguing with you is a waste of my breath."

Following the last announcement, she launched into a lecture on workers' rights. She felt gratified to see everyone ignore Liszt's attempts to regain attention.

Ten minutes later, Kate watched Slater push his pleading manager aside and storm into the crowded yard. His face was nearly purple with anger and restrained violence, his hands curled into fists. He pushed and shoved a path as he walked up to Kate who was elevated on her peach crate. Given the extra height of her platform, she was still a few inches shorter than his towering bulk.

"You're trespassing, causing a riot, and costing me money. I could have you thrown in jail." His voice was calm, but Kate recognized rage in the fire blazing from his heavily browed eyes. "You're leaving."

Kate winced as he roughly latched his huge hand onto her upper arm and yanked her off the box. Instinctively, she lashed her reticule against the side of his head and her foot made solid contact with his leg. Slater's other hand came up defensively to ward off her attack.

The crowd threw ugly words at the man, accusing him of brutal misuse of a fragile woman. When he scowled and dropped her arm, she ceased her wild struggle.

"Mr. Slater, I did not think you are the sort of man to mistreat a woman. I hope I was not mistaken." Kate was surprised by Rebecca's statement as the lady came to stand beside her.

"You would not want to do anything foolish." As Kate heard Caroline's voice she looked behind her to find her friend had returned with Sam Wakely in tow. A fresh wave of excitement zinged through her blood.

"Matt, call Chief Gallagher. We'll let him handle this."

Slater's voice brought her attention forward again and she watched Liszt disappear into the building.

"That was a wise move, Hank," Wakely commented while he scribbled notes on a well-used note pad.

"What are you doing here, Sam?" Henry asked.

"I'm covering a labor dispute. It seems your workers are unhappy. What's your side of it?" The reporter had a pencil at the ready.

"I don't know what this is all about. My people never complained before. These three women are trespassing and causing a commotion."

Kate thought this a first-rate opportunity to get a punch in. "They complain. You just don't listen. Do you have any idea what your workers think of the conditions here?"

"My girls have no reasons to complain. If they don't like it here, they can quit."

"They are women, not girls. You treat them with no respect, demanding late hours, locking the doors and windows, allowing dangerous conditions. If women had the vote, we would make such violations of human decency a crime."

Several women cheered.

A flurry of activity at the gate distracted Kate and she mounted the peach crate to see over the crowd. The horse drawn paddy wagon was parked outside the fence, and she shuddered at sight of the ominous iron bars over the ventilator holes. She looked toward the gate. Two men entered the yard and made steady progress toward the building. The early morning sunlight broke through the mist, glancing off their badges. There was no mistaking John Gallagher and his deputy. They strode with determination, their shoulders set proudly with authority. Kate's stomach flipped over in anticipation of the coming battle.

She felt the anxiety of the crowd pulsate around her as Slater moved among the people to intercept the policemen. An uneasy murmur rippled through the workers. Kate sensed a shift of the women toward the door and the security of their work stations.

"You really did it this time, Katydid. Just back off easy and let me handle the badges." She appreciated her friend's offer, but this was her fight.

"No thanks. I never back off, Sam. It's not in my nature."

The women in front of Kate stood aside to let their boss and the lawmen pass. Gallagher's blue eyes stabbed at her, promising no mercy. She tried to swallow the cantaloupe lodged in her throat.

"Mr. Slater says you three women are trespassing on his property." The chief eyed each suffragist in turn. "Jase, escort Miss Willis and Miss Parkhurst to the wagon. I'll deal with Miss Moore."

"Stand your ground, ladies. Don't let these barbarians bully you," Kate exhorted her helpers.

"Nonsense, Katherine." Rebecca's voice held a no nonsense ring. "We have broken the law and I know these officers to be gentlemen. I do not mean to be disloyal, but this madness has gone far enough."

Kate regarded her with dismay. Without the backing of her team, her own efforts would be barely noticed. She eyed Caroline in a silent appeal for support. Her young friend turned away, embarrassment over her lack of courage stamped on her features. Officer Taylor led his prisoners out of the yard.

"Henry, speak to your people. Their show is over. You can come to the jailhouse later and press charges," Gallagher said.

He turned toward Kate. She surveyed the crowd of workers to gauge their willingness to stand behind her. Many of them were striding toward the factory door. Within a few moments, there would be a general stampede in that direction. The glory time was over and now she had to pay the price in humiliation. If she were alone in this, the lawmen would feel her sharp teeth, but there were Cary and Becca to consider.

The chief firmly took hold of her arm and steered her toward the gate. "You're coming with me. There's a cell waiting for you."

She walked beside him, her shoulders thrown back in a display of pride and courage. Satisfaction swelled within her as they passed Sam Wakely still holding his notepad. Her publicity campaign was well launched.

"After my last visit, I didn't think you would be so eager to invite me again." She kept her tone light in an attempt to hide her growing anxiety.

"Lady, I'd rather face down two crazed killers than deal with you. They're more predictable."

When they joined Officer Taylor and his two prisoners at the paddy wagon, the chief unlocked the door and swung it wide.

"In you go." Taylor helped Caroline hoist herself up onto the high step.

Kate watched her companions swing up, then maneuver awkwardly through the broad doorway and onto the wooden bench. When it was her turn, the step was too high to place her foot. Without warning, she was lifted from the waist and deposited inside the wagon. She turned to see which of the two men had treated her so abruptly, only to have the door slammed inches from her face.

She sank onto one of the wooden benches built in along the sides of the wagon. Opposite her sat her fellow prisoners. With the door shut, the enclosure was twilight dark, the only light filtered through the small barred opening high on the wall. Her gorge rose at the stench of sweat and urine permeating the air. The board seat bumped her bottom with a jostling motion as the wagon started forward.

Tentatively, Kate turned her attention toward her companions. Caroline's huge, blue eyes were alight with exuberance. The naive nineteen-year-old would slam into reality quickly enough when her parents learned about this morning's adventure, she thought. Her gaze shifted to Rebecca, expecting to find the quiet-mannered lady steeped in tears and mortification. To her relief, the woman's straight back and guarded expression exuded controlled stoicism.

"Everything went perfectly." Kate forced enthusiasm into her announcement. "The workers were receptive and Sam Wakely will give us space in his newspaper. This is an excellent beginning."

"I would hardly consider being arrested as part of an excellent beginning. To what advantage is our being locked up like common criminals?" Miss Willis spoke in a tight voice.

"We made ourselves and our cause noticed and people will know that we are serious. Sitting in a cell may be degrading, but it won't do us any harm. It's a small price to pay for advancing our cause," Kate answered with conviction.

"Perhaps some of us are not prepared to pay such a price," Rebecca said. "The next time your plans include jail, please let me know. I would prefer to make that decision for myself."

After assuring Becca she would be warned of such plans in the future, Kate leaned back to relax for the remainder of the ride.

The blanket on the cot where Kate sat was rough under her hand as she rubbed it in nervous repetition. Conditions in this jail were not nearly as disturbing as her similar experiences in New York City had been. At least, here she did not have to endure the company of prostitutes and vulgar drunks. That was not to say that these accommodations were luxurious. A flimsy cot was the only furniture in the cell. She looked through the bars to see Cary and Becca sitting on the bed in the cubicle they shared. They appeared absorbed in their private thoughts.

"What are they going to do to us?" Caroline's voice was tremulous. Her earlier bravado seemed to Kate to be wearing thin while she was enveloped in the bleak jail.

"If Mr. Slater presses charges, we could be fined for creating a disturbance and he could sue us for damages. But I don't think he'll do that. Both of your fathers know him well and men aren't comfortable prosecuting women, especially ladies. We'll probably get off with a slap on the wrist," Kate answered, remembering back. As a result of her eight arrests in New York, she had only been required to pay two light fines.

"How long do you think we will be here?" Rebecca asked.

"That depends on how soon Chief Gallagher decides what to do with us. We could speed up the process by annoying him." Kate perked up at the thought.

"I do not consider that a wise idea," Becca commented.

As the women lapsed into silence again, Kate spent the next twenty minutes throwing mental darts at the Police Chief. Her curiosity piqued as the door to the office opened and Gallagher entered the room. He made no move to unlock the cells and Kate wondered at the purpose of his visit.

"Ladies, this is your lucky day. Henry Slater decided not to press charges against you on the condition that you're released into the custody of a responsible male. That means

I'll be calling your fathers." He looked at Misses Willis and Parkhurst. Kate's stomach bounced when he turned to her. "In your case, we'll call your attorney, Jeff Carlisle."

She blanched. Her lawyer, that long winded prig, was the last person she wanted to rescue her. In an attempt to hide her consternation, she gave the policeman the view of her back. Vaguely, she heard him ask her companions where he could find their fathers.

When he returned to the office, she scrutinized her jailmates' reactions to the latest development. Becca was rigid and expressionless. A surprising inner strength poured from the blandly dressed woman, giving her a becoming glow. Cary, on the other hand, was slumped forward, tears swamping her huge eyes, but not spilling over. Her control appeared marginal.

"My father will be furious, being pulled away from his work," the nineteen year-old moaned.

"I expect my father will be displeased with me, but I am a grown woman and not subject to his discipline," Miss Willis announced.

Kate would not air her opinion of being subjected to a scolding by her tart-tongued lawyer. She did not relish the prospect, but it was certainly preferable to facing an irate parent. These unfortunate women might be ostracized for weeks, while her ordeal would last only a matter of minutes.

Memories of the occasions Ralph Keeler, her stepfather, had bailed her out of jail, raised an acute sympathy for her two friends. Ralph had vacillated between scathing tirades and ignoring her existence for days at a stretch. His punishing moods would not have affected her at all, except for her mother's strong support of his actions. The arrests contributed heavily to their decision to banish her to River Run.

In an effort to change the direction of her painful memories, Kate concentrated on her present circumstance. She was in jail ... Gallagher's jail. Part of her was constantly aware that he was in the next room, likely to appear at any moment. That possibility kept her in a nervous state.

On a conscious level, she loathed his high-handed attitude and would consider it a treat to knock him senseless with a baseball bat. Her barely controlled primitive instincts brought a more intimate pleasure to mind. Like an addicted gambler, she yearned to try her hand again at besting the arrogant lawman. Perhaps, next time she would draw four aces and flatten his overblown pride.

The police chief walked into the room, keys jingling on the big brass ring he held.

"It's time to go home, ladies. Your fathers are waiting in the office." He unlocked the cell that held the two women.

In their eagerness to leave the cage, Caroline and Rebecca barely waved a farewell to their companion. Kate felt abandoned.

"What about me?" She called out as Gallegher started to leave.

"Mr. Carlisle says he's too busy to come for you this morning. He'll be here around noon." He left the lock-up and closed the door.

Kate was alone. She did not plan on spending the entire morning staring at those loathsome bars, but obviously, Carlisle was intent on punishing her. Frustration that she was helpless to change the situation, beat at her composure. She kicked out at the cot, but the pressure relieving gesture did not alleviate her disappointment. A long sigh of resignation whistled from between her lips. She sat on the cot and pushed back to prop herself against the wall. This was going to be a long morning.

Time inched by as Kate sat on the narrow bed and fingered the yellow beads which she had removed from her skirt pocket. For the fourth time, she checked her lapel watch. It was only ten-thirty and already the heat in the airless room was forming beads of dew above her upper lip. By noon, she expected to be roasted like a Thanksgiving turkey. Her hands tugged at the material clinging to her knees and hiked the skirt hem upward nearly ten inches, flapping it to create a breeze on her legs.

Thirst had plagued her for the last half hour, her tongue feeling thick and coated with flannel. She could have requested a drink of water, but that would only intensify her other, more urgent problem. Using the slop bucket sitting in the corner was not an option she cared to dwell upon. Men might find it acceptable to relieve themselves in such a manner, but the thought of her using that convenience made her skin crawl.

Her decision made, she walked to the barred door and inhaled deeply.

"Mr. Gallagher! Mr. Gallagher!" She shouted at the top of her voice, hoping he would hear her from the next room.

It took a few more tonsil blasting efforts before her jailer appeared. He opened the door to the cell room, but did not enter.

"What's all the commotion about?" His voice sounded gruff to her, intensifying her embarrassment.

"I need to use the water closet," she whispered.

"Speak up," he ordered. Kate suspected he understood every word.

She repeated the statement in a clear steady tone, although she felt her complexion deepen with heat.

"That's what the bucket's for." He pointed toward the receptacle in the corner of her cell.

Kate caught the glint of amusement in his blue eyes. He was teasing her. Her mortification quickly turned to anger. How dare he take advantage of his position to humiliate her? She would wet the floor before humbling herself for him further.

"I should have known better than to think you might behave like a gentleman." She turned her back to him in dismissal.

There was a pause while Kate waited to hear the door to the office close and she would again be alone. The rattle of the key in the lock to her cell startled her. She turned to find Gallagher standing beside the open iron door. His expression was unreadable to her, but she liked to think he felt embarrassed for trying to humiliate her when she was defenseless.

Silently, he motioned for her to follow him. She did as bidden, eager to rid herself of her discomfort. The play of the Police Chief's muscles under his shirt caught her attention and held it, no matter how she tried to pry her gaze loose. His body so engrossed her that she almost missed seeing him point to the lavatory.

When Kate emerged from the washroom, she avoided looking in Gallegher's direction and headed toward the back room to let herself into the cell she had been occupying. The less she had to do with him the better.

"Don't run off. I want to talk to you."

His command stopped her in mid-stride. She was tired from the long, harrowing morning and his special attention to torturing her. He seemed to take pleasure in it. Kate spoke without facing him.

"Do I have a choice?"

"None."

Holding her chin out, she strutted to his desk and stood before him. Pride surrounded her like battle armor.

"Have a seat," he directed.

"I prefer to stand." She did not look at him. Kate did not want to relax and lose her edge.

"I said sit." His words were low, but spit out with force.

Kate perched on the edge of the chair. She would reserve her energy for more important causes.

"It looks to me like you wanted to be arrested. Is that true?"

Expecting a scolding, she was surprised by his reasonable tone. A calm, straightforward approach to his question seemed appropriate.

"Yes. Publicity is difficult to come by in this town."

"Is this the kind of publicity you want? Ruining your reputation won't help women to get the vote. If anything, it shows that you're irresponsible. No one will take you seriously."

"No one takes me seriously, anyway. At least, this way people will notice women's suffrage is an issue. I've always had a reputation for social misconduct. That doesn't concern me. I don't live to please others." She paused to consider the policeman's thoughtful expression, his wrinkled forehead and narrowed eyes. "Why are you talking to me like this? You know it won't stop me."

"I'm not trying to stop you, just keep your activities legal. Why can't you behave like a lady and be noticed?"

"Ladies are given orders, patted on the head, and ignored. No man would give the vote to his lap dog."

Gallagher sat back, pensively running his forefinger over his lips. She squirmed under his scrutiny. Could he see past her brave front to her soft bruised heart? Kate fervently hoped not.

"I advise against you being a regular customer here. That would make me very unhappy and when I'm unhappy, I get downright mean. You wouldn't like what happens next."

"By now, you should know threats are wasted on me." Kate stood up. "Our discussion is over."

"Not yet. I want to make a deal with you."

"No deals. There's nothing you could possibly do for me." Kate headed toward the cell room.

"Come back here. We're not finished talking." His raised voice did not impress her in the least. She continued to walk. Just as she reached the door Gallagher leaped in front of her to bar her way.

"Would you agree to stay legal, if I got Sam Wakely to cover your suffrage activities?"

It was a full minute before his proposal sank through to her brain. She stood so close to him she could see his chest move with each breath. Golden hairs curled where his shirt opened at the collar and her hand nearly came up to touch the soft looking mat. When she spoke, her voice was breathless.

"Sam said he doesn't believe in my cause and won't give me free publicity. You can't keep your side of the bargain."

"I can handle Sam. Just give me your promise to obey the law."

Kate stared at him incredulously. After all the trouble she had caused, he was willing to trust her word . . . the word of an enemy. She read the warmth in his eyes and a hard chunk of her defense melted. Perhaps, he was not the ogre he seemed to be.

"You have my promise on the condition that Sam cooperates."

"That's a deal."

Gallagher extended his hand to shake on the agreement. She hesitated a moment before clasping it. His long, strong fingers engulfed her delicate hand, sending electricity up her arm. For a moment her eyes closed as the heat flowed through her and fogged her mind. No man ever had this physical power over her before. A danger signal flashed through the delicious sensations his touch evoked. Men were the enemy. Abruptly, she pulled her hand from his grip.

He stood before her, barring her escape to the safety of the cell. She reached around him to grab the doorknob, but he moved sideways bumping her hand against his thigh. Kate pulled her arm back as though she were burned.

"Please, let me pass." Her words trembled despite her effort to calm herself.

She did not want to give him the satisfaction of seeing her physically back off from him, but could not stop herself from turning her face aside. The gentle touch of his forefinger on her jaw moved something warm and glowing inside her, the melting sensation terrifying her. Pressure from his finger forced her to face him. The door to her innermost secret self was open, exposing her vulnerability to someone capable of doing her harm. It took all of her mental strength to put back the protective wall.

"What's wrong?"

"You're standing in my way." To Kate's amazement her voice was steady.

"You're in a big hurry to get locked up again. Don't you like my company?" She detected a teasing curve to his mouth.

"I would prefer a trip to the dentist to spending time with you. Am I free to go now?"

"Why are you afraid of me?"

"I'm not afraid of you or any man." Kate felt like a wounded doe fighting off a hungry wolf. The deer was doomed to lose, but the instinct for survival kept her from quitting.

"You're a feisty little critter. I'll give you that. Too bad you don't know the difference between the truth and a whopper. I know you're shaking inside. Don't you know by now I wouldn't hurt you?"

She flinched at the sweetness of his finger caressing her jaw.

It's my own feelings I'm afraid of, not anything you could do to me, Kate told herself. But she was not willing to divulge such personal information to that cocky bastard.

"Mr. Gallagher, my feelings are none of your concern and not a topic for conversation. I would like to go to my cell or do you have intentions of standing here for the rest of the morning?"

He pushed the door open behind him and stepped aside to let her pass.

"Lady, you've got the disposition of a rattlesnake. You're welcome to that hot, stinking cage."

Kate darted past him, anxious to leave his disconcerting presence. When he did not follow her to lock the door, she turned to eye him questioningly.

"Let yourself in. I know you're not going anywhere." Gallagher nonchalantly turned his back to return to his desk.

Kate slammed the office door shut. She would fester in that vile cell until noon. The thought infuriated her that if she were civil to him, he probably would allow her to wait in the more comfortable office. Sometimes, that beast made it incredibly difficult to hate him and she needed to hate him. Her emotional safety depended upon it.

Kate entered the cell and sat on the cot. The barred door stood open, offering an escape from her self-imposed imprisonment. Release from the cage meant exposing herself to the danger of his magnetic body and surprising gentleness. But her heart was still too sore to take a chance. Freedom beckoned to her through the open door, but her fear kept her from answering the call. She could not put a name to the emotion that stilled her hand from pulling the bars shut.

CHAPTER VII

Kate stopped in the middle of Jeffrey Carlisle's office. When her lawyer let go of his bruising grasp on her arm she relaxed a bit. Her pride smarted from the grueling forced march from the jailhouse a few streets away, during which she had been treated to an ominous silence. No doubt, he had waited for the privacy of his office to flay her with a tongue lashing. The familiar feeling of awaiting punishment in the headmistress' office at Durham's Ladies' Academy hit her like the sharp rap of a ruler. Her knuckles hurt just thinking about it.

While Carlisle removed his derby hat and hung it on a rack, Kate let her gaze slide over the room. Its dark wood paneling and rich oriental carpet attested to the lawyer's financial success.

Her gaze landed on Carlisle looking in the gilt-framed wall mirror as he patted his thickly pomaded hair and preened his handlebar mustache. She watched him straighten his appearance, then cross the room to stand behind his desk. His blizzardous glare prepared her for an upbraiding.

"I cannot understand, Katherine, why a lady of your high social standing would jeopardize her reputation by behaving in such an outrageous manner . . ."

Kate shut her ears to the tirade. He could do no more than repeat her stepfather's cutting words, an experience she would do well without. Besides, she had made a deal with Chief Gallagher to stay within the law. Unless he did not keep his end of the bargain, her intention was to honor her word. Therefore, Mr. Carlisle's rescue services would no longer be required.

"And furthermore …" The flood of invective seemed to be slowing. "I shall not extract you from jail again. You can suffer the full consequences of your actions. Is that clear?"

Kate was caught off guard by the sudden question. It took her a moment to focus.

"Quite clear, Mr. Carlisle."

"Then you may go. I have more important things to do than scold a silly woman."

The morning had been a torturously long, frustrating ordeal. Her temper, never far from the surface at best, was near bursting whenever she was in her counsel's presence. His last shot was too much to be endured.

"You forget you work for me and I do not have to tolerate your abuse. Your advice hasn't been in my best interests and your mightier than thou attitude is an insult to all women. Your services are no longer required."

Kate felt gratified to see Carlisle's complexion turn grape purple.

"You are just like your father, Katherine. You have no shame. After that terrible scandal, I wondered how you could live in that house so near the Slaters. Now I know. You share your father's lack of decency."

Light flashes went off in Kate's head. Carlisle knew what happened between her father and Henry Slater. He thought she already knew and was trying to hurt her with that knowledge.

"I don't know what you're talking about."

She saw the feral gleam in his eyes, a predator closing in for the kill.

"I thought you would know by now. The whole town knows. Your father and Beatrice Slater were having an affair. The night your father died, she was found waiting for him across the river in a lovers' nest."

Kate felt the blood drain from her face. She wanted to reject the story as a cruel lie, but too many puzzle pieces fit into place around it for the story to be untrue. A roaring crash filled her brain as her father's memory toppled from its pedestal. She desperately needed to cry, but would not give Carlisle the satisfaction of seeing it.

"You are a despicable man to take pleasure in hurting people. I am well shut of you."

Kate stomped from his office, not waiting for his reply. Although she longed to flee until the pressure stopped pounding in her skull, she kept her gait to a determined march.

Once outside, she found refuge in an alleyway deep in shadow where her emotional release would remain private. She seldom permitted herself the luxury of tears, considering them a useless display of weakness. But this was one of those times that her intensity of emotion gave her no choice. Silent tears cooled her disappointment.

She removed a handkerchief from her reticule and dabbed at her wet eyes. With shaking hands, she straightened her skirt and blouse and tucked a few stray wisps of hair under pins before venturing onto the sidewalk.

Her auto was parked outside the Montezuma Cannery, a healthy hike's distance from here. The walk would give her time to make sense of the disturbing discovery. It would also put her in the direction of the river and Captain Tom's houseboat. He might be able to help her sort out her feelings.

As Kate settled into a steady stride, she collected all the pertinent information and put together the pieces. The tragic end to her father's affair with Beatrice Slater would explain the woman's panicked reaction to the mention of Nathan Moore's death. It also explained why Henry Slater was questioned as to his whereabouts that night. If he knew of his wife's affair, that would be a motive for murder. His alibi that he was working late with one of his managers was enough for Chief Peach to drop the investigation. But Kate considered the possibility of him hiring someone to kill her father. Hank Slater had likely paid the Chief of Police to keep his wife's name out of the police report. Kate's mother, who never liked small town living, could have used the scandal as an excuse to sell the freight business and move back to New York. These thoughts, intermixed with doses of betrayal by her father and mourning for her lost innocence, crowded in a jumble inside her head.

By the time Kate reached her auto, she was emotionally exhausted, her mind numbed in defense. With leaden limbs, she cranked the auto handle until the engine started. She climbed in, and headed the Pierce-Arrow in the direction of Captain Tom's river mooring.

Kate drove the Motorette along the narrow road. It was hardly more than a path, running parallel to the Sacramento River. She loved this flat delta countryside with its intricate network of waterways and fog laden marshes.

Ahead, she saw Captain Tom's weathered houseboat tied to the shore. Low shrubs prevented her from driving off the road to get closer and Kate stopped the auto at the side of the road. She walked the last hundred feet to the simple wooden structure, with its deck covered along one side. The captain, who relaxed on a creaking old rocking chair with his feet up on the rail, stood as his visitor hopped onto the houseboat deck.

"What's wrong, Kitten? You look like you just came back from a funeral."

Having no patience for small talk, she blurted out what was on her mind. "Jeff Carlisle just told me about Bea Slater and my father. You should have told me. It would've been easier coming from you."

Tom seemed to age before her eyes, his more than seventy years suddenly heavy on his shoulders. In the next second, Kate flung herself into the fold of his comforting arms, fighting the powerful urge to weep.

"I knew you'd take it hard. I wanted you never to find out." He stood back from her, but kept one arm around her shoulder. "Come set with me a while."

They sat on the time worn wooden chairs looking out at the rippling river. Kate knew her old friend had wanted to spare her the pain of discovering her father's dark secret and did not blame him for his silence. The old man's voice came to her deep and calm, blending in with the peaceful surroundings.

"Your papa loved this river and the people who live by it. He loved your mother, too, at the beginnin'. Jane was proud of bein' New York society and hated this place. She wanted to live in San Francisco; spent a lot of time there with friends. Nate would never move from here. When she knew she was stuck here, somethin' died between them. He would come to visit me of a night to fish and talk. Sometimes, he wouldn't go home 'til the sun was up. I hated seein' him so sad, all pulled in like a turtle in his shell. When he started seein' Mrs. Slater, he perked right up. Now, I ain't sayin' what he done was right, but it sure made a new man outta him. A man who worked hard as he did, deserved a little happiness in his life."

As Kate sat silently listening to her old friend reminisce about her father, an inkling of understanding shone through the dark cloud of her disappointment. She was not the only family member treated to her mother's frigid disdain. It was small wonder he sought warmth elsewhere.

"Did he love Beatrice?" she concentrated her gaze on the soothing rhythm of the river. "I hope he did."

"Yes. I think he loved her. Leastwise, he talked like he did." Tom's eyes misted over. "You look like your mother, so tiny and delicate. But you're warm and talk straight, like your papa. Nate'd be proud of his little girl."

While Kate basked in the tranquillity of the river and the Captain's encouraging presence, the nerve shattering turmoil that had been shaking her when she arrived at the houseboat eased. Her loyalties on this issue were difficult to sort out. Originally, she had sided with her mother for being the wronged wife, but Jane had not behaved as a loving wife. It came down to two imperfect people doing what they needed to do in order to survive. Now she saw the cause of her mother's bitterness, although it was no easier to bear.

"Are you all right, Kitten?"

"Yes. Thank you for your help." Kate patted the age gnarled, but still strong hand that rested on the arm of his chair.

"How did Carlisle come to tell you about Beatrice Slater and your father?"

"He was angry with me for firing him and wanted to hurt me." She did not look at the old man as she spoke, hoping he would not pursue the subject.

"I never did like that greasy haired conniver. Why did you fire him?"

"He insulted me and treated me like something to scrape off the bottom of his shoe." She bristled at the memory of the lawyer's condescending attitude.

"Why would he do that?"

From the cast of his probing, blue eyes, Kate saw he was determined to keep at her until he discovered what she wanted to hide. She breathed a long sigh of defeat. He would probably read about it in the newspaper next week, so she might as well tell him and get it over with.

"I was arrested and he came to get me out of jail. I only caused a minor disturbance at Henry Slater's cannery. It's nothing to get upset about."

"Exactly what did you do?"

Her anxiety drained away at the calm tone of the captain's voice. The day had been too emotionally taxing for her to stand up to his disapproval.

"The women workers needed to know how much having the vote could do for them. I simply told them."

"I take it, Chief Gallagher wasn't too pleased with you."

"That beast is never pleased with me. He kept me in jail all morning waiting for Mr. Carlisle. I just got out about an hour ago."

Kate felt the heat rise to her cheeks as she spoke about the lawman, involuntarily recalling how her hand bumped against his leg when she tried to open the door to the cell room.

"Sounds like a man who knows his job. Maybe, you'll think twice about causin' another ruckus." He sucked on his pipe for a minute before continuing to speak. "I bet you could use some lunch after your busy mornin'. Come inside and I'll see what I can find for you."

The old man stood and walked into the house, ducking his head through the low doorway. Kate gratefully followed. She had not eaten since breakfast, just after dawn, and her stomach loudly protested her neglect.

Her eyes wandered over the familiar, Spartan room. There was no frill or decoration, except for the painting hanging on the wall over the narrow bed. The picture was of her father's steamboat "Cherokee". Tom had captained it for over twenty years. His tiny house was shipshape, not a thing out of place. Seated at the table in the kitchen area of the single room, she watched the river through a canvas-curtained window.

The Captain put biscuits, cheese and strawberry preserves on the table. He poured a glass of milk for her, since it was too hot to light the wood burning stove to make coffee. They sat in close comradeship, munching as they conversed.

"How are your plans for the boardinghouse comin' along?" Tom asked.

"Very well. The house is ready and my friend, Abigail, will move in after I return from the suffrage convention in San Francisco."

"Will you be stayin' with the Endicotts, like you planned?"

"Yes. I'm really looking forward to it, except for the man they want me to meet. He's a lawyer from a well connected family in Rio Vista." She wrinkled her nose in distaste. "He sounds like a stuffed shirt, but I can't refuse gracefully."

"The attention of a young man is just what you need. I bet you had plenty of beaus sniffin' after you in New York."

One beau too many, she thought bitterly. The scar tissue on her heart left by Trevor Freebush would be a formidable barrier for any man to break through.

"Not many men will accept my suffrage work. That narrows the choice considerably. Besides, I'm not ready to settle down yet."

The Captain chuckled. "When the right man comes along, he'll make you ready soon enough."

Kate thought of telling him about her disastrous engagement, but held her tongue. Captain Tom wasn't the only one who could keep a secret.

CHAPTER VIII

Kate sucked in her breath as Mrs. Endicott's maid gave the corset lacing one last tug. She wondered which sadistic man had invented this whale-boned torture device. The stays began just below the bust and continued to a few inches above the knees. It was designed for the straight figure fashions coming into style, which did not suit her feminine curves. She slipped a ribbon bedecked camisole over her head and stepped into the first of three petticoats.

A light rap on the door accompanied a soprano voice. "It's Prissy. Can I come in?"

Kate nodded and the maid opened the door. Priscilla Endicott Johnson rushed in and Kate went to her childhood friend. They hugged with exuberant warmth, Kate trying to soak up all the love she had missed in the six years since their last meeting. When her emotional needs were sated she stood back to assess the changes time had made on her school companion. Kate marveled at the elegant picture of decorum standing before her. Prissy's auburn hair, which Kate remembered as an unruly mass of curls, was now swept up into a neat bun and pompadour. The only evidence of the mischief maker from Durham's School was the devilish spark in the cool, green eyes. Marriage and a baby had transformed her into a lady.

Kate was pleased when Priscilla dismissed her mother's maid and helped her finish dressing.

"When Mother told me you were going to visit her, I was thrilled. I've been wanting you to meet my new family."

Kate shook her head at the prospect of lively, tree climbing Prissy becoming a staid matron at the age of twenty-one. What a terrible waste of a free spirit, she thought.

The women chatted easily about old acquaintances. After a separation of years, it seemed to her, they picked up their relationship as though they had never parted.

The gown of white lace over mint green silk with a green satin sash at the hip glided easily over Kate's head. After Prissy fastened the row of eyes and hooks down the back they were ready to leave the room. This English custom of dressing for dinner had been an accepted part of Kate's life until she returned to River Run. Living alone, the practice seemed without purpose. For the first time, she wondered at the affectation of such formality for one's close family members and friends.

On the way downstairs, Kate hardly noticed the pictures and mirrors hanging on the red and gold damask walls of the elegant hallway. She had lived in such splendor in New York, but the absence of love had made her miserable. Possessions could not give her happiness and so were not important.

"David should be here soon," Priscilla commented with practiced nonchalance.

"Who is David?"

"He's that brilliant lawyer Mother told you about. Actually, my husband roomed with him in college. She invited him to dinner tonight."

Kate winced. The last thing she wanted was to have her first evening in San Francisco ruined by ill conceived match making. Her honesty would not allow her to play the role of a dignified lady to please the Endicotts or their guests. She was determined to dislike the undoubtedly proper, socially elite gentleman and would do all she could to discourage his attentions.

A long, curved stairway led to the marble floored entry hall below. Many of the furnishings on the lower level appeared new to Kate. She remembered the Endicotts were forced to redecorate the smoke damaged first floor after the earthquake and fire which destroyed much of San Francisco four years before.

Kate entered an ornate parlor done in delicate French period pieces and her footsteps were muffled in a rich, flowered carpet. The room's rose, blue and creme hue settled an aura of peace around her.

"I see you found her," Phillip Endicott said to his daughter as he rose from his chair. "My girls look ravishing tonight."

Kate thought her host looked distinguished in his dinner jacket, his blond hair slicked back, steel gray sideburns the only hint of his middle age. He had the same mischievous green eyes as Prissy, who kissed him affectionately on the cheek.

A pleasant looking young man of medium height, with wavy, brown hair joined the small group. Priscilla introduced him as Granger Johnson, her husband. His warm handshake welcomed Kate.

When they were all seated, Kate found herself on a sofa beside Grace Endicott, her friend's mother. She was an older version of Prissy, except for her eyes, which were a mellow brown.

"Katherine, how is your mother?" Grace asked.

"She wrote to me recently and seems to be well. She is reasonably happy; her husband is well suited to her."

"I'm glad to hear that." Phillip's expression showed concern. "When you both left for New York, she was very upset. Being your father's friend, I looked into the sale of Moore Freighting and advised against her selling it to Star Enterprises. The price was so low, they practically stole it from her. I discovered that Jeffrey Carlisle owns Star. He was your father's lawyer, wasn't he?"

This revelation stunned Kate.

"Yes, he was. Did my mother know he was the buyer?"

"No. His name was well hidden. I had to use considerable influence to discover who was behind the business. Your mother would not hear anything I had to say. Are you all right? You look a little pale."

"I'm fine."

She felt as though another piece to the puzzle of the mystery around her father's death was in her hands, but she did not know where it fit. Carlisle had tried to convince her to sell the house and move back to New York, as though he was eager to be rid of her. He also had given her cause to suspect Henry Slater of trying to do away with her father. Was that intentional? There was no time now to work the bits of information into place, so she filed it in her mind and brought her attention back to the people in the room.

"No more talk of business," Grace chided her husband. "That is not a subject to interest young ladies."

The conversation turned toward the latest fashions which soon bored the gentlemen and they soon bowed out.

A few minutes later, the butler entered the room with a guest. "Mr. David Peters," he announced before leaving.

Kate watched the new arrival walk toward Phillip and Granger. A disappointed groan almost escaped from her lips. She had wished the lawyer would resemble a hairy baboon so she would not be tempted to encourage him, but her hopes for a comfortable evening shattered like a window with a brick hurled through it. He was one of the most devastatingly handsome men she had ever seen. Inside the impeccably fitted, formal, black suit, his tall frame moved with an elegant, controlled grace. The glimpse she had of his face before he turned away from her revealed piercing eyes hooded by dark eyebrows. A well-clipped mustache framed a sensuous mouth and light reflected off his raven black hair. Something about his studied perfection dared her to loosen his precisely knotted tie and muss his glossy, perfect hair. What grand fun it would be to shock his starched sensibilities.

David extricated himself from the company of Phillip and Granger to briskly advance on the women. Upon entering the room, he had been smitten by a stunning nymph whose bold stare promised an amusing challenge. Her eyes seemed to look down at him as though she did not entirely approve. It was years since a woman regarded him with anything but fawning admiration and the prospect of confronting the mysterious lady intrigued him.

He greeted Grace and Priscilla warmly before letting his attention fall on the dainty woman with the demure smile, hiding the boldness he had detected earlier.

When Mrs. Endicott introduced him, Kate was startled as the gentleman's warm fingers closed around her hand

and lifted it to his lips. She disliked the European custom, thinking it affected and too personal for a first meeting. As his mustache brushed intimately against her knuckles, the feeling was pleasurable but uninvited, therefore, unwelcome. Not one to suffer in silence, she pulled her hand from his grasp. Their glances locked and she noticed humor dancing in his light gray eyes.

"Katherine has recently returned from living in New York. Her home is now in River Run," Grace offered.

"I know River Run very well. It is down river from my parents' home in Rio Vista." He seemed to recall an article about a Miss Moore in the *River Run Gazette*, but the memory was too vague to place. "What brought you back from New York?"

"I'm here by parental decree. Exile would be a more accurate description. They didn't approve of my controversial politics."

"I am also active in politics. To what, exactly, did your parents object?"

A playful gleam leaped from her amber eyes and her dimples were prominent. "My stepfather grew tired of bailing me out of jail and my mother thought it improper for a lady to lecture in the streets. Do you approve of women's suffrage, Mr. Peters?"

He remembered the article now. Sam Wakely had covered an incident at the Montezuma Cannery. The editor had portrayed Katherine Moore as a harmless buffoon, dabbling in issues far above her head. He had dubbed her group of women the Petticoat Gang. "Yes, I do. I consider myself a progressive, but your penchant for attention should be curbed, my dear. There is no gain in behaving like a hoyden. Your recent exploits as leader of the Petticoat Gang will do your reputation little good."

David felt gratified to see her complexion deepen to a bright shade of pink.

"What's this? Are you still playing pranks, Katie? You were always in trouble at school." Priscilla giggled.

"It isn't funny, Prissy. The reporter made light of a serious effort. The cannery workers need the vote so they can improve their conditions through legislation," Kate explained.

She considered the tall gentleman. The well mannered Mr. Peters had the social graces firmly in command, but he was not above putting a lady in an uncomfortable position. When she had intended to shock him with mention of her outrageous adventures, he had put her on the defensive by bringing up the Petticoat Gang. He certainly presented a challenge. Although Kate was annoyed with him, she liked the studiously correct dandy. She would enjoy ruffling his smooth feathers.

The butler announced dinner was ready to be served. Grace and Priscilla were escorted from the parlor by their husbands, while Kate found herself accompanying David.

"I look forward to discussing your political views over dinner, Miss Moore. A lady seldom admits to having opinions, much less is willing to defend them."

"I shall be delighted to bend your ears, Mr. Peters, if Mrs. Endicott will allow such serious conversation at the dinner table."

Kate felt devilment bubble up inside her. The evening promised to be interesting.

Seated beside David, she took in the elegant dining room with a lingering glance. The crystal chandelier cast a golden glow over the china, silver and lace, and softened the features of the diners. She caught Mrs. Endicott, seated at the foot of the table, eyeing David and her with a victorious gleam in her eyes. Let the old girl think what she would, but she was not star struck by the gentleman seated beside her.

Kate attended to her shrimp bisque until she heard David address her.

"How did you get involved with women's suffrage, Miss Moore?"

"The cause was popular at Barnard College while I was attending there. Later, I worked with Harriot Stanton Blatch at the main headquarters. Those were exciting times."

"Ah, now I see from where your tendency toward public display springs. I've heard Mrs. Blatch leans toward your British counterpart's violent inclinations. Is it true a suffragette actually whipped Winston Churchill with a riding crop?"

"Yes, it's true, but we in America don't condone that sort of thing. I must admit I've been provoked to do bodily harm to a policeman, but it was never premeditated or without justifiable cause."

Kate watched his penetrating eyes during their conversation, but they gave no clue to his thoughts. She was disconcerted by his cool restraint, wondering if he hid a warm heart under his impeccably tailored jacket or if he was as cold as the steel of his gray eyes.

"Did it ever occur to you that a policeman could inflict far more pain on you than you could on him?"

The lawyer's calm, calculated speaking style pushed her to imagine how he would perform in court, every word calculated, every move controlled.

"That is entirely irrelevant when a principle is at stake. Haven't you fought for your beliefs in the face of opposition?"

"Of course, I have. My progressive political stand is not always popular, but I have learned to use an agile tongue instead of my fists. It saves wear and tear on my wardrobe, not to mention my body."

David considered the animated lady with her intensely impassioned voice. Our little soldier has intelligence, determination, and a glib tongue, he concluded. If she would only channel her enthusiasm in a less self-destructive direction, no adversary would have a chance against her. He admired her youthful enthusiasm and fearlessness and hoped the rigors of time and life would not erode them.

"As a man, your words are respected. Sometimes, a woman must go to extraordinary lengths to get anyone's attention." He heard her voice take on a hard edge, hinting at her succinct public speaking style.

"I take it then, you would have preferred being born a male." He had trouble concealing the beginning of a smile.

"Not at all. As a woman I have the opportunity to bedevil you men without fear of severe reprisals. A man with my rebellious ways would be shown no mercy."

Kate watched David's face transform from a handsome mask to a sunbeam as he laughed at her answer. This was her first glimpse of the person he guarded behind his controlled expression. Within seconds the light she sensed emanating from him disappeared, leaving her to wonder if she had only imagined the fleeting sign of warmth and humor. Perhaps he needed someone to encourage his spontaneity before he relaxed his rigid restraint. The idea fascinated her.

Priscilla interrupted their conversation with a question that drew Kate's and David's attention to the other diners, and for the remainder of the meal, Kate was forced to share her dinner partner.

After the meal, as was the custom, the ladies left the men to their brandy and cigars. Kate had always detested her exclusion from the political discussions. She reluctantly settled on the sofa in the back parlor with Grace and Priscilla.

"I am pleased you and David are getting along so well." Prissy's broad smile showed the extent of her pleasure. "He's a marvelous catch."

"I'm not in the market for a husband just now, but I've got to admit, he has much to recommend him. His one fault is his too proper facade. Does he ever let it down?" Kate's curiosity was unbounded.

"I've never seen him anything but perfect."

"What a pity. A perfect person is intolerable. What he needs is for someone to tweak his mustache until he loses his maddening composure."

The Endicott ladies laughed.

Soon after, the men entered the room and Granger announced it was time for he and his wife to return home. Hugs and kisses abounded as Priscilla bid everyone good-bye and promised to see her dear friend again before her return to River Run.

After the Johnsons' departure, Kate was not surprised when David asked the Endicotts' permission to walk with her alone in the garden. Phillip jovially agreed to the request and she allowed the young gentleman to lead her through the French doors into the star-filled night.

The garden was dark and they walked only as far as the fountain, where a beacon filtered out to them through the dining room window. A spicy scent of jasmine tickled her nose. Blowing off the bay, a chill breeze penetrated the light fabric of her gown and she shivered. David removed his jacket and gently draped it around her shoulders.

The coat lining, still warm from his body heat, soothed her chilled muscles and the scent of Bay Rum emanating from the collar surrounded her. Kate noticed how slender he appeared in his shirt sleeves and vest, certainly not the muscled physique of a man used to physical labor. Still, he was very masculine in a refined way.

"Are you sure you want to be out here with such a notorious woman?" she teased. "Association with me might ruin your reputation."

"What reputation is that?"

"Rigidly proper, not a hair out of place, polite at all costs. Need I go on?"

"Have you always been this outspoken, or is this a recent affliction?" His voice did not reflect the humor alight in his eyes.

"Always. I prefer to be disliked for who I am, rather than liked for who I am not. And who are you, under the charming manners and well tailored suit?" She enjoyed goading him to see how far she had to push before the gentleman let down his guard.

"I am a man longing to teach a certain young lady the virtues of silence."

"Then teach away." She challenged him, aware of the intensity smoldering in his words.

His strong fingers imprisoned her arms and his warm, firm mouth pressed hungrily against her lips, the soft mustache brushing her nose. He was gentle, but insistent, deepening the kiss until she responded by bringing her hands to the back of his neck and sliding her fingers into his raven hair. A sweet warmth spread through her like honey, but she did not lose awareness of her surroundings. When he finally removed his mouth from hers and stepped back, she was in full control of her senses.

"So much for your unyielding propriety," she quipped.

David released her so fast she almost fell. "Please forgive me, Miss Moore. I am not in the habit of acting on my impulses. That shall not happen again."

"How unfortunate. Your impulses are not without merit, Mr. Peters. You should indulge them more often."

"What? And lose my reputation for being a pillar of virtue?" His eyebrows lifted in mock horror.

Kate laughed. She could not help liking this man, even though he represented the restrictions society tried to impose on her and she rejected. His dry sense of humor did much to neutralize his stiffly formal conduct.

"Your reputation is in no danger, but mine will be, if we stay out here in the dark much longer." She remembered the elder Endicotts waiting for their return.

"Before we go inside, may I have your permission to call upon you during your stay in San Francisco? Perhaps we could go for a drive or to the theater."

"I would like that. Tomorrow I'll know my schedule for the convention. Call me on the telephone and we will plan an outing."

Kate watched a slow smile spread to his eyes until they shone like polished silver. He was magnificently handsome in the diffused light, shadows accentuating the angular planes of his jaw. How odd, she thought, that she admired his good looks as she would a work of art, with no passionate stirrings of her female senses.

"Thank you. You have made me very happy."

David took her arm and they returned to the parlor where Grace and Phillip Endicott awaited them. Kate shrugged the heavy jacket from her shoulders and handed it to its owner. She caught the knowing glance that passed from Grace to her husband.

When David took his leave, Kate was in an expansive mood. As he kissed her hand, she did not pull away, but let her fingers rest across his knuckles. His eyes smiled at her with a promise of intimacies to come. Her gaze followed the tall, stylish gentleman as he left the house. He was just the type of man she needed now, amusing yet no threat to her heart.

Phillip announced it was late and time to retire, to which Kate heartily agreed. She accompanied the couple upstairs and was soon in the seclusion of her room.

The fringed lamp on the vanity table illuminated the elaborate bedroom with a mellow glow. Her fingers reached behind her to painstakingly undo the long row of hooks running down the back of her gown. Once the dress was hung, Kate shed the petticoats and corset until she was clad only in her chemise. Seating herself at the vanity table facing the mirror, she removed the hairpins holding up her curly hair.

An elfin smile formed on her lips as the attractive image of David Peters formed in her mind's eye. He was delightfully teasable with his stuffy formality, and his keen wit kept her on her toes. His kiss was pleasant, if not as stimulating as some she had experienced. One smoldering occasion leaped into her memory. Strong arms crushed her against him, his mouth hard against her lips, demanding a response. The breeze rustled a wayward lock of blond hair across a masculine forehead. Gallagher!

Why would she think of that uncouth lunatic now? She pushed against the direction of her thoughts, but the sensual tension he drew up clung to her until her hands shook.

"Damn him," she muttered, wrenching out the last of the hairpins. How dare he creep into her imagination!

She tugged the hairbrush through her curls while trying to control her wayward thoughts. The unbidden image of the lawman barring the door to the cell room flickered in her mind. Heat rose through her body like a well-stoked steam engine, building up burning hot pressure until she thought she would explode. In desperation, she squelched the mind picture, and replaced it with an unrelated thought.

During dinner, she had put the tidbit of information Mr. Endicott had dropped about Carlisle into a compartment of her memory to take out and examine later. Curiosity urged her to consider the connection between the lawyer and Moore Freighting.

Kate understood her mother's need to escape from River Run in the face of the scandal brought about by her husband. She had needed money in order to return to New York and, due to her husband's recent financial problems, she had decided to sell the business. The house went to her daughter in the will and could not be sold. Carlisle, as her attorney and owner of Star Enterprises, took advantage of the new widow's misfortune and urged her to sell the company at a ridiculously low price. As a financial advisor, the lawyer could steer his clients into deals with Star Enterprises which would be extremely lucrative to him, so long as his connection with Star was kept secret.

Questions about Carlisle's company crowded her thoughts. What did Star deal in or was it only a holding company? Did it own other companies besides Moore Freighting? Before her visit was through, she would ask Mr. Endicott for all the information he had on Star Enterprises.

Wearily, she placed the brush on the vanity table and walked to the bed. Her sheer, white nightgown lay across the blanket that had been turned down by a maid. In anticipation of a restful night, Kate put aside all thoughts of Carlisle and his unscrupulous business dealings. She needed a clear head for the convention tomorrow.

CHAPTER IX

Kate peered around the restaurant, thinking how well suited to David it was, with its subdued air of genteel masculinity, the darkly paneled walls and subtle lighting. Her gaze came to rest across the table at David. He looked dapper in his pin-striped suit. This was the first time she saw him without formal evening clothes and he appeared less stiff this afternoon, but proper as ever.

She had enjoyed his company this week, having accompanied him to the opera one evening and for a leisurely, romantic dinner last night. This lunch date was in answer to his plea to see her again before she left San Francisco. She had promised to have dinner with a few lady conventioneers on this last evening in the city and noontime would be their only chance to be together before she returned home.

David's expression was pensive as he spoke.

"I read an article in the *Chronicle* this morning about the suffrage convention. It seems there is a movement to put women's suffrage on the California ballot again next year."

"Yes. It was voted down in 1896 because the Republican Party withdrew its support. We'll be counting on their help again. I wonder if that's wise." She enjoyed discussing politics with David. He was one of the few men who respected her mind.

"More than just lack of promised support defeated the bill. The liquor industry was lobbying against it. They claimed women voters would force through a temperance bill and ruin their business. There were handbills against the women's vote posted in every saloon and pool hall in the state. You will be up against those same people this time. They are a rough lot. You and your ladies are in for a tough battle."

She wondered if he was trying to discourage her, but decided to take the comment at face value. David had a way of playing the devil's advocate for the pure fun of it. "We've never expected or received anything less than a rousing fight. This time we'll push the bill through. The liquor interests aren't the only ones with lobbyists in Sacramento."

"Yes. I ran into one of your lobbyists while I was on business at the Capitol. Lillian Coffin was her name. She was an acidic woman with a vile temper." David's mouth twisted in distaste. "The harpy had the audacity to interrupt a meeting of the legislature. She called our state government degenerate and Governor Gillette advised her to go home where she belonged."

Kate read disapproval in his sharpened voice and pinched lips, but she did not let that deter her from voicing her opinion. "Mrs. Coffin is one of our finest generals and a moving speaker. My hope is to be just like her."

Kate was not surprised when David groaned. "I should have guessed. Your forwardness will get you nothing but an unsavory reputation. Diplomacy will get you much further."

"I leave diplomacy to the statesmen. Men listen better when I negotiate with a sword."

Lunch arrived and David sampled his bay shrimp before remarking, "He who lives by the sword, dies by the sword. Beware you do not become a casualty. I would hate to see you broken and bloody and still unable to vote."

"I don't intend to lose." She dismissed the subject by turning her attention to her food.

David was enchanted by her unchained enthusiasm and witty display of bravado. She was also possessed of a stubborn will and quick mind. A gentle but firm guidance was needed, he believed, to subdue her rebellious inclinations and bring out her deeper, more serious nature. She presented a challenge and a temptation he found impossible to resist.

"Have you ever fought for a cause and lost?"

Kate's question brought him away from his deep thoughts.

"A person does not lose until he quits trying. I have suffered several setbacks, but have never lost." David chose his words carefully.

"Exactly, what are you working toward? You've mentioned your progressive politics, but I have no idea what you believe in."

"I am for changing social attitudes to be more compatible with our new industrial age. My pet project is to get the state to set safety standards and mandatory inspections in factories. I lobby in Sacramento and plan to run for a seat in the state legislature in a year or so."

"That sounds impressive. If you run for office in my district, you'll have my vote." She spoke as though suffrage were already granted her.

They laughed together and toasted their future successes. Kate enjoyed David's company more than the excellent food. When the plates were empty and the wine carafe drained, her gaze met his wistfully.

This was the last day of a wonderfully hectic week. She had attended fascinating lectures and prominent suffragists from all parts of the nation had infused her with their dynamic energy. Kate was prepared to lay waste to the opposition, shake up the apathetic, and move the unmovable. Yet, in spite of her eagerness to put into action for the cause all she had learned, she longed to put off her return home.

David was the first man she had allowed this close to her since the disaster with Trevor, and although she was apprehensive of his intentions, her placid attraction to him did not pose a threat. His aloof manner kept her at a comfortable distance so she could enjoy his company without involving her heart.

"I can manage another hour away from the office. Would you care to take a drive by the beach?"

David 's offer came as a reprieve.

"That sounds wonderful." This was a perfect way to delay their parting.

They left the restaurant and emerged onto the busy street. Women with hobble dresses and elaborate hats and men in conservative suits clogged the sidewalk. The roadway was alive with horse drawn carriages and wagons, and a healthy smattering of automobiles and trucks. Motorcars chugged and horses clopped, while a cable car clanged its warning. David steered her to his new black, Oldsmobile touring car parked along the curb. The long, open auto was a luxurious triumph of automotive splendor with its supple leather interior and shining chrome.

Once on their way, noise from the traffic made it difficult for them to converse, leaving her to contemplate their blossoming relationship. Last night, David had expressed his desire to call upon her in River Run. His intention was to spend alternating weekends at his parents' home in Rio Vista in order to be closer to her. Kate was stunned by his willingness to go to such extraordinary lengths for the dubious pleasure of her company.

Her feelings toward the appealing man were not so strong as his appeared to be. Given time, she hoped her affection for him would grow. They were compatible in many ways and where they were at odds, compromise could surely lessen the friction. He rarely criticized her breaches of decorum, but seemed amused by her spontaneous, often outrageous actions. Once determined, she was certain she could erode his neat corners. Their discussions on politics and other, so called, masculine subjects were on an intellectual level men seldom considered her capable of achieving. She deeply appreciated his respect for her intelligence.

An unruly thought occurred to her and she laughed aloud at the ludicrous notion. She noticed David eyeing her inquisitively.

"I was thinking my mother would approve of you."

"Is that cause for celebration?"

"Certainly not. It's been years since she's approved of anything I've done. The shock might give her apoplexy. We wouldn't want that, would we?"

She forced the smile to remain, but feared her pain would show in her eyes.

"You very much want your mother's good opinion, don't you, Katherine?"

"I want it, but not enough to change who I am. A mother should love her child even if they don't agree." She turned away as though inspecting the passing scenery and struggled to replace the disturbing thoughts of her mother with happier ones.

The drive to the beach was exhilarating. When they were out of the congested downtown area, the wind tugged at Kate's hat as they sped along the less crowded roads at twenty-five miles an hour. She took pleasure in the wisps of hair dancing freely against her cheeks and neck. Kate was enticed by the salty aroma of the Pacific Ocean.

"Can we stop at the beach for a few minutes? It wouldn't take too much time."

"We can manage that."

David parked, stepped down from his seat and came around to Kate's door to assist her.

"Don't open the door yet," she commanded.

He watched her bend down, his curiosity piqued. She giggled with a mischievous note.

"What on Earth are you doing?" She was so unpredictable he could imagine any number of improprieties she was likely to commit.

When she opened the door and emerged, he caught a glimpse of pink toes before she sprinted past him like a deer, out of his restraining reach. He removed his shoes, threw them into the auto, and grumbling, followed the lithe young woman onto the sand toward the surf. He compromised his dignity for the sake of speed as the sand sucked at his feet.

Kate raced for the waterline, the hem of her simple, white linen dress hiked up near her knees to keep it from encumbering her progress, unmindful of her bare legs. She picked up fleeting impressions of women in daring bathing costumes, dresses with hems at the knees, showing black-stockinged legs and men in tight, striped pants and tops. Her feet sank into the cool wetness left behind by the high tide, but she did not slow down until the frigid salt water lapped at her ankles and splashed her shins. She chased the foamy flow as it receded and laughed gleefully as a wave chased her back, grabbing at her heels and spraying brine onto her naked limbs.

From his vantage point on dry sand, David watched her challenge the sea to join in her joyful game. He was annoyed that his socks would feel gritty with sand for the rest of the day. Wet, sandy pant legs would be unbearable.

Sunlight glinted off her hair, catching his attention. It bathed her face in a magical glow as she danced with the waves like a sea nymph. Spellbound, he felt his pulse quicken at the ethereal scene. He envied her the ability to suck the sap of life. Many years had passed since he had confined himself to the restrictions of polite society.

Kate dashed toward the beach, away from the chilling water. She looked up to discover her ever proper beau standing in his stockinged feet, hands in his pockets. He stared at her with an unreadable expression. The sight of him brought the realities of her limiting world closing around her. She stood still a moment, allowing the sea to swirl over her toes and attempt to drag her back to play. The dry sand was warm against her wet feet as she trudged in David's direction. Sometimes, he had a sobering affect on her that meant death to her spontaneity. Unsure of his reception, she decided to brazen it out.

"You should have joined me." She was still breathless from her exercise. "We could have had a water fight."

"You continue to amaze me, Katherine. One moment you intelligently discuss the finer points of politics and the next you behave like a ten-year-old urchin. I do not know whether to applaud or scold you."

His voice was not unkind and Kate was encouraged.

"Do neither." She reached up to plant a loud, smacking kiss on his cheek.

Kate watched a thin smile form on her escort's lips as he wrapped her arm around his own and led her off the beach. Maybe he's not such a dreary stick, after all, and only needs someone to show him how to have fun, she thought. She instantly assigned herself the task.

At the auto, she took a few minutes to remove as much sand from herself as possible before heading downtown to resume her responsibilities. Sand still clinging between her toes, Kate sat back in the seat while David cranked the starter and climbed in beside her.

During the drive to the convention hall, she managed to subdue her free spirit enough to concentrate on this afternoon's closing of the women's suffrage convention. By the time David left her off at the convention hall, she was eager to join her fellow suffragists.

Kate tugged up the yellow suffragist band around her arm as she entered the huge, crowded room where hundreds of her sisters in the cause gathered to plan their war against their exclusion from the polls. She reached the spot where delegates from the Sacramento Valley congregated and recognized two women with whom she had grown friendly during the week. They saved a chair for her beside them and she maneuvered down the row of people to seat herself.

At the podium, she recognized John Hyde Braly, the banker from Pasadena who was instrumental in rallying men to the suffrage cause. Kate was encouraged to hear a man confirm her right to vote. She sat back to listen, but her restless thoughts raced forward to starting the campaign to win the vote in 1911 in her town. The state legislature had not yet discussed the issue, but she was gearing up for the challenge. With the backing of men like John Hyde Braly and

California State Senator Lee Gates, women's suffrage was certain to win a place on the ballot.

Kate listened as other speakers took turns haranguing the delegates with calls to action, exhorting them to be visible and make news with rallies and other events. When one of them referred to attending town meetings, Kate laughed to herself. She knew from experience the River Run Town Council was not ready for feminine faces intruding on their territory. One suggestion she intended to explore, though, was getting a speaker from out of town to address a gathering in River Run. Hearing a new prospective from women living in Wyoming, Colorado, Utah, Idaho or Washington, where females could vote, would be a valuable experience.

As Kate witnessed the convention's closing ceremonies, she contemplated the uplifting experience this convention had been for her. The classes she had attended as well as the excellent speakers in the hall provided fresh ammunition for her own speeches. Her strategical expertise was enhanced and reinforcements from out of town would be available. She would return to River Run on the train tomorrow armed for battle.

CHAPTER X

Downtown River Run was in the middle of its bustling Saturday afternoon routine on this warm September day. Farm owners and their hired help were in town to buy supplies or enjoy their leisure with a game of billiards and a mug of beer. Children chased after one another in a riotous game of tag, their voices screeching in glee. Buggies, horse drawn wagons and an occasional motorcar passed on the road near City Hall.

Wilhelmina Christian stood in front of the municipal building where her husband reigned supreme. A rainbow colored dress draped her robust figure. Its design was so hectic a person's eyes would cross from looking at it. One of her still life aviaries balanced on her head. Surrounding her, stood her loyal army of eight women, arrayed in the armor of their conviction and carrying as their weapons, signs expressing their anti-women's vote sentiments. The parade was about to begin.

Kate watched with gleeful anticipation as Wilhelmina raised her hand and brought it forward in a signal to start marching. One of the ladies pounded a drum that hung from a strap around her neck and feminine voices rose in an enthusiastic rendition of *Onward Christian Soldiers*.

Excitement raced through Kate's blood as she watched the enemies to her cause head down Superior Avenue. Let the battle be joined!

"Too bad we couldn't get our hands on the rest of those signs." Caroline Parkhurst whispered near her ear.

At the reminder, Kate hid her paint stained hands in her skirt pockets. She recalled last night's raid on the newly painted posters propped against the inside of Wilhelmina's fence. Caroline and she had blacked out the neat printing with paint and replaced the pillowcases covering them. The damage would not be discovered until too late to make new signs. The placards carried today had not been in the yard.

Kate looked at her soldiers Abigail Penny, Rebecca Willis, and Eulalia Ericson. Thank goodness they knew nothing of the raid. They were her staunch followers, but would not understand the need for destruction of an enemy's property.

As the parading ladies progressed down the road through Willis Park Square, Kate instructed her band of suffragists to stay on the sidewalk beside them and match their stride. A surge of power rushed through Kate's body as Wilhelmina glared at her, then faced forward again, continuing to sing with renewed vigor. The foe had recognized the danger stalking her. She had seen the flicker of uncertainty in the older woman's eyes.

"Lincoln freed the slaves. Now it's our turn." Rebecca's voice sounded strong and clear above the hymn.

Kate noticed Becca had grown in courage and conviction since her experience in jail. She added her voice to the chant.

"Obedience to God and men," Mrs. Christian announced. Her ladies picked up the slogan, trying to outshout their rivals.

Much to Kate's pleasure, they were the center of the town's attention. The drum boomed, horses shied out of control and a band of stray dogs tagged behind, yapping and howling their pleasure. Children romped along with the procession adding their laughter and piercing whoops to the growing din. People appeared in windows and doorways to watch the spectacle pass. The carnival atmosphere lured loitering men to follow and join in the fun with derisive hoots at the ladies supporting either cause.

"No ladies in dirty politics," the marchers insisted.

"Let's clean up men's politics." Kate responded in an imperious voice.

A man in rough work clothes jostled her arm.

"Go home where you belong and learn some manners, girlie," he said to her, his mouth set in a twisted leer.

Suddenly, he doubled over as she rammed her elbow into his stomach. She was satisfied to hear air forced through his lips with a loud whoosh. His eyes turned murderous, but she felt no fear. Caroline and Abigail flanked her, their stance showing they were ready to defend her. The rude man backed away, letting them pass.

As the boisterous throng left Willis Park Square and moved down Superior Avenue toward the river, Kate noticed Sam Wakely emerge from the *Gazette* office. He held a notepad and pencil in his hands. If the "antis" were going to get publicity, so would her side. With renewed zeal, she rallied her team to heap verbal abuse on the marchers until flaming anger leaped from Wilhelmina's blood congested face.

A pebble struck a marcher's sign and Kate smiled. Her throwing arm was still accurate. She saw Caroline's eyes grow huge and round and her hand clamp over her mouth.

"The next person who throws something goes to jail." The voice of authority came from directly behind Kate. She did her best to ignore it.

"Cary, we're not doing anything illegal. Just keep moving," she told her friend loud enough for the Chief of Police to hear.

The heckling continued, but Caroline and Rebecca had lost their enthusiasm. Kate reckoned their incarceration was still fresh in their memories, and the two schoolteachers were subdued by the presence of police authority. He did not have to do anything but be there in order to control the women. Kate wanted to scream in frustration. She doubled her efforts to make up for the slack.

They entered the less affluent side of town and Kate felt uncomfortable. Men stood in doorways and behind windows of shoddy clapboard poolhalls and saloons, cigarettes dangling from their smirking mouths, their eyes removing her clothes with lecherous hunger. She read the distress signals in her companions' tension wreathed expressions. Wilhelmina's ladies seemed to cower behind their signs to ward off the leering stares. Kate believed she was not the only one relieved when Mrs. Christian crossed to the other side of the road and headed back toward City Hall.

She led her suffragists in pursuit. The annoyed glance she cast the two policemen, for Officer Taylor had joined the group, was only for show. Secretly, she was thankful for their presence. Without them, the drunken patrons of the area might not limit their sport to gawking.

As the drum beating, song singing spectacle passed police headquarters, Kate felt the police chief's strong grasp on her shoulder. Gallagher hauled her to an abrupt standstill.

"Jase, escort the ladies downtown. Miss Moore and I are gonna have a little discussion." Gallagher steered her toward his office.

"I won't leave my ladies. They're my responsibility. Let go of me." Kate tried to pry his fingers loose and pull away from him. "You have no right to detain me. I haven't broken the law."

"Should I wait for you at the auto, Kate?" Caroline asked.

"I'll make sure she gets home safely. You run along, Miss Parkhurst." The policeman's voice was perfunctory.

"I'm coming with you now, Cary. He can't make me stay." She tried to wrench her shoulder free of his restraining grasp. Her anger burned in her chest like a glowing coal. She wanted to kick him, but there was no telling how he would avenge himself and she did not want to be further humiliated.

"Good afternoon, ma'am." Gallagher politely touched the brim of his Stetson and nodded to Caroline in dismissal.

Kate resisted as he pushed open the door to police headquarters and propelled her inside. As his confining hold left her shoulder, she turned seeking escape, but found the infuriating officer leaning lazily against the exit. His broad shoulders, sheathed in a fitted beige shirt, braced against the door and his long, muscular legs crossed at the ankles in a relaxed pose. He watched her, a broad grin signaling mischievous intent like a cat batting at a mouse. She silently vowed to ruin his amusement. She would not be toyed with.

"How dare you haul me off the street like a Saturday night drunk? Only a bully would manhandle a woman like that. You had no right to stop me from following the parade."

The sound of claws clicking against the wooden floor and a sharp bark brought Kate's attention to the yellow dog bounding toward her. Rufus licked her gloved hand until she scratched him behind the ears. His tail whipped about furiously. He was an ally in enemy territory and she was grateful for his appearance.

"How did such a good dog like you get mixed up with this reprobate?" she cooed to the mutt.

Gallagher watched the defection of the mongrel with mounting annoyance. He did not want his efforts to subdue her to be diluted by an animal's affection.

"Rufe, out!" he commanded, pointing toward the open door to the cellroom.

The dog looked at his master, glanced longingly back at Kate, and whined before obeying the order.

"You broke your promise to behave." He strode toward her with menacing purpose, but her bold glare did not waver.

"I did no such thing. The agreement was for me to stay legal, which I did. Nothing was said about me not exercising my constitutional right to free speech. You're the one who broke a promise," she shot back.

Gallagher felt a flash of guilt, but shoved it aside.

"You got your news article."

"Not _my_ news article," she bellowed. "Sam flogged us. Now, everyone in town calls us the Petticoat Gang. You could have stopped that."

"You got exactly what you deserved. Anyone who breaks the law and behaves like an undisciplined five-year old should be paddled. I hope Carlisle gave you hell."

"Mr. Carlisle is no longer my attorney. He failed to see the important contribution I've made to gaining freedoms for women." Her voice sounded haughty to him, not the reaction he hoped for. Damned fool woman didn't know when she was being intimidated.

"The only thing you've done for the women of this town is make them a laughing stock. What man would give the vote to a loud-mouthed street brawler?"

"Loud-mouthed street brawlers vote at every election. They're called men. How often do you lock up a woman for being drunk and disorderly?" She had him there, but he would ignore it.

"It makes no difference what men do. We already have the vote and we don't have to play fair. I wouldn't let you vote until you prove to me women are capable of making decisions that will rule my life. So far, you've only proven what an uncontrollable nuisance you are."

"Of all the ignorant, arrogant, incredibly senseless reasoning I have come across, yours wins the blue ribbon. A caveman was more forward thinking than you are."

He was amazed by her bravado as she moved closer to him and shouted up into his face. Gallagher looked down at her amber eyes ablaze with fury, her perky curls framing the impish face. She was the most adorable female he had ever seen. Heat pumped through his blood in a heady rhythm, urging him to crush her lips under his mouth while she raged at him, clawing and biting until he subdued her with her own body's need. He fought for control of his untimely desire as his male anatomy reacted to his runaway thoughts.

Kate saw the passion smoldering in his blue eyes and the telltale ticking of the muscle in his jaw. Defensively, she stepped back. The fear motivating her retreat was not of his overpowering strength, but of her own willingness to answer his desire with her own.

"If you're through with your tantrum, we can talk about a truce."

His voice was even, although she still felt the heat emanating from his body.

"What kind of truce did you have in mind?"

Kate was uncomfortably aware of him standing near her, but she would not step away. Let him be the first to retreat.

"The deal is, you behave like a lady and I won't cut out your liver and feed it to my dog." His attempt at humor insulted her. This was serious business, not cause for teasing.

"That's not a deal. It's a threat."

"Call it what you like. I'm tired of fighting with you. This is the third time I've had you in my office for disturbing the peace. Don't you ever give up?" He allowed his frustration to enter his voice.

"Today, I haven't done anything wrong and you have no right to keep me here and abuse me."

When he grabbed her wrist and held her hand up, stripping away the white lace glove, she pulled frantically to free herself. He had her now! Spreading out her fingers, he examined the black traces around her nails.

"Mrs. Christian came to me about an hour before her parade started and complained about someone painting over her signs. She thinks you did it."

He sniffed the faint odor of turpentine on her fingers. A deep shade of crimson crept over her face and she turned it away from him. That was guilt, he had no doubt of it. Still firmly holding her hand, he pressed his advantage.

"You know they'll retaliate. Then you'll do something worse to them and they'll come back at you. And I'll be in the middle trying to keep the peace. I can't let that happen."

Gallagher caught her chin in his hand and tilted her face up to force her to look at him. He put steel in his voice.

"The next time you're arrested, I won't call someone to get you. I'll deal with you myself and nothing will protect you from me."

He searched her eyes for the fear he intended to instill in her, but found defiance glaring back at him. Her courage assaulted his masculine pride. Theirs would be a long, cruel war when he would have preferred her friendship. His fingers moved along her silken cheek and throat, evoking a sweet torture in him.

Kate was hypnotized by the strong, gentle fingers caressing her face, while his words and voice sent a message of violence and unrelenting mastery. Would he make love like that, she wondered, strong and domineering, yet gentle and sweet? She heard him softly swear as he backed away from her and dropped his hands to his side.

His expression was composed, all residuals of passion carefully hidden under a veneer of easygoing charm as he offered her a seat.

"No thank you. I won't be staying. It's a long walk home and I'd best get started." She hoped to catch up with the parade before it reached City Hall.

"I'll take you home after you hear this story." He picked up a chair and placed it beside her.

Sighing with resignation, she seated herself and watched him lean against the corner of his cluttered desk.

"Is this another of your endless barnyard fables, Mr. Gallagher?" She showed her lack of enthusiasm in her long-suffering tone.

To her annoyance, he smiled at her before he began his tale.

"My mama used to have a little dog. I don't know what kind it was, but it had long, white hair. Mama was always brushing and pampering it. She named it Caesar after the Roman emperor. He thought he was royalty, the way he strutted around, yapping and nipping at people. We kids hated that spoiled little showoff, but we couldn't do anything about it. If Mama caught us so much as raising our voices to him, we'd get the switch for sure.

"We had a big old yard dog named Jasper. Caesar used to tease the life out of that old hound, eat from his dish, bark at him and nip at his tail. Every once in a while, Jasper would chase that little stinker around the yard, ready to rip him apart. Then, Mama would come tearing out of the house with her broom and take off after poor Jasper. You could hear him yelping as she whacked him good.

"After a while, he stopped chasing Caesar. He learned that he might be able to beat that silly little dog, but he was no match for the power that backed him up." Gallagher paused to let the moral sink in. "Wilhelmina Christian has the mayor and town council behind her. You'd be wise to watch your step."

"Thank you for the advice, but your story was wasted on me. If I was Jasper, the satisfaction of sinking my teeth into that little beast would have been well worth a few whacks from a broom." Kate faced him squarely. If he thought he could scare her off with warnings of the powers that be, then he didn't know her at all. She'd been trounced by the best and still came back fighting.

She doesn't scare off easy, but I already knew that, he mused. We all have a breaking point. I wonder what hers is. Maybe, it's better I don't know. I don't mean to break her, just keep her out of serious trouble.

"It's your hide." He lifted himself off his desk. "I'll saddle my horse now and take you home."

"I can't ride a horse dressed like this." Kate held out her legs and he saw the confining hobble skirt that reached to her ankles.

"Don't worry about it. We'll think of something."

A glimmer of mischief winked in his eyes and dimples appeared in his clean shaven cheeks. She frowned. He was enjoying the situation far too much for her liking. His face was alight with a toothy grin as he left the office through the back door. The door remained ajar.

Rufus padded in from the back room and followed his master outside. Kate sat staring at the partially open door. It seemed to offer an invitation for her to join them. Politeness ruled that she not wander around someone's property uninvited, but manners had never entered into her dealings with Gallagher. Curiosity won out.

She opened the door wide and stood at the threshold, taking in the details of the large yard. A small house, little more than a shack, stood to one side, its whitewash in need of a new coat, but otherwise in satisfactory repair. That was probably where the police chief lived, she surmised. Her gaze moved on to a small shed with a fence around it. Gallagher was leading a horse out of the shed. It was a broad-chested roan with a white blaze face. Kate watched the lawman lift the saddle off the fence, his muscles bulging against his shirt with the effort. Rufus bounded toward her and greeted her with a bark.

"Come out here and keep me company," Gallagher called to her without turning around.

She hesitated. This compelling, rough hewn man was dangerous when they fought, but when they were not at odds he was downright lethal. His natural warmth and protective instincts brought out a tenderness in herself that nudged her bruised heart, causing her to flinch with the pain. Should she risk getting close to him? Coward! When you fear your enemy you've already lost the war. Firmly, she stepped outside and shut the door behind her. There would be no running for cover when he aimed his penetrating charms in her direction.

Her shoes kicked up dust as she crossed the bare yard. She stopped outside the small corral where Gallegher stood saddling his horse. A pungent smell of horse dung floated out to her from the shed. Idly, she peered inside the makeshift hut for the other horse. The shed was empty.

Red heat spread up from her throat to her hairline. That conniving weasel expected her to ride double with him! The thought of her body so intimately close to his was not unpleasant, but she could not allow him to put her in such a position without regard to her opinion.

"Mr. Gallagher, it appears you intend for me to get on this horse with you."

"Yes, ma'am."

"Perhaps, I don't approve."

"We have no choice. I'm taking you home and there's only one horse." His voice was matter-of-fact as he continued to work.

"I would prefer to walk."

"I wouldn't." He turned to face her, his mouth set in a teasing grin. "I won't take advantage of your body, if you don't take advantage of mine."

She felt her color deepen. His jest was crude, but that was not the reason for her blush. The realization that he knew how her body reacted to him disconcerted her.

"That remark doesn't deserve an answer."

This man could be a pain in the posterior, yet she was drawn to him and not only because of his physical magnetism. Much of the discord between them was caused by him just trying to do his job. On occasion, he showed remarkable patience and concern. She had to admit she enjoyed his folksy stories, although they were hopelessly corny. Also, the day she read the accident report in his office, he did not mention her father's affair. Was he trying to protect her? She hoped that was the reason.

"I found out who my father was going to meet the night he died. You know who it was, don't you?"

"Yes, ma'am." He adjusted the saddle cinch.

"Why didn't you tell me?"

"I figured knowing would do you more harm than good. Besides, I don't like making women cry. How did you find out?"

"Jeffrey Carlisle told me."

Gallagher shook his head.

"That doesn't surprise me. Sometimes I think he has a stone where his heart should be."

Kate wondered how much he knew about her former attorney. She had questioned Phillip Endicott before leaving San Francisco, but he was not able to give her any more information.

"I heard he secretly owns Star Enterprises, the company that bought my father's freighting business. Why do you suppose he would keep his ownership a secret?"

"I don't know. If I were you, I wouldn't ask too many questions about Carlisle. He can be ruthless. I've seen what he does to people in court. You wouldn't want to stand on the wrong side of him."

She considered the advice for a moment before discarding it. Possible unpleasantness had never deterred her and she was not about to alter her style now. The lawyer's activities piqued her curiosity and she would not stop asking questions until she received answers. The police chief did not have the information or was unwilling to share it with her. In either case, questioning him further would be useless.

Gallagher led the horse out of the corral and came to a stop beside Kate. He easily mounted and kicked his boot free of the stirrup. She grasped his extended hand to steady herself as she hiked her skirt up to her knee and placed her foot in the metal loop. She had boosted herself only a short distance, when his other arm caught her around the waist and he lifted her across the saddle, both legs dangling on one side of the horse. Her back rested in the circle of his supporting arm. Her side snuggled against his chest, hip pressed against his pants. The intimacy and reliance on his strength to keep her upright disturbed her and she struggled to find a more comfortable position.

"Lady, if you don't stop bouncing around, my horse won't be the only gelding in this yard."

Abruptly, Kate stilled, holding herself rigid to minimize her body's pressure against him.

"Sorry," she murmured.

He felt the tension in the muscles along her back and hoped she would trust him enough to relax. She was light, nestled against him, her feminine curves burning him with awareness. One of her hands grasped the saddle horn, the other rested in her lap and he wished she would put her arm around him.

As the horse moved rhythmically beneath her, Kate enjoyed the ride. Before moving to New York, she had ridden often. She smiled to herself as passers-by turned to watch them riding double. Kate loved creating a stir, especially a scandalous one.

Traffic downtown was heavy, with motorcars passing near horses and making them skittish. The town council had banned use of auto horns in River Run. An automobile backfired with an earsplitting boom in front of Gallagher's horse. Both riders were almost unseated as the steed reared and came down prancing. Instinctively, Kate threw her arms around the man who held her as he fought to calm his horse. She choked back a scream, fearing it would further unsettle the animal.

"Whoa, Buck. Take it easy, boy."

The reassuring, deep voice Gallagher used to soothe his horse also seemed to calm the young lady who clung to him. Her fingers which dug painfully into his flesh loosened, but she did not let go. Through his shirt, he felt her racing heartbeat jump against his chest. When the horse was quiet, its sides heaving from exertion, Gallagher enfolded the frightened female in his arms and held her to him.

"Everything's all right now. It's all over." His nose brushed her fragrant hair and the soft curls caressed his lips, the scent and feel of her intoxicating his senses.

His softly crooned words and strong, comforting arms evoked a trust and protectedness in Kate which surprised her. Knowing how dangerous this man could be to her emotional stability, she had raised a shield against him, but he had slipped behind her defenses. He tapped sweet sentiments she thought were long dead.

Slowly, Kate loosened her hold on him and sat up straight. She left one arm around his waist, unwilling to relinquish the illusion of safety.

"I'm fine now. Thank you, Mr. Gallegher." She intended the formality to put a comfortable distance between them, if there could be such a thing after their bodies had touched so intimately.

"Call me John. We haven't been polite to each other from the moment we met." He prodded his horse into a slow gait.

She eyed him speculatively. Friends called each other by their given names. After all of the inconvenience she'd caused him, could he be offering her his friendship? If that were true, then his motives were suspect. Perhaps, he thought she would cooperate with him if they were friends. In that case, he would be wasting his time. On the other hand, he might be feeling the same physical attraction she did. Kate decided to follow his lead with caution and see where the path ended.

"You may call me Katherine."

"I'll call you Kate. It suits you better."

"I suppose it does." Considering all the liberties he took with her, using a nickname seemed minor.

They passed City Hall where Wilhelmina Christian stood on the sidewalk staring in shocked disapproval at the man and woman sharing a saddle. Kate was delighted with her enemy's reaction and blew her a kiss. The mayor's wife huffed and turned her back to the street. Kate laughed as the horse took them toward The Hill.

They neared Kate's house, the late afternoon sun casting a pink glow over the wealthy neighborhood. Gallagher noticed the new sign on the Moore mansion's lawn. *Boardinghouse for Genteel Ladies.* A smaller sign below it read *Piano Instruction.* He'd thought she was wealthy, living off her father's estate. Her working woman status pleasantly surprised him. Perhaps, she was not as spoiled as he supposed.

A movement on the porch caught his attention. The man stepping out from behind a honeysuckle bush seemed familiar, but from this distance, he could not make out his features. Curiosity ran rampant through his mind. Could that man in a city suit be this hellion's suitor?

Kate's pulse raced in alarm at sight of the familiar Oldsmobile roadster parked in front of her house. David was not due here for at least two hours. She glanced toward the porch, hoping he was in the house and unable to see her sitting on another man's lap. Her heart sank to her stomach when she saw David standing at the top of the steps, his body set in a rigid stance.

"Oh, damn," she murmured under her breath. "Thank you for the ride, John," she said aloud.

She tried to slip off the saddle and land on her feet. Gallagher's strong, supporting hand eased her descent. After straightening her skirt, she started at a slow pace toward the house, trying to regain her composure. She opened the gate before realizing Gallagher had dismounted, and tied the reins to a lamp post. He was following her.

"I'll walk you to the door." His gaze was glued to the man standing on the porch.

Before the lady could protest, Gallagher had her elbow firmly in hand and propelled her up the porch steps. Recognition hit Gallagher like a bucket of cold water. He had met the man a few years back when Dave Peters had been an Assistant District Attorney for Solano County. The dandy was known for his charm with ladies and relentless prosecution in court. People in the legal community had dubbed him the Ice Man.

Kate was astounded as David captured her in a no nonsense grip and kissed her on the mouth. When he faced Gallagher his arm remained possessively around her shoulders. This was not an affectionate greeting. She resented this branding of her as his property. No man owned her.

Apprehension seeped into Kate's pores as she watched the men stiffly shake hands and appraise each other as though squaring off for a fight.

"Miss Penny informed me that you detained Miss Moore while she was protesting an anti-suffrage parade. Did she break a law?" David's voice was tight.

"Not yet. I prefer to avoid trouble when it's possible. That's part of my duty."

"Was it part of your duty to ride through the town with her draped over your saddle, subjecting her to the gossip of the entire town?" The calm tone was like a sheathed knife.

"No. That was my pleasure. And hers too, if I don't miss my guess."

Kate watched the two men stand like stallions striking their hooves on the ground, preparing to do battle over a mare. She could not imagine why the lawman behaved like a jealous beau, when there was nothing between them but nasty arguments and one punishing kiss. He didn't even like her . . . or did he? Now, that was an interesting question, but consideration of it would have to wait. The men's eyes glowed with blood lust and she had to defuse the situation.

With an air of purpose, Kate stepped between the men who towered over her. She sensed the tension flow from them, thick enough to touch.

"Thank you again for the ride home, John. I think I've taken enough of your precious time." Holding his gaze steadily, she willed herself not to smile.

The dismissal was no more than Gallagher expected, although he accepted the use of his first name as a small victory. He was a fool to let his impulses get the better of him and barge into the imp's private affairs. It was none of his business that the cold, proper lawyer was all wrong for the lively leprechaun. Yet, he cared. Even when she was a royal pain, he felt protective of her.

He chucked her under the chin. "I'll be seeing you, brat."

With satisfaction, he noted the other man's fist clench convulsively. He repressed a grin and tugged on the wide brim of his hat as a means of taking his leave.

Halfway to the gate, he shuffled a few steps and puckered up to whistle *Beautiful Dreamer*. He'd give that fancy man a run for his money.

CHAPTER XI

David watched Gallagher mount his horse and ride away.

"I was unaware you were on such amiable terms with the local law enforcement. Am I to assume you did indeed enjoy that cozy ride on the back of his horse?" In spite of his intense jealousy, he managed to speak with his usual aplomb.

"Assume whatever you please. John offered me the only means of transportation he had." He detected annoyance in her clipped voice.

"John, is it? You appear familiar with the man. Should I consider him competition for your affections?"

He chided himself for allowing the rough-edged police chief to unsettle him.

"Of course not. My running feud with him is a town joke. Your assumption is ludicrous."

"I'm relieved to hear that, my dear." Although David remained unconvinced she had no romantic interest in the lawman, he was pleased to hear her denial. "Shall we go inside? I believe we've given your neighbors enough of a show for one day."

Kate sighed to expel her irritation with both men. A foul mood would serve no purpose other than to ruin her evening. She preceded David into the house and led him into the front parlor.

The room appeared light and airy with much of her mother's original Victorian clutter removed. She had left only the baby grand piano, two yellow striped sofas, a couple of chairs and a small table. Bright flowers on the wallpaper and carpet gave the sitting room a charming touch.

"I'll have a cup of coffee sent out to you before I go upstairs to change into something more suitable." She briskly kissed his cheek in a peace offering.

Her informal, dark skirt and ruffled white blouse were inappropriate for an evening out with David. He patronized only the poshest establishments. She also needed to wash away the horsy odor clinging to her.

Kate walked down the hall to the kitchen where Blanca was cutting vegetables at the table. After a short greeting, she asked the housekeeper to bring a tray of coffee and sweet cakes to the front room for Mr. Peters. Normally, Blanca did not work on Saturdays, but came to prepare and serve dinner for the two boarders while Kate was out with her gentleman friend.

Abigail Penny and Gladys Smith, the typewriter at the Montezuma Cannery, had moved in over two weeks ago.

The thick carpet on the stairs muffled her footsteps as Kate climbed up to the second floor. Abigail's bedroom door was open and she paused at the entrance to find her friend busy at a small writing desk. She rapped lightly on the doorframe to attract her attention.

"Mr. Peters is being served coffee in the front parlor. You are welcome to join him, if you like." When she had introduced Abby to David two weeks ago, they had struck an intellectual accord. Interesting company while he waited might improve David's mood.

"Thank you. I'll do that as soon as I'm through with this letter." The teacher paused a moment before asking, "How did your chat go with Chief Gallagher?"

"As usual, he raved and ranted, but to no avail. The man likes to roar, but is as dangerous as a pussycat."

"One of these days, you'll push him too far. I wouldn't want to be you when that happens." Abby shook her head.

Kate laughed at the faint-hearted reply. She pushed that man without letup and he showed her his temper, but she was still eager to enter the fray. What real harm could he possibly do to her? Not a thing, she answered herself.

"I'll see you later."

Kate turned toward her own bedroom. As soon as the door closed behind her, she unbuttoned her blouse and threw it across the canopied brass bed. The sunny room, decorated with a light hand in white with splashes of vibrant color, raised her spirits.

Kate undressed while her thoughts lingered on the lawman. She remembered the tantalizing warmth of his chest against her side as the horse moved beneath them, their bodies rubbing against each other, the musky, masculine smell of him calling to her. Under the sheer chemise, she noticed her rosy nipples standing out in reaction to her reverie.

"Damn the man."

He had the affect on her of a prairie fire. Uncontrollable heat spread through her, destroying every sensible thought in its path. Annoyed with herself, she tugged at the corset stays with a vengeance

While undressing, she tried to center her mind on David, that strait-laced, reasonable, safe man. A man who did not tumble her composure into chaos, could not start a roaring furnace in her belly. With him, her head was firmly in control, her heart not clamoring to make outrageous decisions; decisions that could destroy her faith in men and rape her once innocent soul. Her innocence was long gone, sold for a brief glimpse of heaven with a man she trusted, a man who helped to kill her baby and any chance of her becoming a mother.

The doctor had said her womb was so scarred there was little chance of conception and practically none that she could carry a child to full term. Would the proper gentleman waiting for her downstairs be eager to court her if he knew of her past? She doubted it.

Undressed, Kate entered the adjoining bathroom and ran water into the claw-footed bathtub. A door on the far side of the room led to the bedroom her father had used. She'd entered the room only once since returning from New York. His clothes and other possessions remained untouched. Someday, when the pain of his loss abated, she would clear his things out and ready it for occupation.

Warm water enveloped her as she lay back in the tub, relaxing her muscles and soothing the disturbing thoughts caused by shadows from her past. Reluctantly, she picked up the washcloth and bar of perfumed soap. A leisurely soak was exactly what she needed to settle her nerves after the tumultuous events of this afternoon. Unfortunately, there was no time for such a luxury. David waited in the parlor. She smiled, picturing the dark haired man seated on the sofa. He was her safe haven from the turmoil of her feelings and she needed his shelter tonight.

The descending night faded the road to Rio Vista. Kate blinked as David switched on the headlights of his

Oldsmobile, catching a bounding rabbit in its glow. Her fingers twisted a handkerchief in her lap in an attempt to dissipate her growing annoyance.

"Couldn't you appeal to your mother's sense of pride? I can't believe she would allow you to lower yourself by taking in boarders without offering to help you financially." She read his distaste for the situation in his voice.

"My mother doesn't know about the boardinghouse because I do not want her help. Actually, I enjoy the company of the ladies. I was lonely in that big house by myself."

"Be that as it may, a lady of your genteel breeding should not be required to take in boarders. And, considering the three of you to care for, not to mention the large house, it's a mystery to me how you can make do with only one servant."

"Blanca helps me with the housework and cooking. We do quite well sharing the work between us." She was gratified when he turned an appalled glance in her direction.

"I didn't realize you have been reduced to a chambermaid. We'll remedy this problem as soon as possible. You can depend on me, my dear," he declared like a noble knight coming to the rescue of his lady fair.

Kate groaned. He seemed to understand her position less, the more she explained it. How could she make him grasp that she enjoyed her new social status . . . or rather the lack of it.

"David, I do not have a problem. If you cannot accept the way I earn my money, that's your problem, not mine. I will not allow you to dictate to me."

"Let's not argue, sweet. I only meant to help you." He covered both her tiny hands with one of his. "You are quite right. It's premature of me to take on the duties of your husband."

Kate blanched. Considering his progressive politics and support of women's suffrage, she had concluded he would be a liberal spouse, not driven by the concept of the man in the house being the absolute ruler of the roost. Obviously, she had miscalculated. This fine gentleman was a true politician, spouting democratic theory, but practicing male supremacy. He was no better than that overbearing lout behind a policeman's badge. Both of them felt free to give her advice as though she did not have wits enough to rule her own life.

"It seems we do not agree on the duties of a husband. I believe he should allow his wife the freedom to pursue her own interests without interference. He should give her support, not a ball and chain. She is entitled to the same deference as he is."

David laughed.

"I'm afraid your model husband hasn't been invented yet, love. You will have to be content with one of us poor specimens."

Kate brooded, staring out at the shadowed night. Perhaps, he was right about her ideal not existing, but she would not settle for any man who sought to control her. Spinsterhood seemed a likely choice.

The dining room in the hotel in Rio Vista reminded Kate of the elegant restaurants in San Francisco, with its sparkling chandeliers, thick carpet and fine linen tablecloths. Ladies draped in silk or lace and their formally attired escorts appeared to be residents of this town's version of The Hill. On the way to their table, David detoured repeatedly to introduce Kate to his acquaintances. She was uncertain whether he was showing her off as his prize or was trying to impress her with his wide circle of successful friends.

Kate sat primly at the table like a little girl in church, knowing what was expected of her, but not happy with the situation. She had grown up in this stifling atmosphere, the confining world of her socially elite mother, but chose to avoid it these last few months, except when she was in David's company. Even then, she lured him into less formal surroundings when he could be persuaded, which was not often enough for her liking.

Why did she force herself to re-enter this glittering social stratum when, for her, the gold plating had long since been worn through to base metal? The answer was painful to investigate. She still hoped for her mother's good opinion, although she knew her mother's style of living did not suit her. Her father's more down-to-earth ways were more her style.

Thoughts of her father imbued her with guilt. In the three weeks since leaving San Francisco, she had done nothing to uncover the business dealings of Star Enterprises and Jeffrey Carlisle. Her suspicions weighed heavily on her mind, but she felt uncomfortable about taking her next step. David's contacts would make him the perfect person to sleuth for her, yet she did not want to be obliged to him.

As they waited for their entree to be served, David could not keep his eyes off the dazzling vision in cool blue silk seated across the table from him. He was well pleased with Kate's debut into his world. He was about to launch his dream of entering state politics and needed to see how she would fit in with his supporters. Choice of a suitable wife was an important decision for a man with his goals. Her natural warmth and candid remarks were a delight. On the other hand, he was convinced she needed a determined husband to dissuade her from misbehaving in public. He was willing to take on this formidable task in exchange for the joy of possessing the refreshing elf.

David noticed the lady's unusually pensive mood and wondered at its cause. There was still much he had to learn about her.

"Why are you so quiet, my dear? Have I displeased you?"

Kate came aware with a start. She had been deep in thought, her surroundings nonexistent. Blinking twice, she brought her dinner partner into focus.

"Pardon me, David. I didn't mean to ignore you." She smiled at him to reinforce her apology. "There's a puzzle I've been trying to unravel and it pops up at the most unexpected moments."

"You needn't hide your problems, my dear. You know I'll help you any way I can."

The opening was too good to pass up. She explained about the sale of her father's business without interruption. His silence and blank expression unnerved her.

"I understand your frustration, Katherine, but what do you hope to accomplish by asking questions about Star Enterprises? Jeffrey Carlisle is a powerful man. If he takes advantage of people's misfortune, there isn't a thing you or anyone else can do about it."

She was reluctant to voice her dislike for Carlisle and her suspicion that his business practices were illegal. Her credibility was at stake.

"I don't expect anything can be done, but that doesn't stop my curiosity. Until my questions are answered, I'll have no peace of mind."

"If I get the information you want, will you promise to let the matter rest?"

"Absolutely. You have my word." She crossed her fingers under the table. "Thank you, David. I didn't know who else to turn to."

Already her thoughts were racing ahead to what she could do with the information if her speculation proved true.

The Oldsmobile pulled to the side of the road and stopped. When the motor shut off a chorus of cricket song emerged. Then the headlights went off. Kate turned to David. He was little more than a looming shadow.

She had enjoyed the evening in Rio Vista, first dinner, the two of them alone, then joining friends of David at their table. Her partner seemed pleased with the outcome of their outing and in a generous mood.

Now he turned toward her and she caught the silver gleam of his eyes. His voice was husky.

"I wanted to be alone with you, my dear. Do you mind? I wouldn't want to offend you."

"You would have offended me if you didn't want us to be alone."

Tentatively, his fingers touched her cheek near her ear and she relaxed into it. His kiss was gentle, sweet, enticing. Impatiently, she waited for the pressure of his lips to gain force, to take possession of her. When the wait became unbearable, she slid her arms around his neck and moved her lips, careful not to lead him to think she was a hussy. David deepened the kiss, his hands roaming her back and neck. Kate realized he intended the intimacies to go no further and relaxed to enjoy what he was willing to give.

His affection was pleasant, if not passionate, and did not arouse her desire. There was something comforting about staying in control of her body's responses. Her heart was safe from him.

Kate was not used to being treated like a porcelain doll. She found his gentle care flattering, but unsatisfying. A sensual memory crept into her awareness. She leaned against a man, his strong arms surrounding her as a horse moved beneath them. There was more sexual power in the mental image than in the reality of David's gentle hands stroking her back and his lips moving softly along her neck. Disgusted with herself for allowing the vexatious lawman to intrude on her love life, she tried to exorcise him from her thoughts by concentrating on the man she was with. The ploy did not succeed.

David was careful to keep a close rein on his lust. This was a lady in his arms, to be treated with respect and consideration. From her eager response he guessed at her passionate nature, but wished not to indulge himself lest he lose control and do something which they both might later regret.

He noticed the subtle change in her mood. She seemed passive, as though his ministrations had little affect upon her. He backed away and waited for her to open her eyes which remained tightly shut for a long minute. When she finally looked at him, her eyes were unfocused and slightly confused, as though she was surprised to find him there. Upon closer scrutiny, he realized the confusion was not caused by passion and this unsettled him. Of what or whom was she thinking?

"I think we'd better continue on our way," he said.

Kate nodded in agreement, not caring to prolong the unsatisfactory experience. This polished gentleman might know how to treat a lady, but he fell far short of pleasing her. As he stepped out of the auto to crank the starter, she wondered if the feeling of safety she felt when with him was worth the passion missed.

CHAPTER XII

The gate clicked shut at Gallagher's back and the Moore mansion rose up before him like a fortress. He had grown up in a large farmhouse, but it had not been nearly as huge or ornately decorated. Its obvious worth did not impress him so much as define the social barrier between him and the house's socialite owner. For an instant he wondered at the wisdom of attempting to penetrate this bastion of class distinction. The lady already had a wealthy courter, someone of her own background who could restore her to the ranks of the idle rich. Besides, they'd been at each other's throats since that night on the back road when she'd aimed a gun at his private parts. What the hell am I doing here? he thought in panic.

He picked up piano music coming through an open front window. Someone haltingly played *Dance Of The Sugar Plum Fairy*. The familiar melody reminded him of his sisters practicing on their old upright when they were kids. Between his four sisters and his mother, the music had seemed one continuous flow.

Thoughts of his family soothed his jangled nerves and he started up the stone pathway to the porch. He removed his broad brimmed hat and finger combed his hair. Before leaving his cottage, he had changed his shirt to put on the best one he owned and shaved close. He would never be better prepared to face her than he was now. His hand went to the knocker.

The music continued as he waited. Just as he began to wonder if anyone heard the summons, the door swung open and a small woman, evidently Latin from her dark complexion and features, stood there inspecting him.

"I'm Police Chief Gallagher, here to see Miss Moore." He used his best formal voice.

"She gives a piano lesson now, but you can wait inside."

When the housekeeper stepped aside, he entered the house and looked around. There was a long stairway to the right and a narrow corridor leading to the back rooms. Gallagher followed the woman into the hall.

As they passed the entrance to the front parlor, he peeked inside. The lady he came to visit sat at a piano beside a little girl in pigtails. The youngster labored at the keys. For an instant, Kate turned toward him and her honey colored eyes locked with his. Surprise and confusion registered on her face before she returned to her student.

He waited alone in the back parlor. The silk and tapestry covered chairs and sofas did not lend themselves to comfort and Gallagher wondered why anyone would want to furnish a parlor you would not want to sit in. His gaze rested on the sunlit window, and he strode up to it to look out. The garden looked like autumn with leaves just beginning to turn color and late season blooms. He was startled when a gruff voice spoke from the doorway.

"Hello, young fella. Blanca told me you was waitin' out here alone. Come on back to the kitchen and join us. There's a whole passel of folks in there eatin' cookies."

Gallagher grinned as he recognized the long white beard and officer's cap of Captain Tom Macaphee. They'd shared a few beers and swapped a few tales down at the docks over the years. The lawman made it his business to know who patronized which saloons and where the trouble spots were. The captain was a valuable asset, knowing the docks and the river people. He'd proven his willingness to help the law on many occasions.

"Thanks, Cappy. I was getting kind of lonesome in here."

He followed the old man two doors down the hallway to the kitchen. Before he reached the entrance, he heard women's conversation and the shrill voices of young children.

As Gallagher's boots touched down on the shiny linoleum floor, he felt the illusion of entering his mother's kitchen. This room was fancier than the one in the farmhouse, but the aroma of baking bread and cookies, and the cheerful sound of relaxing people brought up comfortable memories.

Lit by the late afternoon sun, the kitchen took on a golden hue, highlighting the gleam of the floor and the stained glass cabinet doors. Platters of cooling cookies and breads covered the polished maplewood table. The woman who had answered the door stood at one end of the table, icing a cake.

"Good afternoon, Miss Penny." Gallagher addressed Abigail who was seated at the table.

"Good afternoon." The teacher's greeting was reserved.

"Have a seat and grab a couple of cookies," the Captain urged.

Gallagher crossed the room to the other side of the table. Two children sat on the floor among a scattered pile of pots, pans and wooden spoons. The younger child was a boy about a year old and the other was a girl no older than two. They had the dark features of the housekeeper.

"These yours?" He indicated the babies.

"My grandchildren." She beamed.

"Cute kids."

He turned a chair backward and sat on it, leaning his arms across the wooden frame of the back.

"Kate in trouble again?" Tom asked.

"Not that I know of, but with Kate, you can never be sure." Gallagher's grin added dimension to his vague reply.

"Know what you mean," the Captain chuckled. "She's always up to mischief. Been that way since a tadpole."

Scratching and mewling sounds came from just below the police chief as he felt a pressure on his booted calf. He looked down in time to see an orange blur scoot up inside his pant leg and out of sight. He stomped his foot on the floor to dislodge whatever it was and was amazed as a kicking ball of fur dropped onto the toe of his boot. When he picked it up, the clawing, biting creature was so small he could almost close his fingers and hide it completely.

"Chica had kittens." The maid nodded toward the corner near the iron stove.

Gallagher saw the gray mother cat lying on her side in a towel lined box, one tabby offspring suckling in contentment. He set the squirming kitten on the floor and gave it a gentle push toward its mother, but the tiny adventurer turned around and scampered under the table. The older child chased after the fuzzy animal.

"Kitty, kitty, kitty," she shouted with glee as she ducked under the table after it.

There was a loud thunk and the table shook. Two seconds later, a bawling toddler crept out near Gallegher's feet, holding the side of her head. The second oldest of eight children and uncle to nine, he was used to dealing with crying babies. He lifted her, and sitting her on his knee, kissed the sore spot on her head. She stopped crying long enough to size him up, then scrunched her face in preparation for a new fit. Before she could suck in enough wind for a good howl, he wrapped her chubby fist around a cookie and cuddled her back against his ribs. He grinned in satisfaction as she brought the cookie to her mouth and eyed him with a flirtatious batting of long, dark lashes.

This warm kitchen filled with unaffected people spanning three generations felt more like the farm the longer he sat here. Totally at ease now, he munched on a raisin cookie, oblivious to the crumbs he and the toddler dropped onto his lap.

"You do Kate an injustice by not taking her seriously." Abigail defended her friend, bringing the focus back to the original conversation. "Her methods may be unconventional, but her heart is in the right place. The town is benefiting from her spirited support. Did you know that the shepherds' children have been allowed to remain in the River Run schools due to her intervention at the Town Council meeting?"

"Yes, I remember that night." Gallagher's lips twitched with suppressed amusement as he recalled the hellcat handcuffed to the chair.

"That night was unforgettable." Kate's voice came from the doorway. "As I recall, you behaved like a beast."

Realizing the object of his visit had entered the room, Gallagher removed the child from his knee and stood. He silently damned himself for jamming his foot into his big mouth.

"We can both take some credit for that," he retorted.

Kate saw his discomfort and was almost sorry to have brought it on. He had appeared so endearing crunching a cookie and holding the little girl. It was a side of him she would like to get to know.

"Perhaps so," she conceded. "To what do I owe the pleasure of your visit?"

She watched Gallagher look around at the room full of attentive people.

"I'd like to speak with you in private, Kate, if you don't mind."

"Certainly. Follow me." She stepped into the hallway.

Kate heard him say a brief good-bye to everyone before coming up behind her in the hall. In the front parlor, she seated herself in a chair so he would not have the option of sitting with her on a sofa. His physical presence was too unnerving to invite him that near. He took a nearby chair.

"I've been thinking we always seem to be fighting. If we got to know each other, maybe it would make our jobs easier." He ran his fingers around the rim of his hat in nervous repetition.

"Are you suggesting we get to know our enemies?" she asked, putting on her sparring gloves.

"I hope you don't think of me as your enemy. I'd much rather be your friend. There's a dance at City Hall this Saturday night. I'd like for you to come with me."

Kate's jaw dropped. A social invitation was the last thing she expected. The baffling scene on her porch a few days ago between him and David came to mind. She remembered wondering if he behaved like a jealous ass because he liked her. Now, she had her answer.

"Before you refuse, hear me out," he rushed on. "You only know me as a policeman chewing your ears off and getting in your way. That's my job. There's more to me than that. Just like I'm sure there's more to you than being a stubborn pain in the neck. I'd like to get to know who you really are."

She thought of this rugged man relaxing in her kitchen, showing a gentle and generous nature only hinted at from her previous contact with him. He seemed to belong in the informal setting surrounded with the family she had created for herself. The part of her seeking a warm, down-to-earth man urged her to accept his offer. But there were other considerations to ponder. The erotic need his nearness triggered was both a blessing and a curse. If he chose to use her cruelly, giving in to her physical needs could be disastrous. Her battered heart could not take more abuse. She would not give her body without also giving her love. Yet, the titillating thought of touching him and being touched by him overrode the danger signals. Another point to think about was how he would expect this friendship to affect her suffrage activities. She had no intentions of altering her plans to suit him.

"Before I give you an answer," she said. "I want to assure you my support for suffrage would continue as before, no quarter given. My principles will not be betrayed for the sake of an alliance. If you can accept that condition, then I'll go to the dance with you."

Gallagher grinned.

"Agreed. Until we compromise, whatever happens while I'm wearing my badge will be put aside when I take it off. We won't let business interfere with our personal lives."

"There will be no compromise." Her voice was firm.

His grin broadened.

"We'll see about that." The light in his eyes danced with devilment. "After I put you across my knee and spank your bottom, you'll compromise soon enough."

Kate recognized the humor in his expression and knew he was teasing.

"Do you often abuse your badge for your private gratification?"

"Never. Paddling you would be a personal pleasure and I would gladly remove my badge for the occasion."

She felt like the rodent in a cat and mouse game and decided to change the subject.

"It seems we have an unresolvable difference of opinion. Let's call this match a draw and work on the truce you suggested."

"We'll have to work on the truce Saturday. I have to get back on duty now." He rose from the chair, his smile still in place. "I'll pick you up at eight o'clock."

Kate walked with him to the door. She was surprised when Gallagher tentatively brushed her cheek with his fingertips. After a moment of gentle contact, he pulled his hand back as though stung by a bee.

"Thanks for agreeing to come with me, Kate."

"Don't thank me too soon." She led him into the hallway. "Our attempt at peacemaking could be a disaster."

"War can be fun too."

"Then I'll come armed to the teeth."

They stopped at the door. After a brief good-bye, she watched Gallagher cross her porch and pass the garden gate. No matter how poorly they would get along, Kate was certain the evening would not be dull. She shivered at the thought of dancing in his arms. Heat suffused her cheeks in anticipation. Annoyed with herself for allowing her mind to tangle with romantic illusions, she closed the door to shut him out of her view.

A black buggy slowly rolled down The Hill behind a high stepping chestnut mare as it made its way toward City Hall. The borrowed conveyance was not new, but was in acceptable repair, its wheels greased, the leather seats supple and clean, and the canopy without holes. It was a reminder of a less hectic age, before motorcars pushed such modes of transportation off the road.

Kate sat back watching the lamplit street slowly slide by. The last time she rode in a buggy was eight years ago, before her father bought the Pierce-Arrow. Accustomed to the speed of automobiles, she found this lazy pace maddening.

She looked at the strong hands competently holding the reins. In her estimation, John belonged in this rig which seemed to deny the advancing era of new machines and changing ideas. If he clung to his belief that women were happiest while keeping in their place and serving their men, he would soon become a relic, as was the destiny of this buggy.

"I hope you don't mind the dance being sponsored by the Ladies' Aid Society," Gallagher remarked. "The proceeds go toward the school fund for the shepherds' children."

Kate looked at him. He appeared ill at ease in the dark blue suit and black string tie. She considered him exceptionally handsome in the semi-formal attire.

"That organization does worthy work and many suffragists belong to it. I don't mind that Wilhelmina Christian is president of it. I'm happy to be going tonight."

"You'll want to steer clear of her. She's still angry about the signs you painted over. I'm trying to talk her out of pressing charges, but she won't give in."

"Thanks for trying, but it isn't worth the worry. Whatever comes of it, I'll live to fight again."

"You really don't care about the consequences, do you?"

"Not in the least."

"Then, in the interest of peace, you won't mind if I negotiate a settlement."

"Do as you please, but don't expect me to apologize." Kate was uneasy with the turn of the conversation. He had something in mind, something she was not going to like.

"An apology is not what I'm thinking of. I need your word that you'll abide by my decision."

She examined his face closely, trying to determine whether to trust him.

"If there's no apology or public humiliation involved, I'll accept your judgment."

A self-satisfied grin spread across his face. Already, she regretted her promise. She trusted his sense of fair play, but not his concern for her dignity. Kate wished she could retrieve her pledge without losing honor.

They reached City Hall and Gallagher helped Kate down from the buggy before parking the rig nearby. As she waited for him to return, people also headed for the dance passed her. The women's pretty, but inexpensive clothing reaffirmed her decision to wear a simple blue silk dress with a single strand of pearls at her neck. Overdressing in one of her couturier gowns would have been an embarrassing blunder. She took the hint from Abigail and Gladys who showed her what they intended to wear to the dance.

When Gallagher joined her, he linked her arm through his and led her up the steps. He had left his hat in the buggy and Kate noticed his usually unruly hair was slicked back with scented oil of Macassar. Although he appeared dashing, she preferred his locks in their natural condition.

Gallagher paid for their admission and they entered the meeting hall that was converted to a ballroom for the evening. Brightly colored streamers and ribbon festoons decorated the room in a festive feast for the eyes. The room was crowded and noisy, loud, popular music overpowering the chatter of the people.

Kate recognized a few familiar faces as her escort guided her to the refreshment table. Abigail and Eulalia stood with a group of teachers, Gladys was on the dance floor doing the turkey trot with a young man who worked at the cannery, and Sam Wakely conversed with a couple of merchants. Residents of The Hill were conspicuously absent. Except for the Mayor, his wife, Kate, and her two boarders there was no one from The Hill. Kate was aware that ladies from the wealthy section of town had helped to organize the dance, but would not be seen socializing with the common folk.

Gallagher handed her a cup of fruit punch and she sipped from it. Kate could not fathom why her escort appeared ill at ease. He seemed to be waiting for her to make the next move.

"This music is wonderful. Do you dance the Bunny Hug?"

"Yes, ma'am."

With enthusiasm, he led her to the crowded dance floor. They moved well together to the steps of the Bunny Hug, Turkey Trot and Cakewalk. These daring new dances exhilarated Kate and she felt her partner's energy. When the band played a waltz, the sweet music made her achingly aware of their clasped hands and the rough weave of his jacket under her fingers. The scent of him drifted to her, whispering of masculine strength, courage, and passion. He drew her to him like metal to a lodestone.

Kate had never danced with such abandon before this night. The formal affairs she usually attended demanded polite decorum. She was surprised this big, rough man could dance so well and was even more astonished by his gentlemanly behavior. He did his best to impress her and she appreciated his effort.

In spite of the late September breeze wafting through open windows, Kate felt the crowded room become stifling. She fanned her flushed face.

"It looks like you could use a rest and some punch."

Gallagher led her to a chair beside a window. "I'll be right back."

Kate watched him disappear in the direction of the refreshment table. She felt dizzy and turned her face to catch the fresh air floating by. Her eyes were closed as she concentrated on cooling herself. A melodic voice called her name and she came suddenly alert to find Blanca's seventeen-year old daughter, Dorothea, standing there.

"Miss Katherine, this is Carmela Cabrillo." The young woman introduced her companion. "We would like to speak with you for a moment."

Kate graciously invited them to sit with her. There was something familiar about the dark woman in her early twenties who was with Dorothea.

"If I remember correctly, Carmela, you stood at the door of the factory, keeping the workers outside on the day I came to speak there."

"Yes, that was me. You were very brave that day. Do you still want to help us at the cannery?" The young woman's Portuguese accent sounded pleasant to Kate.

"I'd like to help you, but I don't want to cause any more trouble for Mr. Slater. It's a personal matter." Kate thought of her father cuckolding Henry Slater and cringed.

"This would be a favor to him. The union men are back, trying to get us to join. If Mr. Slater treats us better, the union will not be necessary."

"Why wouldn't you want the union, Carmela?"

"The women don't trust outsiders, especially men. The union will never happen at Montezuma, but we want to use the threat to get what we want."

"I understand. What is it you want me to do?" Facing the cannery owner would be uncomfortable after her unwitting bungle at his home and the scene she had caused at his factory. But with finesse Kate hoped to allay his disapproval.

"There will be a meeting of cannery workers Wednesday night at eight o'clock, at the old Number Three warehouse on the South Street dock. We would like for you to be there." Carmela's voice was heavy with hope.

Attendance at the meeting would give Kate a better idea of the employees' situation at the cannery without committing herself to take action. It was an ideal opportunity and she accepted the invitation. Dorothea and Carmela soon took their leave.

A few minutes later, Sam Wakely sat in a chair beside her and handed her a cup of punch. She could not remember seeing the newspaper publisher so spruced up. He had a close shave and his dark suit was devoid of wrinkles. Even his mop of hair was neatly trimmed and combed. His ever present notepad protruded from his jacket pocket.

"Chief Gallagher asked me to bring this to you." He indicated the drink. "Some young bucks with a bottle of hard liquor started a fracas at the other end of the hall. He went to quiet them down. My guess is he'll be here soon."

"Thanks, Sam. I was beginning to wonder if he'd run out on me." She smiled to show she was not serious.

"A lot of people are surprised at you two showing up together, especially at one of Wilhelmina Christian's functions. Does this mean the end of the Petticoat Gang?" She saw a merry sparkle in his eyes.

"It means no such thing. I'm not against the work of the Ladies' Aid Society just because I don't agree with the politics of its president. So far, I've managed to avoid Mrs. Christian. If I'm lucky, there won't be any friction between us tonight."

"I think your luck just ran out, Katydid. She's got you in her sights and she's charging like an angry buffalo."

Indeed, when Kate looked up, she saw the leader of the town's anti-suffrage movement bearing down on her. The fire of vengeance burned in her eyes. In lieu of an ornate hat a long, red feather ascended from her full blown hairdo, waving over her head in a gigantic question mark. An entourage of Wilhelmina's supporters flanked their leader in battle array.

"Good evening, Wilhelmina. Congratulations. It appears your fundraiser is a rousing success." Kate spoke with as much nonchalance as she could muster. It ate at her craw to be polite to her arch enemy. But the last thing she wanted was to break tonight's truce with Gallagher.

"That is none of your concern." Wilhelmina's face was red with rage. "How dare you show up here under the protection of Chief Gallagher? You flaunted yourself like a cheap tart on that horse to help him forget his duty. You're nothing but a common vandal. I have power in this town and you'll pay for what you did!"

Kate stood to meet the challenge. Her temper straining on its tether, she fought control of her voice and lost it.

"I don't need a man to protect me from a ridiculous old bat like you. If admiration for you was part of admission, this room would be empty."

"Ridiculous am I! You'll change your mind when no decent woman in this town will speak to you. You'll come crawling to me for forgiveness, you little savage."

Kate formed a fist and was about to smash it into Wilhelmina's face when Sam stepped between them. "Now ladies, this is no place to start a rucus. You ought to be ashamed of yourselves."

"Shut up," Kate shouted at him, annoyed to hear Wicked Willy' s voice echo her own. She hated to agree with her on anything.

As Sam moved out of her way, Kate caught a glimpse of Gallagher's approach. She had no time to land her punch before his arm surrounded her shoulders, relaying the message that he was in charge now.

"How nice to hear you ladies having a friendly chat." The deep, blunt timbre of his voice demanded attention and respect. Kate glared at him, but he continued politely as though serving tea in a parlor. "I was just thinking what a sweet example you two are setting for the town."

Following his gaze, Kate noticed the small crowd of onlookers intently listening to the exchange. She saw Wilhelmina flush with embarrassment and shift her view to the floor. Kate was not so affected. Trying to wriggle free of the lawman's confining grasp, she only succeeded in having him tighten his hold.

"You'll be happy to know Miss Moore has volunteered to replace the four signs that were ruined." He addressed the mayor's wife. "I think that's a fair peace offering."

Kate bristled as a wide grin adorned the matron's gloating face.

"That will do nicely," Wilhelmina said.

"You're insane!" Kate renewed her attempt to loosen his grasp. "I never said such a thing."

"There's no need to be modest. Your generosity is overwhelming," he said.

Stealthily slipping her hand under the side of his jacket, Kate grabbed a bit of his flesh through his shirt and gave it a bruisingly vicious pinch. His muscles flinched in reaction, but he gave no further acknowledgment of the attack.

"I won't do it," she announced with finality.

"Of course, you will." Gallagher's answer was matter-of-fact as he turned to Mrs. Christian. She wore an expression of triumph. "The signs will be delivered Wednesday. Now, if you'll excuse us, Miss Moore looks a bit pale and needs some fresh air."

Before Kate could comment, he led her toward the door. She resisted being forced to retreat, but he overpowered her, nearly lifting her from her feet.

"Let me go, you barbarian," she railed in vain.

She considered kicking him, but recalled how he retaliated the last time she had used that tactic. The price of physically abusing him might be more than she was willing to pay. Besides, she had the pinch for which to answer.

They reached the empty entry hall and he released her.

"What in the devil were you doing in there?" She shouted, venting her anger and frustration. Her voice bounced off the walls with a roar.

"Settle down and we'll talk. On the way here, you agreed to abide by my decision on the signs. You gave me your word, Kate. Doesn't that mean anything to you?"

"The deal was for no public humiliation."

"I didn't cause the scene in there. You two were going at it claw and fang. If anything, I saved you from humiliating yourself. Will you honor your promise?"

His gaze steadily held hers, demanding an answer.

Kate felt tricked, trapped, and betrayed, but she had no choice. She must stand by her pledge. If she turned away from it now, she would lose not only his respect, but her own as well.

"That self-righteous bully will get her signs. Just don't expect them to be delivered with a smile. As for you, I'm very angry. You paid no attention to anything I had to say, then dragged me away with no regard for my feelings . . ." She continued to ramble on, berating him for his treatment of her.

Gallagher watched the fire spring from her as she dragged him over the coals. He appreciated her most when she was fierce like this, crackling with temper and feral heat. His hand came up to touch her, but she backed out of his reach.

"Stay away from me. I'm not finished saying what I think of you." She retreated as he advanced on her until the wall at her back made her halt. He closed in until their bodies nearly touched. Before she could bolt, Gallagher clapped his palms against the wall on either side of her head, imprisoning her between his outstretched arms.

"Let me go," she demanded, although she knew there was no stopping him.

"When I asked you to the dance, we decided not to confuse business with pleasure." His voice was low and throaty, giving off sexual signals which to Kate were both an invitation and a threat. "Wilhelmina Christian was business. Now it's time to put her aside and take some pleasure."

As his head came toward her, his lips moving ever closer to their target, Kate warred with herself. She had anticipated this moment all evening, yet was unwilling to let go of her anger. When she turned her face away, his mouth followed hers and made contact. While her mind could still resist, her hands pushed frantically against his chest, pommeling it when he showed no signs of relenting. His fingers gently stroked the sensitive area of her neck just below her ear as his lips applied more pressure and she could no longer ward off her yearning. She reveled in his touch. Her hands came to rest on his chest, feeling the hard muscles beneath the material of his shirt, her fingers gliding in tiny circles under his jacket. She opened her mouth to taste him, her tentative tongue flicking lightly at the warmth of his lips, until they parted and his tongue met hers in a wickedly sensual dance.

Now that she was responding with willingness, Gallagher was on fire, his desire barely under control. His hand braced against the wall kept his body from pressing against the delicious little witch, a safeguard from losing his reason. His raging blood urged him to wrestle her to the floor and savagely take her. He nibbled at her earlobe and continued his lips' journey down her throat, feeling a low moan vibrate in her sweet flesh. God, how he wanted her.

Footsteps and voices broke into their circle of passion and he reluctantly pulled away from her, trying desperately to shake off his languor. Kate looked as dazed as he felt. Her eyes sparkled as though beholding a treasure and her ravaged mouth was half open in wonderment.

"People are walking by," he managed to say. "Do you want to go back inside or leave?"

She shook her head and blinked her eyes to dispel the fog lingering in her head. Her body wanted them to find privacy where they could bring what they had started to its natural end. Unfortunately, that was not one of her choices. Preservation of her pride urged her to leave rather than return to the dance and face Wilhelmina and the crowd, but avoidance of a challenge was not her way.

"I'd like to go somewhere quiet where we can talk, but first I need to show my face in the hall so the old battle ax won't think I'm hiding in disgrace."

He nodded his understanding. Kate laid her hand on his offered arm and accompanied him toward the ballroom. The lively strains of a George M. Cohan melody streamed out to them. Gallegher had won the contest, she contemplated, yet she felt as if she had the prize. It was only a kiss, but its promise of future delights glittered like a perfectly cut jewel. He had her so confused that losing to him felt like winning. She would have to ponder that phenomenon when he was not around to addle her thinking.

A hoary mist floated above the river, subduing the moonlight's reflection on the rippling water. Dim lantern light glowed eerily through the window of a houseboat moored on the bank upstream and the soothing sound of the current mingled with insect song.

Kate sat on the seat of the parked buggy, snuggled in her shawl. Surrounding night lingered on the periphery of her awareness. Her attention centered on the shadowed features of John Gallagher who sat beside her, his leg nearly touching her own. He had removed his string tie and opened the top button of his shirt. His relaxed appearance eased her own nervousness.

"I'm glad you enjoyed the dance." The deep, mellow music of his voice drew Kate closer to him. "I thought you might not feel comfortable there, you being used to fancy society balls and men with shiny new motorcars. By the way, I hope Dave Peters wasn't too upset the other day." Kate caught his roguish grin, betraying the falsity of his last statement. He was full of the devil.

"If he was he didn't show it."

"Are you still seeing him?"

"I don't discuss my male friends with other men. It isn't seemly." Let him wonder about her and David. It was none of his business, anyway.

She broke eye contact with Gallagher to close the subject. Kate did not want to think about David now. When he took her hand in his and stroked the palm, she could not keep her fingers from trembling.

"What I really want to know is how much you care for him. Is there any room for me?" She heard hesitation in his voice. This was not easy for him.

Kate squirmed. In light of the danger signals he set off, she found it difficult to accept her increasingly favorable opinion of this warm, magnetic man. If she let him know how he affected her, he would have more ammunition against her weakened defenses.

"Mr. Peters and I are friends. The extent of that friendship doesn't concern you." His tender touch exploring her hand disconcerted her and she had trouble speaking.

"Am I also your friend?"

"I don't know. Are you?"

"I'm your friend and more, if you'll let me be."

He brought the palm he stroked to his lips. Her hand jerked with a slight withdrawing motion, then lay rigid in his grasp. His fleet glance at her eyes confirmed his suspicion. Fear flashed at him from the amber orbs for an instant before she shielded it with a neutral glaze. Recall of that pained look flitted through his memory. She had feared his gentleness those many weeks ago and the emotion was still there. Although this hellion had more courage than a bobcat, she was still afraid of him.

"Why are you frightened of me?" He knew she would deny it, but was unable to keep from voicing the question.

"I'm not afraid of you." Was that false bravado he heard?

Gallagher was surprised when she leaned over and planted a hearty kiss on his cheek. While she was still off balance, he found her mouth with his own and clutched her to his chest. He nearly dragging her onto his lap. She seemed determined to prove to them both that she was no coward as she answered his ardor in kind. Soon, he was lost in sensation, carnal heat throbbing through his veins, her touch urging him to devour her.

The lady's sexual expertise startled Gallagher. Certainty that this was no naive maiden emboldened him. His hand homed in on her bodice, molding it to the curved globe pushed up by her corset. His thumb found the nub at its peak and massaged it until it stood out hard.

Kate floated in a luxurious dream, barely realizing the exquisite stirring in her breast was caused by his fingers. Not until his hand slid inside the neckline of her dress did she become aware of his purpose and clear the fog from her head. Appalled that she had lost control of herself, she struggled wildly to fight free of his encircling arms and spell-binding lips. When he let her go, she watched his eyes open wide in surprise and confusion. She knew she could not explain her actions. Giving way to her instinct to escape, she leaped from the buggy, nearly stumbling to her knees before running into the tall grass.

Gallagher swore at the lunacy of the young woman trying to lose herself in this isolated area at night. Swiftly, he took off after her. She ran surprisingly fast, but she was no match for his long stride and he soon overtook her. He latched onto her arm and swung her around to face him. When she strained away from him, he shook her once to let her feel his determination. Her struggling stopped.

Kate let her head hang forward, staring at the grass at her feet. How could she look at him when she had behaved so irrationally? She wanted to disappear.

"There was no need to run from me. All you had to do was say 'no'. I don't attack women."

His soothing voice surprised her. She had expected anger. Perhaps, he was not disgusted with her and their fragile friendship could be salvaged after all. Kate knew her own lack of control had precipitated his boldness. If she could keep her passion in check, he might be able to do the same. Unfortunately, with this man, curbing her desires was like trying to stop an ocean tide from coming in.

When she did not speak, Gallagher tilted her face up to read the play of emotions on her face. At first, her eyes avoided him, but with persistence, he persuaded her to look his way. Fear and pain flickered on her features as she tried to conceal them. He was certain she had been cruelly hurt by a man and was afraid to risk it again. He did not relish paying for another man's mistakes, but he had sampled the delicacies waiting behind her protective barrier. The prize would be well worth the price in patience.

"I didn't mean to upset you. Are we still friends, Kate?"

She nodded in the affirmative, but could not find her voice. He made this awkward time easier for her and she appreciated his tact. When he slid his arm around her shoulders she did not protest. Kate allowed him to guide her back to the rig,

"Don't worry. I may be an ogre, but brats are only on the menu every second Tuesday. You're safe tonight," he said with mock seriousness.

Kate laughed and looked up at him. He smiled, squeezing her shoulder. She returned the smile. Many times he'd seen her at her worst, yet he accepted her, warts and all. No matter how outrageous her behavior, he still wanted to be her friend.

The ride back to The Hill was companionable. On her porch, she guardedly returned his good night kiss. Gallagher whistled on his way to the gate as Kate watched him from the open doorway. She allowed herself a contented sigh as she shut the door.

CHAPTER XIII

Crumbling walls and layers of filth gave the Number Three Warehouse on the South Street dock a derelict atmosphere. The wooden building had not been in use since the flood of 1907 when the rampaging current had carried off sections of its walls. Pockets of debris afforded homes for rats and crawling insects, and cobwebs decorated the rafters. A thick, clinging stench of mildew overpowered the fresh scent of the river flowing not far from the back door. One hundred and twenty people, mostly young women, stood in the middle of the vast room where kerosene lamps dispelled the night and discouraged the rodents from venturing forth.

Kate stood at the side of the crowd, careful to stay within the protection of the light, her distaste for rats brought near the surface in this forbidding place. In this room full of strangers the presence of Gladys Smith, her boarder, comforted her.

Kate looked at Gladys. The sweet-faced blonde was fashionably plump, her long, beaded necklace resting on a softly pillowed bosom. Her plain, but stylish dress set her apart from her fellow cannery employees whose clothing was threadbare and utilitarian. Kate understood her boarder's purpose in attending the meeting was only to accompany her and assuage her own curiosity. As a typewriter in the office, Gladys was not subject to many of the conditions from which the factory workers suffered and had informed Kate she was not interested in unionizing.

A sturdily built man sporting a derby hat and a red plaid vest stood on a platform composed of empty fruit crates. In a booming voice, this union organizer extolled the benefits of membership in his group. The men in the audience applauded, but most of the women frowned.

"A union would get you higher wages," the man in plaid boasted.

"If my job paid well enough, Mr. Slater could hire a man to do it and I'd have no job," one woman called out.

"A union gives you bargaining power against management. The threat of a strike can be mighty convincing," the union man argued.

"The Waistmakers' Union in New York was on strike for three months last winter. The workers were beaten, arrested and starving and the best they got was a fifty-two hour work week. I'm a widow. I can't afford to strike. My children would starve."

The proceedings enthralled Kate. Never before had she been so close to the plight of women forced to factory labor. She realized that, but for the accident of her birth to wealthy parents, her situation could be as ugly as the women's who worked at Montezuma. Her father's legacy and her education were the only things standing between her and poverty.

By the end of the meeting, it was obvious to her that interest in the union was not strong enough for it to succeed. Yet changes at the factory were desperately needed. Even more pressing than the desire for higher wages, was the necessity for healthier and safer working conditions. When Carmela Cabrillo climbed onto the platform and called for unity even if the union was voted down, she was met with a half-hearted reception. Convinced of their helplessness and fearful of losing their jobs, the women workers would not risk stirring up trouble.

As the crowd slowly dispersed, a discouraged looking Carmela approached Kate.

"Thank you for coming." Carmela's welcoming smile was lopsided. "Now you can see we need help. There is too much fear and too little courage for us to stand against Mr. Slater on our own. If I go to him with our complaints, he will fire me. Will you help us?"

"Unless you all band together and challenge Mr. Slater with a show of power, anything I do for you would be wasted. Besides, I'm not on good terms with Mr. Slater. He might not agree to see me."

"Please try." The young woman's plea touched Kate's sympathy "We are just beginning to grow strong. I am sure soon we will be able to stand up for ourselves."

Kate doubted that with the lack of enthusiasm at tonight's meeting, the women employees of the Montezuma Cannery would ever unite. But for her own reasons, she saw merit in a meeting with the factory's management.

"I'm not promising anything, but I'll try to speak with Mr. Slater."

Carmela thanked her profusely before taking her leave.

"Why are you willing to speak to Mr. Slater about factory conditions, Kate? You can see nothing will come of it. When the women aren't willing to fight for themselves, why would you do this for them?"

"I'll be collecting ammunition for suffrage speeches, Gladys. Many of the injustices against working women can be changed by making laws. With women at the polls, politicians will have to listen to us. The eight hour work day for women was passed in California last April, but canneries were excluded because the food will rot if it isn't canned immediately. They could hire a second shift instead of overworking the women who start at dawn. That law must be changed to include canneries."

Most of the people had left and Kate heard the scurrying of tiny feet in the dark behind her. She shivered and started toward the door.

"Let's get out of here. This place gives me the willies."

She heard her companion follow close behind as she left the decaying building.

Kate stepped into the cannery's outer office. She thought of how austerely decorated it was, all its components dedicated to utility, with no concessions to pleasing the eye. Her breath came in shallow spurts to minimize the overpowering odor of pears in different stages of processing. Low wattage light bulbs hung from the ceiling, emitting a jaundiced, yellow hue over the entire office. The round clock high on a wall announced it was ten o'clock. She was right on time.

Kate stood at the clerk's desk just inside the entrance to the room. Searching out the source of the clatter of a typewriting machine, she spied Gladys engrossed in her work on the far side of the office. Men occupied the two desks reserved for the bookkeeper and Mr. Slater's personal secretary. Women filled the lesser clerk positions.

She pulled her attention back to the matter at hand, and asking for assistance from the clerk at the desk in front of her, was directed to Henry Slater's secretary. The pale bespectacled young man politely rose as she approached. He showed her into his boss' office.

Yesterday, Kate had called the owner of the cannery, apologizing for barging into his home and upsetting his wife. With a bit of fancy talking, she had managed to finagle him into granting her a tour of his factory. She'd led him to believe if he could prove his fairness to his employees, she would use her influence with the workers to discourage unionization.

Henry Slater stood behind his massive desk as she entered his room. He rolled down his shirt sleeves over his furred forearms and buttoned them at the wrists. Kate noticed his suit jacket remained hanging on the coat tree.

"Good morning, Katherine. Have a seat. My Operating Manager will be here in a few minutes to take you through the building." His rumbling voice sounded friendly to her. He called to his secretary who was closing the door on his way out. "Calvin, tell Matt to come in here."

The young man nodded and shut the door.

"Thank you for allowing me this visit. I realize that you and your people are busy and I'll try to disrupt everyone as little as possible." Kate's tone was clipped with her effort to sound confident.

"You won't interfere with anything. My girls know they have to put the work out. They wouldn't do anything to jeopardize their jobs." He paused for emphasis. "and that includes union agitation."

She watched him innocently, as though she did not pick up the threat to her contacts. In order to protect Carmela and Dorothea, she would have to be careful not to appear to recognize them.

"Tell me, why did you pick on my factory for your speech? The women who work here don't have any influence and most of their men aren't citizens and can't vote. What good came of it?"

"I wanted to show how women are not protected by our laws and do not have the same work opportunities as men. It was done for the publicity and to gain support of the female workers here."

"Of course women don't have the same opportunities as men." He laughed. "There's no reason they should. Men have to support families. Women don't. Besides, women aren't dependable. They go off and get married and quit their jobs. A woman can't be a man, no matter how hard she tries."

A light knock sounded on the door before it was opened and Matthew Liszt entered the room. Immediately, Kate recognized the young man with the pomaded hair and impressive handlebar mustache. He was the manager who had tried to eject her from the yard last July.

Slater introduced Kate to his employee, then said, "Matt, I want you to give Miss Moore the grand tour. Show her why we're proud of Montezuma."

"It will be my pleasure, Mr. Slater."

After thanking Henry, Kate left the inner office with the manager. As they made their way across the outer office where the clerks pored over their paperwork, he mentioned that the company employed nearly two hundred people, mostly women.

"Mr. Slater said women workers are unreliable because we get married and leave. If that's true, why do you hire us?"

"We don't have much of a choice, Miss Moore. The men laborers, mostly Filipinos, Mexicans, and Chinese, work in the fields for higher wages. Women who can't do such heavy work come to the factories. It's a matter of economics," Matthew explained.

"You mean, it's a matter of exploiting cheap labor."

"Not at all. Everyone benefits from this arrangement. The women would have no place to work, if not for the cannery."

She clung to her original evaluation in spite of his reasoning.

The office was on the second floor and they descended a stairway to start the tour where the produce was graded, washed and peeled. Mr. Liszt was pleasant though formal and kept up a barrage of facts and boastful opinion concerning the factory. Pears were in season as Kate's nose had told her upon entering the yard. A long conveyer belt wound around the huge room, moving the yellow fruit as workers processed it. Their hands moved rapidly in the familiar patterns. Wide doors were open through which men hauled the recently picked crops into the room, but Kate felt claustrophobic with the absence of windows and inadequate electric lighting.

"How often do the women rest?" She considered the monotony of their tasks.

"They get a half hour for lunch. Now, this is where we cook the fruit. This is the most modern equipment on the market."

"How many hours do they work a week?"

"When we are busy, about sixty to seventy, but in winter we are slow. Do you see how that machine fills the cans exactly each time?"

She noticed that the knowledgeable manager answered her probing questions about the workers as quickly as possible, then extolled the qualities of the mechanical equipment.

As they passed the gigantic vats of cooking fruit, the heat formed beads of moisture on Kate's upper lip. The women working in this wilting temperature showed soggy clothing where the perspiration had soaked through.

"Mr. Liszt, are there many accidents here working with the hot food?"

"Occasionally it splatters or spills when a worker is careless, but we don't see many serious burns."

She scrutinized a few of the women who worked in the cooking area and could not find one who did not have red scars on her hands, neck or face. Kate wondered what he considered a serious burn. Would he have more compassion for a dented machine than he had for the scarred women?

Upstairs, where the caps were soldered over the holes in the tops of the cans, she spotted Carmela and Dorothea at work. She quickly averted her eyes. The grimy windows were shut and did not offer much light.

"Do you ever open the windows? The air is stuffy in here." She could not seem to fill her lungs for a complete breath.

"The windows were painted shut a few winters ago and are stuck. It isn't important."

She imagined the door and windows locked on a stifling summer night while the women worked with the dripping hot solder. How could they stand it?

By the time she stood at the front entrance to the building, thanking Matthew Liszt for the tour, Kate was more than ready to leave. She was angry that the condition of the machinery was considered more important than the comfort and safety of the employees. The certainty that these women would not unite to better their lives depressed her. She had seen the bitter acceptance in their stoic faces and shoulders rounded in defeat. Centuries of inbred subservience to men would not be easily overthrown. Though the women's rebellion gained power, the majority were still too fearful to lift their heads and consider the possibilities. Kate renewed her determination to boost women out of their degrading circumstances.

CHAPTER XIV

During the months when autumn slipped by and River Run's mild winter took over, Kate adjusted to an easy flow of events. Days blended into one another like blurred images in a water color painting, peaceful and dreamlike. Even her suffrage activities did little to upset the placid balance of her life. Her truce with the Chief of Police held firm ... until an event in Sacramento changed everything. On January twenty-sixth, the California State Legislature put women's suffrage on a special fall ballot.

Kate stood just inside the entrance gate of Willis Park, watching the townfolk and Saturday visitors take advantage of the temporary sunshine. She looked up at the glaring sun, then to the north where black clouds shrouded the sky. More rain was on the way. She eyed the empty flower beds that were now mud puddles due to two days of rain. They had better hurry if they wanted to beat the weather.

Stepping nearer to the crowd listening to Abigail Penny speak for women's rights, Kate watched for trouble. She knew the saloon owners and their patrons disrupted the ladies' speeches in any way they could. If the police were not there, the men's protests became physical. Kate watched a group of men standing around a crate of eggs, eyeing the lecturing schoolteacher with speculative malice. A broadside across the crate with her umbrella seemed a delightful idea. But she must bide her time and not make the first move. Perhaps the police would arrive before she needed to act.

"Our call for the women's vote is gaining support rapidly among the men of this state. Our Senate voted to put women's suffrage on the ballot by a vote of thirty-three to five. With such encouragement from responsible men, you must realize our cause has merit." Abigail's voice sounded confident.

Kate watched the men in charge of the eggs. Their language became increasingly offensive. She saw Abigail dart apprehensive glances in their direction, panic growing in her eyes.

Sam Wakely came up beside Kate. "It looks like they mean to do some target practice. What are you going to do about it?"

"I thought scrambled eggs might be a good idea." She tapped the point of her umbrella against the gravel pathway.

"An admirable thought, but dangerous. You'd do better to retreat."

"You know better than that," she chided.

The rhythmic booming of a drum approaching from the park entrance caught her attention. She turned to see Wilhelmina Christian marching at the front of her anti-suffrage supporters. The voluminous hat perched on her head was a landmark of ribbons, bows and ostrich feathers. The demeaning signs they carried outraged her, especially the four she had painted herself. The drum drowned Abby's voice, yet she continued to speak. Kate was proud of her and hoped she could hold out until the parade passed hearing range. An irate gasp escaped her when Mrs. Christian turned off the path, leading her ladies across the damp lawn straight at Abigail.

With growing irritation, Kate watched as Caroline and Rebecca tried to head off the mayor's wife. Wilhelmina and her women swept the two suffragists aside like dust motes before a broom.

Kate was furious. Racing toward her harassed colleagues, she paused at the men's egg cache, picked up two in one hand and dumped the remainder onto the grass, smashing every one. She escaped before the stunned men had time to stop her. Heavy footsteps pounded behind her as a couple of the men belatedly gave chase. She managed to stay ahead of them until she stopped in front of Wilhelmina, who was intent on routing Abigail. A quick sideways glance in the direction of her pursuers assured her they were more eager to watch her confrontation with Mrs. Christian than throttle her themselves.

Although she did not reach Wilhelmina's shoulders and was outweighed by nearly one hundred pounds, Kate stood up boldly to her. She stumbled back a few steps when Wilhelmina's meaty, beringed hand caught Kate in the chest and shoved her. Enraged, Kate sprang forward, her arm outstretched. She dropped an egg into the neckline of Wicked Willie's jacket and whacked her hand down hard on the ample bosom where the egg had lodged. Wilhelmina's eyes rounded in surprise as Kate heard a satisfying crunch.

She aimed the egg in her other hand at the sign Wilhelmina lowered as she surveyed her damaged dress. Suddenly, the sign jerked away and a glowering face took its place. Too late to stop her arm's forward momentum, Kate thrust the delicate shell against the woman's forehead. She watched with a mixture of glee and horror as the yellow slime oozed down the matron's nose and onto her cheeks.

Kate saw Wilhelmina's sign descend toward her head and parried the attack with her umbrella. They dueled in this fashion, with Kate managing to avoid injury thanks to her superior speed and agility. When Mrs. Christian unsheathed a long hat pin from her treasured creation and wielded it like a sword, Kate reached up and snatched her opponent's hat, tossing it into a nearby mud patch. The pin stabbed through her jacket and blouse, piercing her upper arm. She fought the urge to yelp with the surprise and pain. When Wilhelmina grabbed her shoulders from behind and pushed her toward the mud where the hat floated, Kate struggled to free herself. But Wilhelmina was much larger and stronger than Kate and her protests failed.

As she sailed toward the brown muck, she hooked her foot around Willie's ankle and they toppled together into the mire. Kate landed in the oozing slime, flailing her arms and kicking at her likewise floundering enemy. Mud coated Kate's clothes, stuck to her hair, squished in her shoes, and splattered her face. Anger ruled her actions and she struggled in a crimson haze, unaware of everything except her desire to pulverize her arm swinging, mud flinging foe.

Suddenly, Kate felt herself lifted by the back of her collar and stood up on solid ground. Her eyes still shut against flying mud and her mind focused on battle, she fought the unidentified force.

"Settle down." A familiar voice issued the command.

A red mist still engulfed her and she lashed out with her arms and legs toward the speaker, failing to make contact.

"That's enough!" A vigorous shake emphasized the words.

Slowly, her temper receded and her surroundings registered with mortifying clarity. First, she saw the mud begrimed mayor's wife splashing in the slop and bellowing insults as Officer Taylor tried to help her to her feet. Then she turned around to confirm the identity of the person who still clutched her collar. As expected, John Gallagher glared into her face, his unrelenting blue eyes promising she would pay dearly for this fiasco.

"It's not my fault. She tried to bully Abigail and push us out of the park and ..." Her words spilled out in a rush to mitigate his fury.

"Hush. You'll explain later," he said through clenched teeth.

Kate saw Wilhelmina standing a few paces from her. Jason Taylor's hand on her arm restrained her from a physical attack, but that did not stop her from shouting her indignation.

"You're both under arrest for disorderly conduct. You can come along quietly or be handcuffed." Chief Gallagher looked meaningfully at Mrs. Christian who continued to howl her resentment.

When Jason produced handcuffs, the tirade suddenly stopped. Kate watched with satisfaction as her opponent recognized a force that would not buckle beneath her loudly proclaimed power.

Kate's satisfaction turned to apprehension when Gallagher headed her toward the jail.

A glob of mud plopped onto the floor of the cell as Kate removed her soiled jacket. The room was cool, but she could no longer stand to be wrapped in the filthy garment. Her skirt hung heavy with wet earth and she would have to wait for it to dry before brushing off the mess. She sighed at the condition of her high-buttoned shoes. They looked beyond redemption.

"You brought me to this, you brazen chit, debased scoundrel. Blackard! My good name is ruined because of you. I'll make you sorry for this."

She saw Wilhelmina ranting at her from the other cell. Filthy and disheveled, the older woman lost her impressive bearing. With the egg and mud clinging to her face she looked like a clown. The insults and threats Wilhelmina heaped upon Kate delighted her for they demonstrated the depth of her foe's distress and Kate offered the mayor's wife the ultimate affront. She laughed. It bubbled up from deep inside her like a mountain spring, gaining strength until it gushed like a geyser.

When Kate finally ceased, she realized that, from the adjoining cell, huge gulping sobs replaced the angry tirade. Mrs. Christian sat on the cot, her shoulders hunched forward and face in her hands. Kate understood the despair of a person who treasured pride in her public standing above all else, being humiliated in front of half the town. She would have felt sorry for her if their feud were not so deeply rooted.

Her own consequences of the debacle in the park now invaded her thoughts like ants at a picnic. Gallagher refused to let Captain Tom accept the responsibility of reproving her when she was let out of jail. He vowed to see to the task himself. He only waited to deliver Mrs. Christian into the hands of her husband so Kate would receive the full force of his displeasure without interruption.

She was not frightened of him in a physical sense. Gallagher would not abuse a woman's body. Since their first evening together at the charity dance she had grown to know him well. She held his attentions at bay for fear the bonfire he ignited in her body would consume her and he accepted her restrictions with good grace. He terrified her with his ability to make her drop her guard and respond to him without reserve. Eventually, she would have to turn him away or succumb. The thought of him as her husband was ludicrous. His manipulative and overbearing ways set her teeth to gnashing. Due to her careful avoidance of breaking the law, their truce held firm . . . until today.

Blaming Wilhelmina for the fight would not work. Both women had tried to convince him of their innocence, but he would not listen to them. Perhaps, with ample pouts, doleful bats of her eyelashes, and a kiss or two she could dampen his resolve and get off with a tongue lashing. What further punishment he might deal out she could not imagine, but she knew him to be creative in such matters. Thank goodness the pillory was no longer in use, she thought with relief.

Officer Taylor came into the room from the office and unlocked both cells.

"Your husband is here for you, Mrs. Christian." He pulled open the barred doors and let them out.

Kate followed them into the next room, holding her head up in a show of bravado. If defending her principles and friends was a crime, then there was fault with the law, not her. She would admit to unladylike behavior, nothing more.

The Mayor and Chief of Police stood together facing the tousled, dirt encrusted women as they entered the office. Clearly dismayed by the appearance of his wife, Arnold stared dumbfounded for nearly a full minute before finding his voice.

"You've really done it this time, Mina," he managed to say.

"But it wasn't my fault. This little toad pushed me into the mud and jumped on top of me," Wilhelmina wailed.

"Oh, be quiet! This time I'll do the talking." The Mayor turned to Gallagher. "I promise you, this will not happen again. Good day."

"How dare you speak to me that way?" His wife protested as he led her from the police headquarters. "It was not my fault, I tell you . . ." Her voice trailed away as the door closed behind them and they walked down the street.

Kate glanced at Gallagher, uncertain of his mood. Perhaps, while she was locked up, his anger had waned. When she caught the blue fire in his eyes, her hope for leniency withered like flowers after a funeral. Still, it would not hurt to try softening him. She caressed his cheek, two fingers playing with his earlobe.

"Surely, you don't believe all those vile things she said about me. You know I'm no monster," she cooed.

His stern face did not change expression as he locked his hand around her wrist and removed the distracting tickle from his ear. He was certain if he was not careful, she would wrap him in her erotic spell and he needed his wits about him. The time had come to unmask the ghost causing her to distrust men. Such a showdown called for a firm hand and assured privacy.

"Jase, take over for a while. I've got some business to take care of," he called out to the officer sitting at a desk across the room.

"Sure thing, boss."

Kate stiffened as Gallagher unpinned the badge from his shirt and tossed it onto his desk. That small act declared this a private matter with no rules except those of his own making. She reinforced her backbone for the coming battle.

With his hand on her back she felt him guide her to the rear door. He pulled it open, revealing rolling gray clouds. A few fat drops splattered on the ground as she looked out. He lifted her jacket from over her arm, and draped it across her shoulders. When he led her into the yard toward his tiny house she tried to pulled away, but the pressure of his arm on her back was insistent. She side stepped and spun around, in full flight. Kate had declared his rooms off limits at the beginning of their friendship and she would not relax that rule now. As he caught her above the elbow and swung her around to face him, her gaze threw off sparks.

"I'm not going in there with you," she declared, her anger rising. "If you try to force me, I'll scream. I swear it."

Recalling how stubborn this pint sized hell-raiser could be, Gallagher knew arguing would be a waste. In one swoop he lifted her from her feet, tucked her under his arm and clamped his free hand over her mouth. He crossed the yard in a dozen strides and kicked open the unlocked door of his cottage.

Once inside, Gallegher lowered her to her feet in the middle of his kitchen. After he took his hand away from her mouth she screamed in long, ear shattering shrieks. He stood aside to watch her performance, resigned to let her tire herself out. There was no one within hearing distance, except for Jase and he would not interfere. Leaning against the table, he removed a cheroot from his shirt pocket and lit it, letting the smoke relax him as he waited.

Kate's lungs filled and emptied again and again while she waited for her tormentor's submission. She knew there was no physical danger in entering his home and the sole purpose of this vocal exercise was to let him know he could not bully her. Her eyes were shut to keep her resolve from wavering.

The smell of burning tobacco told her the ploy did not work and she might as well stop. Besides, her throat hurt. The commotion ceased in the middle of a long high note. She slowly opened her eyes to see Gallagher leaning comfortably against a table. It held dishes with the remains of breakfast on them and a jar of grape jelly. Behind him the sink was piled high with dirty dishes, at least three days worth. Aside from the wooden chairs around the table, the only furniture in the room was an overstuffed armchair, comfortable looking, but certainly not decorative. There was a closed door which she suspected led to a bedroom.

"Are you finished?" he asked calmly.

"For the moment."

She watched him squelch the cheroot in a dish, then turn his full attention on her. His narrowed, blue eyes glinted like sunlit ice.

"Do you have any idea of what you look like?" Not waiting for an answer, he continued, his voice gaining volume as he spoke. "You look exactly like what you are; a common street brawler with no respect for the law, womanhood, or yourself. I don't see how hitting another woman and flopping around in the mud is gonna help you get the vote. There won't be a person in this town who doesn't laugh at you. You oughtta be ashamed of yourself."

"You sound just like my mother." She interrupted his tirade. "I don't care what either of you think. Men made the rules that say a woman can't fight back. Well, I don't believe it. There's nothing you can do to change my mind. You can all go to hell in a wheelbarrow."

Gallagher watched her as she ranted, enthralled with the mixture of conviction and pain that molded her face into a tortured mask. He sensed her feelings were close to the surface now and he hurt for her, but he could not allow her to retreat to safety.

"What happened in New York to make you distrust men so much? Was there a man you loved? Did he turn his back on you ... for another woman, maybe?"

He saw the panic growing in her eyes and instinct told him she prepared for flight. He grasped her arms and brought her up close to him, giving her no space to think and barely enough room to breathe.

"Did he take your innocence then turn you away? Is that why you're afraid to let another man near you? Tell me, who did this to you?"

"My past is none of your business." Emotion choked her. Anger with this meddling fool mingled with the rage and pain she felt at the thought of Trevor.

"Yes, it is my business. I love you."

Caught in her angry whirlwind, she recognized and dismissed Gallagher's shock at his declaration of love. An ugly laugh escaped her as tears threatened to overflow.

"Love is just a word people say to use each other. What is it you want from me? I have nothing worth taking anymore."

"You little bitch, I didn't deserve that."

Overwhelming remorse flooded Kate. He had offered her a part of himself and she had cruelly trampled it. He shook her, his bruising fingers biting into her arms.

"There's an ugly secret hiding inside of you, rotting your mind and I'm going to hunt it down and kill it." His voice shook with raw emotion.

Terror struck her a dizzying blow. If she allowed herself to feel too much for this man, he could destroy her and she suddenly knew the time for preventing him entrance to her heart had passed long ago. The power to hurt her lay in his rage driven hands and her need to escape him overcame all else. She struggled to free herself from his punishing grasp until, in desperation, she swung out, delivering a cracking blow to his cheek.

For a long moment, she wondered how he would retaliate as he stood motionless, his features etched with fury. Her trepidation grew as he tossed her jacket from her shoulders onto the floor, pulled a chair away from the table, and planted his boot firmly on the seat.

Kate found herself face down across his knee, skirt and petticoat hiked up to expose the seat of her lace trimmed bloomers. A mighty whack to her bottom elevated her temper still further before he roughly stood her on her feet again. Venom and humiliation took turns battering her. She wanted to hurt him, brand him with hot irons, gouge out his eyes, damage him so deeply that he would run away and leave her in peace and safety.

"You want to know my secret." Her voice trembled, barely under control. "You're right about the man, if that's what you would call an animal that takes a woman's life and crushes it to dust for a handful of money. He took more than my innocence when he left. He also took the life of our child. Do you know what an abortionist can do to a woman, how the blood flows and you can't stop it and your baby is dead before you've even held it?"

She was openly sobbing now, tears spilling down to her chin, arms wrapped around her middle to cradle herself. She continued to speak in a rush as the floodgates to her soul opened and spilled the pent-up misery into a tempestuous river of words and emotion. Unable to see the man in front of her through the tears, she looked inward as she relived the events that had emotionally crippled her.

"How much money are a lover and baby worth these days, a thousand dollars, maybe two? I doubt my stepfather paid him even that much to drug me against my will and have my child done away with. To butcher me so I can never bear children."

Kate was relieved that Gallagher stood motionless during most of her terrible outpouring. She feared his touch would unleash the tormenting memories she took such care to restrain and she would never get them under control again. When he reached his arm out to her, she shrugged it off.

"I see that look of disgust on your face," she accused. "Slut, you're thinking. Why should you be any different? My own mother thinks the same, can't stand the sight of me. She never could." Her voice broke and she could not go on.

With him in possession of the key to her past, she felt naked to his eyes. Was that hurt she saw on his face or disappointment? No matter. He would not want her in any case.

She needed to run, to escape from the tremendous burden of her feelings and the man who tried to make her love again . . . and succeeded. Kate rushed for the door, on her way lifting her jacket from the floor. She reached for the doorknob and pulled, but the door would not open. Looking up, she saw Gallagher's hand directly above her head, holding it shut. Her temper unleashed, she beat at the door with fists and feet as she threatened and begged him to let her go. When the futility of her pounding dawned on her, she rounded on her captor, fists flailing at his chest and arms, mindless of where they struck. Her bleeding emotional wounds reopened after a year of festering and her agony was horrendous.

His arms wrapped around her shoulders crushing her against his chest, pinning her arms to her sides until she felt trapped and suffocated. Guttural sounds of a tortured animal issued from her throat as she tried to wrench free. She struggled against the comfort of his body's warmth and his deep, soothing voice. Finally exhausted, she sagged against him and gave herself up to the tears.

Gallagher held her as she wept, sensing the depth of her suffering. Her silent heaving as she trembled touched him and he absorbed her anguish, his shirt soaking up her tears where her face rested against his body.

"I'm sorry," he murmured, pressing his lips to her tangled hair. "I had no idea it would be this rough on you. Hush now."

The tears continued unabated until she felt empty and battered like a milking pail filled to overflowing then kicked across the barn. Awareness of her surroundings returned to her in the comfort of his sheltering arms and the steady beat of his heart against her cheek. She allowed his body heat to nourish her starving spirit, drawing from him the strength to face his disappointment in the person she had revealed herself to be.

When Gallagher felt her calming, he stepped back, one arm still around her shoulder to help her regain her emotional balance. She faced away from him, her eyes shut tight. He removed a clean handkerchief from a back pants pocket and gently blotted away the tears clinging to her lashes and the corners of her mouth. Hesitantly, he brushed back the wet curls matted to her face.

"After all you've been through, it took a lot of courage to become the strong, decent lady you are." His low voice held conviction. "It would have destroyed most women. I'm proud to know you."

She opened her eyes and he detected a shadow of her fear returning.

"How can you say that after what I just told you?" Her voice sounded dead, like wind blowing through the tattered sails of a ghost ship.

"You're not to blame for what those men did to you. And neither am I. Don't punish me for their crimes. I love you too much to let you run from me."

She wanted to believe him, but her wounds would not allow her to reach out so far. Most of her anger had drained away with the tears, and his touch felt healing. For the moment, it was enough for her to know she loved him. She would unravel the complicated knot of her emotions when her thoughts were more rational.

"I don't want to run from you." Her voice was almost a whisper as her fingertips tentatively touched his cheek, then slid to the curves of his lips.

He bent to kiss her gently, his tongue tasting her lips until they parted, permitting him entry to the soft warmth of her mouth. The knuckles of one hand nestled under her jaw, the thumb roaming her throat, sliding up to explore the small, silken ear.

She undid a shirt button and slid her hand beneath the material, flattening it against the hard, smooth muscles of his chest, delighting in the soft curls lapping around her fingers. Finding the flat male nipple, she circled it with her forefinger before flicking and rubbing it. She felt him flinch and his muscles go rigid. Confusion seized her when he pulled away and extracted her hand from under his clothing.

"You'd best leave while I'm still willing to let you go." He spoke in a strangled voice. His eyes smoldered.

"I want to stay. Please, don't send me away." Her unwavering gaze held his. She needed his warmth, his strength, his love. She needed him. No matter if it was just for this moment and she would pay for it tomorrow.

"You don't know what you're asking for."

"I know exactly what I'm asking for." She undid two more of his buttons.

Kate was unprepared for the force with which he crushed her to him. He lifted her six inches above the floor and possessed her mouth in a fierce kiss. She was breathless, but unprotesting when he walked with her still clutched against him, feet dangling in air, across the kitchen and pushed open the bedroom door.

She got a swift impression of an unmade double bed, and a man's clothing strewn on crude furniture, before he sat on the edge of the bed and deposited her on his lap. Gallagher shooed Rufus off the pillows where he had been napping.

The brief interruption heightened her anticipation and she was not disappointed when he nuzzled her below the ear and wrapped his arms around her to undo the buttons on the back of her blouse. With a few adept movements, she opened his shirt entirely, pulled it loose from his belt and bared his impressive shoulders, leaving his chest exposed to her exploring hands and mouth.

As the last of the damnably tiny buttons came free, Gallagher stripped the blouse from her and dropped it to the floor. His shirt joined hers before he cupped her chemise covered globes in his hands, then tackled the hooks down the front of her lace trimmed corset. He ignored the feel of her hands at his belt buckle, but came abruptly aware when she fumbled at the buttons of his pants, jostling his swollen manhood. As near as he could tell, her clumsiness was deliberate. If he did not control her bold hands, he would be rushed into taking her before he had a chance to touch and taste her as he had dreamed of since last summer.

When the corset came undone, he set her on her feet between his legs, and discarded the skirt, petticoat and chemise, not allowing her time to touch him. He captured both her hands in one of his and held them behind her where they could not work him to a frenzy. Her rounded breast filled his hand and left soft flesh exposed for the loving ministrations of his lips.

Kate moaned at the sweet torment of his touch and her inability to pleasure him with her hands. His imprisoning grasp of her wrists annoyed her more for his intent to control her than her inability to use them. Wedging her knee against the crotch of his pants, she pressed her mouth to his ear. When he lifted his head, she claimed a kiss, and pushed against his chest using her leverage and the element of surprise to try to force him back onto the bed.

Not willing to relinquish command Gallagher stood, taking her with him and tossed her onto the middle of the mattress. After stripping away the last of her clothing and then his own, he straddled her, entwining his fingers with hers and securing them above her head.

His kiss was demanding yet gentle, taking and giving at the same time. Although his domination annoyed her, she was also intrigued by it. When he placed both of her hands together to leave one of his free to roam and tantalize her and his mouth left hers to trail down her throat, branding a path to the rosy tip of a breast, she realized the extent of his determined mastery. There would be no escaping it. She relaxed and settled into the slow, pulsating rhythm that his touch evoked, riding the crests and gullies until he would set her free.

Gallagher froze for a moment, considering the possible consequences of their intimacy. Then he remembered her say she could not conceive a child and the circumstances leading to her sterility. Gentle emotions floated to the surface and he directed them toward the sweet woman who lay beside him. His empathy, prompted by her vulnerability, softened his lovemaking and he allowed her the use of her hands, letting her bring him to a throbbing need. When she tried to take the initiative and slide above him, he rolled over with her, pinning her back to the mattress and entered her moist, secret place with a powerful thrust.

Kate writhed beneath him, trying to set the pace, but his unrelenting strength dominated, pounding into her with increasing force as she rebelled, until she finally yielded and they moved together to his rhythm, their hearts galloping in a wild stampede, lifting each other to another world where only their dew sheened bodies and passion existed. Until he exploded inside her and she clung to him, moments later experiencing her own release as it came in shock waves that rocked her again and again.

They lay together, his leg still possessively thrown over hers, his hand cupping her jaw, fingers tangled in her hair. She reveled in the intimacy, the musky aroma of love enveloping them, his toughened body warm against her, the tousled hair falling over his eyes. For the first time since entering this room, she was aware of the sound of rain beating at the window.

"You're a tyrant," she complained with a mock pout. "I doubt I'll be able to walk after your abuse."

"Some fillies need a stronger hand than others. You need a steel fist, brat." Gallegher kissed the tip of her nose.

"Not always." She traced her hand along the outline of his throat and brushed her lips against his.

"Too bad I don't have the time to go another round with you right now. Jase will wonder what happened to us."

Gallagher swung his legs over the side of the bed and sat up.

"Do you need a ride home?" he asked while tugging on his trousers.

"No. My auto is waiting for me outside Willis Park."

"Then you can wait here until the rain lets up."

Kate wistfully watched him as he dressed and lit a cheroot. The sweet glow of lovemaking dissolved as she saw him readying himself to leave her. Thought of her growing love for him set in like an unwanted boarder who would disrupt the careful order of her life.

"I've got to go. I'll see you soon."

Gallagher kissed her cheek. On his way out of the room, he stopped to scratch Rufus under the chin.

"Go get her, boy." He nudged the dog toward the bed.

An instant later, Kate fell back amid the tumbled linens as the huge, hairy mongrel trampled and licked her. She squealed and laughed while trying to ward him off.

When the dog finally quieted, Kate dressed herself while surveying the haphazard display of John's belongings draped on every surface. She imagined the wooden wardrobe and dresser were empty, considering the number of garments strewn around the room.

Reaching out to clutch his shirt from the bedpost, she brought it to her nose and breathed in the scent of him. Instead of the warm, protected emotion she had experienced before he left the bed, the dark wings of fear swooped down on her. Love for him left her vitals open to attack, inviting a death blow that would come when she was at her most fragile. If experience had taught her anything, it was not to trust her heart to a man's mercy. Reluctantly, she returned the shirt to its perch. Her inevitable self-preserving decision turned thoughts of him sour.

Kate reached into her skirt pocket for the comfort of her yellow beads, but her hand came out empty. Frantic she might have lost them, she hurried into the kitchen to search the pockets of her jacket that lay crumpled on the floor. When her fingers clamped around the well worn glass bubbles, her features relaxed with relief. Those small globes emanated her father's nurturing love. Without them, she would be set adrift on a hostile sea.

Tears struggled to the surface as she searched for utensils to write a note. She found a scrap of paper and a pencil on top of the wall telephone in the bedroom. Ten minutes later, she propped the message on his pillow and left his house.

As she crossed the yard, a steady rain pelted her mud sodden hat and mingled with her tears.

Gallagher walked through his dark kitchen and shivered as he removed his coat and threw it onto the overstuffed chair. It was two o'clock in the morning and the storm had passed, leaving a cold clear night. He passed a weary hand over his eyes as he flicked on the bare electric bulb that hung from the bedroom ceiling. The Saturday night drinkers had been a rowdy bunch tonight.

Pleasant surprise touched him as he noticed his bed had been made, the blanket neatly tucked over the pillows and under the mattress. The rest of his belongings remained where he had thrown them. She had not tried to rearrange his life, had only straightened the one thing she had used. He admired that in a woman.

His mouth pulled back in a grin as he saw the paper on his pillow. Expecting to see a love note, he picked it up and read eagerly.

This afternoon was a mistake. It must never happen again. Do not call on me. Good-bye. K.

Gallagher was dumbfounded. How could the joy they had shared be a mistake? No! his injured heart screamed. I won't let her go like this! He passed his hands over his face, pressing his burning eyes. Calm down. Calm down and think. She's scared, don't crowd her. Give her some time to miss me, then take her back. She's mine, she just doesn't know it yet.

He took a deep relaxing breath and crumpled the note in his fist.

CHAPTER XV

Sunshine glinted off ripples in the river as ducks hunted for wet vegetation near the marshy shore of Sherman Island. One bird flapped its wings and squawked at the loud plop of a pebble hitting the water nearby.

Kate looked toward the source of the noise to see David toss another stone into the water. Her annoyance rose as she returned to setting out the picnic David had supplied. Everything he did today irritated her. She had nearly laughed aloud with derision while unpacking the food hamper. No doubt the Peters' chef had supplied it. The fare resembled a British high tea with tiny watercress sandwiches, crusts carefully removed, and dainty, frosted petite cakes. French wine, exquisite bone china, and Irish linen napkins completed the elegance.

She knew she should not fault David for her nasty humor. He could no more change being who he was than she could turn him into the man she loved. Gallagher monopolized her thoughts since she had left his bed a week ago. Wanton memories of a picnic with Gallagher tiptoed into her awareness; fried chicken and chocolate cake, laughter and sensual delight as they licked crumbs from each other's fingers and lips. Resolutely, she set aside the daydream.

"Katherine, are you listening?"

The insistent voice came from the other side of the blanket she sat on. Upon glancing up, she saw David kneeling across from her, his expression intent.

"You are distracted today. What's the matter?" he said.

"I just can't seem to concentrate. What were you saying?" She focused her attention on him.

"I have finally come up with the information you asked for concerning Star Enterprises. It's taken all these months to get it. Your Mr. Carlisle hides his tracks well." He paused a moment, watching her intently.

"Go on. What did you find out?" Kate thought he was stalling on purpose.

"First, you must again give me your promise to carry the matter no further. This entire affair has an unsavory stench to it and Carlisle could ruin you."

"I've already given you my word. Besides, how can I, a mere woman, hope to thwart an influential man like Jeffrey Carlisle?" Kate carefully worded her reply without giving the assurance he requested. She remembered her crossed fingers when she had given her promise.

David looked at her askance, but she treated him to a wide-eyed expression of innocence.

"Star Enterprises is a holding company with six acquisitions in the Sacramento Valley. They keep their original names so most people don't know that Star owns them. All were bought out cheaply after suffering financial setbacks. There were accidents, fires or machinery suddenly breaking down. Sometimes, mortgages were bought and foreclosed. A few of the circumstances were suspicious, but not enough evidence was found to accuse anyone. This sounds like nasty business. You promised to stay clear of it and I expect you to hold to your word."

"I wonder if there were accidents at Moore Freighting?" Kate's curiosity overshadowed her caution. Let him suspect her motives, she needed to know every detail he could give her. "Can you give me the list of companies owned by Star?"

"No, Katherine. I can see the wheels in your devious mind turning and I won't let you use the information to put yourself in danger."

Kate wanted to punch him. The last thing she needed was an overprotective man standing in her way.

"If you don't give me the names of the companies, I'll tell Sam Wakely from the Gazette about this and he'll get the information for me." With nonchalance she handed him a sandwich and bit into her own. Let him think she didn't need him. He'd cave in soon enough.

"Giving this information to a newspaper would guarantee you trouble. I forbid it." David knew his last words were a mistake as soon as they passed his lips. Why couldn't he fall for a tractable lady with a healthy sense of self-preservation? He tore at his food with frustration.

"You can't forbid me anything, David. I'm free to do as I please. One way or another, I'll get the names of those companies." She smiled at him sweetly, but he heard the steel in her voice.

"The names won't do you any good. There's nothing to accuse him of. Can't you see I'm only trying to protect you?" He heard himself pleading and hated it. She was determined to get what she wanted.

"I don't want your protection. Maybe I can't accuse him yet, but some day I might uncover proof of his wrongdoing. Forget it. I'll ask Sam for help." David threw his napkin aside in a gesture of defeat.

"I'll send the list to you, but that will be the end of it. You will not pursue this matter further. Do I make myself clear?"

"Perfectly."

Although part of Kate's face was hidden as she sipped wine from her goblet, David recognized the tiny, satisfied smile, broadcasting her sense of victory. His pride bristled as he detected the devilish glitter in her eyes.

"You seem to dispense with caution a lot lately. I read in the Gazette of your escapade in the park last week." David noticed her complexion turn a deep rose hue and her glance moved away from him. He felt gratified. "The article said you were arrested. Were charges filed against you? Somehow I can't imagine John Gallagher being so hard on you."

Mention of the disastrous incident with the Mayor's wife, reminded Kate of the event later in the cottage behind the jailhouse. As she gave her imagination rein, she almost felt John's hands and lips on her body. Heat crept through her as her escort's voice droned on. Suddenly, strong fingers tilted her chin up and she blinked to bring David's face into focus.

"Have you been listening to me?" he asked for the second time that afternoon.

Kate latched onto the question prior to his last sentence before it slipped into oblivion with the rest of his conversation.

"John let me go after a severe scolding." She would not look into his eyes and wished he would let go of her chin.

"I get the impression there is more to the story than you're telling me. Did he hurt you in any way?"

"Of course not." She took the hand at her face in both of hers and moved it to her lap, masking it as an endearment.

"Talk of the incident embarrasses me. Let's change the subject."

Her confused feelings for Gallagher had not abated since she left his cottage that rainy afternoon. Kate's love for him became a constant throbbing pain, but she could not give up her fear. No man was to be trusted.

"Is it too much to hope the scolding did any good? Knowing how stubborn you are, I think that was not the last of your mischief."

"You sound as though I play childish pranks and will eventually grow up and stop doing it. I assure you, my activities are not child's play. Attacking problems head on is the way I do things. Nothing will change that."

Seeing Kate's intractable expression, David accepted her words as truth. People did change, but she would never allow a man to do her thinking for her. He adored the vivacious unpredictability of this nymph and it was exactly this quality in her he hoped to control and might destroy in the process. Yet his ambitions might not withstand the strain of a sometimes embarrassing wife.

"I didn't mean to belittle your efforts, Katherine. My concern for your reputation goes deeper than you imagine. I intend to make a bid for the Republican nomination for the state assembly this fall. I'll be returning to live in my parents' home in Rio Vista to campaign in that district. Aligning myself with a controversial firebrand like yourself could compromise my position." David tightened his hold on her hand and peered into her eyes. "I love you dearly and want you for my wife. Your promise to act with prudence would go a long way toward providing a successful future for us."

Kate was not surprised that he spoke of marriage. She had expected such an offer eventually. But his other request stopped her cold. He asked her to control the spirited instincts that ruled her life, as he controlled every aspect of his own existence. Could she make him happy without giving up the spontaneous part of herself that gave her life flavor? Would she ever be content with his sterile life?

"I'm very fond of you, David, but I'm not sure I can give what you ask of me. I'll have to think over your proposal."

David is what you wanted, the scarred guardian of her heart reminded her, a man who could not take your heart and smash it to mush. Yet, when she closed her eyes, she saw Gallegher, his teasing eyes daring her to trust him. Kate shook off the intrusive image and concentrated on the man seated on the blanket in front of her.

"Does John Gallagher have anything to do with your reluctance to accept my proposal? I know he's been courting you." David thought himself much the better match for the lady, but knew love did not always take such matters into consideration.

"Not at all." Her tone projected finality. "In fact, I've stopped socializing with him."

"I'm relieved to hear that." In fact, he felt jubilant at the news. Now he was certain she would soon consent to be his wife.

Kate was startled when he pulled her to him and kissed her with more warmth than usual. The pressure of his mouth on hers, meant to arouse a virgin's passion, fell far short of its purpose. It left Kate hungry for Gallagher's touch. She wondered if the affect on her of David's lovemaking would improve when he was her husband? Probably not. His reserved manner was too ingrained to let her believe he would treat her differently as his wife. The prospect of cold coupling dampened any spark he might ignite in her.

Impatiently, she waited for him to relax his grip on her arms so she could draw away from him.

Her eyes closed and the amused image of a blue-eyed man with a wayward lock of hair across his forehead seemed to say, "You gave up our passion for this sorry kiss?" His taunting laugh echoed in her mind.

Kate only half listened to David's endearments. Her thoughts were with Gallagher and that ill conceived note she had left on his pillow. She sighed with remorse. The damage was irreversible and there was no use in digging up the specter of his love. He had not tried to contact her since her fateful visit to his house.

David held out a glass of wine to her and she took it gratefully. Sipping the heady liquid would help to numb the regrets and thorny decisions tumbling around in her mind.

CHAPTER XVI

The narrow levee road was coal black on this moonless night. Hulking shadows of houses on stilts lurked along the sides of the manmade protection against the swollen river. April brought an abundance of run-off water to the Sacramento Delta region, flooding parts of it almost every year.

A beam of light from the Pierce-Arrow's front lamp was the only illumination on the otherwise deserted road. The handle of the steering stick was warm beneath Kate's sweating palm. To the left of the road a steep decline led into a farmer's field; to the right was the river, roaring with the power to swallow the automobile and her along with it. She kept her attention on the narrow levee road, wide enough for only one vehicle.

Kate felt blessed to have Abigail's cheerful company. Without her she might have given into the tension that stiffened her shoulders and whitened the knuckles of her clenched fingers. She was thankful that next week's meeting of the suffrage association was to be held in River Run and there would be no need to drive around the countryside in the dark.

The deep rumble of a truck coming up behind her slow moving Motorette triggered a groan from deep inside her. She imagined the impatient driver bedeviling her until the road widened enough for his truck to pass.

As the huge vehicle behind them closed in and its headlights lit up the interior of the motor car, she blinked her eyes, trying not to lose her night sight. The truck bumped the back of the auto, bouncing Kate into the air. She honked her horn like a mad woman, not comprehending why the driver behind her did not slow down. The powerful truck pushed the one cylinder Pierce Arrow faster than it could go with its own engine.

Abigail screamed as Kate reached for the small pistol hidden under her seat. When her auto swerved toward the river under the control of the truck, her steering stick proved useless to change their direction. Expecting at any moment to be plunged into the cold, swift river, she turned to Abby to tell her to jump before she would be trapped. But the words never formed.

As suddenly as the attack started, the truck stopped, backed up, and drove around the Motorette. Kate heard two words flung at her as the truck passed.

"Leave town."

She turned off the motor and slumped over in relief. Her heart pounded wildly, seeming to her to drown out the roar of the river. A quick look out the side window told her the car was half off the levee, its side wheels spinning in air. Kate still held the gun in her hand.

"Leave town." The words echoed with each thudding beat of her heart. This was the second time she had heard them in one week. The first was an instant before a rock came sailing through the window of her front parlor.

Abigail's voice sliced through the fog of Kate's thoughts.

"When the window was broken, you wouldn't go to the police. I understand your reluctance to see John Gallagher, but this time we could have been killed. Tomorrow, this will be reported. If you won't do it, I will."

"Yes. The situation is entirely out of hand." Abby was right. There was more at stake here than her pride. "I'll go to the police in the morning."

The thought of seeking out Chief Gallagher set her nerves throbbing. During the six weeks since their romp in his bed, he seemed to be playing a maddening game of tag with her. When she was downtown he would suddenly appear to caress her cheek or hand with tentative fingertips. Once he had stolen a kiss before retreating, leaving her body trembling for him, her heart in tears. Sometimes, he spoke to her before disappearing. His message was always the same; he was determined to have her back. The part of her that was terrified of love wished he would fall off the face of the Earth. But her other instincts cheered him on. Anticipation of their next meeting spurred her to take unneeded trips downtown.

Her tumultuous feelings for Gallagher bid her avoid him, but she would be foolish to refuse help when the lives of her friends, as well as her own, were endangered. A confrontation with John was inevitable and she could put it off no longer. Setting her impending visit to the police aside, she concentrated on getting the car back onto the road.

When Gallagher heard the front door of the jailhouse open, he glanced up from the papers on his desk. As he recognized the lady in the lacy white blouse and shawl to be his Kate, he stood and advanced two steps before stopping to control his impulse to hold her. She seemed appealingly fragile and uncertain of her reception, with her eyes fixed on the floor and her cheeks flushed a flaming pink. He had the advantage, and intended to make full use of it. His pulse raced, and he waited for it to calm before he spoke.

"What brings you into my lair? I thought you've been avoiding me."

"I have a problem that needs police attention." She still stared at the floor.

This must be serious, if she's willing to brave facing me, he thought.

"Have a seat and tell me what's wrong. Then we have other things to talk over."

Kate's gaze shot to him, panic written in her wide open eyes, like a doe that has caught the scent of a prowling wolf.

"No! We have nothing else to discuss."

He had waited six weeks for a sign that her resolve to shut him out was weakening. Her longing gaze at him when she thought he was not watching or a hasty touch on his sleeve before she retreated to safety hinted at her crumbling determination. He would not allow her to escape him before she voiced her fears and gave him a chance to ease them.

Slowly, he went to her and rested his hands on her shoulders, feeling the delicate collarbone beneath his fingers.

"I've been patient with you, but today we'll do things my way. You're not leaving here until I've had my say. I know you're not a coward, so stop acting like one."

Gallagher felt her muscles stiffen before she shrugged out of his grasp. Golden sparks flashed at him from her eyes.

"I'm not a coward."

He half smiled. This was the feisty Kate he loved to torment. It was easier for him to deal with her temper than her fears.

When he gestured toward the chair facing his desk, she seated herself in it. She removed her hand from her skirt pocket and lay it in her lap. The string of yellow worry beads coiled around her fingers, giving her comfort. He perched on the near corner of the desk, his long, muscular legs stretched out close enough for her to touch. With a monumental effort, she focused on the reason for her visit.

As blandly as she could manage, she told him about the broken window of the week before and the incident on the road the previous night. His brow knit with concern as he listened.

"You should have come to me with your problem last week. I might have prevented what happened last night." Of course, he knew why she hadn't come to him before this. Nothing short of a life or death situation would force her to face him. At least she didn't intend to die for her stubbornness.

"I'm used to people throwing things at my house. I'm not exactly popular in some circles."

Gallagher could attest to that. He'd heard enough idle talk in the town to know Kate was laughed at and scorned by many men and quite a few women in River Run.

"Could you recognize anyone in the truck or the truck itself?" He held a notebook and pencil, ready to take notes.

"No. It was too dark and my attention was on trying to control the car." That did not surprise him.

"Do you have any idea who could be responsible for this?"

"There are the Southside saloon owners or any other antiwomen's vote group, Jeffrey Carlisle, or Henry Slater," she suggested.

It was evident to Gallagher why she would mention the saloon keepers and he also understood why she suspected Slater. Although the union organizers had left town, she continued to stir up sympathy for the female workers at his factory. But the reference to the lawyer baffled him.

"Why Carlisle?"

"I've been investigating Star Enterprises. That's the corporation he owns."

"Yes, I remember. You told me it bought out your father's company."

"That's right. All the companies Star bought have two things in common. They all had suspicious accidents before being taken over and Carlisle was their attorney. I think he caused the problems so they would be forced to sell at rock bottom prices."

Warning bells went off in Gallagher's head. She could put herself in trouble with shoot-from-the-hip thinking like this.

"Whoa, girl. It sounds like you're putting the cart before the horse. Maybe the people who run Star just look for businesses in trouble and can't climb out. You're talking about arson, fraud and murder. You can't accuse anyone without hard proof."

Gallagher wanted to halt her enthusiasm before it got out of control. With her stubbornness and lack of fear, he pictured her marching bare-handed into a lion's den, ready to do battle.

"A few days ago, Captain Tom told me my father was investigating accidents at Moore Freighting when he was killed. A boiler on one of his boats had blown up and one of his warehouses had caught on fire. I think he was getting too close to the truth and they silenced him."

"Hold on a minute. Your father died in a boating accident. The way you talk, it sounds like murder. I think you're borrowing trouble when you already have more than you need." Her preoccupation with her father's death disturbed him. This was an emotion-charged subject she could not think about rationally.

"It was murder and I intend to prove it. You can believe your almighty police report, but I don't have to. I've made telephone calls to previous owners of Star businesses and I think someone is nervous I might find out too much. If that same someone had my father killed, then I'm in trouble. I wouldn't be here talking to you, if I didn't think I was in real danger."

Gallagher watched Kate roll the yellow beads between her fingers in agitation. She had cause to fear. He found it difficult to believe a man of Carlisle's stature would feel threatened enough by a powerless woman to try to frighten her into leaving town. Yet, her danger did exist, and until he discovered its source, he had to consider all the possibilities.

He leaned over and placed a reassuring hand on her shoulder.

"I'll find out who's behind this harassment and have it stopped. Until then, you're always to have someone with you, especially after dark. No more riding out in the country at night. I'll check up on you every day and I want you to call me immediately if you have any more problems. As for Carlisle and Slater, leave them alone. I'll finish your investigation of Star Enterprises, just to ease your mind. This is not a game. You have to do as you're told or somebody could get hurt. Promise me you'll do this my way."

She hesitated before giving her answer. His plan included speaking to him every day, which would be an ordeal. How could she get over him, under those circumstances? Also she would have to agree to obey this insufferable man whom she had been at odds with more often than not. Kate thought of Abigail and Gladys endangered because of her and knew she had to give her consent.

"You needn't worry. I'll take the precautions you suggest."

"Good girl. Now we can go on to our other problem."

Kate heard his voice grow husky. A warning vibrated through her body. She could not allow an intimate discussion with him and hope to retain their distance. Escape foremost in her mind, she stood and faced the door.

"You'll excuse me. I'm late for an appointment. Thank you for your help."

She had taken only one step toward freedom when Gallagher grabbed her arm and plunked her back onto the chair. Kate was terrified. He could harm her more with a few words than he could hurt her physically.

"You can't go on avoiding me." His face was stern. "I've let this go too far already. I thought by now you would've come to your senses, but you're too stubborn to admit you were wrong. The two of us being together was not a mistake. What we had that afternoon was beautiful."

Her hands flew to cover her ears and shut out the delicious memories he conjured up, but her imagination clung to them; the feel of his hands caressing her breasts, his lips trailing fire. She shook her head to dislodge the disturbing images.

He gripped her wrists and dragged her palms away from her ears. Kate felt naked, her emotions bare for him to see.

"Look at me," he commanded. "You'll hear everything I say. I've wanted to talk to you ever since I read your note, but I knew you wouldn't listen. Well, I'm through waiting."

She hated when he pressed her like this, forcing her to see his view of life, a view so much more innocent and trusting than hers. His words pounded at her, and she tried to fend them off while she clutched her pain to her.

"Why are you afraid of me? I didn't seduce you. Why don't you trust me?" Kate offered no answer and turned her face away. If she ignored him, he would eventually give up. "You're not afraid of Dave Peters. Are you going to marry him, with his fancy motorcar and his family's money? I didn't take you for a gold digger."

A gold digger? How could he think that of her? She spoke before thinking of the consequences. "Money has nothing to do with it. I don't fear him because I could never love him. He'll never have the power to hurt me."

Kate watched Gallagher's features go all soft before she realized what she had implied.

"You don't fear him because you can't love him, but you're terrified of me. You love me, don't you?"

She did not want to admit the truth, yet she could not bring herself to lie. Not answering would be an admission. Damn him for confronting me, she cried inside her mind.

Before she thought of an appropriate answer, he drew her from her seat by her shoulders and crushed her lips under his mouth. As she struggled to back away, he held her firmly to him until his touch transformed her fears into passion. Keeping herself away from this compelling man for six weeks while her imagination summoned him to her again and again had been a unique brand of torture. The conflict between her deep caring for him and her mindless sense of danger when he was near, warred within her as the kiss deepened, escalating the punishment to new heights of anguish. With the force of her confusion she dug her fingers into his arms.

When he finally released her, she trembled uncontrollably before calming herself. Coherent thought soon followed. His duty as her police protector would give him frequent access to her and the besieged wall of her defense could not tolerate a concerted attack. She needed to slow his advance.

"I haven't admitted such strong emotions toward you and I would appreciate your restraint." Kate stepped away from him.

"You haven't denied your love, either. I've already used too much restraint lately, trying to stay away from you. I don't have much left. I won't be put off."

"I won't be your whore." Her voice was uncompromising.

"You were never that and never will be. The only thing I want from you is your love. Someday, you'll trust me enough to accept that. Until then, you won't shake loose from me. That's a promise."

Kate stepped back from the intensity of his probing eyes. Beneath the anxiety of knowing he would pursue her affection, she felt strangely elated, as though a black veil had been lifted from her heart.

"I'm impressed with your dedication. I hope that virtue extends to your work as a policeman. Then I won't be plagued with unknown attackers. I would only have you to worry about."

"I don't molest women, although in your case, I might make an exception. I always have trouble controlling myself when I'm around you." Gallagher's eyes twinkled with amusement as he ran the back of his hand down her cheek and along her throat.

Hastily, she moved out of his reach. Even as she realized he only teased her, his warm fingers on her skin played havoc with her already churning emotions. Escape from him seemed the wisest move.

"I must leave now. I trust your control will have returned by the next time we meet. Thank you for your help, John."

He watched her retreat backward toward the door, still keeping him in her sight. Did she expect him to pounce on her? he wondered, chuckling to himself. He remained near the desk until she was one cautious step from her goal. Then he dashed across the room toward her and heard her startled gasp. Gallagher grinned as he swung the door open and stood aside, allowing her to pass. The relief and annoyance playing on her adorable features almost made him laugh aloud.

"You can count on my help, but I can't guarantee my self-control," he announced as she crossed the threshold.

He caught her withering look at him from over her shoulder before she pertly crossed the sidewalk. In spite of her rebuffs, Gallagher knew he was on the way to winning her.

CHAPTER XVII

The sun dipped behind the hills, casting the mansion lined street in pink shadows. The boardinghouse sign on the lawn of the Moore house swayed and creaked on its hinges in the breeze. Gallagher sat astride his blaze-faced roan, staring at the shiny Oldsmobile parked on the street in front of him. He recognized it as the lawyer's machine and scowled. His thoughts turned to his sweetly packaged bundle of trouble being courted by another man. Jealousy burned in his gut. He removed a cheroot from his pocket and lit it, savoring the soothing smoke.

Every day in the four weeks since Kate had appeared in his office, he had spoken to her either on the telephone, during her forays downtown, or on his visits to her home. He used concern for her safety as an excuse to be near her or just to hear her voice.

She had reported no further dangerous incidents, but that did not surprise him. While scouring the Southside for information about the attacks on her, he had spread word that she was under his personal protection. Gallagher was almost certain the saloon owners were not responsible for the broken window or incident on the road, but he was sure his message had reached the culprit.

He also worked on her other problem. The information he had gathered about Star Enterprises led him to believe the organization's holdings might have been obtained under suspicious circumstances. Unfortunately, he could not prove them guilty of wrongdoing. A couple of years had passed since the last company was purchased. With time, the memories of the previous company owners grew foggy and evidence was destroyed. One interesting piece of information was uncovered this week, which was the excuse he used for this visit.

Gallagher eyed the showy motorcar. When he found it parked like this, he knew Peters was inside the house and he usually turned his horse around and left. Lately, he saw the auto a couple of times a week, which was far too often for his comfort. Tonight, his ornery streak refused to allow him to retreat. He would take the measure of his competition and challenge him.

Fortified with determination, he dismounted and tied the reins to the lamppost. After taking a last drag from the thin cigar, he tossed it on the ground and crushed it under his boot. While he strode on the path to the porch, soft voices wafted to him through the open parlor window. At the door, he rapped loudly. When he heard the feminine footsteps from the hall, he snatched the broad-brimmed hat from his head.

The door opened to reveal a petite angel standing in the hallway. Gallagher was speechless at the sight of Kate swathed in white lace on aqua satin, emeralds at her throat, her hair pulled up with cascading curls down the back. She looked the perfect lady for any gentleman's drawing room. For the first time, he wondered if she might be happy with Perfect Peters, after all. Then he gave himself a mental shake.

Thought of his hot blooded bobcat in bed with the Ice Man lit a fire in his gut. He couldn't let that happen.

"John, I wasn't expecting to see you tonight." Her eyes were huge with surprise. "I have company."

Kate's nerves jumped with apprehension. She and David were soon to leave for Rio Vista where she would meet his parents. He was already tense and she did not want to disturb him further with the appearance of a man he considered his rival.

"What I have to say won't take long."

His words did not reassure her. Her temper piqued as he pushed past her into the entry hall.

"Really, John, this is most inconvenient. Perhaps we can discuss this tomorrow." Gallagher thought her formal tone belonged to the upper social order of Peters and his ilk.

"Don't sound so eager to be rid of me, Princess. We haven't even said hello properly, yet." He spoke loudly enough to be heard in the parlor.

Gallagher shoved the door from her grip and it closed with a wall shaking shudder. Kate foresaw disaster, but could not detour this lunatic from his purpose. Before she had a chance to protest, his arms encircled her shoulders, trapping her against his warm body, his mouth capturing her lips to keep them prisoner until he granted amnesty.

She struggled to free herself, her heartbeat frantic at the sound of footsteps approaching from the parlor. Abruptly, the overhead light switched on. She sagged against the man who held her as her heart nearly flew from her chest with the surprise.

"Am I interrupting something?" David's voice rumbled with a forbidding timbre. Kate was too embarrassed to speak. This uncomfortable situation was no fault of hers, but her defense would only make it worse.

"Don't mind us." She winced when she saw Gallagher's grin. His teasing humor could start a fight. "We were just saying hello."

"I think you were just saying good-bye." David held his hands at his side, fists clenched. She knew there would be trouble if she did not step in.

Gallagher's grasp loosened from around her and she stepped out of his embrace, regaining enough composure to take hold of the situation. Stabbing the police chief with a poisonous glare, she addressed them both.

"Gentlemen, I will not be fought over like a bone between two dogs. John, if there is a reason for this visit, please get to it. I have no desire to see my home become a battleground."

"I'm just checking, like I do every day, to see if you're having any more trouble."

Kate noted the lawyer's narrowing eyes.

"What trouble?" David inquired.

"Everything was fine today. Is there anything else you need to know?" She would deal with the business at hand and see to her disgruntled suitor later.

"You just tell me if the drunks accost you on the street again and I'll take care of it." Gallagher continued as if the other man was not there. "By the way, I found out something interesting about the companies owned by Star Enterprises. Before the accidents started, all the companies hired the same man. He gave a different name in each place, but the description is the same. He's big, with dark, shaggy hair and he's missing the last joint of his right pinky. He would disappear right after the last accident. If you see anyone who fits that description, I want you to tell me about it."

"Katherine, what is going on here? You promised to drop the Star investigation. And what is this about drunks?"

The attorney's usual calm showed signs of cracking. Kate knew she was in for trouble.

She groaned. The blue-eyed beast grinning at her had deliberately intruded on her evening and made a shambles of it. She would need to do some nimble explaining later to smooth the knots John created. The cocky grin on the lawman's face begged to be smashed and she itched to oblige it.

"David, we will discuss this later." With deliberation, she opened the front door wide and faced Gallagher. "We can talk another time. You've done enough damage for one evening."

"I certainly hope so," he whispered, his mouth nearly touching her ear. Briefly, his lips came down hard on hers, branding her. "I'll see you tomorrow."

By the time Kate caught her breath, Gallagher had crossed the porch and was halfway to the gate. Slowly, she closed the door and turned toward David. His features appeared rigidly controlled, his temper on a short leash. Stalling for time to gather her thoughts, she took hold of his arm and headed for the parlor.

"You seem to enjoy special privileges from the local law enforcement." A thick layer of jealousy flavored David's words. "Daily reports on your safety and personal detective work go far beyond his duties. Now that I live in Rio Vista again and see you more often, might I expect to see more of your self-appointed bodyguard?"

Kate sat on the end of a sofa and waited while he settled beside her, before launching into her defense.

"I've had problems lately, probably caused by my suffrage activities. Someone broke a window in my home and drunkards sometimes stop me on the street. Most of that has stopped since the police took an interest, but a few bartenders still incite their patrons against me. I appreciate Mr. Gallagher's concern."

"I don't object to his concern for your safety, but he carries it too far. And you haven't explained your continued interest in Star Enterprises. You promised to put that subject aside, young lady."

Kate felt like when she was a child and her mother had caught her in red-handed disobedience. The familiar sensation jogged a spark of rebellion.

"That promise was a mistake and I do not apologize for following my conscience. Now that the police have taken over, you do not have to be involved anymore."

David recognized the glint of temper in her penetrating gaze. He knew he could never hope to control her, but that was not his major problem. The real danger to his future with this enchanting nymph was the man with the badge. Katherine saw him as her white knight, and judging from their performance in the hall, was enamored of him. He needed to remove Gallagher from her life immediately. As David's fiancee she would be duty bound to keep other men at a distance.

He gently held her hand in both of his.

"I realize I have no jurisdiction over your private life. You've apprised me of that fact often enough. I would like to change that. Katherine, I want you to be my wife as soon as possible. We could be married in a month. Please, say yes."

Kate felt trapped in an airless room, gasping for life giving breath that did not exist. She had avoided answering his proposal these last weeks and was still unprepared to do so. David was kind to her, handsome, successful, wealthy, and her mother would approve of him. She was not in love with him, but that was desirable. There was less chance of being controlled and hurt. If becoming Mrs. David Peters would be so beneficial, then why did she feel suffocated at the thought of it?

A blue-eyed visage with a cocky smile floated through her thoughts. This is silly, she upbraided herself. John did not deserve serious consideration. To him, she was just another notch on his bedpost. Besides, with his overbearing personality and her penchant for freedom, they were poorly suited for a lifetime match. All reason pointed toward her wedding the patient man holding her hand, yet she could not say yes. An unnamable presence held her back from committing her future to her mother's world.

"David, this is an important decision for me and I need more time to think it over. Much depends on my meeting with your parents tonight. Give me a few more days to consider."

"My parents will love you, as I do. I know you'll decide in my favor." He kissed her gently.

Indeed, the decision to become his wife seemed inevitable to her, except for a tiny romantic hope hidden in the corner of her mind. Something monumental would happen to alter her decision. Such an occurrence would be a miracle and Kate did not rely on fantasies. She resigned herself to becoming a staid lady.

Window shades shut out the moonlight, locking Kate's bedroom in total darkness. She turned over in the brass bed again, rearranging her pillow to find a more relaxing position. This was the fourth night since David's last marriage proposal, and though exhausted from three nights' lack of sleep, the relief of oblivion eluded her. She hurled sharp words at the tangled sheet binding her feet together.

Her evening at the Peters' home had gone rather well, she recalled. David had prepared his parents for her refreshing vivacity, as they referred to her lapses in propriety, and Kate comported herself with commendable control. A future ruled by restraint was not appealing to her, but safety from heartbreak would compensate for the sacrifice.

John Gallagher had wheedled back into her good graces. She could not withstand another of his devastating attacks and engagement to another man would slow him down . . . she hoped.

Sounds from outside her window shattered her contemplation. The tapping of men's boots on the stone path of her front yard mingled with excited deep voices. A red danger flare shot through her. Men on her property at this ungodly hour could only mean trouble. With a nervous flutter deep in her chest, she pulled open the drawer of the nightstand beside the bed and drew out her pistol. The cold iron in her hand restored her confidence. At the banging on the front door she catapulted out of bed, threw a silk robe over her thin nightgown and headed for the stairway.

Halfway down the steps, Kate heard someone call her from above and saw the hall light switch on. She stopped and turned to see Abigail at the top of the stairwell. The teacher wrapped a woolen robe around herself, her long braid hanging over her shoulder.

"What's happening?" she called down in a loud whisper.

"There are men at the door. I don't know who they are, but don't worry. This will scare them off." Kate held up the gun.

Abby's eyes widened at sight of the firearm.

"I'll go down with you and call Chief Gallagher on the telephone." She started down the steps.

Both women descended to the dark entry hall, the only light filtering from the top of the stairway. Kate crossed the room to the front door, while her boarder went to the telephone. The door vibrated from the pounding.

"Who are you and what do you want?" Her voice was strident with fear.

"Open up. We come for some girls. Murphy sent us." Raucous laughter accompanied the words.

"You've made a mistake. Now, get off my porch."

"Come on, Sweetie. Murphy says you're real high class whores and I got somethin' in my pants special for you."

Already in a foul mood from lack of sleep, the vulgarity shoved Kate over the edge of her control. She unlocked the door and jerked it open. Holding the pistol out straight in her two hands, she clicked the hammer back.

Two young men stood on the porch swaying in liquor induced imbalance. Their eyes were glazed and she gagged from the stench of cheap whiskey radiating from their breaths.

"I think we better go back to Murphy's and play a game of pool." one of the intruders eyed the gun and backed away.

His partner took a step toward Kate. "I come here to get laid and I ain't leavin' without it."

Kate's shoulder took the brunt of the recoil as she pulled the trigger. The young man stood in front of her, his hand covering his ear, eyes wide with wonder.

"She shot me." His voice was incredulous.

The pistol barrel moved up to aim between his eyes and the hammer clicked back. Both men bolted from the porch and hurled themselves over the picket fence.

Kate stood in the doorway, shaking with anger.

"Damn! Damn! Damn!"

She punctuated each word by whacking her hand against the doorframe. She wished it was Murphy's head she was slamming. Although she knew him no better than the other Southside saloon owners who hazed her, he seemed a perfect target for all her revenge. The tension caused by David's marriage proposal also needed an outlet, no matter how displaced it would be to dump it on Murphy.

"I'm going Downtown. Don't wait up for me." She called behind her to Abigail who was cranking the telephone.

"Where are you going at this time of night?" Abby's voice was tight.

"To Murphy's saloon on South Superior. He's earned a lesson tonight."

The teacher replaced the receiver on the telephone box, giving Kate her full attention.

"You can't go out dressed like this, especially to the Southside. Just look at yourself. You're an invitation to every man in sight. We'll call Chief Gallagher and let him take care of Mr. Murphy."

"You're right. I can't go out like this." Kate surveyed her clinging silk robe.

She removed her coat from the hall closet and shrugged into it. The coat reached down to her ankles. Kate chose to ignore her bare toes. When she returned to the open front door, she still held the pistol.

"You can't shoot him," Abigail protested.

Kate contemplated the gun before dropping it into her coat pocket.

"I suppose not."

She lifted a stout handled umbrella from its stand beside the door and took a practice swing with it. Her bare feet slapped against the boards as she crossed the porch.

"Gallagher here." His voice was gruff with sleep.

"Thank goodness I've reached you." The piercing, female voice slapped him fully awake. "This is Abigail Penny. Kate has a gun and she's headed down to Murphy's saloon to beat him. There were two men at the door and she shot one of them. You've got to stop her."

"Slow down. I can't make head nor tail of all this. Start at the beginning. Who was at the door?"

"Two men. They were drunk and said a man named Murphy sent them here. They were told this was a . . . oh dear. This is so embarrassing." He heard her rasp in two deep breaths before continuing. "A house with loose women. Kate told them they were mistaken, but they wouldn't leave. That was when she opened the door and shot one of them in the ear."

Gallagher groaned. "Was he hit bad?"

"I don't think so. I didn't see much blood. Anyway, that scared them off. Then Kate got it into her head to chastise this Mr. Murphy."

"You said she was going to beat him and she has a gun. Did you mean shoot him?"

There was a pause before the high pitched voice blared at him with a hysterical ring.

"Oh you've got to do something! I hear her driving onto the street!"

"Miss Penny, settle down. It'll take her a while to get Downtown. Now, answer my question."

"She wants to beat him. She has an umbrella, but the gun is in her pocket."

"Don't worry about it. I'll head her off before she gets there. You go back to sleep. I'll take care of Kate. Thanks for calling me."

Gallagher slammed the receiver on the hook and turned on the light switch. Within two minutes he dressed himself, grabbed his gunbelt, and dashed out of the house. If that female maniac managed to get by him and reach Murphy's Saloon, some fire power might come in handy.

As he stood in the dark street waiting for the Pierce-Arrow to appear, boisterous sounds reached him from the pool hall across the road. A picture formed in his mind of the rough horseplay and foul language that went on in saloons. Those men would eat this puny mouse of a woman and spit out the bones. Anger and frustration built up inside of him like a steam engine. No matter how he tried to persuade the little she-devil to avoid trouble, she courted it with a suicidal bent. He would have laughed at the thought of her marching into a saloon, armed with an umbrella, if he was not so frightened for her.

Gallagher heard the rumble of the motorcar at the same time he saw the headlight shining on the road. He moved to the middle of the street directly in its path and waved his arms.

"Stop the car!"

Kate saw the man standing in front of her and swore under her breath. She had worked herself into a glorious frenzy and would not allow sight of a badge to deprive her of smashing Murphy. The steering stick in her hand jerked to the side as her bare foot on the gas pedal hit the floor. Missing John by a hairbreadth, she straightened her course and the auto continued to chug along the street. He would certainly come after her, but she hoped to finish her business before he arrived. What would happen then, she did not care to contemplate.

Murphy's Saloon appeared on the left side of the street and she stopped the auto beside the horses tied to the hitching post. The nervous animals stomped and complained at the noisy machine. Armed with her wooden handled umbrella and the pistol hidden in her pocket, she stomped onto the sidewalk and swung open the door to the male sanctuary.

Her nostrils twitched at the stench of cheap cigars and even cheaper liquor. Deep voices rumbled in hearty comradeship. Through the thick smoke, she made out men standing around two pool tables and a long bar in the back of the room. On the wall above the bar, hung a picture of a voluptuous, naked woman in repose. Kate looked away in embarrassed astonishment, but soon regained her composure. A few of the patrons had already noticed her and she knew if she did not move quickly, she would lose the element of surprise.

Clutching her sturdy umbrella, she marched up to the balding man behind the bar.

"Are you Murphy?" She gave her voice full power to catch the attention of every man in the room.

"Yeah, that's me, but you can't come in here, Missy. We don't serve ladies." His grin was an insult.

The high bar came up to her chest, but Kate hoisted herself onto it and scrambled to her feet. She grasped the unwieldy umbrella with both hands and brought it down with a solid blow on Murphy's shoulder. He lunged for her, roaring like a wounded boar, but she nimbly sidestepped out of his reach, and swung at him again. This time, the wooden handle made contact with the side of his head. Finding her rhythm, she danced away from his grabbing hands as she belabored his head and body. Finally, he backed off, his arms held up as a shield. Laughter and jeering hoots encouraged her to go after him. Her blood was up and she followed him, kicking over glasses and bottles, hardly noticing her surroundings.

Gallagher burst into the smoky room. Atop the bar stood Kate, a five foot tall virago with golden curls in tangled disarray, bare feet sticking out from beneath a coat with two inches of a silk robe peeking from the bottom. She belabored the bartender as he fended off the blows with one arm and tried to grab her ankle with the other. Thankfully, she appeared unhurt.

Kate heard a voice from nearby order her to stop and get down, but she ignored it. Strong hands encircled her waist from behind and dragged her off the bar, but she was prepared for an attack. Holding the umbrella in one hand, she reached into her pocket for the pistol. When her feet touched the floor, she whirled around and pointed the barrel at the attacker's chest, intending to scare but not shoot him.

As she lifted her gaze to the man's face, her mouth dropped open. Gallagher's eyes were ablaze with blue fire. She had never seen him look so angry. When he took the gun from her hand, she relinquished it without a word. For the first time, she considered the consequences of seeking her own revenge. She winced at the memory of nearly running John down in the street. He would make her pay dearly for that.

"Outside." He nodded toward the door.

Not waiting for Kate to respond, he clamped his fingers around her arm and propelled her across the room. She resented his high-handed treatment, especially in front of the male audience that hooted and laughed at her predicament. Unfortunately, there was nothing she could do about it. Her protests would only incite him further.

Out on the street, a blast of cool fresh air greeted her, but Gallagher gave her no time to savor it before beginning his tirade.

"I swear, you've got no common sense at all, going into a place like that, assaulting a man twice your size. Have you lost your mind?" He hauled her in the direction of her car.

"There was no problem. I had my gun."

"That gun was more of a danger than a help. The only person you pointed it at was me. And every bar on the Southside has a firearm hidden behind it. You could've been trading bullets with a shotgun."

They reached her car and Gallagher forced her to sit on the passenger side.

"Stay here," he admonished before heading back toward the saloon.

What was he going to do in there? she wondered. Curiosity overcame her caution and she made her way to the window to peer inside. The police chief stood at the bar, talking to Murphy. When the saloonkeeper laughed and shook hands with Gallagher, Kate fumed. That bald-headed slime had insulted and humiliated her and the man who swore to protect her supported him. In a fit of temper she kicked the building with her bare foot and yelped with pain.

Mumbling curses, she hobbled to the front of her auto and cranked the starter. She was so angry that if she saw John now there was no telling what she would do to him.

In the saloon, Gallagher wrapped his hand in the front of Murphy's shirt and hauled him halfway over the bar. He had just convinced the proprietor not to press assault charges against the little bobcat. Now, he was going to teach him the folly of offending a policeman's woman. His fist smashed against Murphy's face and blood spurted from his nose. He let go of the dazed man and watched him reel until his back hit the wall and he slumped to the floor. Satisfied, Gallagher headed for the door.

Stepping onto the sidewalk, he noticed the sputtering sound of an automobile engine starting up. He made out a short, shadowy figure in front of the Pierce-Arrow, straightening up from the cranking position. The little stinker was trying to run off! Gallagher raced to the driver's seat, handily beating her to it.

"Get out of my car, you two-faced son of a bitch." She pounded on his body.

He had no clue as to why she was in such a rage, but no matter the reason, he would not put up with it. Lifting her by the waist, he dragged her across his legs and plunked her onto the passenger seat.

"How dare you take his part when my back was turned. I hate you!"

Gallagher clamped his palm over her mouth and waited for her to stop struggling.

"For once in your life, shut up and listen." His voice was harsh. He was fresh out of patience. "I didn't take his part. He could've had you arrested for assault. What you saw was me talking him out of it. You missed me putting my fist through his face. Now, I'm taking you home and I don't want to hear another word from you."

He tentatively removed his hand from over her mouth. She remained silent, although her bottom lip protruded in a prominent pout. She looked like a ten-year old to him, with that naughty girl expression and her wildly tousled mop of hair. Gallagher denied the powerful urge to kiss her and concentrated on the levers and pedals before him.

Many years ago, his father had taught him to drive the farm tractors so now he could back the auto onto the road and head toward his office. The vehicle lurched and veered until he managed to control it. Soon they putt—putted along the road at a fine clip.

While John brushed off his dusty driving skills, Kate built up a head of steam. This night was not going at all well. Within the past hour, she had been insulted, humiliated, laughed at, bullied, and physically subdued. And this was not to be the end to it. She expected to be scolded, if not worse, for defending her honor. This maddening oaf, presently misusing her motorcar, treated her like a criminal instead of congratulating her for defending herself. By the time they reached the jailhouse, she was gnashing her teeth.

When the auto turned into the alley leading to the police chief's cottage, she could no longer remain silent.

"You said you were taking me home."

"Yes. My home, not yours."

"I won't go in there." Kate remembered with erotic clarity what happened the last time she set foot in his house. If she shared his bed and body again, she could never force herself to settle for a passionless life with David.

Gallagher turned off the engine and stepped down from his seat, dragging the stubborn female behind him. As he tried to lift her down, she lashed at him with her arms and legs. Coming at her with his head down, he heaved the flailing bundle over his shoulder and carried her the few yards to his house.

Once inside, he put Kate down and she found herself standing in the middle of his kitchen. The only light in the dark room came from the moon glowing through the curtainless window. A silver stream illuminated Gallagher's features. Deep shadows accentuated the rugged bone structure and her angry thoughts were pushed into the background to make room for physical desire that pounded through her blood. With a Herculean effort, she kept the maverick emotion at bay until he switched on a dim lamp, dissipating the moonlight.

"I will not permit you to bully me." She fought to keep the desperation from her voice, but had only partial success. "You have no right to cart me around like a piece of your property. I refuse to stay here."

She watched him close in and tower above her until all she saw were his shirt buttons. Relying on her reserve of courage, Kate stood her ground.

"In case you haven't noticed, I'm bigger than you are and you'll stay until I say you can leave." His voice rumbled from above.

Undaunted, she pulled a chair away from the table and stepped onto it, now able to see the top of Gallagher's head.

"I've had enough of your male posturing. I've been insulted and humiliated by drunken bums and you treat me like the wrongdoer. I was the victim and deserve some consideration. Instead, you behave like a rampaging grizzly bear."

Gallagher peered up with amazement at the tiny warrior.

The nervy brat was trying to take the upper hand. Wrapping his arm around her waist, he swept her off her pedestal and sat her on the edge of the kitchen table.

"I ought to blister your backside," he raged at her. "For weeks I've done my darnedest to keep you safe and you run out in the middle of the night smack into a nest of snakes. How am I supposed to protect you when you avoid my help? And I didn't appreciate you nearly running me down in the street."

He saw her bold glare soften and aim toward the floor in embarrassment. A bright flush colored her cheeks. He lifted her chin with his fingertips.

"It terrifies me to see you in danger." His voice was soft and warm now, melting through her antagonism. "I love you too much to let you hurt yourself."

Kate felt her body stretch toward him and, without thinking, pressed her face against his spellbinding fingers. When she saw him leaning in, his mouth on a collision course with her own, panic seized her. She threw her hands up to hold him away and struggled to slide off the table.

"No! We can't do this."

Her legs were trapped against the table edge by his muscular thighs. In a last ditch effort to escape him, she covered her face with her hands and announced the one thing she knew would stop him.

"I'm marrying David Peters."

Gallagher stood still, too shocked to function. Then he came alive, motivated by a driving desperation. He tightened his fingers around her jaw and grabbed her arm, shaking her.

"You're lying."

"He proposed a while back and I'm going to say yes." Did he only imagine the uncertainty trembling in her voice? If he accepted her words without question he would do himself and her an injustice.

"Then you haven't told him yet and you won't go through with it. You don't love him."

"How do you know that?"

"Because you love me."

His mouth came down hard against hers, denying her feeble attempt to protest, plundering her sanity. She thought of never being held like this by him again and wanted to cry with the pain. Her loving response was tentative at first, picking up intensity as his hands slipped inside her coat, slid fleetingly over her robed body, and lingered at the tips of her firm breasts.

Kate could not deny the power he had over her. Deftly, she opened the coat buttons to allow him better access to her body and he slipped the garment from her shoulders, letting it drop on the table. His movements were rough with urgency as he untied her robe, and with his mouth, found a turgid nipple through her nightgown. Heat rose in her female core. Pushed backward until she was flat on the table, she was pressed against the hard wood by his weight, her coat offering a cushion. He reached above her head and she heard the clatter of crockery hitting the floor as he swept the table clear. She felt herself lifted further onto the wooden surface. Then John was beside her, his body half covering hers.

His mouth claimed hers again, glorying in her avid response, spurring his maddening need. The material of her nightgown was nearly weightless in his hand as he lifted the hem to her waist. Dampness met his fingers as he probed the moist core of her, then delved them inside. Her internal muscles pulsed around the two digits, inflaming his desire to a firestorm.

Kate was caught in a sensual maelstrom, her body begging for release. When he positioned himself between her legs and thrust his hardness deep inside her, she clutched his back, her nails embedding in his flesh. Their joining was a frenzied storm almost violent in its intensity. At the peak of her pleasure, she bit down on the smooth flesh of his shoulder, driving him to his final surge as his passion spewed forth within her.

She fought back the tears as she clung to the man she loved. The terrible war she waged with herself was finally over, but she could not decide if she had won or lost. Conflicting emotions overwhelmed her. Would he abuse her love, use it to rape her soul? Only time would reveal the answer. Now, she belonged to John, no matter the outcome.

She opened her eyes and Gallagher noticed a teardrop overflow and run across her cheek. Remorse whipped him. He would have sworn she was a willing partner. Could he have hurt her?

"I'm sorry. I didn't mean to hurt you. Forgive me."

"No. I'm fine." Her voice was so low he barely heard it. "You were right. I do love you."

"What about Peters?" He did not breathe while awaiting her answer.

"I can't marry him."

Gallagher laughed with relief. He sat up on the edge of the table, taking her with him, and encircled her in a crushing hug. When she giggled at his exuberance, he held her away from him and gave her a playful, smacking kiss on the mouth.

His joyous mood was contagious. Her hands clasped behind his neck and she leaned back to see his eyes sparkle like the North Star. He lightly kissed the tip of her nose. Before he could back away she locked her lips onto his. A new excitement enveloped her when he slid from the table, lifted her into his arms and strode toward his bedroom. She felt an exhilarating freedom in allowing herself to be John's woman and she was eager to explore it.

CHAPTER XVIII

The Nickelodeon Theater, located on Willis Park Square opposite City Hall, was filled to standing room only on this evening in early June. The motion pictures, starring Bronco Billy and the Keystone Cops, were finished and the California Equal Suffrage Association and their guest speakers from San Francisco took the stage. Anticipation of the rally ran high in the town, affecting its supporters as well as the anti-women's vote groups. Southside hecklers and Wilhelmina Christian and her ladies sat among the audience.

Kate stood on the side aisle, her nerves jumping with high tension. She had worked long and hard to make this event happen. Her attention was on the stage where Victoria Simpson, the suffrage association's local president, introduced the three visitors. First to speak was Martha McCan, responsible for the campaign's state wide press releases. Next up was Elizabeth Gerberding, who wrote for the "Overland Monthly" and supplied skits for rallies. Gail Laughlin, originally from Colorado, was to be the last speaker. She represented the National Business and Professional Women's Clubs.

During a break between speeches, Kate sat at the piano to the side of the stage, playing an accompaniment to a rousing popular suffrage song led by Mrs. Simpson. After the last note faded and Victoria called forth the remaining speaker, Kate let her gaze wander the room. She recognized many cannery workers in the audience, Carmela Cabrillo and Dorothea Mendez among them. Sam Wakely, with his ever present notepad and pencil, sat toward the front.

Her vision focused on Gallagher who stood on the side, his back against a wall, eyes alert for trouble as he surveyed the crowd. Early in the program, he had extracted a couple of hecklers from the theater and the disruptions had been minimal since then. She smiled as his gaze locked with hers, seeming to tell her that he wished they were alone.

Much to Kate's disappointment, during the three weeks since the incident at Murphy's Saloon, they had managed to see each other frequently, but seldom in private enough to release their passions. The presence of her boarders was a mixed blessing. They preserved her maidenly reputation, but made it hellishly difficult to allow a man in her room or spend the night in John's bed when they knew she was with him.

David still called on the telephone, although she had refused his marriage proposal and informed him of her emotional involvement with Gallagher. She allowed his continued friendship, not willing to hurt him further than she had already. It was true John did not mention marriage, but even if their relationship was to be only temporary, she would not reconsider David's offer of a restricted existence.

She brought her wandering thoughts under rein as she honed in on the form of Gail Laughlin at the podium. The speaker was long past her youth, but her forceful voice testified that she had not lost her energetic vitality. A plain, dark blue dress helped her to attain an aura of dignity.

"Business women and ladies who own property pay taxes and should have the right to representation in government. We stand by the old revolutionary cry of 'no taxation without representation'. That which was unjust over a hundred years ago is as unjust today."

Kate listened to the eloquent message and reaffirmed her dedication to the cause. She was aware that the unsympathetic elements in the audience grew restless and hoped they would remain under control. As Gail Laughlin's speech drew to an end, she permitted questions on her experience with women's suffrage in her home state of Colorado. Women had won the vote there in 1893. The wisdom of allowing the "antis" a chance to speak was lost on Kate, but no one had asked for her opinion. She saw no way to reverse the invitation to disaster.

Audience participation was lively, but did not become unruly. When the speaker made her closing comments and left the podium to Victoria Simpson, Kate sighed with relief. She had invited the speakers, hired the meeting hall, and offered her home to the out-of-town guests. The special police security was also arranged by her. If a major fiasco occurred, she would feel responsible.

Applause vibrated the walls at the end of Victoria's graceful statements which concluded the successful gathering. While most of the audience filed out of the theater, a few suffrage association members advanced to the stage to speak to the ladies from San Francisco. As Kate gathered her sheet music, Gallagher came up beside her.

"Will you ladies need an escort to your house?" he asked.

"No. We'll be fine. Thank you for standing guard. This place would have been Bedlam without your help." She smiled at him with appreciation.

"If you need me, just call. I'll be going now."

Gallagher touched his hand to her cheek for an instant and winked at her. Her gaze trailed him as he turned and descended the steps from the stage. Kate watched him walk through the theater until Caroline Parkhurst caught her attention.

"Since the guests will only be here one night, a few of the ladies from The Hill would like to visit with them now.

Would you mind having company at this hour?" The young suffragist's eyes were alight with excitement.

Kate nodded in consent. Stimulating conversation would be a fitting end to this remarkable evening.

"Everyone is welcome. We can serve tea in the front parlor."

The stage cleared as the women headed for the private exit behind the platform. An ancient, seven passenger touring car waited in the alley. It had been dubbed the "Blue Liner" by the suffrage ladies who used it to tour the state in this campaign. Kate felt honored to be among those few to ride in it.

All the ladies were settled comfortably in the front parlor. Kate and Caroline prepared a tea service for ten while Abigail and Gladys helped the company feel welcome. Among the socially elite guests from The Hill, only Rebecca Willis and Carolyn Parkhurst were members of the Petticoat Gang. An atmosphere of refinement permeated the gathering.

"How is the campaign doing state-wide?" Rebecca asked this of Mrs. Gerberding, who had been touring with the "Blue Liner" much of the Spring.

The fifty-three year old writer sipped her tea for a moment before answering.

"We are doing well in the countryside, but the cities seem determined to hold out. Of course, we still have four months before the special election in which to improve our position, and we are winning more converts every day. This is the largest suffrage campaign yet."

"The leading daily newspapers are against us, but we have the backing of the small ones," added Martha McCan, who was in charge of press releases. "How are you faring in this area?"

"We're experiencing quite a bit of resistance," Abigail explained. "But we're steadily gaining strength. The packed house tonight was evidence of our success, although a few of the audience were hostile."

Persistent knocking on the front door interrupted the conversation. Kate excused herself and entered the hall. Surprise and annoyance raced through her as she swung back the door and recognized Jeffrey Carlisle.

Although she took an interest in the lawyer's business affairs, she had not spoken to him since their clash the past summer. The mocking tilt to his mustached upper lip did not bode well.

"Good evening, Miss Moore. It's imperative that I have a word with you. May I come in?" His tone was exceedingly polite and devoid of warmth.

"It's late, Mr. Carlisle, and I have guests. Perhaps, you can return at a more convenient time."

Kate fumed as he pushed past her and entered the house.

"I'm here now to emphasize a point. Our little talk will not take long. For your sake, I would suggest more privacy than this hallway provides."

A malicious glimmer in his eyes warned Kate to tread lightly. She decided the wisest course of action would be to grant him the few minutes he asked and get him to leave with as little ado as possible.

"Follow me." She led the way to the den.

Kate switched on a Tiffany lamp that left the corners of the room in deep shadows. Carlisle closed the door and faced her. She did not offer him a seat. There were to be no amenities observed here.

"It came to my attention that you show an unhealthy interest in Star Enterprises." The attorney spoke as though presenting a case in court, slowly pacing the floor, hands clasped behind his back. His actions and voice showed a theatrical inclination. "My business affairs are no concern of yours. All of my transactions are airtight and legal. Any attempt to besmirch my name will be rewarded in kind. In fact, Miss, if you and your policeman friend do not stop snooping into my private matters, I will make life quite unpleasant for you."

"If you try to harm me, you'll face Chief Gallagher, even if you are on the Town Council." She forced herself to sound confident.

"Your problem is not quite so simple, Katherine. My hired detective found a young man in New York who gave very personal information about you. His name is Trevor Freebush."

Kate felt the blood drain from her face and her legs turn to jelly. She did not have to guess what the money motivated turd had revealed to this unscrupulous man. A respectable reputation in a small town was a social passport.

Without it, doors would close in her face and her position in the suffrage association would be destroyed.

"I see you remember the gentleman." She wanted to smack the smirk from his face. "Conceiving a child out of wedlock is shocking enough, but having it aborted is double damning. What do you think the genteel ladies in your parlor would say, if they knew of your sordid past?"

The hand she placed on the desk to help steady herself trembled uncontrollably. Worse than the fear of having her good name crucified, was the idea of betraying her father's memory by allowing this man to go unpunished.

"I will not submit to blackmail."

"I advise against a hasty decision." He seemed to enjoy her evident upheaval. "I'll give you time to think about my proposition. Your secret will be safe with me until you or Chief Gallagher further intrude on my privacy."

"Get out of my house." She kept her voice low, but it quaked with anger.

Carlisle laughed aloud.

"Sleep well tonight, Katherine. I'll see myself out.

She watched him leave the room and listened until she heard the front door close. On wobbling legs, she made her way to the oversized leather chair behind the desk and lowered herself onto it. Her throat ached from tears held back. It would not do to reappear in the parlor with telltale red, puffy eyes. With a shaking hand, she reached into her pocket and removed the string of beads. The smoothness of the glass on her fingertips and her father's armchair supporting her back lent her little comfort. This problem could not be alleviated with the memory of a loving touch.

Feeling like a rabbit caught in a trap, she tried to think of a possible means to escape. Should she ask John for his help? No. There was no way to stop wagging tongues and he might stop investigating Star Enterprises to save her reputation. Or he might even become angry enough to endanger his job by confronting Carlisle and speaking his mind. She would not risk hurting him. To her way of thinking, there was nothing to do but wait for the disaster to descend on her. Amid the multitude of thoughts whirling through her head, giving into Carlisle's demands or leaving town never occurred to her.

"Are you all right?"

Kate was surprised to hear Abigail Penny's concerned voice come from the doorway.

"Yes, of course." She forced a crooked smile.

No matter her personal problems, she was still committed to suffrage and important guests waited for her in the parlor. Determination stiffened her back as she returned the beads to her pocket and rose from the chair to resume her duties as hostess.

Kate stepped inside the newspaper office. Her nose wrinkled at the sharp odor of printers' ink. A stack of the current week's edition of the *Gazette* sat on the counter. Kate picked up a copy of the publication and placed a coin beside the stack.

"Hello, Katydid."

She turned toward the voice to see Sam Wakely standing behind his desk that overflowed with paper, books, and ash trays heaped with cigar butts. His sleeves were rolled up and the top button of his white shirt was open. Heat emphasized his florid complexion.

"Come and sit with me a while."

"Sure, Sam. I'll be glad to rest for a minute. This heat makes me lazy." She seated herself in a chair beside the publisher's desk.

Her friend seemed uncomfortable and his eyes shied away from contact with hers.

"Is something wrong?" she asked with concern.

"I don't know how to say this." He grimaced and fidgeted with the cigar he held between his fingers. "Someone is out to hurt you. Five days ago someone slipped this under my door."

He held a typed sheet out to her and she took it. Curiosity mingled with fear. The first sentence set the tone of the note. She did not need to read further to understand that Carlisle had carried through with his threat. Her past in New York was spelled out in every damaging detail. Even her arrests for disorderly conduct were included. All coherent thought fled, her hands grew clammy and she wanted to retch. Kate shut her eyes and breathed deeply. Sam's gruff voice penetrated the numbness.

"I checked out the information and it's reliable. Don't worry, I won't use it. I wouldn't hurt you for anything in the world. I'm only warning you. This story will probably get out and you should be prepared for it."

He lifted the condemning paper from her hands. She watched Sam drop it into one of his oversized ashtrays and light a match. When he touched the flame to the paper and it blackened to ash, she wished she could destroy the memory of Trevor Freebush as easily.

"There's more to the story than what you read. I was in love. We were to be wed, but my stepfather didn't like him and paid him off. He got rid of the child against my will. I paid a high price for blind trust and stupidity."

Sam's huge, comforting hand covered her fingers resting on his desk.

"No need to explain to me. I won't judge you. Do you have any idea who would try to hurt you like this?"

"Jeffrey Carlisle." There was no reason to keep it a secret. He was doing his best to ruin her. "Two weeks ago he tried to blackmail me with this information."

The incredulous expression on the publisher's face attested to his shock.

"He wanted money?"

"No. I've been gathering information on a company he owns. He wants me to stop asking questions. I refused."

"This sounds interesting. Is it anything I might be able to use?"

"Eventually there will be. I can't prove anything yet, but I must be getting close. Mr. Carlisle is nervous."

Kate was purposely vague. She did not want Sam blabbing to Gallegher about this latest problem. That had to be kept secret from him until she could no longer be spared by halting the investigation.

"I have excellent resources. If there's any way I can help you, let me know, Katy."

"Thanks, Sam, but there's already someone working on it for me. When we find the answers, I'll tell you everything." Kate stood in readiness to leave. "I appreciate your warning. You're a caring friend." She kissed him on the cheek.

They said their good-byes and she left the newspaper office.

She could do her downtown errands in peace today, but she knew the comfort would not last for long. This week's edition of the *Gazette* came out this morning and Carlisle would discover his initial attempt at publicizing her past indiscretions had failed. She knew he would try again. In a small community like River Run, gossip flew through the town like a cyclone and Kate was certain she did not have long to enjoy her respectable name.

CHAPTER XIX

On July Fourth, the River Run picnic grounds provided space for a clamorous, high-spirited independence celebration. Most of the population of the town was in attendance along with a goodly portion of farm folk from the area. A noisy baseball game was in progress on the playing field, boats were launched from the pier and glided onto the calm river. Local politicians and social improvement groups harangued an audience from the grandstand from early morning on. Ladies of the California Equal Suffrage Association now occupied the stage.

Kate sat on the platform in a chair between Victoria Simpson and Abigail Penny. Although the sun had started its descent over five hours ago, heat penetrated through her sheer, white cotton dress and cooked her body inside the sweltering oven of her corset. She resisted the urge to fan herself with a handkerchief in order not to divert attention away from Rebecca Willis, who now delivered a speech. An expectant quiet hovered above the audience as though the people awaited a signal to burst into activity. Surreptitious glances aimed her way might have stemmed from her imagination, but she thought not.

For days she had been snubbed not only by her enemies, but also by women whom she had counted among her friends. *And so it begins,* Kate sighed. Carlisle planted the seed of gossip and the town now bore its bitter fruit. This morning, at the start of the parade from City Hall to the picnic grounds, three of her sister suffragists, who lived on The Hill, refused to march with her. Mrs. Simpson enforced Kate's right to participate and the disgruntled dissenters left. Making matters worse, Wilhelmina Christian made remarks in her speech against the women's vote, about the "depraved morality" of certain suffragists. Many gazes had turned toward Kate.

As a campaign veteran, she was used to being the target of barbs, but the vicious intensity of these attackers went beyond her experience. She decided to continue about her business as though nothing untoward happened. Eventually, a new scandal would take the public's interest. Until then, Kate was prepared to toughen her hide against public opinion.

Her staunch resolve did not mean she was fearless. As she marked time until her turn to speak, the tension of the crowd worked havoc on her nerves. Anxiously, her vision panned the area for Gallagher or the extra policeman he had hired for the day. With nearly everyone gone to the celebration, Jason Taylor guarded the town against easy pickings. Her stomach flopped over. No police protection was in sight.

Scattered applause accompanied Rebecca's return to her chair. Victoria stood to introduce Kate and expectant excitement seemed to ripple through the audience. One woman booed. Kate squared her shoulders and forced herself to the center of the stage. Malevolence exuded like a poisonous cloud from the people facing her. She tried to

S

shut them out of her mind, and concentrate on her speech. No more than thirty seconds into her message, the verbal attacks began.

"Whore! Slut! Leave town!"

"Baby killer! Murderer!"

Kate tried to swallow the emotional pain that settled in a huge choking mass in her throat. As the invectives continued, she raised her voice above the stinging words, determined not to run from the abuse. An overripe tomato hit the platform beside her, splattering her shoes and the hem of her white dress. Stoically, she continued with her speech.

"Hussy! We don't want your kind here!"

The air was thick with missiles, but she would not hide or raise a hand to protect herself. Something hard and sharp hit her shoulder. She felt someone grab her arms from behind and try to pull her from the stage.

"Kate, please," Abigail begged. "You must leave."

Although rotten produce and eggs slimed her face and clothes and there was no letup in sight, she refused to budge. She rang out her speech with defiant force, further inciting the audience. A stone hit her beneath the eye, the pain stunning her. She staggered, but found her balance. No matter what they threw at her, she would not leave.

Kate felt a firm grip on her arms, replacing Abigail's ineffectual strength. The broad body of a man suddenly stood in front of Kate, shielding her from the punishing mob. She struggled against the power that propelled her from the platform.

"Take it easy. I'm trying to help you."

Gallagher's welcome voice cut through her fogged senses and she knew the ordeal was done. No one would accuse her of running away when she could not possibly prevail against the police chief's muscle. With his protective arm around her, she allowed him to lead her to the shade of a tree. She sat on the ground, her back against the tree trunk.

Gallagher squatted beside her to examine her bloody and swelling face. There were no tears in her eyes, only unspeakable pain and fierce anger. Why would they be so cruel to her? The insults the crowd shouted had nothing to do with suffrage. This was a personal attack.

He noticed Abigail standing nearby.

"Abby, we need some clean water and ice. Could you find some for us, please?"

"Of course, John." She started toward the picnic area.

He turned toward the crowd in front of the stage and saw them dispersing. The show was over and they went about their business as though nothing happened. Wrath settled in his chest like a burning coal. He smoothed her wispy hair back from her face.

"Everyone knows about Trevor Freebush and the baby." Kate's voice was small.

He watched her in silence as he tried to grasp the implications of this development. Someone was trying to ruin her.

"Who did you tell about it besides me?"

"No one. Jeffrey Carlisle had a man in New York dig up dirt about me. He threatened to expose it if I didn't stop you from investigating Star Enterprises."

Gallagher's anger leaped like flames. He smashed his fist into the tree above her head, skinning the knuckles.

"Damn!

The ire boiling up inside of him was not all reserved for the lawyer. This baby faced schemer had deceived him into believing she trusted him. Yet, she did not inform him of Carlisle's threats, depriving him of the chance to defend her.

"Why didn't you tell me when it first happened? I could've found a way to keep him quiet."

"I didn't want you to stop asking questions about Star or face down Mr. Carlisle and jeopardize your job. This is my problem, not yours."

"Your problems are mine. Don't you know that by now?" He smoothed her hair, hoping to comfort her with his touch. It hurt him that she still felt alone in the world. "Carlisle will hear from me before this day is done."

"That would be foolish. Why warn him of our intentions? We'll eventually get to him through his company."

"It wouldn't hurt to roust him. He already knows we're after his hide. I'd rather him go for my throat than yours. You can't fight back like I can. No more arguments. We'll do this my way."

She opened her mouth to protest, but his fingers covered her lips. Through her resentment, she felt heat leap from his touch and spread through her body. Curse him. How could she remain annoyed when he made her feel so warm inside?

Abigail returned, carrying a tin cup of water and a piece of ice wrapped in a handkerchief. Kate winced with the shock of the cold against her tortured flesh when Gallagher placed the ice on the swelling beneath her eye. The pain soon subsided into numbness. She closed her eyes while he tenderly wiped the blood and egg from her face with his wet handkerchief.

"Are you all right?"

"I'll be fine, Abby. I'm just a little shaken."

"This is Wilhelmina Christian's doing. She's told everyone about an anonymous letter saying terrible things about you. She never forgave you for that fight in the park." Abigail's voice lowered to a near whisper. "I can't believe what she says is true."

Kate saw the doubt in Abby's eyes, pleading with her to say the rumor was a lie.

"We'll talk about this at home. I don't know exactly what you've heard, but I'm sure it's not entirely true."

As feminine voices drew near, she looked up to see Caroline, Victoria, and Rebecca arrive. Their expressions showed concern.

"You poor dear. I had no idea you were this badly hurt. Is there anything we can do for you?"

"There is something you can do, Mrs. Simpson." Gallagher looked up at her from his squatting position. "The leader of your Action Committee is resigning. You can see how dangerous it is for her to call attention to herself. You'll have to find someone to replace her."

Kate flung his ministering hands from her face and sprang to her feet.

"I will not resign. You have no right to make decisions for me. Nothing will stop me from fighting for the vote."

"I'm afraid Mr. Gallagher is right, Katherine." Victoria's voice was firm, but kind. "It would be dangerous for you to continue and the scandal would lose us more supporters than you would win. Some of our members have already threatened to leave the organization if you remain active. I'll allow you to work for us behind the scenes, but for your own good and the good of the cause, I can't allowed you to represent us to the community."

Kate felt stricken to her marrow. The trust and respect she had toiled for during the past year had been destroyed in a few days. Not even her colleagues would permit her a show of pride.

"After I gave new life to the organization at great personal expense, you throw me out like an old shoe." Her voice shook with the tears she refused to shed. "Whatever happened to loyalty and friendship?"

"It's because we are your friends that we will not let you be tortured." Caroline rested a consoling hand on Kate's shoulder. "Those of us who still believe in you want to keep you safe to fight again when this blows over."

With the defection of her staunchest defender, Kate recognized the futility of persisting. She allowed her proud bearing to slump forward and turned her back to the ladies. As Gallagher enfolded her in his arms she felt as if he tried to protect her from the emotional beating. Although she was still angry with him, she did not push away from his sheltering embrace.

"I think you'd better leave her alone for a while." His words annoyed her, but she did not have the energy to protest. "She'll understand what you're doing for her once the shock wears off."

"I'm sorry, Katherine." Victoria spoke softly. "I wish I didn't have to make such a difficult decision. We'll be expecting to see you at the meeting Thursday evening."

From inside the cocoon of John's reassuring arms, she heard the ladies' mumbled good-byes and departing footsteps.

"It's best you go home now. I'll have Captain Tom stay with you."

Kate backed away from him, shrugging off his arms. Her temper soared.

"I refuse to run away and hide my head as though I'm ashamed. Jeffrey Carlisle won't win that easily."

He saw her stubborn stance and knew the only way she would leave would be if he took her home himself, kicking and screaming all the way. Then he would have to keep her occupied in her house to insure that she would not return to the picnic grounds. The prospect of such a delightful sacrifice almost brought a grin to his lips. Unfortunately, his police duties at the celebration did not allow him the time to indulge his private pleasures.

"Have it your way, but you'll still have to stay with the captain. I don't want you getting into any more trouble today."

"That's ridiculous. I don't need a nanny."

"No arguments. I want you safe."

Gallagher clamped his hand around her upper arm and started toward the picnic tables where he had last seen Captain Macaphee. He needed a strong ally to keep this explosive, pint-sized package out of harm's way.

Kate grumbled all the way to their destination. She enjoyed having someone who cared for her, but John was so overbearing that she wanted to kick him into the next county. With each step she took, her frustration rose another degree. By the time they reached Captain Tom, who was playing checkers at a table with one of his cronies, she was as testy as a wounded cougar.

The old man's eyes flew wide with astonishment when he saw Kate's face.

"That's one heck of a shiner you got there, Kitten. What happened?"

"Someone threw a stone at me, but I'm fine."

"Cappy, we need your help. Kate's in trouble and insists on going out to look for it. She needs a bodyguard until I can straighten out this mess. Could you get some of your things together and move into her place tonight? I sure would feel better knowing you're looking after her." As Gallagher spoke he ignored the storm cloud spreading across Kate's face.

"Be happy to help any way I can. Just tell me what you want me to do."

"I don't want or need a bodyguard. How dare you try to arrange it without consulting me?" She rounded on the lawman. "I'm capable of taking care of myself and making my own decisions. You can't order my life to suit yourself."

"You don't have a choice and your jawing at me won't change my mind." Gallagher gave her his no nonsense look, hoping to intimidate her. "I'd rather have you angry and safe than standing in line for another black eye or worse. Now, you stay with Cappy and behave yourself. I'm going to find Carlisle." He turned to the old man. "Thanks, Cappy. I'll be back in a little while to explain what's happening."

Before Kate could object, he turned and walked away, his long stride soon taking him out of earshot. A swift look back assured him that she took a seat on the bench beside the captain. He let out a long breath. The little stinker was exasperating, he acknowledged before setting his thoughts toward his next task.

He had to convince Carlisle to stop tormenting Kate. A knuckle busting punch on the nose was his first choice, but he couldn't do that and keep his job. His position as Chief of Police depended on the mutual respect between the Town Council and himself. If he physically attacked one of its members, the uneasy balance of respect could tip against him. In other circumstances, the satisfaction of flattening the obnoxious lawyer might have been worth the price. Unfortunately, he needed his badge to investigate Carlisle. He cautioned himself to control his temper.

Gallagher spotted the attorney a distance away, speaking to Mayor Christian. Dressed in a stylish gray suit and Derby hat, although the temperature reached into the nineties and the picnic was informal, the lawyer appeared impervious to the heat. When Carlisle saw him approaching, Gallagher noticed a malicious smile curve under his carefully waxed mustache. He watched the lawyer excuse himself from the mayor and come toward him.

"Hello, John. This is quite a shindig the town is putting on. It's been peaceful, I hope."

"Quiet enough, except for some unscheduled target practice at a suffragette."

"I heard about that incident. There's no telling what can happen when gossip starts flying. She might be wise to leave town. People can be vicious when they're incited."

Gallagher chose his words carefully. He wanted to accuse and threaten without making it official. "They might even break a window or attack defenseless women on a dark road. Is that what you mean?"

"Such things are possible and you could never prove who was behind them. Even if you could prove anything, there are certain people who cannot be touched. Power and money do have their advantages."

Gallagher's fists clenched at his side. The fool thought he was invincible. Well, he would soon learn he didn't control everyone. The law counted for something when it was in the right hands.

"If you don't stop bothering Kate Moore, I'll let it out that you own Star Enterprises."

Carlisle laughed.

"If that's all you have against me, I have no worries. it's not a crime to be a businessman. As for bothering Katherine, there's no need. Town gossip has beaten her to the ground and I don't foresee her rise to grace anytime soon."

Impotent rage fired through Gallagher like a blast furnace, urging him to wind his fingers around the fastidious fop's throat and squeeze the life from him.

"One day, you'll make a mistake and I'll be there waiting for you."

"Do I detect a threat, John? That would be a mistake. Your job might not survive it. I'll leave you now to think on our interesting conversation."

Carlisle touched the tip of his bowler in a mock salute. His mouth turned up in a self-satisfied smirk before he strutted toward a group of businessmen a few yards away.

Gallagher lit a cheroot as he headed back toward Kate and the captain. The veiled conversation went much as he had expected it would. Neither man had spoken his mind, yet they understood each other perfectly. Threats and challenges were exchanged and accepted.

In the last few weeks, although Gallagher had continued to ask questions, the investigation into Star Enterprises had hit a dead end. He did not have enough evidence and the lawyer knew it. Then why would he try to stop them from snooping when he knew he was safe? Could it be that Carlisle was preparing another company for a cheap buy out and he didn't want anyone snooping around him? The thought rattled around inside Gallagher's head before taking root. He would keep his eyes and ears open.

Kate relaxed across the tapestry covered sofa in the back parlor, her feet up on the cushion, face turned toward the back, away from the dim lamplight. Her silk robe was tucked snugly around her legs to keep it from slipping open. The cut and bruise under her eye that she had received earlier in the day had swollen painfully. Her body was also bruised and she felt as though someone were using her head for a bass drum.

She would have gone upstairs to sleep, but Gallagher had promised to visit her tonight after Jason Taylor relieved him from duty at the picnic grounds. Music and dancing would continue there until midnight. Kate loved parties and would have been one of the last to leave, but she could not combat the people's insults and physical abuse. Captain Tom had convinced her that leaving the battlefield sometimes took more courage than staying. Her old friend now sat like a sentinel in a rocking chair on her front porch. She felt comforted that someone trustworthy was there for her protection, but she was annoyed with Gallagher for forcing the guard upon her.

The front door clicked shut and footsteps sounded from the hallway. Kate recognized the cadence of John's long stride and struggled to sit up. It would not do to let him to see her laid low. When she looked up, he stood in the doorway, sympathy softening his features.

"Don't stare at me. I look like a raccoon." She turned her face away from him.

Gallagher crossed the room and sat on the sofa beside her.

"You make an adorable raccoon." He kissed her forehead.

"Don't try to humor me. I'm in a wretched mood."

She looked so small and childlike with her bottom lip thrust forward and her amber eyes huge and soulful that his protective instincts took over. He folded his arms around her narrow shoulders and clutched her to him, hoping to infuse her with his strength. His lips touched her hair and he inhaled the light scent of lavender.

"It doesn't matter what other people think of you. The people who love you are still here. We won't let you down."

She wrapped her arms around his waist, and pressed her cheek against his warm chest. At moments like this, she was tempted to trust him implicitly, then she took into account the way he forced her to his will. Captain Tom acting as her bodyguard was only one case in point. She believed this intolerable personality trait could never be changed. Kate laid her annoyance aside and soaked up the solace of his enclosing arms.

"You need someone to depend on and look after you." His voice gentled her. "I love you, Kate. Marry me."

Her heart stopped for a moment before confusion set in. No question she loved him, and if not for his commanding ways, she would have rushed him to the altar before he could change his mind. The fact remained that she would not allow him to dominate her and their marriage would resemble the Civil War.

She moved back from him to look into his eyes before answering. His love poured out to surround her, and the words backed up in her throat.

"I love you, John, but we'd kill each other inside of a month."

"Then the second month would be heaven. Two people in love can work out anything."

She wanted to believe him, but experience told her men were not to be trusted. More than likely, he thought he would teach her who was boss and after that the going would be smooth. He certainly did not have compromise in mind. A little voice inside her head reminded her that loving a man opened the door for betrayal.

"We would fight and grow to hate each other. Besides, you would want a big family and I can't give you children. We could never be happy together."

"We've been fighting since the first night we met, but that didn't stop us from falling in love. Think of it this way, our marriage would never be boring. As for having a family, orphanages are full of children who need homes."

He held her close, his hands roaming her back, infusing her with his strength. His love surrounded her like a fragrant steaming bath, seeping through her pores, healing her hurts, both of body and mind. Her resistance wavered.

"I can't think straight when you're with me, John. I need some time alone to decide. There's no hurry and I want to be sure."

"You'll be sure."

His mouth covered hers softly at first, then gained pressure. Her senses responded with a heat that matched his own. She felt the tension in the muscles as her fingers glided across his back, reveling in the masculine firmness of his body. His hands inside her robe sent a liquid heat through her, caressing her ribs, the thumb reaching to the underside of a smooth mound. The crest tingled in anticipation of his touch.

Gallagher heard the front door slam shut. He groaned in frustration and moved back from Kate as Captain Tom's heavy footsteps sounded from the hall. He watched Kate straighten her robe and try to compose herself. She wasn't the only one who needed time to think things over. Gallagher stood as the captain entered the parlor.

"I'll be leaving now. I have to patrol the town while Jase is at the picnic grounds."

Before leaving, he kissed Kate's cheek and thanked the captain again for keeping an eye on his woman. He nearly raced down the hall toward the door.

On the porch, he stopped to light a cheroot and calm his nerves. His thoughts steamed ahead like a speeding locomotive. When he had entered the house this evening, a marriage proposal had not been in his plans. The frightened urchin hiding behind Kate's facade was never more evident than it was tonight and the lost expression in her eyes pushed him to offer his protection.

In his daydreams, he often pictured them wed, but he did not think she would marry someone who was not her social equal. He would never fit in on The Hill, and despite her earthy nature, Kate was used to fine clothes and gentle manners. He couldn't provide her with either one. They were well matched between the sheets, but he knew a successful marriage depended on more than a healthy romp in bed. She had not mentioned any of these concerns in her refusal and he wondered whether she truly did not care about money or social status. He thought of her rebellion against his mastery as merely spice for the pot.

Gallagher suspected her delay in saying "yes" was due to her distrust of men. He was determined to sway her decision in his favor, but as she had pointed out, there was no hurry.

Revitalized with a sense of purpose, he jauntily descended the porch steps.

CHAPTER XX

The sun at dusk threw off a veil of color that turned all it touched a marigold tint. Through the open kitchen window, Kate noticed the rose bushes in the garden needed to be snipped back again. She sighed wearily and dipped her hands into the sudsy water to wash the dinner dishes. Housework and keeping up the garden had not seemed such a chore before she had felt like a prisoner in her home.

Since the fateful Independence Day town celebration, the townsfolk's loathing stares and unkind whispers had pushed her further and further from public contact. Now, at the tail end of August, she felt like a recluse. A few people, whom she thought could be counted on for support, had abandoned her with the first wave of ostracism. She had not heard from David Peters since before the debacle at the picnic grounds. Word had probably reached him of her disgrace and association with her might damage his reputation. She did not miss his friendship, but the implied insult still stung.

To Kate's satisfaction, many of her friends remained loyal. Captain Tom had moved into her father's bedroom the night of the attack and faithfully stood guard over her. He now relaxed in his favorite rocking chair on the porch.

Both of her boarders refused to abandon her, although some of their landlady's taint had rubbed off on them. In any case, Kate would soon lose Gladys, after the typist wed Matthew Liszt, the Production Manager at the cannery. They had recently became engaged. Of the suffrage organization, only Caroline, Rebecca and Abigail welcomed her to the meetings. With the women's suffrage question to be decided at a special election on October tenth, the suffragists were in a frenzy of activity. As the former leader of the Petticoat Gang, Kate felt pained to stand aside while others fought on the front lines.

Surprisingly, a new friendship had emerged for her through the quagmire of social ridicule. Beatrice Slater, once herself the target of social abuse, offered her support to her former lover's daughter. Knowing that the older woman had once loved her father, Kate felt a kindred spirit and accepted the extended fellowship.

Her exuberant nature, quick to rebound from devastating blows in the past, now recovered slowly. Instead of springing back with her own attack, she was forced to sit on the sidelines. The inactivity frustrated her, but with extra time to contemplate, she discovered qualities in herself she had not known she possessed. In spite of the condemnation of the people of River Run and the spurning by her mother for not living up to her expectations, Kate realized she was a good person. Her standards of excellence in character were different from most other people's, but they were just as stringent and sometimes more so. She would never permit herself to back away from a tough fight or let an injustice go unchallenged. The shame other women attached to physically enjoying a man before marriage was incomprehensible to her, so long as she loved him. Swimming against the tide of opinion was never easy and she recognized that people who did so were endowed with special courage.

Kate smiled to herself with pride at the thought of the letter she had written to her mother. She had told her about turning her home into a boardinghouse, her decision not to marry David, a romantic involvement with the Chief of Police, and the part she played in the fight for suffrage. The tone of the letter had been light and devoid of defiance. If her mother could not accept the woman her daughter had become, then it was her mother's problem. Kate refused to feel guilty any longer.

She plunked a dish onto the drying rack with more force than was necessary. She hated succumbing to the town's censure. It was contrary to her proud nature. Gallagher's decree that she not challenge the gossips by continuing her public life would have gone unheeded if Captain Tom were not constantly watchful. She could not leave the house unless the captain tagged along to keep her out of mischief. Only her fear of a physical attack kept her from protesting. Kate would have thrown off the restrictions after the first week, except for an astonishing possibility.

Her hand gently rested on her flat belly and she half-smiled in anticipation. Kate's feminine monthly flow was over a week late, a phenomenon that had occurred only during her brief pregnancy nearly two years ago. She could not yet be certain and the New York doctor's opinion that she was barren did not hold back her hope that a new life started inside her. If by a miracle she were pregnant, she knew the chances were high her scarred and weakened womb could not carry the burden. She would need to take extra care to keep from losing the child. For this reason alone, she complied with Gallagher's stringent rules.

Kate considered marrying John. Perhaps she would accept his marriage proposal, but would not do it only because she carried his baby. Strong ideas died hard, and she still feared betrayal by men. John was no exception. She also feared he would whisk her into a shotgun wedding as soon as he suspected her condition. The prospect of being his wife did not upset her so much as losing the choice. As for the notoriety of conceiving a child out of wedlock, her reputation could not be any muddier than it already was.

A startling jangle erupted from the telephone in the front hall. She dried her hands on a dishtowel while heading toward the front of the house. Sometimes John called at this hour. As she reached the phone, she saw Gladys descending the stairway from the bedrooms.

Kate picked up the receiver and pressed it to her ear. "This is Matthew Liszt. There's an emergency at the factory. Please tell Gladys I'll be late."

She heard distracting noise in the background and his voice seemed so frantic she barely understood him. "What's going on, Matt? I can hardly hear you."

"Fire at the cannery. Can't talk now. I'll see Gladys when it's over."

The telephone connection cut off. She replaced the receiver on the hook and turned to Gladys.

"Matt said he'll be late. There's a fire at the cannery. He hung up before I could get any more information."

A deep frown puckered Gladys' brow.

"I'm worried, Kate. If the fire is out of control, people could get hurt. Workers were staying late to finish packing a load of tomatoes. I wish I knew what's happening there."

"I know what you mean. I have friends there, too." Kate thought of Dorothea and Carmela. "Let's drive down there and see for ourselves."

"What about Captain Macaphee? Will he let you go?"

"He can come with us if he wants, but he can't stop me."

She removed her shawl from the hall closet and let herself out the front door. Gladys was right behind her.

Kate stopped the automobile outside the fence and sat for a moment watching the pandemonium. From an open window, orange flames reached long arms to rival the sunset, lighting the sky behind the Montezuma Cannery. Thick black smoke billowed from several other windows on the second floor. In the front yard, people milled in dazed anxiety, all eyes trained on the upper story of the brick building. Some faces were smoke blackened. Men shouted orders amid the sounds of people coughing and crying in the yard and the screams of victims still trapped in the burning rooms. River Run's sleek new firetruck stood amid the chaotic scene, one volunteer firefighter manning the water pump that supplied the hose. Another man steadily climbed a ladder that led to a smoke filled window.

The prospects were not encouraging. Although only a small portion of the upstairs rooms seemed to be involved in the conflagration, many workers could be hurt. She remembered when the employees worked late, many of the doors were locked to keep them from leaving and windows were stuck shut with layers of paint. If no one could get to those rooms, the outcome could be disastrous.

Kate hastened to join Gladys and Captain Tom who had left the car and waited at the gate. She and her friends entered the yard and merged with the stunned and disorganized crowd.

Many of the laborers' faces were familiar to her through her work for better factory conditions, but she did not see

Dorothea Mendez or Carmela Cabrillo among them. In the failing light, she noticed the bulky figure of Henry Slater and the narrower build of Matt Liszt across the yard, standing with John Gallagher. She started toward them. Enroute through the crowd, she saw the tear drenched features of Blanca, and Kate made her way to her loyal old friend. She heard Blanca mumble prayers in Spanish.

"Blanca, what's happening? Where's Dorothea?" She clasped the woman's shoulders.

"Up there." The woman moaned and pointed toward a window from which smoke streamed.

As Kate watched, a man leaned a ladder against the window ledge and two firemen climbed up, disappearing inside the room. When one of them emerged, he carried an unconscious woman on his shoulder, but with her face against the fireman's back she could not identify who was being rescued. With Blanca in tow, Kate followed the man and his burden to Dr. Morrison's first aid area in the corner of the yard. She noticed Captain Tom trailing behind them while Gladys headed toward her fiance.

As Kate neared the victims of the fire, the stench of charred flesh and singed hair overpowered her and she breathed deeply to help control her urge to spew up her dinner. Five bandaged women sat on the ground, their eyes glazed with pain and shock. The fireman deposited the injured woman on the ground and returned to the burning building. Kate studied the smoke blackened features of the young worker who lay inert. She was not Dorothea or Carmela. The harried, middle-aged doctor knelt beside his newest patient and checked for a heartbeat. He nodded with satisfaction and continued to work on her.

Blanca's long wail of anguish brought Kate's attention back to the firemen at the building. Another woman had been carried down the ladder and brought to the makeshift hospital. She recognized her housekeeper's daughter.

Although Dorothea was unconscious, Kate heard her groan as she was put down on the ground. Her skirt and blouse were partly burned away and charred, the exposed skin of her limbs roasted. Tears welled in Kate's eyes as Blanca threw herself across the injured girl, weeping and imploring God to spare her child. The doctor gently lifted the overwrought mother to her feet and placed her in Kate's care.

"Keep her quiet so I can do my work," he directed, before returning to his patient.

She held the sobbing woman in her arms until the shaking ceased. From a short distance away she heard Captain Tom speaking to Doctor Morrison.

"Doc, there anything I can do to help?"

"You can tell Chief Gallagher to hitch up his paddy wagon and bring it down here. Then you can use it to drive these people to the hospital."

"On my way." The captain started across the yard.

A fireman approached and wearily laid another woman on the ground. "This is the last one. Nobody else is up there. The fire is almost out." He loped back to the building.

Under the soot that begrimed the face of the newly arrived victim, Kate recognized Carmela Cabrillo, her staring eyes showing white in the moonlight. The doctor closed the lids.

"She's gone."

Kate tried to swallow back the tears, but they brimmed over, trailing down her cheeks. Her nerves reacted fiercely to the sight of pain, destruction and death. She needed to take part in controlling the disaster.

"My auto is available. I can take someone to the hospital and help your wife get ready for the others."

"Fine. Drive through the side entrance on this side of the building."

As she passed through the crowd on her way to her car, she glanced at the cannery's second floor windows. The smoke was reduced to wisps and four gaping black holes stood where windows had once reflected the light. From the outside, most of the building appeared unaffected by the calamity. A more devastating toll was taken in human suffering.

Glaring electric lights welcomed Kate as she entered the ten bed hospital on Superior Avenue. Only two of the beds lined against the gray walls were occupied, most ill people preferring to be cared for at home. She knew the injured young cannery worker accompanying her thought the ride uptown had been torturously long.

Kate was relieved to see Nancy Morrison, dressed in her white nurse's uniform, meet them before they were halfway across the room. The doctor's wife had her silvering auburn hair neatly rolled in a net at her nape.

"Come this way, please." She showed them to the examining room at the far side of the ward.

"The doctor said to prepare for six more burn patients. You'll be needing at least three beds in the women's section. He also suggested calling in the Ladies' Aid Society to help." Kate spoke as they walked. "I'll stay as long as you need me."

"Your help is appreciated. While I tend to this patient, you can call Wilhelmina Christian and ask her to send a few ladies here to help us. The telephone is there." Nancy waved toward a corner of the doctor's office. "When you're through, I could use your help with this woman."

At the offhand request, Kate's stomach felt as though she had swallowed a cannonball. She stared at the wooden callbox that had suddenly grown horns and looked prepared to attack her. With squared shoulders and forced determination, she picked up the receiver, cranked the handle, and asked the operator to connect her with the mayor's home. In order that the self-righteous snob would not refuse to work with her, she did not identify herself and requested aid using the doctor's name. There would certainly be an uncomfortable confrontation with the arrival of The Hill's self-appointed queen, but Kate was resolved not to let them chase her from the hospital.

After reporting for duty with Mrs. Morrison, she was too busy to think about the imminent arrival of Wilhelmina and her cohorts. She spread linens on beds, set out instruments and supplies, and assisted the nurse.

Kate was tucking a sheet corner under a mattress when she heard footsteps behind her. Upon looking up, she saw four women standing in the middle of the room gawking at her. The mayor's wife was in the forefront, a haughty expression pinching her mouth.

"What are you doing here?" the matron demanded.

"The same as you." Kate's voice was steady. She continued to work as though nothing of importance were happening.

"I shall inform Nancy that I refuse to be in the same room with you. She didn't take into consideration my aversion to you when she spoke to me on the telephone."

Kate straightened up and faced Wilhelmina toe to toe.

"You spoke to me, not Mrs. Morrison. In spite of our differences, we are all needed here. Helping injured people is more important than your moral prejudices or my pride. If you don't think so, then you're free to leave. I'm staying."

From the corner of her vision, Kate noticed the door to the examining room open and the nurse stand at the doorway.

"Ah. there you are ladies. You're just in time. Patients are arriving at the office entrance. Come along quickly."

Without hesitation, Kate turned her back on the mayor's wife and walked toward the examining room for further instructions. She was determined to do whatever was needed and ignore the poisoned barbs aimed at her. Not a word passed between them as the the other ladies filed out of the ward behind her.

Kate worked at a hectic pace set by the rapid-fire instructions of the Morrisons. She was not surprised when two aid society volunteers could not tolerate the sight of tortured flesh and begged to be put to use away from the victims. Her own courage was sorely tried by the gory sight. Forced to work beside Wilhelmina, Kate held her antagonism at bay while she put her energy toward a more constructive purpose.

When Dorothea was brought in, Kate went to her and helped the doctor minister to the burns. The young woman was conscious and wept with agony. A liberal dose of morphine brought the suffering under control. Kate spoke to her softly and held her hand while the wounds on her arms and legs were cleaned and treated. She knew her housekeeper's daughter was too drugged to understand what was happening.

"She's a friend of mine, doctor. Will she be all right?"

"There's always a chance of infection. We'll keep her here for a while so we can watch her. She's young and strong. With the proper care, there's a good chance she'll come out of this with only a few scars. Once we have her settled into a bed, you can speak to Mrs. Mendez in the next room. She can sit with her daughter for a while." The doctor patted her arm in reassurance.

"Thank you." She was grateful for his consideration for Blanca.

As the physician lifted Dorothea and carried her into the ward, Kate went out the opposite door into the narrow waiting room. She spied Blanca standing against the wall, all the seats taken by those more in need. Kate went to her and slipped a sympathetic arm around her shoulders. She repeated the doctor's hopeful comments and permission for her to stay by the sickbed. Blanca hugged her before heading for the door to the ward.

Panning the waiting area to estimate how many more people still needed to be cared for, Kate noticed Sam Wakely speaking with Captain Tom. Henry Slater was on his way out of the back door. She joined her two friends.

"Hello, Katydid. I didn't expect to see you here with Wilhelmina's Ladies' Aid Society. What kind of miracle is this?" Sam raised his eyebrows in surprise.

"I'm not here with them, but in spite of them. We're all here to help. Tomorrow they'll probably return to their old spiteful selves. I just saw Hank Slater leave. What was he doing here?" Kate felt more anger toward the factory owner than usual, and she was looking for more reasons to hate him.

"He wanted the names of the people who are injured so he can notify their families." The publisher spoke around the unlit cigar butt jutting from his mouth.

"It's about time he thought of the welfare of his employees." She surveyed the waiting room, filled to capacity with hurt cannery workers.

Kate was certain the unsafe practices and neglect of the management was responsible for the severity of the wounds and Carmela's death.

She looked at Captain Tom. "I'll be staying here for a while. You can go home without me. I'll be fine."

"These folks'll be needin' a ride home and I still have John's wagon hitched up." The old man nodded toward the fire victims waiting for medical care. "I'll be here long as I'm needed."

Kate flashed a tired smile in his direction.

"I'd better get back to work." She turned toward the examining room.

With a weary shake of her head, she eyed the people still waiting for treatment, smudged with smoke, pain haunting their eyes. A long, demanding night loomed ahead for her. With firm purpose in her step, she returned to the next room to assist the doctor.

On an evening two weeks after the fire, Kate answered a knock on the front door. She expected to see Gallagher and was disappointed when the visitor turned out to be Matthew Liszt. The cannery manager, his resplendent mustache fashionably curled and pomaded hair slicked flat to his head, greeted her with an expectant glitter in his eyes. She welcomed him with a familiar easiness as he entered the front hall.

"Gladys should be downstairs soon. We can wait for her in the parlor."

She led the young man into the sitting room and motioned him toward a sofa. Kate settled into a chair.

"I understand the cannery will be back in full operation tomorrow, Matt."

"Yes. We've been working hard to put the factory back in order, but the man who started the fire hasn't been found yet."

"I didn't know the fire was started intentionally. Does anyone have an idea who did it?"

"John Gallagher questioned everyone about a dark haired man who's missing half his small finger. He was an employee of ours before the fire. Then he suddenly disappeared."

Her awareness came alive with a jolt. There possibly was new information on the Carlisle investigation and that snake with a badge was keeping it from her. Kate seethed.

"Is there any speculation why the man would have set that fire?"

"Why would any arsonist start a fire? Maybe he has a grudge against the company or he's just plain crazy."

"Did Mr. Slater ever mention to you the possibility of selling the cannery?" The appearance at the cannery of the man Gallagher was looking for was too much of a coincidence to be innocent. Carlisle had to be linked to the fire.

"No, he hasn't, but I'm only one of his managers. Its not likely he would discuss such an intention with me. Why do you ask?"

"There seems to be a lot going on under the surface here. I was just wondering what it all meant." Kate tried to sound nonchalant so Matt would not continue to wonder at the motive for her questions.

"Would you know how Dorothea Mendez is doing? I know she's your housekeeper's daughter."

"She's mending well and should be out of the hospital in another week. Her friends from the cannery visit her regularly. They want safety reforms at work and are prepared to fight for them. I was asked to speak with Mr. Slater on their behalf. Do you think he'll be more receptive since the bad publicity on the fire?"

Matthew smiled, although his eyes showed regret.

"You can speak with him if you like, but it won't be necessary. We've already instituted new safety and health measures to begin when we officially reopen tomorrow. There'll be no more locked doors during working hours and windows will be open for ventilation, among other changes. I'm certain Mr. Slater would welcome you to take another tour of the cannery. He's invited Sam Wakely from the *Gazette* to look around."

"I'm glad he's taken the initiative. I wasn't looking forward to clashing with him."

Kate was pleased with Henry Slater's new concern for his employees and made a mental note to take Matthew up on his offer of a tour. She looked up as the sound of footsteps drifted in from the hall.

Gladys, her lustrous blond hair neatly swept up in a pompadour and bun, and her ample figure draped in a waistless blue dress, entered the room. Her betrothed immediately rose and went to her, kissing her lightly on the cheek. From the engrossed light in their eyes, Kate was certain they forgot her presence for the moment. When they finally looked her way, it was to announce their departure.

She walked with them to the door to see if she could spy Gallagher. Kate had expected him when Matthew had appeared. As the young couple made their way across the lamplit lawn, she caught sight of John tying his horse's reins to the lamppost. He exchanged a few words with the two people exiting through the gate before he entered the yard.

Gallagher saw Kate standing on the porch, her fists on her hips, elbows out. One foot tapped rapidly on the floorboard. If he could see her face in the dark shadows, he was certain it would be tight-lipped. As a boy, he had often seen his mother stand in such a way just before going for him with a switch. He knew he was in for an earful now, unless he could manage to soften the little tiger's temper.

Without a word, he bounded up the few steps to the porch and wrapped his arms around her. His mouth came down on hers for a devouring kiss. He felt her resistance, but refused to relinquish his hold until she pounded on his arms with her tiny fists.

"You can't jolly your way out of this, you deceitful worm," she declared, breaking free of his hold.

"What've I done this time?" He expected a petty complaint about his safety precautions.

"You didn't tell me about Jeffrey Carlisle trying to move in on the Montezuma Cannery."

"Who told you that?"

"I figured it out for myself. Matt told me you've been asking about the man with half a finger who worked at the factory. You and I know that Star Enterprises will try to buy out Hank Slater. What're we going to do about it?"

"*We* aren't going to do anything. I can't move until I have proof of a crime and you'll stay clear of this mess. I don't want Carlisle coming after you. You've suffered enough because of him."

Kate ignored his no nonsense tone of voice.

"That's exactly what we *do* want. If he tries to hurt me, it'll prove he has something to hide. Besides, Captain Tom is watching over me. Nothing can happen when I'm so well protected and Henry Slater should be warned. You can't let the cannery be practically stolen from him."

"Keep away from Slater and Carlisle, young lady, or I'll lock you up in this house until it's all settled. This could get dangerous and I don't want to have to worry about you."

His moonlit gaze held hers prisoner, but she would not let him intimidate her. She needed to play a part in crushing Carlisle. Her loyalty to her father demanded it.

"I have business with Henry. His workers want me to represent them. They're counting on me." She knew it sounded like a weak excuse even as the words passed her lips.

"It'll wait. You'll have to trust me and do as you're told. I won't hear another word about it. Now, let's go into the house."

Gallagher opened the door and stepped aside for her to enter before him. She scorched him with a hostile glare as she stepped inside. He was not fooled by her supposed surrender for one minute. No doubt, the stubborn little schemer would find some way to get herself into trouble. His job was to head her off.

"Where's Cappy? I need to speak with him alone for a few minutes."

"He's in the kitchen, but telling him to keep a close eye on me won't do any good. I'll do what I want anyway." Gallagher watched her step into the front parlor and seat herself in front of the piano.

He shook his head in exasperated acknowledgment of the truth she had just spoken, but he had to try for his conscience's sake. The lively rhythm of Scott Joplin's ragtime music accompanied him on his way to the kitchen.

Captain Tom sat at the table with a San Francisco newspaper spread out before him. He looked up as Gallagher entered the room,

"Hello, John. Looks like someone's been stompin' on your toes. You and Katie been fightin' again?"

"Not exactly." Gallagher turned a chair around and straddled it backward. He rested his arms across the back.

"She suspects Carlisle is after Slater's cannery and she wants to warn him."

Tom let his breath out in a long whistle.

"Knew this would happen eventually. Surprised she didn't think of it before. How much does she know?"

"Not as much as she thinks she does, but she's a good guesser. I don't want her in on our plans. She could get hurt. We've got to keep her away from the Slaters and that means Bea also. Do you think you can handle that?"

"Reckon so. I may be an old man, but no little gal's gonna walk over me." He spoke with surety. "By the way, how's it goin'? Did the fish bite yet?"

"We got a nibble. A Sacramento lawyer called Slater with an offer to buy him out and they set up a meeting. He represented Star Enterprises. Too bad we lost track of the man we think started the fire. Without him we don't have a case. But we'll keep trying." Gallagher rubbed his hands over his face as though to scrub away the weariness.

"You'll eventually catch him. He's bound to make a mistake sometime. Meanwhile, I'll keep a watch on our little handful so she don't get into mischief."

"Thanks, Cappy. Without you here, there's no telling what she's likely to do. I'd best get back to her before she gets curious about what we're talking about for so long." Gallagher rose to his feet.

He did not want to chance her overhearing any part of this conversation. She was difficult to control at best and if she set her mind to working against him, all his well-laid plans could end in ruins.

Kate gently returned the telephone receiver to its hook and tiptoed down the hall to the rear of the house. In an act of acute frustration, she had secretly called Bea Slater and begged to meet with her discretely around the corner of the street.

Since her discovery two weeks before that the fire at the cannery was possibly set by the man who was missing a finger, Captain Tom had thwarted her every attempt to speak to the Slaters. He sat now like a sentinel on the front porch, ready to keep her from visiting her neighbor across the road. A short telephone conversation with Bea might be managed without the captain's knowledge, but the two operators at the town's switchboard were notorious for eavesdropping on conversations. What Kate had to say was not for public announcement.

She let herself out through the back door, crossed the garden, and circled around the carriage port at the side of the house. Before covering the short distance along the driveway to the street, she furtively checked the porch to find Captain Tom ensconced in a rocking chair, his face turned away from her. Kate flitted across the open area and disappeared on the far side of the high hedges belonging to the property next door.

A nervous giggle escaped her at the ease with which she avoided detection. Her brisk gait soon took her to the corner and she turned right, passing the imposing mansions of her neighbors. Kate finally halted under the partial cover of low, leafy branches of an oak tree extending above the sidewalk.

Her mind turned somersaults as she waited for her friend to appear. John was up to something and she had to discover what it was. She was directly responsible for bringing the activities of Star Enterprises and Jeffrey Carlisle to his attention, and he would not exclude her from the final showdown. His oppressive protection seemed ludicrous and would intensify once he discovered their impending parenthood.

Kate was certain, since she missed her second feminine course, that a new life grew inside her womb. Although her waist was as tiny as ever, her breasts were exceedingly tender and spells of nausea plagued her. A trap had to be set for Carlisle soon or her overbearing protectors would keep her away from the action even if they had to cart her out of town. It was imperative that she warn the Slaters and ferret out John's plans to end the case.

Kate saw the gracefully tall figure of Beatrice Slater round the corner and head toward her. Her neatly coifed dark hair glowed with a rich patina under the turned up narrow brim of her hat. Warm brown eyes greeted Kate with an amused glimmer.

"This is rather melodramatic, Dear. I know we are being kept apart, but wouldn't a talk on the telephone have done just as well?"

"This is too personal to be said over the public phone lines, and no one will bother us here."

"What could be so important that you need to see me? You look peaked. Have you been ill?" Concern furrowed Bea's brow.

The discomfort of early pregnancy was the cause of her wanness, but Kate chose not to disclose that information just yet.

"I'm fine." She tried to sound convincing. "I have to talk to you about the cannery."

"That's Hank's responsibility and he doesn't confide in me, but I can relay any questions you may have. It probably wouldn't do any good, though. You and I aren't supposed to be communicating. It puzzles me deeply why John Gallagher is so vehement about keeping you and me apart. When I questioned him about it, he suggested I ask my husband. Hank simply told me that there were some problems because of the fire and you were determined to cause more trouble. What's happening, Kate?"

"There's a corporation that's been buying out companies having financial problems. It bought Moore Freighting. All these companies had costly accidents before the sale. I think the mishaps were planned to get the owners to sell cheaply, but I can't prove it. I want you to warn Henry not to sell the cannery to Star Enterprises."

Bea's eyes rounded in surprise and apprehension.

"A man from Star Enterprises called Henry on the telephone at home. They made an appointment to meet. Right after that call, Hank asked the operator to ring up Chief Gallagher. Then he told me to leave the room. It sounds like Hank has already been warned."

"It seems so. Maybe Jeffrey Carlisle won't get away with it this time."

Mrs. Slater's creamy complexion turned pasty white.

"What does Jeffrey Carlisle have to do with this?"

"He owns Star Enterprises. I think he killed my father."

In thick silence Kate watched the rapid play of emotions cross Bea's features.

"Your father's freight company experienced a rash of accidents and he suspected Mr. Carlisle was somehow connected with it. He was determined to discover the truth and came very near doing so when he died. I was so distraught over his death and harassed by scandal that it never occurred to me Jeffrey Carlisle might have been at fault. And now Hank is involved with him." Her voice ended on a desperate note.

Kate wrapped her arm around Bea's back in a comforting gesture.

"I'll do my best to see that vile man comes to justice and I'm sure John will protect Henry."

"No! You must promise to stay away from this. I would never forgive myself, if you came to harm because of something I told you. Besides, Henry and Chief Gallagher seem to be working together on the problem. Promise you won't interfere."

Kate considered for a long moment before giving her reply. With Captain Tom guarding her so closely and the solution to the case imminent, she did not have much choice but to stand aside. Common sense dictated a passive role, but her instincts were in full rebellion. The investigation had been initiated by her and her pride was insulted when they shunted her into a corner while they played out the last critical moves of the game. She would offer a compromise.

"I promise to stand back for one week. If nothing is accomplished by then, my promise will be withdrawn. You can't ask more of me."

Bea paused before answering. She chewed her fingernail and grimaced.

"All right, if that's the best you can do."

"I knew you would understand. Now, I have to return to the house before Captain Tom realizes I'm gone."

As they started toward the corner at a leisurely pace, a tentative plan to set fate in motion took form in Kate's mind. She set her target on the special election date ten days away.

CHAPTER XXI

Sunlight and tangy autumn air poured through the open windows of the City Hall meeting chamber. A steady trickle of men entered the polling place on the afternoon of October tenth. Although it was not the major election day of the year, local interest in the women's suffrage question ran high and the voter turnout was brisk. For the first time in the history of River Run, women were permitted entry to the room where men filled out their ballots. Kate, Rebecca Willis, and Blanca Mendez stood behind the ballot boxes as the voters straggled past.

Kate stifled a giggle as Mayor Christian gingerly dropped his ballot into the box and bestowed a warm smile on her. She remembered how she had conned him into allowing the California Equal Suffrage Association to supply poll watchers to insure the honesty of the election. Her mentioning that women in New York had been poll watchers for years, even though they could not vote, had not swayed the Mayor. But when she had pointed out that he was up for re-election next year, his attitude changed. If women won the vote now, they would remember his confidence in them when his name was on the ballot.

The musical sound of the Spanish language floated to her from a few yards away. Blanca questioned a man who had the appearance of a migrant worker. This morning, the housekeeper had rooted out at least a dozen aliens who were paid a dollar each by Southside bartenders to vote against women's suffrage. The women had caught a few men trying to vote twice and had thwarted several attempts to drop more than one ballot into the box at a time. once word had circulated that cheating would not be tolerated, attempts had slowed to a sparse few. In fact, Officer Taylor, who handled offenders with firm assistance to the door, stood idle for the past hour.

Unconsciously, Kate rested her hand on her belly and gave it a maternal pat. She had let out her corset ties a bit at the waist, but that did not show in the loose fitting current fashions. No one seemed to suspect her condition except for Blanca who clucked over her employer's queasy stomach and would not permit her to lift or push anything heavy. Given another month, her figure would change noticably and her secret would announce itself to the world.

She did not look forward to the resurgence of disdainful glares and nasty whispers as she passed. Antagonism toward her had calmed since she had worked beside the Ladies' Aid Society volunteers at the hospital on the night of the fire. A mutual respect had developed during that trying episode. The repaired feelings did not approach the point of friendship, but even a shaky tolerance was a vast improvement over the venomous attacks. Sam Wakely's coverage of the volunteer effort at the hospital had also gone a long way toward boosting her public image.

Today at the polls, men eyed her with curiosity, but the lascivious leers she was subjected to since the damaging rumors began were absent. Although there was little danger now of an attack by the townsfolk, Captain Tom continued his guard duty. While the men voted, he stood vigil against the wall behind his charge. Kate knew that so long as Star Enterprises maneuvered to gain possession of the cannery, Jeffrey Carlisle posed an ugly threat.

Throughout the day, she watched for the arrival of Jeffrey Carlisle so she could launch her plan. Her proposed course of action was dangerous, but caution had produced unsatisfying results and it was time to challenge the devil.

Now in the late afternoon, Kate looked up and surveyed the room, spotting the hated attorney as he marched into the meeting hall. Her heart picked up its tempo and adrenalin pumped through her blood. Knowing the captain would watch her every move, especially when her nemesis was in the room, she had prepared an indirect method of communication. She removed a small envelope from her reticule and turned toward Blanca who stood a few steps away. From the side of her vision, she glimpsed Captain Macaphee, his gaze fixed on Carlisle. In an instant, she stood beside Blanca, pressed the envelope into the woman's hand, whispered instructions, and pointed out the man with the handlebar mustache. The housekeeper frowned and hesitated for a few seconds before leaving her station. Kate's shoulders sagged with her relief.

She returned to her assigned spot, once again looking at the captain who regarded her with apparent curiosity. Her rapid sweep of the room caught Carlisle staring in her direction, holding the closed message in his hand. She allowed herself a subtle smile while he extracted the small slip of paper from its envelope and read the short note. Kate recited the written words in her mind as she imagined him reading. *I know why you killed my father.* Not overly poetic, she judged, but to the point. His eyes came up to meet hers, incredulous at first, then changing from shock, to malice ... to murder. Fear smothered her like a pillow held over her face and she moved closer to the captain. This malevolent reaction was what she had hoped to evoke from him. Yet, now that it was attained, she could not help feeling she had made a mistake. She brazened out the uncomfortable moment with a broad smile and a salutary nod of her head. He broke eye contact and headed toward a ballot box on the far side of the room from Kate. Carlisle voted and left without turning toward her again.

It was done. There could be no retreating to safety while John took his time setting his trap. Her enemy would stalk her like a wolf does its prey and there would be nowhere to hide. She would have to warn Captain Tom, but not just yet. He would immediately force her into seclusion and she would miss the suffrage jubilee planned for that evening. She had worked too long and hard to miss the excitement as they waited for the election results. While surrounded with a crowd of people and guarded by the captain, she thought the chances of anyone attacking her would be small. Besides, she planned to carry her pistol in her reticule for extra protection. Tomorrow was early enough to apprise John and Tom of her action. Until then, she needed to be alert to the added danger.

Crackling bonfires illuminated the river bank, the red and yellow light reflecting in the dark flow of water. Nearly two hundred enthusiastic people milled in the firelit River Run picnic ground. Grotesque shadows danced in answer to the flicker of flames. Many of the revelers were not staunch supports of women's suffrage, but came to enjoy the lively music and festive atmosphere.

Kate's nerves tingled as she moved through the crowd. She was aware that not everyone might wish her well. This had been a long, tension infused day for her and she felt drained. Again, she checked beside her to see that Captain Tom was not separated from her by the jostling crowd. Three hours had passed since the closing of the polls and she impatiently awaited word of the local election results. After that she would take her leave with great relief.

She thought of Abigail Penny and Victoria Simpson watching over the vote counters to insure against chicanery by the opposition. The two ladies would bring news when they knew the outcome. Women's suffrage needed a huge win in the rural areas to overcome the expected losses in the big cities. If this area lost, there would not be much hope of the law passing.

Carolyn Parkhurst approached Kate, her eyes glimmering with exhilaration.

"Victoria just arrived and is ready to make an announcement. Hurry."

Kate felt her arm clasped by her friend who hauled her through the press of people toward the platform where the brass band stood. A blaring trumpet fanfare called attention to the tall, buxom lady ascending the stage. Her voice rose over the hushed murmur of the audience. Kate leaned forward in expectation.

"The count is in. Women's suffrage won a resounding victory in River Run. Let us hope that the rest of the state voted as wisely."

Roaring cheers drowned out the remainder of Mrs. Simpson's speech. Firecrackers exploded outside the circle of bonfires while women hugged each other in elation, dancing, laughing, clinging together with sheer joy. Kate exulted in the small triumph, unwilling to consider that other parts of California could overrule their decision. She joined in a rapid succession of feminine embraces as the Petticoat Gang descended upon her in a madcap celebration. The heat of the fires and bodies surging around her combined with the excitement brought a high flush to her cheeks. Flickering yellow flames added to the dizzying whirl of motion. Her lungs struggled for air, but she could not raise her head above the shoulders of the people who blocked her from the fresh river breeze. As the familiar nauseous roil in her stomach threatened to erupt, panic gave her the extra strength to force her way through the noisy throng to the river's edge. She inhaled the cool air in deep gulps until her discomfort eased.

"You all right, Kitten?"

The captain's concerned voice reassured her.

"Yes. A little too much excitement, that's all. This has been a busy day."

"Too busy, looks like to me. A hot bath and bed is just what you need."

"That sounds like heaven. Let's go."

Kate turned back to wend her way through the crowd, with Captain Tom positioning himself in front of her to open a path. Gratefully, she followed in his wake. Friends questioned her early departure as she passed them, shouting above the clamor of music, firecrackers and happy voices. To each she pleaded fatigue and a promise to visit soon.

As she left the bonfires and noise behind, darkness wrapped itself around her like a shroud. The moon had not yet risen and Kate could not see the sparse grass that she knew grew near her feet. Dry stalks rustled in the breeze and crickets sang their courting song while the people noises grew fainter with every step. Captain Tom appeared no more than a shadow beside her, the thud of his footsteps more an indication of his presence than the sight of him. Her heart sounded loud in her ears. Instinctively, she fumbled in her cloth purse to feel the cool iron of the pistol. The string of glass beads nestled against the backs of her fingers as she disturbed their resting place beside the gun.

Kate knew they reached the road when a steep incline leveled out to a packed dirt strip. The nerves along her shoulders relaxed a notch. They would come to the parked Pierce-Arrow at any moment and she could turn on the headlight. She almost bumped into the auto before seeing its angular line. Relief brought a tired smile to her lips.

From behind her, a muffled groan caught her attention. Before she could turn to investigate, a brutal hand covered her mouth and pulled her head back against a thickly muscled chest. The pistol was in her hand, the velvet of the purse still covering it. She could shoot through the material if only there were a target. Furiously, she fought for a foothold to twist and face her attacker. Her elbow caught the assailant in the ribs, and his hold tightened convulsively, forcing a meaty finger between her lips. She bit down hard and tasted blood. The hand dropped from her face and she spun around, aiming the pistol at the hulking shadow. Kate stumbled sideways as the man hit her with the force of a battering ram. The pistol barked, firing harmlessly into the night. An oath rose in her throat. The side of her head exploded in a stunning pain, shattering into thousands of tiny stars. She drifted into darkness.

CHAPTER XXII

Kate opened her eyes to the familiar surroundings of an office. She found herself seated on a wooden chair facing a large desk. Pictures of shallow-hulled river vessels hung on the walls and glimpses of her youth flashed through her mind. This used to be her father's office at the Moore Freighting warehouse. How did she come to be here? An abrupt movement of her head brought a pounding pain to her left temple. Gingerly, she probed the sore place with her fingertips and they came away with congealed blood. Memory of her terror on the dark road returned with shattering force. Captain Tom! She prayed in silence that he was not badly hurt. Masculine voices from behind her chair snared her attention. Kate turned slowly to see Jeffrey Carlisle conferring with a tall grizzly bear of a man. The coarse, unkempt appearance of the stranger contrasted incongruously with the meticulous lawyer.

"Ah, I see you are finally awake, my dear. You've been asleep for nearly an hour. My assistant is too enthusiastic in his duties, but highly effective. Unfortunately for you, you are not in a position to appreciate his talents." Carlisle chatted easily, seeming to savor her discomfort as he might a well seasoned meal. "Lester and I have had a long, successful acquaintance. I believe your father met him shortly before his death."

She read the malice in his eyes, while her fingers worked at the drawstring of her reticule that was wrapped around her wrist. The purse felt too light to still contain the pistol, but she hoped the yellow necklace remained in her possession. Her racing heartbeat calmed when the string of beads spilled onto her lap.

Carlisle strode past her to stand in front of the desk where she could see him without turning. Lester's hands rested on her shoulders. She cringed at his touch and ventured a peek at the thick fingers covered with a mat of dark hair. The last joint of the small finger on his right hand had been sliced away and healed, leaving the bone exposed. She swallowed back the revulsion and fear rising in her throat.

"That charming note you sent to me lacked finesse, but it certainly caught my attention. I wonder why you sent it when you think you could destroy me. Why the warning?"

When Kate did not answer, the attorney continued.

"I see you're not in a talkative mood. Perhaps, my friend can persuade you to be more cooperative. How did you find out your father was killed because he discovered Lester?"

The fingers on her shoulders tightened painfully and she thought it prudent to answer.

"I didn't. You just told me."

His eyes bored into her and he shook his head.

"This is such a waste. What did you hope to accomplish with your deceitful little note? Did you think you could make me sweat?" His laugh was mirthless. "That was a deadly mistake. Now you'll tell me how much you know and what your policeman friend is up to. He's seen a lot of Henry Slater recently and you're going to tell me about their plans."

Although Carlisle spoke softly, Kate recognized a maniacal gleam in his eyes that did not bode well for her future. Knowing her captors were capable of murder and would not set her free, she fought back the panic threatening to paralyze her mind. Her survival depended on her alertness. If an opportunity for escape presented itself, she needed to be ready to avail herself of it. Her best chance was to stay alive long enough to be rescued. John would eventually realize she was missing and search for her. Carlisle would top the list of his suspects. But, as certain as she was that he would look for her, she could not depend on his intervention. Her plan was to keep the lawyer talking and hope to give John enough time to find her.

"I don't know if they're planning anything. Chief Gallagher doesn't discuss business with me. Do you plan to take over the cannery?"

"You amaze me. my question goes unanswered and you ask me one of your own. Don't you understand who is in charge here?"

"I answered your question as honestly as I could. He's investigating the possibility of arson at the cannery fire. That's all I know."

"Why do you insist on lying? My money and power will win over them in the end. Their efforts are useless. You can save them the trouble of prolonging Slater's struggle to save his factory. He will lose it anyway."

"Is the cannery your only concern? Don't you think kidnaping me will cause you any problems?"

"Kidnaping is the least of my sins." Amusement pulled his lips up into a near smile. "Your disappearance won't lead anyone to me. If they ever find you, you won't be in any condition to talk. The old man who was with you saw nothing. This chitchat is becoming tiresome, Katherine. Answer my questions or I will allow Lester to be creative. For him, brutality is an art."

Thick fingers dug into her hair and pulled until a moan nearly escaped from her clamped lips.

"How much does Gallagher know?" Carlisle asked.

"I don't know. He doesn't tell me everything."

Carlisle nodded and the big man removed his hand from her hair and lowered it, grabbing her breast. He tightened his fingers like a vice and she gasped at the pain, clawing at the punishing digits. Her tormentor finally laughed aloud and released her.

"A fighter. Good. I'll have some fun." The deep voice came from above her head.

Kate looked up at Carlisle and was surprised to find distaste evident on his features. Perhaps, he would not allow the brute to inflict too much damage on her. She had no information to give, but would have remained silent even if she did know something useful to them.

"There's no use torturing you. The police can't touch me without proof." His gaze switched from Kate to Lester. "Take her downriver to the marsh below Sherman Island. Make sure she doesn't come back."

"Sure thing, boss."

He yanked her out of her seat by her arm. Her breath caught on a sob as her beloved yellow beads slid from her lap and rolled beneath the desk.

"The police will come looking for me," she warned.

"They won't find you here. You truly are a nuisance. No wonder your mother threw you out. Lester, get her out of here."

The crude man secured her hands together behind her back with a heavy rope and gagged her mouth with a kerchief. He pulled her by the arm to the rear door of the office while panic rose in Kate's belly. She had to stall for time or she would be dead before John could find her.

"Come along. We have a nice cozy boat ride ahead of us, just you and me."

When his knuckles brushed along the side of her breast, searing anger sparked inside Kate and she retaliated with a kick to his shin. If her balance had permitted, she would have chosen a higher target. His fist met her jaw and she felt nothing before blackness overtook her.

A half moon rose over the road to the River Run picnic area, lending enough light to distinguish shapes but not much else. On horseback, Gallagher nodded with satisfaction as he recognized the Pierce-Arrow parked on the side of the road. He would take Kate home and make certain she stayed there. If what Beatrice Slater had just told him were true, his headstrong rebel was looking for trouble in Carlisle's direction. Turning his horse toward the river where bonfires lit up the shore, he reached the edge of the crowd of celebrants. Gallegher dismounted and tied the reins to a bush.

Even from the added height of the saddle, he had not been able to catch a glimpse of Kate in the crowd, but he had noticed a few of her friends. Gallagher approached Rebecca Willis and Abigail Penny.

"Have either of you seen Kate around?"

"Captain Macaphee took her home about half an hour ago," Abby replied.

Gallagher frowned.

"That couldn't be. Her auto is still here."

The two women shrugged their shoulders. With renewed determination, he looked everywhere in the lit area, but his search for the illusive lady proved futile. Now confused, John sought out other friends of hers only to receive the same answer he had received from Abigail. No one had seen her since she had said good-bye.

A black feeling gnawed at the edge of his composure. Where could she be? At least, Cappy was with her. That was some consolation. From a bonfire, Gallagher separated a piece of wood that was lit on one end to use as a torch light. He untied his horse and walked back toward the road, peering in every direction as he went. His alarm grew greater with every cautious step.

Ahead loomed the shadowed shape of Kate's auto. Holding the torch high, he circled the motorcar, alert for signs of a struggle. He squatted to look closer at grooves in the earth that indicated boot heels were recently dragged through the area. Tense with dread, Gallagher followed the scarred ground to the far side of the Motorette and found a man's body stretched out face up.

It was Cappy. He knelt and pressed two fingers behind the captain's jaw to feel for a pulse. Yes. The flesh was warm and the beat was strong. Captain Tom groaned and his eyes opened. He reached up to touch the back of his head before struggling to sit. Dread wrenched at Gallagher's gut. Kate was unprotected.

"Somebody jumped me from behind and took her."

"I guessed as much. Was she near Carlisle lately? Beatrice Slater told me Kate wanted to bait him."

After a moment of thought, the captain shut his eyes in defeat.

"Didn't think much of it at the time. When Carlisle came to vote today, Kate left her post and spoke to Blanca. I was watchin' Kate walkin' back and forth and when I looked up again, Blanca was comin' back from Carlisle's direction, and he was starin' at Kate. He didn't look too happy."

"Damn." That one word summed up Gallagher's opinion of the situation. He wiped his hand across his face while clearing his mind. "I'm going back to town to get Jase and Rufus. Are you feeling well enough to get to your houseboat on your own?"

"Go on back to town and I'll wait here for you. Was me who let 'em take her and I'll help get her back."

"You're welcome to come along if you can keep up with us."

John handed the torch to the captain and stood. He mounted the roan and headed into town at a gallop.

Before Kate opened her eyes, she was aware of the soft soughing sound of water passing against the boards beneath her. Wooden oars knocked against metal oarlocks as the boat glided on the water. Cold spray sprinkled her face. Her jaw throbbed where the ham sized fist had connected and she moved the joint to discover if it was broken. The bones were intact, but her head ached. A damp chill bit through her clothes and she shivered. The woolen shawl she had worn earlier in the evening had disappeared by the time she arrived at the Moore Freighting warehouse. She tentatively moved her feet. They were free, but her wrists were still bound behind her. The tight binding impeded the circulation in her hands.

Furtively, she opened her eyes halfway, hoping that her captor would not notice she was awake. Hoary fog descended as the temperature dropped and she saw, as though through a veil, the hulking form of Lester pulling on the oars. She raised her head ever so slowly to peek over the side of the boat and get a bearing on where they were in relationship to the riverbanks. Behind them faint illumination flickered on the shore. Bonfires, people . . . safety. Disappointment tasted bitter on her tongue and she swallowed the urge to let a tear escape.

A healthy swim was all it would take to reach the shore, but with her hands tied back, that route of escape was an impossibility. Once they reached the shallow marsh, her chance of surviving a plunge would improve markedly . . . if she lived that long. The shaggy haired man sitting a few feet away was unpredictable. She was certain that he intended to take his pleasure with her, but how long would he wait? There was quite a distance to travel before they reached the end of Sherman Island.

She struggled against her rising panic at the repugnant memory of his hand touching her breast. Fighting his attack might incite him to hurt her. Could the fragile new life in her womb tolerate such treatment? Kate doubted it. Even if she managed to survive this night, there was a terrible chance her child would not.

Kate longed for the soothing feel of her string of beads rolling under her fingertips, but they were gone now, lost forever. Her eyes closed, as she tried to shut out the despair. A strong, smiling image appeared, blue eyes alive with love and humor, a stray lock of light hair falling across his brow. Gallagher's strength was a settling influence in her life, but she could not depend on him to rescue her from this predicament. He would not know she was missing until it was too late and then he could never find her. She had to rely on her own abilities. Her future and that of her child depended on her alone.

Time passed in slow motion as the boat took them downstream. She knew the thickening fog would hide them from the shore. Kate's arms were numb, her head and face ached, and she shivered with cold, but the physical discomfort was easier for her to ignore than her fear of the impending ordeal.

The rhythm of the oars and the passing water halted. Wood knocked against wood and she knew the paddles were being shipped. The boat rocked. He was coming for her now. Terrified, she peered over the side, hoping to see land nearby. Through the swirling fog she barely made out scrub bushes and mud islands in the distance. The dinghy was too far out into the current for her to stand on the river bottom, but no choice remained if she wanted a chance to live. To stay meant being raped and murdered. As slim as they were, the river offered better odds.

Swiftly, she catapulted up from the boat's floor in a desperate lunge to throw herself over the side. The sound of ripping material blended with a coarse laugh when her skirt tore in his hand, but held together enough to halt her flight. Her back hit the wooden floor with a thud, and his thick body toppled across hers, his unwashed stench suffocating her. Kicking and bucking to throw off his massive weight proved futile, yet she continued to struggle. He slashed at her clothing with a knife until they lay in remnants strewn about the boat.

"How much clothes you got on, woman?" He complained when he reached yet another layer of linen and lace.

He sheathed the knife and pulled up her chemise from the bottom, then grabbed her dainty drawers at the waist and yanked them down, exposing her female secrets and slim legs. A scream rose in her throat to be muffled by the gag in her mouth. She saw him balanced on his knees for a moment, one hand squarely on her chest, holding her down, the other fumbled at the buttons to his pants. The garment fell around his knees and she gasped in terror at the sight of his swollen manhood. Her renewed kicking toppled him sideways as the boat rocked and his pants hobbled him. Kate rolled the opposite way, and slid out from under his hand. The boat tipped, sending Lester crashing against its side. She drew a deep breath and hurled herself over the opposite side.

Frigid water enveloped her, dragging her down, down, clutching at her limbs, sucking her into the river's heart. When the initial shock of escape registered, she confronted this new opponent with desperate determination. Free of most of her clothing, her legs pumped easily as they propelled her toward the surface and away from the boat and its deadly passenger. She did not have much current to fight here in the sheltered tangle of islands and marsh, but she fell deeper than she hoped and her lungs screamed for air. Her legs pumped against the pressure that urged her toward the muddy bottom. Her heartbeat drummed in her ears.

Then she burst through the surface, unable to open her gagged mouth to gulp in the oxygen her laboring lungs demanded. Treading water, she concentrated on calming herself. In the dark and concealing fog, she was hidden from her pursuer's sight, but he still might hear her. A short distance off, she made out the vague outline of the boat.

Once her breathing was steady she headed for land, moving her legs like a frog so the splashing would not attract attention. The sound of oars dipping into water came to Kate and she knew the beast followed her. She redoubled her efforts until tall grass loomed ahead, then lowered her aching legs to test if they touched bottom. When she stood, water came to her waist and she waded to the mud bank, keeping to the low shrubs which were the only camouflage available.

"You can't hide from me, my pet. Come to Papa." Lester's voice crooned to her from out of the mist.

He unerringly followed her, although she was certain he could not see her. Her glance down spotted the distinct trail left by her shoes in the mud. She changed direction, seeking the aid of the water and tall grass in this deadly game of Hide and Seek. His demonic voice haunted her, spurring her to a reckless pace that outreached pain or thought. Her shoes sank into the slime, impeding her progress, but with her hands tied she could not undo the buttons and slip them off.

Silence. The nerve bending voice had stopped. Where was he? Kate peered into the gloom, but her sight could not penetrate far into the black night and swirling mist. He was on her suddenly, huge hands grasping, his muscled bulk shoving her off balance to fall heavily. Water exploded around them with the impact of their bodies. Superior agility gave her an advantage over the hulking size of the man who floundered in the shallows. Before his struggles stopped, she escaped into the eerie, danger infested marsh.

A sharp bark sliced through the night on the fog shrouded dock. Gallagher came to a halt from a lung burning run and knelt beside Rufus who stood rigid, attention riveted to a back door of the Moore Freighting warehouse. He surveyed the area while his labored breathing and galloping heart calmed a bit. The mongrel had followed Kate's scent at the picnic ground down to the river, where they had found her shawl and signs of where a rowboat had been pushed off. They had lost the trail until Rufus had picked it up again on this dock.

Officer Taylor bounded across the dock and hunkered down beside his boss and the dog.

"The captain'll be along in a minute. Is this where the boat landed?" Jason whispered.

"Ruf thinks so. I'll check out that lit window. When Cappy gets here, tell him to go around the front and make sure nobody leaves that way."

Gallagher kept low as he advanced to the side of the lit window while keeping to the shadows. His hand found the reassuring coolness of his pistol and removed it from the holster. The window shade left two inches uncovered on the bottom and he knelt to peer through the opening. He peeked in just long enough to recognize Jeffrey Carlisle standing beside a desk, before the light was extinguished and footsteps shuffled on the floorboards in a hurried pace.

We spooked him, was Gallagher's thought as he tried the doorknob and motioned for Taylor to join him. The door was locked, but soon gave way under his powerful kick. They entered the office, guns drawn, to find it dark and empty. A door leading to the unlit warehouse stood open and the tapping of a man's running feet echoed off the walls.

"Go find him, boy," the Chief of Police told Rufus, giving the animal an encouraging pat to get him started.

He circled in the opposite direction from his deputy, through the piles of crated goods, toward the front of the huge storeroom. The dog plunged ahead, slowing now and again to retrace his steps.

"Police, Carlisle. You'd better come into the office and talk to us," Gallagher called into the darkness. "My dog could rip you apart before I can call him off."

As if on cue, Rufus snarled and his claws clicked on the floor in a dead run.

"I'm coming out." The lawyer's voice shook with panic. "Rufus. Here boy!"

The sounds made by the dog changed direction and Gallagher heard a man's slow step coming toward him.

"You should have identified yourself sooner. I thought you were robbers."

The police chief knew that was a lie, but made no comment. They entered the office followed by Taylor while the dog continued to growl.

Carlisle switched on an overhead light. John checked the attorney for a weapon and found none. He returned his firearm to its holder, but made no attempt to stop Rufus from snarling.

"Jase, watch the doors. We don't know who else could be here."

The policeman nodded, his gun in his hand.

"Explain yourself, Gallagher. Why are you here harassing me?" the lawyer demanded.

"Kate Moore's been kidnaped and we followed her trail here."

"As you can see, she isn't here. Now get out. You're on private property."

"You know where she is and you'll tell me."

Gallagher wrapped Carlisle's jacket lapels around his fists and pulled the man toward him.

"If she's hurt, I'll make you wish you were dead."

"This is highly illegal. I'll have your badge for this. You can't just come in here and accuse me."

Gallagher was distracted by Rufus pawing at something under the desk. Taylor stooped down to pick it up.

"Boss, look what Rufe found." The officer dangled a yellow bead necklace from his fingers.

Gallagher's heart lurched. He held out an upturned hand and Jason dropped the trinket into his palm. His fingers closed over the familiar glass beads, but not before he noticed a glob of dried blood on its smooth surface. overpowering fear for his courageous, foolish Kate turned to explosive rage.

John's fist drove into Carlisle's stomach, nearly felling the man as he clutched at the pain. The lawyer's head snapped back as Gallagher's fingers entwined in his hair and pulled.

"Tell me where she is or I'll beat you until your own mother wouldn't recognize you."

"You can't do that. It's assault. Taylor, tell him he's sworn to uphold the law. Reason with him." Carlisle's voice rose with anxiety.

"I don't know what you're talking about, sir. My boss is a regular pussycat. I think I'll step outside for a breath of fresh air while you two have a little discussion. It wouldn't surprise me if you fell down and hurt yourself. A warehouse can be a mighty dangerous place. You could break your ribs or knock out your teeth. There's no telling what could happen in here."

"Don't leave me alone with him. I only told Lester to scare her, but he took her here. He said he was taking her down the river. I tried to stop him. It wasn't my fault."

"You sniveling rat. If she dies, I'll kill you. Exactly where did he take her?" Gallagher's face nearly touched Carlisle's. His fingers still clutched hair.

"On a boat to the marsh past Sherman Island. I tried to stop him. I swear it."

"Cuff him, then take him in," Gallagher ordered.

With a powerful effort, he released the cowering man. He wanted to beat the lawyer to a bloody mass.

The police chief hurried out the back door and rounded the building with Rufus at his side. Nearing the street side of the warehouse, he heard the click of a gun hammer pulling back. He saw Tom guarding the front door.

"It's only me, Cappy."

"Did you find her?"

"No. We've got Carlisle. Someone's taken her downriver past Sherman Island and I need your help. Can you get your hands on a fast boat?"

"Sure can. If there's one thing I know, it's the river. Let's get goin'." Captain Tom was already moving toward the dock.

Kate's feet slipped out from beneath her in the slick mud. Unable to protect herself with her arms, which were still tied behind her, she twisted to the side and fell heavily onto her already bruised shoulder. Her legs, grown weary and numb with the hours of damp cold and forced movement through strength sapping mud and water, gave way often. If the fall could not be stopped with her knees, she preferred another bump on her side than to risk landing on her stomach. A host of discomforts plagued her, but thankfully cramps in her lower torso was not one of them. She prayed she was not spotting blood, foretelling of a miscarriage.

Again she picked herself up and trudged forward. Lester was slow but persistent in his pursuit and she could not afford a moment's rest. Fatigue, aggravated by cold dampness and a rhythmic pounding in her head, took their toll on her stamina.

The immediate future looked bleak indeed. If she managed to evade the hunter until morning when help might arrive, the fog that cloaked her movements would dissipate with the concealing night. She would be clear to her enemy's view in this shelterless morass of water, mud and low vegetation. One well aimed shot at her was all it would take to end this nightmare of terror and pain.

"Are you tired, sweets? You'll be able to rest soon. Look to the east." A demonic chuckle punctuated the baritone voice that had goaded her throughout the night.

Reluctantly, Kate turned her eyes in the direction of the rising sun. A red glow penetrated the mist and a bird twittered nearby. Morning. Despair flooded over her like the crash of a tidal wave. It would be so easy to cease struggling and rest in the soft mud until he found her. There would be a few minutes of degradation, then it would all be finished. No more running, no more pain, . . . no more life. Why fight on when she would die with the coming of the sun no matter how hard she ran?

No, she chided herself. Quitting now would be like handing this animal her honor. Better to die in battle than as a coward.

Kate lifted her head to hone in on a new sound. Hope burst inside her like an exploding star. The chug of a boat engine came from up the river. A moment later, the elation faded. In this near darkness and thick mist no one would see her, and with her mouth gagged, her voice was useless. Tears coursed down her cheeks in silent frustration, while a pleading prayer resounded in her thoughts.

As if in answer to her unspoken plea, the boat's engine slowed nearby, then stopped. Indistinguishable men's voices floated to her across the water. Unthinkingly, Kate stopped her frenzied retreat to listen to the sounds of hope. No longer able to tell from which direction Lester advanced, she was startled by the splash of water and rustling of bushes to her right. Turning away from the ominous sound, she fled blindly into the tall grass, every instinct intent on evasion.

Suddenly, she crashed headlong into a fleshy solid wall. Booming laughter greeted her and she looked up to see the darkly whiskered face of Lester leering down at her. The scream she emitted was muffled by the cloth covering her mouth as he grabbed her. A knife appeared in his other hand.

"Sorry there's no time for a tumble." His voice held regret. "Good-bye, honey."

Kate kicked at him and struggled for freedom, but his grip was unbreakable. She shut her eyes, waiting for the blade to descend. Something huge leaped past her, brushed her arm, and collided with her attacker. A snarl and snapping teeth sounded beside her ear and the bruising hand on her arm fell away. Shocked at her sudden release, she stepped back to see what happened. Recognition of the big yellow mongrel evoked boundless joy. Rufus! John had come for her.

Once the surprise wore off, she saw Rufus was in trouble. The knife had dropped from the man's hand, but his fist sledgehammered into the dog's body. Rufus' teeth still held their trap-like grasp on Lester's arm, which kept the man's attention from Kate. She could have run to safety, leaving Rufus to his fate, but she rejected the unworthy thought. Maneuvering behind Lester, she kicked at him, nearly throwing herself off balance.

Someone's arms enveloped her from behind and hauled her aside as a gunshot rang out. The hulking menace that had stalked her through the night toppled back into the mud. He lay inert.

"You're all right now, Kitten." The familiar voice of Captain Tom surrounded her.

One arm supported her against him as he removed the kerchief from over her mouth. She wanted to speak, but no words would come as sobs spilled over.

Gallagher stood with the smoking gun in his hand, surveying the area. The captain had pulled Kate out of harm's way and Rufus sniffed at the prone body. His first impulse was to go to his woman and hold her until he was certain she was well. But that would have to wait while he checked on the man he had felled. With a cursory inspection, he determined the bullet was not fatal. An errant memory flashed through his mind of the rowboat found a short distance from here with Kate's slashed clothes and underthings lying around. His arm came up to point the gun barrel between the kidnapper's eyes. He pulled the hammer back.

"No, John. Don't do it. You're not a murderer."

Captain Tom's stern voice had little affect on Gallagher. He held the pistol steady, the sweet smell of revenge egging him on. Through his haze of strangling emotion, Kate's voice distracted him. He turned to see her extricate herself from the Captain's hold and stumble toward him. She appeared so weak and lost that all he could think about was holding her. When Tom took the gun from his hand, he felt relieved not to have Kate see him commit murder.

She seemed so frail in his arms, sobbing, clutching at his shirt, trembling with cold that his own tears came close to brimming over. His woman was safe, and he had almost been convinced he would never see her alive again. He removed his jacket and draped it over her bare shoulders. They needed to go home now and let time heal the memory of this horrendous night.

CHAPTER XXIII

The linens were warm and fragrant around her. Kate snuggled deeper under them before opening her eyes to see she was alone in her bed. Gallagher had only promised to stay with her until she fell asleep, but she had hoped he would not leave. He had been sweet and protective this morning, bringing her home after last night's ordeal on the river. By the time they arrived at her house, both Abigail and Gladys had already left for work and Blanca was in the kitchen.

She giggled, remembering the housekeeper's protests when John insisted she stay out of his way while he took care of his woman. Gently, he bathed her and washed her hair as she drowsed in the tub, exhausted and aching. His touch soothed her and swept away the fear that clung to her like cobwebs.

Leisurely, she stretched, threw back the light blanket and sat at the side of the bed. The window shades were drawn, casting the room in gray gloom, but from the warmth of the air, she judged the hour to be late afternoon. As she stood in her nightgown and crossed to the windows to let in the sunlight, her body complained from a dozen bruises and strained muscles. Kate ignored the pain. She had slept away more than half the day and there were important things for her to do. It was time to shut the door on her past and plan for the future.

Her father's murderers were caught and she could allow his memory to rest in peace. With a sad twinge, Kate thought of the yellow glass beads she had lost during the harrowing night. It was a fitting end to a dependency long past its usefulness. She would always hold a special love for her father, but her own strengths would support her now. When she needed help, there were John and a few dear friends who had proven themselves worthy of her trust.

The shade rolled up, letting in the sunshine. Her strong tug on the window opened it and sweet air flooded the room. Kate breathed deeply and stretched, glorying in the penetrating heat of the sun. A new beginning was ahead for her. After a moment, she sagged.

This morning, while riding through town on the way home, John had stopped at the *Gazette* office to ask for news of yesterday's election. The report was not encouraging. Although the official vote count was not available, some San Francisco newspapers had announced the defeat of women's suffrage. She felt discouraged, but not crushed. This was not the last election and someday women would win the vote.

Unexpectedly, Kate's body trembled and a cold sweat broke out on her forehead. Her stomach flipped over and bile rose to her throat. For the first time, she was glad to feel ill, for it meant her baby still nestled inside her. Just as she reached the bathroom, she spewed the contents of her stomach into the bowl. The retching continued until her throat burned and her eyes watered.

A cool touch on the back of her neck calmed her and she turned to see Gallagher standing there, concern reflected in his eyes.

"What's wrong? Do you have a fever?" His fingers touched her brow.

Her head felt cool. He poured a glass of water from the tap and handed it to her to rinse out her mouth.

"I'm fine. This is common for women in my condition."

He knit his forehead in confusion, then his eyes grew wide with understanding and wonder. Coming from a large family, he was familiar with the symptoms of pregnancy. He had noticed the slight rounding of her tummy, but had not equated it with motherhood. Gallagher tentatively placed his fingers on her nightgown over the life-bearing mound. Her smile warmed him and the next moment he hugged her to him with desperate ferocity.

"We've got a date with the preacher, woman." His voice was exuberant. "You don't have a choice."

"I don't want a choice." She stretched up on bare toes to plant a kiss on his chin.

He bent down to kiss her lips hungrily, his mood playful. Gallagher swooped her off her feet and carried her to the bed where he deposited her with a bounce.

"Before we celebrate, I have something for you." He sat on the rumpled bed beside her.

Gallagher picked up a newspaper he had earlier tossed on the bed, and held up the headline. *Women Win The Vote,* proclaimed the special edition of the *River Run Gazette.* Kate rejoiced with an ear ringing shout, and grabbing the newspaper, she pored over the article. The referendum had won by only three thousand, five hundred and eighty seven votes, an average majority of one vote in every precinct in the state. Two counties, including San Francisco, failed to pass it.

She placed the paper on the nightstand and turned to John, wanting to thank him for bringing her the marvelous news. What she saw stopped her cold. He held his hand out to her palm up. In it lay her yellow string of beads. Her heart swelled. She was struck speechless, but not because of the return of an irreplaceable treasure. She had never mentioned the necklace to him, yet he knew how much it had meant to her. The intense expression she read on his face told her the offering was an important gesture. All the trust and security she had depended upon from those beads, she could now receive from the man who held them out to her. Kate lifted the glass bubbles, and without looking, placed them on the edge of the bed. With her other hand, she clasped his fingers and brought them to her lips.

"I don't need them anymore. I only need you."

Gallagher pulled her to him, and tumbled with her across the bed where they caressed each other in sweet celebration. As the bed dipped, the beads dropped unnoticed to the floor. Kate, at last, was at peace with her past, and eager for the future.

EPILOGUE

General Election Day 1912

At mid afternoon, City Hall was crowded with men and women eager to vote. This was a highly contested Presidential election year with incumbent William Taft running against fellow Republican Theodore Roosevelt and the upstart Democrat, Woodrow Wilson.

Kate grinned, forcing back raucous laughter as she stepped into line to wait her turn for a ballot. She had just come across Wilhelmina Christian standing on the sidewalk, encouraging women to vote as though their suffrage was her original idea. No doubt, electioneering for Arnold's continuation as Mayor had changed Wicked Willie's opinion. She had greeted Kate, her old enemy, with a pleasant nod. That nod had nearly toppled the huge botanical creation perched on her head.

A tiny fist popped Kate on the mouth, and she shifted six month-old Nathan to a more comfortable position in the circle of her arm. He had inherited his mother's golden crown of curls and wide smile and his father's penetrating blue eyes. The child's independent will and stubbornness were a legacy from both his parents.

A shadow passed across Kate's pensive features as she recalled a different election day over a year ago. The memory of that terrifying night did not return often any more, especially after the trials were done. There had been more than one victim in Lester's long career of crime and he had been hanged for murder. Jeffrey Carlisle managed to avoid the rope and would spend the remainder of his life in prison.

Her unpleasant thoughts faded when she saw Gallagher enter the room and head her way.

"Hi, brat." He greeted her with a kiss on the cheek. "What've you been up to?"

He lifted his wriggling son from his wife's arms and held him high over his head, eliciting an excited squeal from the baby.

"This morning, a letter came from my mother. She wants to visit us and see her grandson." Kate sounded eager.

Gallagher's nose wrinkled at the thought of his austere mother-in-law staying in their home. Their house was busy with their boarder Abigail, children tramping in and out of their front parlor for piano lessons, frequent visits from Captain Tom, and the multitude of Gallagher sisters, brothers, nieces, and nephews. The high society lady would not approve of their household and his wife would suffer for it.

"How do you feel about her visit?"

"I'm looking forward to it. I'm curious to see if she can live up to my standards."

With a broad grin, he wrapped her in a one-armed hug. His spunky little woman was ready to face anything the future might bring.

ABOUT THE AUTHOR

Sharon Margolis graduated from Brooklyn College with a major in creative writing. In her twenties she moved with her husband from New York to Southern California. She joined the Orange County Chapter of Romance Writers Of America and was on its local Board of Directors. Sharon has published two historical novels, "Swan Maiden" and "Suffragist Hellraiser."

Visit Sharon's website at sharonmargolis.com.

Lightning Source UK Ltd.
Milton Keynes UK
UKOW04f0658010218

317198UK00001B/2/P